THE NEW PLANTATION

By

Sandra Snowden

To Dawn

Reach for your,
Sky Blessings
Sandra Brown

TABLE OF CONTENTS

Acknowledgements... vii
Introduction... ix

Chapter 1 - Ancestor's Speak..11
Chapter 2 - The Journey...41
Chapter 3 - The Blessing...77
Chapter 4 - Safety 91
Chapter 5 - Reassurance Completed..............................101
Chapter 6 - Death Comes Creeping 125
Chapter 7 - Meeting of the Minds...................................141
Chapter 8 - A Place of Hope 171
Chapter 9 - Opportunity Knocks.....................................201
Chapter 10 - Birthing the Vision.....................................231
Chapter 11 - The Convention..259
Chapter 12 - Miracles for Real?......................................281
Chapter 13 - Betrayal 319
Chapter 14 - A Betta Life 335
Chapter 15 -Reality 355

Word Definitions 363

ACKNOWLEDGEMENT

This acknowledgement is actually a cute story itself. I began this book about five years ago. Never having written a fiction I had no idea where to start; but obviously I did. After struggling with the manuscript, I shared my thoughts with my granddaughters, Amber and Akia. They became so engrossed in the story that everyday when they came in from school they would ask, "How are the Baskets? What is Poppa Basket doing now? How is Abunda?" Finally, my struggling manuscript now had a life of its own thanks to "Ber and Kita" as they are affectionately known. Therefore, I publicly acknowledge Amber and Akia Sembly, who were the driving force that kept me motivated to write.

Akia, great job with the first reading and critique you did. Although you were only 13 years old, you did the job of an adult. I still have the critique and will keep it forever. I pray that you utilize that awesome gift of writing that you possess.

Thanks so much to Opal Besay for carefully reading and assisting with the editing.

Tania, my child, your reading of the earlier version helped to set the pace for the rest. Blessings for doing a great job and being persistence in completing the reading!!

Also, I thank my circle of friends who became concerned about the whereabouts of the "Baskets" as well.

I hope that this finished work is as much a blessing to all of you as you all were to me!!!

To God be the Glory!!!!

THE NEW PLANTATION
INTRODUCTION

It's not what you think it is, so don't conclude that you know where I'm going! There are all kinds of plantations that each and every one of us live on whether we admit it or not. Life has all of us enslaved. Even some of the richest people who have everything are enslaved to something.

The New Plantation is new because it makes us take a long look at where we are in the background of the old plantation. The old plantation was only for the Coloreds where slavery was executed and most defined slavery as "the need for labor to enhance a nation," but there was a price paid by all and lessons never learned by many, but today....

Looking back at the old plantation there were so many things that Coloreds never imagined or considered a part of their lives. Though there were those who escaped and fought for the freedom of others, most relinquished their external freedom in an effort to 'just live from day to day'. Internally, they wondered if freedom was a viable option. Could we escape the horrors of this life and live without redress or harm, their hearts wondered?

The Basket family is a typical Colored family trying to endure in a time when they were relegated as unnecessary. Always looking for 'a better life', the Baskets endured tragedy, hopelessness and what they called success. Poppa Basket fought to keep his family together at all cost. Regardless of what he attempted to do his wishes seemed to only live as a butterfly; beauty for a short while!

Momma Basket the strong Colored woman, stood completely beside her man. She possessed the courage, strength and tenacity to stand when he was weak and even when she wanted to lose hope. As characteristic of strong Coloreds, she was not only a mother to her children, but a caring and nurturing woman to others.

Sounds like the old plantation doesn't it?

Will you be able to find yourself and identify your plantation? Or will you resort to the preconceived conclusion that you are, never have been or ever will be on a Plantation?

Chapter 1

Ancestor's Speak

The plantation is a place that takes every imaginative fiber of your existence to behold, understand, grasp in the cerebella of your mind and includes the wonderment of why those who are taken there would want to stay. It dominates the core of your thinking and has the capacity to rob and rape you of your freedom to think, function and act independently.

This same plantation could also provide a freedom that may never be experienced in the finiteness of the human existence. Arrayed in different designs and architectural splendor, breath taking landscaping, and often businesses, whether it is the sale of property or minds, the plantation draws you into its web of intrigue.

History details how slaves were taken from their countries for many years, their liberty was taken away, many lives killed, and an assumption that their wills were destroyed. The slaves found themselves in a strange land, with a strange song and the determination to find their way back home to Africa. Such was the story of one African family.

The headship of an entire Africa family, named Buswasla was kidnapped and brought to a country for slavery. The Buswasla's were from a very prominent tribe in Africa and the oldest man taken was the King of the tribe. This tribe had a history steeped in African tradition and wealth. They possessed precious stones, gems, gold and much land. Educated according to their African culture, they prevailed in maintaining the tribe and caring for all of its members, which numbered over 5,000. Because of the mandate of maintaining the tribe, an inheritance was introduced that would belong to the tribe or family who successfully understood the mystery surrounding the inheritance. Over the years, the rumors about the inheritance grew and decades had passed yet no one had received the inheritance.

King Buswasla was a very religious man according to African standards. He believed in ancestor worship, which was the main form of religion in Africa. Africans believed that their forefathers would rescue them from hurt, harm and danger. They prayed to and worshipped them.

King Buswasla maintained the rituals while they were on the plantation. He was sort of a preacher. Every evening the family would gather around to hear stories from home, about the inheritance and give prayers and oblations to their forefathers. This daily event made life bearable.

On evening King Buswasla was conducting the rituals when he started talking about the inheritance. In his African language he said to the family, "Can you keep a secret?"

"Yes, yes," was the overwhelming response from the family.

"It has to do with the inheritance, something mysterious in our family," the King said, as to bait the family.

"What is it? What is it?" everyone yelled with utter excitement and anticipation.

"Is this the same inheritance that we've been hearing about for years," asked Amuna, one of the teenagers in the tribe.

"Yes," responded King Buswasla. "I heard from my ancestors that if you found out about the inheritance, you will get something precious and very valuable."

"Tell us more, please", the family urged.

The King said, "I can only tell you that you will never have to worry about your life if you get the inheritance. Never!"

Rumors of the inheritance made for interesting stories on the plantation, as the Buswasla family talked and longed for home. This inheritance seemingly kept the tribe strong under very adverse circumstances.

Years went by and the image of the Buswasla clan seemed to diminish. There was no one left to talk about or long for the inheritance that kept the tribe hoping. Needless to say, the toil of slavery was harsh and destructive especially to the African families that sought to stay together at all cost.

The main method for staying together was the telling of stories. While the African families had the chance to share their history, when not in the fields, they told of home. They told of their ancestors, tribal life, and their continued and relenting desire to return home. Many were convinced that they would return home and never succumb to slavery. However, for the Buswasla's it looked as if their desires and traditions had become the victims of slavery?

Years following the Buswasla's, the plantation still continued to flourish. Most southern slaves desperately wanted to flee to the north where they would be free. Such a family was called the Baskets, who were direct descendants of the African family named Buswasla. The name was changed when the ancestors were bought by the Basket Plantation. The Baskets knew of their family history and kept it alive by telling the stories about the Buswaslas and the inheritance.

Poppa Basket was the man of the house and Momma Basket helped him keep the family together. The Baskets had 8 children, 5 boys and 3 girls. Momma and Poppa, as they were called, both carefully instructed and nurtured their children to assure them that their family was not one of despair but one of opportunity.

Poppa Basket was small; frail in stature and he looked much too small to have fathered so many children. He was, however, always concerned about caring for his family. Poppa Basket arose early, before anyone needed to come and get him up for the day's work. Dressing in work clothes with a raggedy straw hat on his head and sneakers on his feet, Poppa Basket headed for his secret place to think about the adventures of the day he was facing; the cemetery. Sitting on a grave in the cemetery where the peace was overwhelming and certainty was nebulous, he pondered his fate.

Poppa Basket starts talking to those who have already gone home, "Why y'all leave us here lik' 'kis? How y'all mad' it 'en git happy? Y'all tell da truth 'bout keepin' us peoples 'gatha. What we's gonna do if we git tooken 'way som' where? I's mad lik' hell at som' y'all 'caus I feel ya jis' la'ing d'ere la'fin at me. Ya tellin' me work it out fo' me self!"

"Why y'all botherin' us, now? We don' git som' peace. Here ya's messin' us! Do what we don' told ya! Work da rest out fo' ya self," came from the center of a grave that Poppa Basket was looking down on.

"Oh, God, I's los' my head. I's hearin' da dead. I's gonna be a basket case if I's keep dis up. But hold on, what's y'all don' told me do? Is I doin' it?"

A silence so eerie filled the entire moment; one that felt like the world had come to an end and nothing was left. Poppa Basket stood in absolute fear, but surprisingly he was not afraid. He sensed a calmness that made him not look at what he was feeling but redirected his thoughts to his ability to overcome today's adventures whatever they may be. Taking a deep deep breath, consciously as if to get enough

14

oxygen for the whole day, Poppa Basket turned and began walking back for work. Still consumed with his thoughts, he tripped and fell over a small log that was hiding in the thick ivy covered pathway through the cemetery.

"What's I doin' here? What dis place is? Who ya?"

Trembling with intensity as his own body rattled, Poppa Basket continued to inquire but received no attention from those around him. Some of them nudged him with little branches as though he was some alien creature that came from another world to do them harm. With inquisitiveness still lurking in their minds, the wonderers left the scene and returned with others who were much older than they.

They picked Poppa Basket up and carried him to a small village. The streets were flawlessly clean. The landscaping seemed to be composed of every type of vegetation on the earth. Massive trees lumbered over the streets providing a type of protection for those who walked under. It seemed to be a sign from the heavens that protection is also provided from anything that might try to intrude from above. An oak tree that appeared to be over 200 hundred years old was stationed in the center of the village. It had limbs that looked sculptured to its trunk. The limbs had crossed each other in some places and gave the appearance of hugging one another. Some limbs shot off in various directions as if to declare their independence from the others. The trunk of the tree was partially covered with ivy that formed a face in the center. Patches of artwork seemed to be present on the tree from the formation of aged nicks and chips. A strange silvery light surrounded it on all sides illuminating the tree but there was no electricity. It almost served as a god but the inhabitants did not worship it, they were just in awe of its beauty and independence.

"It just grows, all by itself with no help from us little ones," a voice pronounced.

"Its destiny was predetermined from the beginning and it continues to live and fulfill it by just being. It doesn't have to work at being because it already is. Being is inherent; it just is! Big people would do well to learn from the tree how to be. They already have what they need so why can't they just be? They are always making things much harder than they really are. Just accept what is; is that so hard?" the companion responded to his friend.

"People, people; who can figure them out?" sighed the other one who was carrying Poppa Basket.

"Why *is* people ain't lik' da tree? Jis' be what dey's 'posa be?" was an unconscious thought that ran through Poppa Basket's mind.

Continuing through the small village, there stood to the left a Promise Store that had a humongous 24 caret gold lock on the beautiful French doors that lead to the pathway of the desires of the human heart. The windows of the Store were trimmed in gold and silver with a translucent onyx for the panes. Strangely enough, the building itself was tattered with a look of sadness that did not reflect the prosperity of its trimmings. Loneliness stuck out as if the Store was trying to convey its feelings and attempts to get someone to come inside and help to ease its pain. As you looked at the Store a voice seemed to speak to your heart saying, "I still have those things you longed for and are still trying desperately to achieve."

"Promises, promises, promises, dey's ain't na'va gonna be. I's work all my lif'. Still ain't gonna git li'l things I's hope fo'. Promises! Dream on 'til 'morrow 'cause dey ain't na'va gonna com' ta lif'. Jis' bein' 'round in ya head makin' ya crazy. Offa folks' promises com' true, but mines...," muttered Poppa Basket.

A volt of what seemed like electricity so strong went through Poppa Basket's body causing him to shake violently for several minutes. Almost as punishment, the volt seemed to announce its displeasure with Poppa Basket's negative mutterings. Afterwards the shaking would subside and Poppa Basket would be peaceful again.

Still being carried by his rescuers through the village, they approached a school but all of the students were grown-ups. No children attended this school. The name of the school was Get It Right Academy. The door was opened and inside was tables and chairs nothing like in a regular school. One big room could be seen and it was divided into sections named: Wisdom, CommonSense, Mistakes, and Accomplishments. The silhouettes of grown-ups sitting at a table could be seen through the door.

"They're still in there. Wonder how long it's going to take before they get it? Don't you think children are much smarter than grown ups 'cause we don't stay in one grade that long," said a little one to a friend.

"Yea," the friend replied. "I think it's because they don't listen and do what they're told to do. They think they know it all 'cause they have grown up. Now they have changed their minds about what they learned."

"I don't think they ever learned it. They can't be that dumb to keep repeating the same wrong thing over and over. Man, I got more sense than that and I'm just a little something."

The school teachers all looked like they could be in Poppa Basket's family. His mother and father. His grandfather and grandmother, even his great-great grandmother was there. She was the head master. One teacher looked just like his favorite uncle that he loved so much. Everybody had something to say. "'Memba don't fo'git; dis. 'En do dat. Why ya ain't fix da thang da way I us'a do it? What's wrong wit' ya prayin'. I don' told ya what'd happ'n if ya' didn't? Let's try dis ag'in, what I sade do when ya needed sup'in?" blasted da head master? "Pray, answered Poppa Basket. Pray, pray, ya's say dat fo' e'rythang," he mimicked, again, under his breath.

"I's gotta do whate'er I gotta git me out dis here school. It ain't me fault I's ain't gon' school. I's ain't git no learnin'. I's a'ways workin'; dey's told me what I gotta do. I's na'va don' git do it as I's was told by 'em. Dey's ain't stay long nuff fo' me see if it worked as dey'd don' sade it could. Why's peoples a'ways puttin' so much on ya, don't kno'. I's jis' wanna git sup'in right so I kin' has som' peace din." All this rolled over the conscious of Poppa Basket.

This small village is full of intrigue and mystery that seems to illuminate as Poppa Basket is being carried, still, to who knows where. The air in the village is therapeutic and fills the body with an aromatic effervescence that removes any stress that could create labor to the body. Inundated with harmony, the air sings to the atmosphere and all of its inhabitants with melodious cords and phrases. It commands everyone to a level of meditation that occurs even while the person is still in motion. So strong is its control that there is no need to stop and be quiet, because the air's calming affects causes an involuntary submission to its commands.

Poppa Basket begins to feel that his body rhythm is slowing down but he cannot seem to find himself. Struggling for feelings, he wrestles, tosses and turns only to lose himself again into something.

"Poppa Basket, Poppa Basket, Poppa Basket," a faint call seemingly from thousands of miles away irritates the peace in Poppa Basket's mind.

"Git gon', git gon', I ain't gonna hear ya, git gon'," Poppa Basket thinks. "I's ain't got dis kin'a peace befo'. E'rythang is work! Fix dis. Do dat. Go d'ere. 'Memba dat I's sade ta ya. He'p me. Git gon'!!! Git gon'!!!"

The mini battle is won. Poppa Basket drifts further into what he does not know. Not knowing enhances his peace and is reflected by his body language that demonstrates his submission to his new surroundings. Tranquility. Peace. Beauty. Awe. Innocence.

As Poppa Basket succumbs to the peace, the movement stops and those who are carrying him gently lay him down in a field of lilies. The beauty is breathtaking and the moment embraces a serenity that could cause someone to want to remain there forever. The fragrance of the lilies is intoxicating and addictive. The little stems inside play a tone as they rhythmically touch each other. The sounds continue to lull Poppa Basket further into tranquility.

"Ya can't sta' y'ere fo'ever! Ya ain't su'pusa be wit' us. Ya ain't git don' wha'ca 'posa do. 'En jis' dem who's don' kin sta' y'ere. Git up!! Git up!! What 'bout da 'heritance? Git up!! Move!" The voice was so stern, it startled Poppa Basket and he began to respond.

His voice trembling, "What don' happ'ned? Where's I? What don' happ'ned? Where's I?"

The faint sound of drums rang for what seemed like an eternity. The smell of incense now was overriding the fragrance from the lilies. Time was traveling backwards and reality disappearing. Listen. Listen. Listen. Watch. Watch. Watch. Remember. Remember, continually resonated through the atmosphere around Poppa Basket. Standing over him was a Witch Doctor who was chanting incantations and scattering herbs. Dancing systemically to a drumbeat, the Witch Doctor continued in African language saying, "Be free. Be free. Keep your mind. Keep your mind."

A horrible fear gripped Poppa Basket, again, but this time it paralyzed him. He struggled to get away from the Witch Doctor but was unsuccessful. He could sense moisture on his face that let him know he was crying from the fear. But a strange thing happened, the fear left and the peace that he had been experiencing returned. For an instance he felt the presence of his ancestors trying to warn him and to help him.

"Be free. How? From what? What dat mean keep ya mind? Y'ere we's go ag'in. Dey's sayin' fo' me what ta do, ain't how I's gonna git it don," wondered Poppa Basket. "I's think dey kno' what dey's talkin' 'bout 'cause I's feels it. How's I git d'ere?" thought Poppa Basket while still almost in a trance.

From what seemed like miles and miles away, "Poppa Basket, where ya at?" could be heard in the back of Poppa Basket's mind. "Where ya at?" called the voice again. Poppa Basket could not respond. His inner man was consumed with his ancestors while his outer man seemed to be held captive.

"I's gotta kno' what da old peoples, who's gon', gotta say 'en how I's git it don', 'cause I's gotta git it ta liv' right now. I's gotta sho' me peoples da way out. Dis coulda be da thang ta our 'heritage. I's ain't gonna leave me peoples wit' nufin 'en I's gon'," thought Poppa Basket.

Above Poppa Basket's head was a figure that contained his ancestors from years back. They stood locked arm in arm with their chests protruding with pride. It gave Poppa Basket a surge of stamina, hope and invincibility. No one spoke but the energy that was produced consumed all the air around Poppa Basket.

The energy began to take on a life of its own. The sound of small pitter-patters began to fill the air symphonicly with a rendition that was so sharp its movements caused the atmosphere to sing. The different sounds of the pitter-patter falling on the lilies created a choir and the sound of the light whistling of the wind served as the conductor.

This awesome display of nature suddenly brought Poppa Basket back to reality. He awoke but was still too drowsy to contemplate all that had happened to him. He quickly surveyed his surroundings to grasp his bearings. He was not yet able to gather himself because he was still captivated by whatever it was that happened to him.

Again, the voice from the distance called to him, "Poppa Basket, where ya at? Poppa Basket pleeeease answer me." He could hear the concern in the voice but still was unable to respond with enough strength to be heard. "I's y'ere," he responded but it sounded like a whisper. He tried again, "I's o'va y'ere. I's y'ere." Nothing. No confirmation that Poppa Basket was heard came from the voice in the distance.

Struggling to open his eyes, Poppa Basket's vision was blurred and he thought he saw what looked like tombstones around him. "Oh my God, I's dead. Is I's gon' ta heav'n or hell?" Trembling, he cried out, "Momma where's ya? Is ya ain't 'ere I's kno' I's in hell."

Scared to death, Poppa Basket began to move frantically. He began to feel better so that he could get his bearings. With stuttered speech, he mustered, "Ooooooh myyyyy God, pleeeeeeease help me. I's sorry fo' ain't bein' a good man. I's sho' sorry."

Suddenly Poppa Basket felt a hand touch him and he said, "God fo'give me. I's ready git my lashin's."

The voice responded, "Poppa, Poppa, I's glad I don' found ya. Ya al'right? What happened?" Crying with joy, Poppa Basket's second oldest son, Jumba, sat down and was holding and rocking his father.

"Ya mean I's ain't dead? Oh my goodness! Thanks ya God fo' givin' me 'nuffa chance. I swear I'll be betta. Ooops, I's sorry, I ain't 'posa swear," Poppa Basket anxiously chattered.

"Poppa what happ'ned? Where ya been? We's all lookin' fo' ya. We's so worried 'bout ya!" exclaimed Jumba.

Poppa Basket replied, "I's don't kno' what happ'ned. I's comin' hom' by da graveyard." He did not want anyone to know that it was his secret place. "When I's, I's don't 'memba. Ouch, my head hurts," said Poppa Basket touching the left side of his head. "I's got a big knot on my head."

"Did ya fall, Poppa?" asked Jumba.

"I's musta," replied Poppa Basket.

"Can ya stand up? We try," Jumba said. He put his hands under Poppa Basket's armpits and started helping him up from the ground.

"Oh, oh, hold on. I's ain't steady yit," said Poppa Basket.

"Ok, Poppa, take ya time," Jumba encouraged.

Jumba got Poppa Basket to his feet and they slowly made their way back home. The family ran outside to greet them and realized that something had happened to Poppa Basket. Momma Basket was extremely frightened at Poppa Basket's appearance, yet she was relieved that he had been found.

"Where ya was? What happ'ned? Ya al'right? I's git sup'in fo' ya?" Momma Basket fired one question after another. "Thank ya God, he safe. Thanks fo' answerin' my pray'rs," she said softly under her breath.

Everyone in the family rushed into the house to find out what happened to Poppa.

"Don't make no fuss fo' me. We's gotta git ta work," Poppa Basket ordered.

"Ya ain't gonna work jis' now," Momma Basket said. "Ya needs rest."

"I's ain't got no time fo' rest woman. We's gotta do work. I's gonna be wit' da resta 'dem," Poppa Basket emphatically stated. Off he went to work.

While working in the hot sun, Poppa Basket started thinking about what happened to him. His mind began to show bits and pieces of the dream. He remembered the little people, the awesome tree and especially seeing his ancestors. He was not quite sure where he saw them but he remembered their taunting words, "Jis' do what I's told ya do."

"What it all is? What it all is? I's wait 'til I's git hom' out dis hot sun. Din I's 'memba som' mo'. I's tell'em 'bout it whil'se we's eatin' suppa," Poppa Basket considered.

"Don't fo'git," a voice from nowhere whispered, "Don't fo'git."

Poppa Basket shook his head to be sure of what he heard but the pain was still very evident. He concentrated on the pain and not the voice.

Humming while he worked, the voice returned, "Don't fo'git, don't fo'git." Poppa Basket remembered not to shake his head but pondered the voice and responded to himself, "Don't fo'git What? The secret. The inheritance. The rules. What? Forget what?" cluttered Poppa Basket's mind. Immediately he realized that he was remembering more of what took place in his dream, if it was a dream? The workday was getting very long and Poppa Basket knew that it would soon be quitting time. The sun had shifted from the east to the west and was beginning its downward spiral to rest from its day.

"Boy, I think I's gonna go all th'ough dis day, ev'n wit' my strange start," Poppa Basket encouraged himself. "What's I gonna tell'em 'bout dis mornin'? I's ain't really 'memba much. But when I's let my mind go back sup'ins com' back. It really strange. But I's kno' it's got som' real good sup'in fo' me. I's ain't think 'bout dat 'heritance in a long time. I's kind'a gave up on it. 'Cause ain't n'body in my daddy's family made much talk 'bout it. Maybe dey's jis' ain't take time. 'Cause its hard 'nuff workin' sun up sun down e'vry day. Who git time fo' som' 'heritance. What hidin' in us? Wonda' what it is?"

Getting his things together, Poppa Basket slowly started making his way home, thinking, "Night's gonna' be in'trestin'."

The landscape was beautiful. Huge majestic trees were situated so that they provided an enclosure for the lovely flowers, manicured lawns and the stately houses. This place looked like something out of a dream book.

Poppa Basket continued to walk until he reached his quarters. Momma Basket came running out when she saw him coming from a distance. Still concerned from this morning, she asked, "How ya is? Ya feel beta? Ya head hurtin'? Com' 'en rest a bit."

Poppa Basket grumbled, "Don't make no fuss, woman, I's ok. I's work hard 'day. I's ok."

"What don' happ'ned dis mornin'?" asked Momma Basket inquisitively.

"I's ain't sho', jis' let me git som' rest. 'Pose I's talk 'bout it lata."

Poppa Basket went to the other room and laid across the bed. His head began to pounce and throb to the point that he wanted to cry, but being a man he held back the emotion and just held his head in his hand.

"God, if ya's dere 'en hears me, pleas' take dis pain from my head. I's kno' I's hardheaded but right now my head feels lik' its don' been smashed in. It's been a while fo' I's com' see ya. But I's got a feelin' I's need start comin' see ya mo' din I do. Was ya fittin' say sup'in dis mornin'? Does I's need to kno' sup'in. Or is sup'in I's not doin'? Look lik' my ancestors ke'p on tellin' me do what dey don' told me 'en do it right. I jis' don't kno' what dey's talkin' 'bout. Kin ya he'p me?" asked Poppa Basket with all seriousness because he wanted the best for his family.

The room was extremely still, kind of reminded Poppa Basket of the stillness of the cemetery that is before this morning. Afraid of falling asleep, Poppa Basket tried to stay awake but was soon in a peaceful sleep.

The aroma of fried chicken, yams, greens and short bread filled the house. Momma Basket was the greatest cook in the world. She was a fine woman who was quite head-smart about many things even though she had very little education. It seems as though she just had a God given knack for figuring things out and or coming up with answers that were needed when no one else could. She was very pretty with an ebony complexion. Amazingly she had a great body after giving birth to so many children. She did not look any way near her age. Poppa Basket was so proud of her and loved to show her off when they got around other people.

As the family all made their way back home, Momma Basket summoned everybody for supper. "Y'all, com' on," she would yell to get everybody together. "Com' on."

Children would start running from everywhere. The little quarters were not enough room but Momma Basket was determined to make them a family. She slipped into the room where Poppa Basket was resting and gently nudged him saying, "Poppa, Poppa git up, suppa time. Com' on fo' ya food gits cold."

Poppa Basket rolled onto his side and slowly opened his eyes. He wanted to make sure that the events of this morning were not repeating themselves. Looking upward, Momma Basket seemed like a statue to him, at first, but when she touched him he knew that it was her. They had been married for a very long time and they knew each other backwards and forwards.

"Ok, I's comin'," Poppa Basket said roughly.

The family stood around the table in rows and Momma Basket said the grace. "Dear Lord thank ya fo' dis food ya give us. Thank ya fo' keepin' us togatha 'en safe. Thank ya fo' lovin' us. Amen."

There was a square table in the middle of the room but everybody could not sit at it, so the oldest sat down and the younger ones sat wherever they could around the room.

"Poppa," called Jumba. "Tell us what happ'n dis mornin'. I waited all day long ta hear da story."

"Yea, Poppa", chimed in almost all of the children. "What happ'n? Tell us."

"Soons we git don' eatin' 'en clean' up, I's tell ya what I 'memba", said Poppa Basket.

The meal looked like it was for an army. There were plates of fried chicken, a deep dish of canned yams, a big pot of greens and two dozens of shortbread biscuits. It was amazing that Momma Basket could do all this cooking and work too. It did help that she also cooked for the people at the estate, so she could get food from them and slip in her own cooking.

Today everybody ate and cleaned up faster than ever before because they wanted to hear Poppa Basket's story. When they finished, they all gathered around the room sitting attentively.

"Ya see, dis mornin' I's goin' ta me secret place ta think 'bout da day 'en git me ready as I's a'ways do's. Sup'in funny happ'n. I's yearin' peoples talkin'. Y'all kno' da graveyard' me secret place. Guess I's gotta git anuffa place now ya's kno's. Well, a people com' out da dirt talkin' 'bout jis' do what I told ya do. I's ain't kno' what he means. I sho' was scaked. Scaked, 'en all, I's talk back, do what? I's was gittin' back, I musta fell, hit my head. I's still hurt. Da mo' I's 'memba, what don' happ'n, da mo' strange it 'tis. Da most 'potant was when I's see my great great granddaddy, my great great grandmamma, my great granddaddy, my great grandmamma, my granddaddy, my grandmamma, my daddy, and my momma. Dey's all teachin' in dis school. Dey's kept sayin' fo' me, jis' do what dey's sade fo' me do. I don' fo'git what dey's told me," said Poppa Basket.

"What'd dey tell ya, Poppa?" asked Jumba.

"I's ain't sho'. It 'potant ta 'em I's 'memba, but I's can't," said Poppa Basket. "Is I's don' told ya'll 'bout our family from Africa? We's gotta 'heritance?"

"Naw ya ain't," spoke up Momma Basket. "I 'memba ya tellin' me su'pin 'bout it years back. We's got maybe 2 or 3 chi'dren 'den. Why's ya's 'memba 'dat?"

"'Cause my ancestors don' told me 'bout it in da dream afta I's fall 'en hit my head," said Poppa Basket.

"Com' on Poppa, tell us 'bout it. We don' had family from Africa? We com' from Africa, too? Poppa, com' on tell us," Jumba insisted.

"Y'ear me, my great great granddaddy don' told us our Africa family name Buswasla. Dey's a rich tribe in Africa. Da oldest man, he cared afta da tribe. He da King. All peoples 'new 'bout 'em all 'round, all over. Deys had precious stones, gems, gold 'en much land. Deys was learned, lik' deys peoples in Africa. Da King don' took care da family 'bout 5,000 peoples. King Buswasla, ya great great great great granddaddy, him was a very religious man in African ways," shared Poppa as the family sat spell bound.

"We had a King in our family, a real King?" asked Sha'myla, the second oldest girl.

"Sho did," Poppa Basket replied. "King Buswasla be'leve ta worship ancestors. 'Dat was what dey don' in Africa. Dey be'leve da ancestors woulda save 'em from gittin' hurt. So deys prayed ta 'em 'en worshipped 'em.

Da main peoples in da whole Africa family was stole 'en takin' ta dis country fo' be slaves. King Buswasla don' ke'p doin' da ancestor-worship thang whil'se dey's on da plantation. Him was lik' a preacha. All night times da peoples git 'round fo' hear stories 'bout home, da 'heritance, do prayers 'en oblations ta da ancestors. Oblations dey poured water on da ground 'en pray fo' safety 'en ta go hom'. Dat's how dey's lived on da plantation: thinkin' dey's git off someda'. Go home, ta Africa. My great great granddaddy says 'cause da King wan' all 'em be 'gatha he com' up wit' da 'heritance. Who don' work it out, git it. N'body don' got it I's kno' 'bout, yit," Poppa continued with the story.

"What it, Poppa? Where it? Is it really gonna make somebody real rich if they get it?" commanded Makita the oldest girl.

"Slo' down. Slo' down," Poppa Basket cautioned. "I's ain't kno' what it 'tis. If I's did we's ain't be y'ere. I's ain't kno' where it 'tis. Dey's sade it really make ya rich. Dey's sade da King was a wise man. It ain't nuffin dumb."

"Please, tell us more. What 'bout da 'heritance?" Jumba asked. "Can we's look fo' it as a family?"

"All I's kno's great great granddaddy says all da time he y'ear 'bout da 'heritance dey's say, ya hold a secret when dey's first be talkin'," added Poppa Basket.

"So it a secret?" asked Jumba. "What ya think it could be? Gotta be sup'in real bad?"

"It don't gotta be, it could be sup'in good," said Makita positively. "You don't kno'!"

"Stop ya fussin'," said Momma Basket. "Jis' list'n."

Poppa Basket continues with everyone spell bound. "Com' think 'bout a secret, I's y'eard a tale when I's li'l. King Buswala was 'den a slave on da Magnolia Plantation. Dey's kept on sayin' ain't n'body kno' 'bout dis. Da King was a looka. Da White ladies, on da plantation, who don' seen 'em a'ways hushin' 'bout him was a looka 'en how good him body look. Da tale sade dey wanna see him wit' nuffin on 'cause dey's y'eard tales 'bout African's parts. One day da King don' gon' ta da big house fo' ta do som' work. Da plantation owna's wife, Mrs. Magnolia, was hom'. Her sade fo' da King ta fix sup'in in her bedroom. Da King ain't wanna 'cause no slave 'posa be 'lone wit' a White woman. Ya be dead fo' sho. Da King ain't kno' whatta do. Him don' sade som' tale ta git mo' time to think. Whil'se he's doin' 'at, lady friends of Missy Magnolia don' com' by. Dey's gon' off to anuffa room. Da King work fast, but jis' fo' he don', Missy Magnolia com' in da room. Da King don' gon' back 'en jis' 'bout fall right on da bed. Him stop 'en sade Miss Magnolia dat he's sorry fo' touchin' da bed. Her sade, "that's all right", 'en her's slowly com' ta 'em. Da King breathin' hard. He jis' 'new he gonna be dead. Her went fo' ta touch 'em 'en don' put her hand on him shoulda. He ain't got no top on. Her was rubbin' 'em shoulda. Her was 'bout ta touch 'em ag'in 'en som'body yell fo' her, Magnolia where ya at, I's home. We's got peoples y'ere. Com' on down. Missy Mangolia went ta go. Da King tried ta git his self 'gatha. Him don' hurry up 'en do him work. Him got don'. On da way down da back stairs, him y'eard Mr. Magnolia talkin' ta a man. Him sade dat his granddaddy killed a plantation ownna 'en don' sade a slave don' it. Him sade, too, 'dat he granddaddy don' took papers from da plantation ownna. He hide 'em fo' safe keepin' so years down da road he git da plantation. Da dead plantation ownna's peoples had lots 'en lots of money, folks even sade som' was buried on da land. One of da mens visitin' Mr. Magnolia was kin ta da dead plantation ownna. Dey's gonna take it o'va. Da King y'eard where's dey hide da papers 'en gon' out da back do'. Missy Magnolia 'en her peoples was sittin' in da garden. Da King git by 'em."

"What happ'n to da papers, Poppa?" Sha'myla asked.

Poppa Basket quickly replied, "Don't kno'".

"What was da name of da plantation where they killed da owner?" In an exciting voice Abunda, the oldest son said. "Can we go found it? Come on y'all let's find da 'heritance and git way from here."

Poppa Basket stopped the excitement by saying, "We ain't got da name of da plantation or where it at. Last I y'eard, da plantation ownna 'en his crooked friend was gonna be gon' from da south shortly fo' da Civil War git too bad. Dey's ain't wan' da north soldiers git all da stuffs. Stories sade lots'a plantations was gonna git burned down. Soldiers was gonna steal all da good stuff plantation ownnas had. Na'va y'eard mo' 'bout da plantation ownna 'en his friend any mo'."

"Poppa, ya think da King really 'new where da papers was? Ya think he hide 'em fo' us? If we git dat money we really could keep our family togatha 'en git 'way from here. We could do some great things like what da White peoples do. We could git som' mo' real learnin'," said Abunda, the oldest son and the outspoken one in the family.

"Well, I ain't kno' where ta 'gin lookin'. We's gotta jis' fo'git 'bout dat. We's gotta keep our heads 'bout stayin' 'gatha 'en be alive right where we is," said Poppa Basket.

"Did da King kno' fo' sho'? Did he really want da family ta git it? If he did, why is we jis' gonna fo'git it? Dat sounds dumb ta me," Abunda blurted out in his insistence for an answer.

"Hold ya mouth," yelled Momma Basket. "Ya betta 'spect ya elders 'en ancestors".

"Look what money do's. We's fussin' ov'a sup'in we's ain't ev'n got. Jis' talkin' 'bout it make us crazy. 'Pose we's jis' gotta fo'git all 'bout dat 'heritance," Poppa Basket said in disgust.

"Dat's 'nuff 'bout dat 'heritance. It's gittin' late. We gotta git ready fo' mornin'," Momma Basket added.

"What 'bout da rest of what don' happ'n to Poppa t'day? When we gonna hear da rest?" asked Jumba.

"We's got much time y'ear ta rest, 'morrow 'en da offa day, 'en da offa day," Poppa Basket said with finality.

Everybody started getting ready for bed. Actually getting ready for bed was really a metaphor because the little quarters hardly had enough space for all the beds they needed.

The quarters were in an old run-down shanty that had four rooms, a porch and an outhouse. The house was a dark gray that had not been painted in years. The outside had a big yard that had no grass, just dirt. Inside the house was a kitchen with two windows and a black wood stove that sent smoke curling through the quarters. It was used for cooking and heating the house.

The older girls in the family made the kitchen curtains from sackcloth. They were really gifted so they would sew little figures on the sackcloth to make designs in the curtains that looked like snowflakes. There was a long table that took up most of the space in the kitchen. The older boys made it and it was very strong and sturdy. Momma Basket and the girls did everything on this table: cooking, washing clothes, sewing, bathing the younger children, everything!

The other three rooms served as bedrooms. Poppa and Momma Basket's room had one big bed for them and one little bed for the younger children where the two little ones slept. The little bed was along the wall and the big bed was in the middle. The little bed had a mattress that was made by stuffing big sackcloth bags with old rags. It was very lumpy but the children did not seem to care. Momma Basket and the older girls hand made a quilt for the little bed with pretty scraps of old clothing.

Quilting was fun for the girls. They would carefully match the scraps before starting. One quilt had patches from a little girl's clothing where Makita worked. The lady of the house was very mean, so instead of giving her little girl's clothes to Makita, the Basket girl who worked for her, she would cut them up and throw them out. Quietly, Makita would go to the trash and get the pieces, stuff them in her clothes and take them home. Laughing along the way she said to herself, "She so mean, she crazy. I got the clothes away. My little sistah gonna love the quilt these things gonna make."

Momma Basket kept the house clean and tried to make it pretty. Sometimes the people that she worked for would give her old wall pictures that she would bring home and put on the wall. She, too, would go through the rubbish and get little knick-knacks, little tables, vases, curtains, sheets and anything useful to take home, clean it up and use it in her own house. The other two bedrooms were very small and only had enough room for two beds and an old bookcase that was used for a dresser. One room was for the boys and the other for the girls. The children slept according to their sizes so that there would be room in the beds.

The boys' bedroom had no pictures or frills, just the bed and the dresser. There was a bucket for going to the bathroom at night.

The girl's room was decorated, a little, with some of the things Momma Basket or the older girls would bring home from work. They had little pictures of White girls on the wall. A small table was sat cozily between the two beds with a vase of fresh flowers; mostly dandelions they would pick. A beautiful soft green cover with designs that looked like trees was made for the top of the old dresser that Mrs. Rouse gave to Momma Basket. It was nearly fallen apart but the girls continued to use it. Little pieces of different colored material was used to make the leaves on the trees for the cover. The window curtains were flowery and they too came from Momma Basket's work place. Although the house was old and very run down, the Baskets made a point of keeping it clean and very nice. They were proud of what they had and lived in anxious expectation of getting more.

Momma Basket said, "Let's do sup'in we ain't don' in a long time fo' we go to bed."

"What's 'at?" asked Poppa Basket.

"Let's pray lik' we usta 'en thank God fo' our blessin's," she replied.

"Women, ya sounds lik' me great grand momma, now. All she kno' was ya gotta pray 'en git thankful fo' e'rythang," Poppa Basket sarcastically voiced.

"Well, she right. Maybe if we ain't stop doin' it things be much betta fo' us now," Momma Basket vehemently replied.

"Okay, women, but make it fast 'cause I's tawd."

"No, ya do it, ya da man of da house ain't ya?"

"Ya's really pushin' my head."

"Poppa, please pray for us, you is our father and you know what to say to God for us," pleaded Makita.

"Ok, ok, shucks. If ya Momma ain't sade nuffin, oh fo'git it. We's pray. God thank ya fo' what ya don' fo' us. Thank ya fo' keepin' us safe 'en 'gatha. Thank ya fo' our ancestors who is wit' ya now. I pray dey he'p us live a beta life 'den da don'. Amen. Now we git to bed?" Poppa Basket barked.

"Yasa," Momma Basket said with pride.

With everybody now in bed and the house silent, Poppa Basket quietly made his way to the front porch. He tried to get to sleep but could not. As he sat on the porch he pondered the events of the day.

"What dat was 'bout?" thinking to himself. "Why it happ'n 'day? I's still wanna kno' what deys mean when deys sade jis' do what I's told ya'."

"Boy ain't I's told ya what ta do 'en how ta say it? All ya gotta do is read dis scripture 'en say a li'l pray'r. Why's 'at so hard fo' ya ta kno'."

"Granny, I's ain't wanna stand up in church in front all 'dem folks. 'Pose I's git it wrong 'en sade da wrong word or sup'in?"

"Don't worry 'bout dat, God don't care 'bout ya messin' up long ya ask fo' fo'giveness. Any how, ya don' learn da scripture in ya head. Boy, ya's blessed ta learn ta read e'vn a bit. Peoples don' git' kil't ta he'p ya learn read. Ya's gonna do it. God ain't gonna a'ways keep us in dis mess dey's call lif'. One day som'body gonna be free. Ya's gotta kno' ta read 'en write. Fo' God sake don't drop or mess up da Bible. We's sneaked it ev'rywhere we's been 'cause dey's don't let us git no books", Granny demanded.

"I's walk in da li'l wood church, scaked death. We's gotta be quiet 'bout it 'cause we's ain't 'posa be d'ere. It ain't e'vn a church. It was a old shack, n'body used but da old peoples made us be lik' it was fo' we have manners fo' God, da sade.

My time com' I walk ta da front. Granny don' put on my best clothes 'cause she a'ways sade we's gotta look good fo' God.

Take ya hand out'cha pocket fo' ya drop dat Bible. Lift ya head boy, I y'eard dis voice sade when I's walkin'. I look up, it was me momma. Her smile; it he'p me 'en I kep' on walkin'.

The Lord is my shepherd I shall not want. He maketh me to lie down in green pastures. He leadeth me beside the still waters. He restoreth my soul; he leadeth me in the paths of righteousness for his name's sake. Yea, though I walk through the valley of the shadow of death, I will fear no evil for thy art with me, thy rod and thy staff they comfort me. Thou preparest a table before me in the presence of mine enemies: thou anointest my head with oil, my cup runneth over. Surely goodness and mercy shall follow me all the days of my life and I shall dwell in the house of the Lord for ever.

Befo' I say Amen all da peoples was sayin' Amen 'en clappin'. Boy, I felt real good, but I's still gotta pray", Poppa Basket recollected.

"Let's pray: God thank ya fo' dis' day. God thank ya fo' what ya don' fo' us. Thank ya fo' keepin' us safe 'en 'gatha. Thank ya fo' our ancestors who is wit' ya now. I pray dey he'p us liv' a betta life d'en dey had. Amen."

"Jis' a minute," Poppa Basket said out loud. "Da's da same pray I us'ta pray when I's a li'l boy. Is dat what dey means when dey says, jis' do what I told ya? Momma Basket she right. I's ain't pray no mo' 'en now my chil'len ain't pray 'cause I's ain't. Wonda, don' dat mess me up? God, ya don' stop blessin' us wit' mo' 'cause I's ain't prayin'? Granny us'ta say dat ya giv' us ev'rythang 'en we jis' oughta 'leas sade thank ya e'ry day 'en e'ry night ta ya. Man, I's don' really messed up, ain't I's? What's wrong wit' me? I's talkin' lik' ya's really gonna talk back at me. I's guess I's mo' tawd d'en I's kno'."

"Boy, is ya e'va gonna list'n at me?" a voice came from nowhere. "Ya us'ta da when ya was li'l."

"Granny? Granny is 'at ya?" Poppa Basked was anxious to know because he missed his grandmother so much.

Tears began to well in his eyes as he started thinking about his grandmother. This was his grandmother on his father's side. She was born on the plantation and was a slave for all her life but she had faith in God. Her family still worshipped their ancestors but the little White girl, Serar, on the plantation introduced her to Christianity and Jesus Christ.

"Jesus loves us, don' matta if we is slaves. We ain't slaves ta Him, Granny us'ta a'ways say. One day He com' git us from dis bad place. We's gonna have a good lif' if we jis' stay wit' Him. Granny, I wish ya was here wit' me now. Lif' is much harder d'en I reckoned it'd be. Ya a'ways kno' da right thang ta say 'en do. I feels lik' I's jis' stumblin' 'en gittin' no wheres," Poppa Basket moaned.

For a good while there was nothing but a stillness that seemed as if this was not reality. Poppa Basket just sat. And sat. And sat. And sat. Feeling very vulnerable, holding his head in his hand, the bewilderment suddenly seemed to consume him. Finally, reality overtook the stillness and Poppa Basket became conscious of his surroundings. Sitting in the dark, on the porch, looking at the sky with the Big Dipper and Little Dipper glaring downward, the vastness of the heavens appeared to be an open door to infinity. A world where everything Poppa Basket ever dreamed of was housed. Poppa Basket rose to his feet, shook his head and sighed, "Oh well, 'morrow's anuffa day. We see what gonna happ'n."

He went in the house and quietly laid on the bed beside Momma Basket. Not wanting to awake her, he didn't undress.

A brilliant sun peaked through the curtains in their bedroom and caused both Momma and Poppa Basket to awake. They laid very still, not wanting to disturb each other, but a cough from Momma Basket signaled that she was already awake.

"Mornin'," Poppa Basket said to Momma.

"Mornin' sir. Looks lik' a beautiful day, what da sun shinin' 'en all, ain't it?" Momma Basket responded.

"Uh huh," muttered Poppa Basket. Poppa Basket took a washrag and towel and went on the side of the house where the water pump was to wash and get ready for the day.

All the children started to rise when they heard their parents. The little ones came quickly to the bedside and looked to Momma for assistance.

"I hungry," said Junna, the littlest of them.

"Oh, baby Momma's gonna git ya som' food jis' now", Momma Basket replied assuredly.

She went to the kitchen and got a big round silver washtub. She called to two of the older boys to come get the tub and fill it with water from the well. While the boys were getting the water she started making breakfast: fried potatoes with onions, flap jacks, and scrambled eggs.

"Sho' smell good out da," said a voice from the other room.

"Y'all git wash 'en put ya clothes on 'en hurri' up. I gotta git da li'l ones don' 'fo breakfast," ordered Momma Basket. "'En when ya don', dump da tub 'en git som' mo' water fo' ya sistahs 'en da li'l ones."

"Shucks Momma, ya kno' 'dat tub heavy. Why can't d'em girls fill it wit' some buckets? Why is we always gotta do it?" questioned Jumba.

"Boy, ya betta not sass me. I tell y'ur Poppa 'en ya kno' what he gonna do ta ya," responded Momma Basket. "Jis' do what I tell ya!"

"Now ya sound lik' Poppa 'en d'em ghosts he be listenin' ta, jis' do what I tell ya," laughed Jumba.

When the older boys finished, they did what Momma told them to do. They took the tub on the backside of the house where the older girls went to bathe.

"Momma, we's hungry," Junna reminded her. "When's we goin' eat?"

Momma said, "I's ain't gonna be long now, baby, jis' wait."

Right about that time a huge bee flew into the house. Everyone started yelling because one of the children had gotten bit before and was allergic. The boy swelled up real bad from that bite and Momma Basket had to get some ice from the house where she worked to put on the swelling.

As fear gripped the entire house, Momma Basket said, "Y'all stay out d'ose. I's kill dis bee. I's ain't got much time. I's gotta git ta work fo' dey comes 'en gits me".

Poppa Basket came running and yelling, "What all da noise 'bout?"

Almost on cue, all the children in the house yelled, "A bee in here. It gonna sting us."

"Woman, I's git dat, fo' ya git hurt foolin' wit' dat bee," Poppa told Momma.

Moments later, Poppa Basket had killed the bee and everyone was feeling much better and safer.

"Food ready yit?" Poppa asked.

"Few mo' minutes 'en y'all kin eat. I's gotta git don' wit' da li'l ones." Momma replied.

"Ok, let's eat." Poppa commanded. But Jayla reminded him, "Ain't granny tell ya we ta pray, first?"

"Yea, com' on. I's ain't got all day," Poppa insisted. "God thank ya fo' dis food ya don' git fo' us. Amen".

"Y'all Baskets better git over here," came a voice from across the way. "We's got work to do and ain't nobody got time for y'all to be late."

"Hurry up boys we ain't wanna git in trouble wit' d'em folks. We's been 'gatha a'ways 'en we's gonna keep it dat way," said Poppa Basket.

"I be glad when we git 'way from here," said Abunda in a dejected tone. "I hate dis place."

"Watch yo' mouth fo' ya git us all in troubl', boy. Ya gonna hate it mo' 'en dat if ya gits y'eard talkin' back," said Poppa Basket.

"I'm jis' gonna runaway. I'm sicka dis place. Ain't no body gonna make me do nothin' I's don't wanna do anymo'," Abunda continued defiantly.

"Boy, what I's jis' say? Ya ain't gonna make life bad fo' da resta us, ya y'ear me?" commanded Poppa Basket.

The boy did not answer but took a resistive stance. He folded his arms across his chest and arched his back as if he was ready to pounce. He glared deeply at his other brothers and then, with no fear, gave the same look to Poppa Basket.

Immediately, Jumba, grabbed hold of Abunda's arms and pulled them to his side. "Ya is gonna git hurt real bad 'en I ain't talkin' 'bout by n'body else. Poppa's gonna git ya. Ya betta say ya sorry right now or else."

"I don't care. I's tawd of livin' like dis. You kin' stay if you wan', I'm running away," defied Abunda.

"Boy, ya betta com' ta ya mind. Git right y'ere by me, now," Poppa ordered.

Abunda did not move. His brothers were now trembling as they anticipated what Poppa Basket would do if their brother did not move quickly. Once before when something like this occurred, Poppa Basket took a 3-inch strap and beat one of the boys for defying him. Poppa Basket always made it very clear that he was the only man and that he was in charge. Momma Basket would sometimes stop him from beating the boys real bad but she was not here to help this time.

"Ya gotta beat me Poppa. I'm tawd a dis', ain't ya? I ain't bein' wrong ta ya but I'm tawd a dis, so ya's jis' gotta beat me, now," said Abunda.

Poppa raised his fisted hand to hit his son and on the way down a strong arm grabbed him.

"Don'cha hit my brotha!" proclaimed Jumba.

Poppa snatched away from Jumba but he stood firm.

"We's don' been hit nuff by offa peoples, Poppa".We ain't need be hittin' each offa no mo'. What don' gon' wrong?" Jumba pleaded.

Poppa said, "Watch out Jumba. Da boy's gittin' sassy. Sayin' he ain't gonna work no mo' 'en he gonna run 'way. He gonna git us all in trouble wit' his sassin'. Maybe he oughta run 'way? I'm tawd 'em wantin' mo' lik' dis ain't good null fo' 'em. Go 'head, run 'way."

"Poppa, no. Please no, don't send our brotha 'way. He's ain't na'va been lik' us but don't send 'em away. Please, Poppa," pleaded Jumba.

What seemed like an hour was now reduced to a few minutes when a familiar voice called, "Let's get moving you Baskets. I ain't gonna tell you again."

"We's talk 'bout dis when we's git back hom', dat's if ya still y'ere," Poppa said authoritatively to Abunda. To the others he said, "Com' on, let's git."

Poppa and the boys headed across a huge field and got on the back of an old beat up truck. The truck driver drove carefully around the beautiful grounds. In the middle of the grounds was a large two story estate house that had four large white columns, oversized cathedral windows, a porch on the second level, sculptured gardens, riding stables, a patio adorned with white wrought iron furniture that had flowered cushions, and a cupid that spouted from a water fountain.

Chapter 2

The Journey

The name of the place was Annapolis Grove. It looked like something from Architectural Magazine, a magazine that spotlighted gorgeous houses. It was something so beautiful that it seemed unreal, let alone inhabited. The owners were the Rouses and their family owned the property for over 100 years. The Rouses, Mr. Jet Rouse and Mrs. Leta Rouse had two children: Storm and Alyon. Mr. Rouse was an attorney and he acquired the family business from a long line of successful attorneys. He was a kind man with very high moral principles. Standing six feet three inches tall, weighing 205 pounds, with light brown hair and mystic green eyes, he was recognized easily throughout Annapolis Grove.

Mrs. Leta Rouse was a compliment to her husband. Socially she was accepted by just about every prominent family in Annapolis Grove. Some even said that she was too nice to Colored people and would often shy away from her. Mrs. Rouse did not give any credence to those people but believed that she was to be nice to everybody as she was taught.

As the truck made its way around the grounds picking up more people, everyone seemed to be in a somber mood. The

beauty of the estate was heavily overshadowed by the emptiness of those on the truck. Their presence was not acknowledged by the estate or their own desires to be there. Everyone
seemed to be longing for somewhere else. Abunda's attitude
engulfed the entire crew on the truck without him saying a
word.

"One day I'll be gittin' 'way from dis place," spoke a
voice in the crowd.

Thinking that it was his son, Poppa Basket immediately became angry. "Boy, ain't I told ya shut up?" he asked
rigidly.

"Dat ain't me," responded Abunda. "See I ain't da only
one who wanna git 'way from here. I gotta kno' who sade
dat anyway, 'pose we runaway to'gatha?"

Poppa Basket now much more angry than before admon-
ishes Abunda, "Ya betta hush. I's ain't wanna hear 'nuffa
word from ya 'bout runnin' 'way 'en I means it, too."

"Uh huh," his son replied under his breath, while thinking
to himself, "I mean I's really gonna git off dis place. I ain't
waitin' fo' too long e'tha. I heard there's a betta way ta live
wit'out e'rybody tellin' ya what ta do. When ta com' 'en
when ta go."

The truck came to a stop and everyone got off going in
different directions to do their work for the day. The day
was beautiful with a full sun and not a cloud in the sky. The
temperature was very pleasant, not too hot but just right for
a day's work.

"Ya really wanna run'way from dis place?" a voice said
to Abunda.

"Yep, I'm really gonna do it 'en I ain't care who lik's it
or no. I wanna betta lif' den dis 'en ain't n'body stop me,"
replied Abunda.

"Where's ya gonna go?" inquired the other boy. "'En
how ya gonna git d'ere?"

Abunda turned and said, "Oh, it was ya what sade dat on da truck?"

"Yep, it me," said the boy. "Me name Bela."

Abunda said, "We's can't talk 'bout it now. We's git ta'gatha suppa time; n'body hear us, ok?"

"Ok, I's meet ya in da field yonda da big house 'bout sundown," his soon to be runaway partner said.

The men and boys worked diligently. Momma Basket and the two older girls also went to work. Momma Basket took the three younger children with her and sometimes they played with the Rouses' children. They also helped Momma Basket by doing little chores, like emptying the trash, dusting and whatever else she needed them to do at their age.

The Rouse children, Storm and Alyon, were very friendly to all the little Colored children. They treated them nicely but could not show their affection for them when visitors came. When Alyon was not in school, she played school with the Basket children. As their teacher she taught them to read and write. She shared her books and made lessons for them to do.

"Mornin' Missy Rouse," Momma Basket spoke as they entered the back kitchen door.

"Good morning Momma Basket and you little ones," said Mrs. Rouse kindly.

"Momma Basket, we are going to have guests for dinner this evening and I want you to make something special. I also need the children to clean Alyon's room. She has made such a mess throwing her dolls and toys all over the place. They can pick up the things and put them back where they belong".

"Wha'cha want fo' dinna', Missy Rouse?" asked Momma Basket.

"What about your bake chicken with dumplings, green beans, parsley potatoes, apple pie with ice cream. The children can be churning the milk for the ice cream when they finish cleaning Alyon's room. How does that sound?"

"Fine, Ma'am. Jis' fine. I gotta git one da boys kill som' chickens 'en pluck 'em so's I 'kin soak 'em," said Momma Basket.

Momma Basket reached for her apron that hung behind the kitchen door. Putting the top part over her head, she quietly surveyed the kitchen and subconsciously arranged things for her day. Momma Basket was a very orderly person and believed in planning before taking on any task. Adorned in her apron and her mental plan in place, she summoned her children.

"Y'all li'l ones git upstairs 'en clean Ms. Alyon's room. Jis' pick up da toys 'en put e'rythang 'way in da toy chest. Put da dolls on her bed. Y'all kno', big ones first 'en da li'l ones next. Don't be all day playin' 'cause y'all heard Missy Rouse I need y'all churn da milk fo' da ice cream. Gon' on, now. I's git ya later, fo' Ms. Alyon com' back."

"Uh, uh Junna Basket, ya be right here wit' me. Ya's too li'l be goin' wit' 'em. When ya git a li'l olda, ya can git wit' 'em," Momma Basket said to her youngest little boy who was so eager to join the others.

"I big now, I go Momma," replied Junna almost crying."

"Dat's ok baby, ya can he'p Momma in da kitch'n. Give me dat big spoon. See Momma really need ya be wit' me," she said in a calming voice.

Junna believed his Momma and contented himself with being with her. After all he would get to taste all the good cooking before anyone else.

"Mother, mother, where are you?" asked Alyon Rouse as she and Storm entered the house. "Oh, hi Momma Basket, where is mother?"

"Her gon' ta town fo' sup'in. Y'all havin' peoples t'night. She wanna git sup'in special. Ya wanna snack? I's made som' brownies."

"Yes, yes, Momma Basket your brownies are the best," Alyon responded. "Where are the other children?"

"Dey's out back churning da milk fo' da ice cream tonight," Momma Basket said.

"This must be special people if we're having homemade ice cream," said Alyon. "Wonder who there are?"

"I don't care," Storm barked. "I don't feel like entertaining, especially if they have girls my age. I always have to be nice to them and I don't like girls."

"Missy Rouse gonna tell ya 'bout it soon she gits back. En don't be fussy it might be fun," advised Momma Basket.

Momma Basket finished the cooking and took down the fine china and silver to set the table for dinner. Mrs. Rouse taught her how to set a formal table.

"Is ya don' churnin' da milk fo' da ice cream, yit? I's ready make da ice cream," Momma Basket asked the children as she was walking towards them.

"Yes, ma'am," said the children in unison.

"I's wanna taste it. Um um dat's good." said Momma Basket. "Y'all is a big he'p ta me."

After Momma Basket finished setting the table and making sure that everything was ready for the evening guests, she made her way around the house finishing her other chores. While making the bed in one of the guest rooms she finds an old letter under the mattress. Wanting to read it, she held off fearing that she might be caught with it and get into serious trouble. Now wondering what she should do with it, her mind analyzes: "'Pose I's tell Missy Rouse? 'Pose I's takes it hom'? 'Pose I's leaves it here 'en say nuffin? 'Pose it ain't nuffin jis' a old letta?" Somehow, though, something was telling her that it was more than just an old letter. Momma

Basket could not shake the thought that it could be something very serious.

Still pondering what to do, a voice called, "Momma Basket, where are you?"

Recognizing the voice she responded, "I's in da guest bedroom," Missy Rouse.

Immediately Momma Basket put the letter back under the mattress as she heard footsteps getting closer to the room.

"My, everything looks lovely downstairs," Mrs. Rouse complimented. "My guests should be arriving shortly and I will need you to be finished so that you can serve us."

"Yes, ma'am, Missy Rouse. I's be sho' I's don' y'ere shortly 'en git da chi'dren out da way."

Mrs. Rouse went off to another part of the house. Momma Basket got the letter from under the mattress and tucked it in her dress pocket. She still could not shake the feeling that something important was in it and that she needed to read it. The Rouses taught her how to read better even though she went to an underground school when she was a young girl. At that time you could not let anyone know that you could read or write because you would be in serious trouble.

"Storm and Alyon are you getting dressed, our guests will be arriving soon?" called Mrs. Rouse to her children.

"Yes, Mother," replied Alyon while her brother remained quiet.

"Storm, did you hear me? I need you to answer me, now," commanded Mrs. Rouse.

Still no answer. "Alyon go to your brother's room and see what's going on for me please," asked Mrs. Rouse. "Tell him what I said."

Alyon started towards her brother's room and upon approaching it she heard a muffled sound. She sped up her steps and called out to her brother. "Storm are you all right? Storm, you're scaring me, please answer me." Still no answer.

Alyon reached for the doorknob when suddenly the door opened and there appeared Storm with the door scarcely cracked. As she proceeded to open the door more, she met with resistance.

"Let me in. What is wrong with you? Mother wants us to get dressed for dinner," she informed Storm.

"I'll be out in a minute and it's my room so you don't have to come in. I just wish everybody would live me alone".

"I thought I heard some strange noise in there. Who's in there with you, Storm? If you don't tell me I'm going to tell Mother," Alyon demanded.

"I don't care what you do. I told you that I'll be out shortly. You need to mind your own business, anyway," replied Storm angrily.

Storm slammed the door in Alyon's face and she began to walk away, but before too long she heard the muffled sound again. Shaking her head, she just said, "Boys, what strange creatures."

Alyon reported to her mother that Storm was getting ready but she did not tell her about the strange sound or Storm's weird actions. Mrs. Rouse was content with Alyon's report and continued her preparations for her guests.

"Missy Rouse, y'ur guest is comin'," Momma Basket called.

Mrs. Rouse proceeded to the front door with her genuine warm smile.

"My, it is so good to see you all. Do come in. Zoey you look lovely and my how the girls have grown. Well girls, how have you been since we were last together? Let's go into the parlor and chat before dinner," Mrs. Rouse requested.

Zoey Pinkerton was one of Mrs. Rouse's best girl friends from elementary school. The Pinkerton's owned the huge estate next to the Rouses.

Mrs. Rouse asked Momma Basket to tell Storm and Alyon that their guests had arrived and to come into the parlor immediately. Alyon came along bubbling with the same warmth as her mother but Storm was reluctant and very tentative. They all gathered in the parlor and after about an hour of chit-chat they had dinner. Mr. Rouse was away on a business trip.

"That was the greatest meal I've had in a long time. You know I've always wanted Momma Basket to come with us. Remember, if you ever want to replace her just let me know," said Zoey Pinkerton.

Momma Basket finished serving and cleaning the kitchen and said, "Missy Rouse, I's don' now. 'Kin I's go now?"

"Of course Momma and thanks for everything. I'll see you in the morning."

Momma Basket gathered the children and headed for home. It was getting dark as the sun had set and she did not want to be walking too long in the dark. It still was not safe for the Coloreds to be out at night.

She was very tired from her day but soon remembered that she needed to take care of her own family. The men would be coming in soon and she wanted to get supper prepared for them. The two older girls had been given the responsibility of starting supper as they got home a little earlier than Momma Basket.

Spotting their house from a little ways, the children started to run. They called out to their older sisters and ran faster until they reached their destination. Even they were tired from their day so they sat down to rest.

"We don' ice cream t'day wit' Momma," exclaimed Jayla. "We taste it; it good. I wanna we git 'dat thing 'en Momma kin' make us som' ice cream."

"One day we git one 'en Momma promises ta mak' ya som' ice cream. All ya kin eat," encourages Momma Basket.

"Sho' smells good in y'ere. Ya girls had a good day?" inquired Momma Basket.

"Yes, Ma'am. We jis' 'bout don' suppa so ya can jis' rest a l'il befo' da men git back," said Makita.

The girls had been taught to read and write by Momma Basket. She also taught them to fake acting stupid so that they would not be hurt for being educated. Momma Basket was a pretty good actress herself as she led people to believe in her stupidity.

"I's hungry, where's my suppa woman?" a gruffy voice barked coming through the door.

"Yea, we's hungry, too," chimed in some of the other boys.

"Suppa is jis" 'bout ready so quit ya fussin'," said Makita.

Everyone gathered around for the evening grace, which was now a part of the Basket tradition along with the family rituals from Africa.

Supper was over and Momma and the girls were cleaning the dishes while Poppa and the boys went their way. Abunda was on the side of the house sulking from the day's experience, thinking, "Somehow I's gonna leave this place. I's still tired of bein' here 'en not havin' nothin'. Momma and Poppa can stay here until they die, but I ain't stayin' here 'en for sure I ain't dying here."

"Abunda, Abunda," called a voice from the far side of the house. "Com' 'ere."

"Who' dat?" Abunda inquired in a nervous tone.

"Me, Bela. I wanna talk 'bout runnin' 'way lik' we's sade t'day. Com' 'ere."

Abunda moved quickly towards the voice and the far side of the house. Rapidly approaching the meeting spot, his anticipation heightened and reality loomed in him believing that he really would leave home and very soon.

"Bela, ya really wanna leave home 'en go som'where else ta live?" Abunda asked. "Ain't ya scaked of what coulda happen ta us out dere? Ain't ya gonna git homesick 'en wanna com' back soon things git hard. It gonna be real hard fo' us at first 'cause we ain't got no money or o'tha stuff we need."

"I don' thinkin' 'bout runnin' way fo' long time. I's sicka stayin' 'round 'ere 'en workin' hard ta git nuffin'. Ya got ya family, I ain't kno' where my is. I's been token from one place ta anuffa. I's see what da White folks got 'en I's e'vn see som' Colored people wit stuff lik' da White folks. I's kno' we's kin git mo' den dis. I's really wanna leave."

For a moment the two just sat engrossed in their thoughts. Neither said a word to the other but just looked up at the crisp clear sky. Suddenly a shooting star ran across the velvet black drop of the sky and both guys responded simultaneously, "Say a wish".

"I's wish dat we git a way ta leave from here 'en som' things we need ta go. I wish dat we don't git hurt 'en our peoples be safe 'en don't miss us too much," Abunda almost prayed.

The boys decided to give themselves a little more time to be positive that running away was what they wanted to do. They departed from one another but planned to meet again very soon to further discuss their plans. Each had an attitude of hope that was not present before this meeting. They felt like they could endure a little longer and could even work with a spirit of excitement because they had a secret.

Momma Basket had put the little ones to bed and was preparing herself for bed. She took off her dress, laid it across the bottom of the bed and reached for her nightgown. Weary from the day, she put on her gown and laid on the bed. She soon fell into a deep sleep.

Poppa Basket came into the room after taking a stroll around the house. It was a habit with him so that he could make sure that everything was all right and his family was safe. Sometimes he would sit up instead of sleeping, almost as if to guard the house against intruders and people who hated the Coloreds. He saw Momma Basket lying straight out and sleeping soundly, so again, he made sure not to make any noise that would awaken her. He prayed, "I's got me a great woman. We's been th'ough a lot to'gatha 'en she a'ways be wit me. I kno' she git betta if she ain't wit me. I's wanna git her mo' 'en one day I's am. Jis' watch me. Amen" Then he, too, fell asleep.

Momma Basket becomes obsessed with the future of her family and their spiritual well-being. Grappling with sleeplessness nights, her growing family and the events that surround them, she longs for a confidence that everything will surely be all right.

Thoughts of concern were bombarding Momma Basket's mind, "What gon' happ'n ta my chi'dren afta me 'en Poppa is gon'? Is dey gonna stay to'gatha if we's die? Whos' see afta da young'ens? How dey gonna mak' it? It gotta be a'way som'where."

As her thoughts continued to devour her, she remembers portions of Poppa Basket's ordeals when they found him in the cemetery. Her mind found its way to what Poppa Basket said his ancestors kept saying to him, "Jis' do what I told ya do".

"What dey mean? D'ere really a 'heritance? God, I be'leve ya d'ere, 'kin ya he'p me?" she prayed.

Momma Basket does not remember her family. She vaguely only remembers her grandmother who always told her that God loves her and will protect her. As she attempts to find some connection to her past, pain sets in and she sees herself being taken from her grandmother but the ache of the pain would not allow her to remember more.

"God is real. Poppa's family gotta diff'rent God but it was still God. Dey see God in da dead, who looks o'va dem from above. I kno' my grandmomma's lookin' o'va me from up d'ere, too. So we's all be'levin' in God," Momma Basket thought empathically. Momma's mental wandering stops as she realizes that it is another day and again time to get her family ready for the day.

While Momma was contemplating the family's new relationship with God, Abunda and his friend, Bela, got together to discuss the plans of their running away. Now, however, Bela tells him of others who want to join them and are ready to leave. Abunda becomes extremely nervous, thinking that too many running away at once will draw attention quickly to their absence.

Abunda questions Bela, "Why ya tell'em? Who dese offa people? Where dey gotta leave from? How we all gonna make it safely?"

"I's ain't don' thought all 'dat. One my brotha 'en I's gonna keep'em wit' me. We's been 'gatha a long time. I's guess'em don' tell da offas," Bela replies.

"Ya kno', dis dangerous 'en we's could git kil't."

"Yea, I kno' but I's gonna try 'en so is da offas. We's gonna' do dis, Abunda."

"Don't tell n'body else, ya hear me?" Abunda barked.

"I hear ya, Abunda. I hear ya," responded Bela nervously.

"Ok, here's da plan."

After finalizing their plans, Abunda and Bela separated.

Momma was serious about having the spiritual ritual every evening. It was now like a service at home. She demanded that the family come together and sing a song, pray and read the Bible that the Rouses gave to her.

Abunda came in just in time for the service. He barked, "I ain't doin' dis no mo'. I ain't. Jis' watch, I ain't gonna be here. Jis' watch."

Poppa Basket slapped him across his face. "Don't talk ta y'ur moffa 'en me lik' 'at no mo'. Ya ain't gotta worry 'bout bein' y'ere if ya's keep dis up."

Abunda raises his hand to his face. Seething with anger he turns to leave the house but his mother's cry halts his steps. "God he'p our family. God he'p our family. Don't let us leave each offa. Please, God. Please!"

The family is still and fear could be felt like a heavy blanket over the room. The little ones were crying because their Momma was crying and the others remained pensive with anxiousness. The older boys surrounded Abunda and attempted to console him. Only their whispers could be heard in the room. The Basket boys had a very strong bond, but Abunda was always different. He was a loner but he made himself fit into his family. He was very outspoken and extremely intelligent in spite of his display of a limited education. Listening and observing were the tools that he used to enhance and improve his education even more.

Momma Basket urged Poppa Basket to start praying. After several promptings, Poppa Basket said, "Let's pray. God thank ya fo' what ya don' fo' us. Thank ya fo' keepin' us safe 'en to'gatha. Thank ya fo' our ancestors who is wit' ya now. I pray dat dem he'p us live a betta life 'den dey had. Amen."

"'En God please don't let Poppa 'en Abunda fight no mo'," says a little voice. And everybody in the room said loudly and in unison, "Amen".

The atmosphere in the house was very solemn as night crept in and the emotions attempted to dissipate. The family prepares for bed but it is obvious that getting to sleep is going to be a problem. Most are concerned as to the validity of Abunda's vehement statements surrounding his running away. His brothers are openly dismayed and their faces demonstrate their heaviness.

Abunda's second oldest brother, Jumba, took him to the side and asked, "Why ya wanna run 'way 'en hurt Momma? Ya's kno' how much she love ya, even mo' den us?"

"I don't wanna hurt Momma", Abunda said, but I jis' can't keep on stayin' here. Ain't ya tawd of this life? Always workin' hard like slaves 'en gittin' nothin', jis' goin' from one day to da next."

"I kno' but I be'leve dat God is gonna he'p us git 'way som'day, all us. If we stay to'gatha, as a family, we can he'p each offa. I kno' Poppa ain't always real 'bout his prayers but I be'leve it when he pray. Ya kno' he always pray da same pray'r."

"Pray'r ain't got us no where yet, 'en I kno' it won't git us no where later. We's still here ain't we?"

Jumba walks away saddened that he could not reach his brother. He is awfully afraid that Abunda will runaway and he will never see him again.

Abunda goes out the house and sits on a stomp. Looking up at the sky he thinks, "I gotta to see her befo' I go. I want her to kno' where I's be 'en that I's gonna come back 'en git her or I's gonna send for her. She's my life line 'en I need her."

While the family sleeps, Abunda, quietly undresses and gets into bed. Thinking, "Tonight ain't da right time 'cause da others ain't ready to go. I ain't sure I want all 'dem to go wit' me, anyway."

As Abunda sleeps, he has a dream that he is away in a big city with a good job, and is making money. He is a businessman who owns a publishing business. He learned the trade as an apprentice when he ran away from Annapolis Grove and decided to have his own business. He saw other Coloreds in prominent positions and the Whites were kind to them. The Whites supported their businesses and everyone seemed to get along with one another. It was so unlike Annapolis Grove where the Coloreds did all the work and the Whites reaped the benefits. No Coloreds had the opportunity of business or anything else other than working for the White people.

Abunda laughed in his sleep as the happiness he was experiencing in his dream bordered on reality. He nestled himself into a fetal position and gave way to his new surroundings.

The family arises the next morning and readies themselves for the day. Momma Basket's day is uneventful and she is concerned about getting home because of Abunda's threats. As she approached their house, she thought she heard someone crying and began to run. Running as fast as she could she almost falls through her front door. Before speaking, Momma looks around to see if everyone is present because her initial thought is that someone had been hurt. Abunda is missing!!

"Where Abunda? Where Abunda?" Momma asks in tears. "Where my son?"

Momma runs about the house going from one room to another, crying out for her son. The other family members try to comfort her, but to no avail. In her despair, she does not notice that Poppa and Jumba are also missing. She is so conscious of Abunda's threats to runaway that his absence sent her into a tail spin.

"Momma, please stop, ya gonna make ya'self sick. Look, Poppa 'en Jumba ain't here either," Makita says trying to console her mother.

Stopping almost in her tracks, she composed herself and realized that what was being said was the truth. "My God I scaked Abunda don' run'way lik' he sade. Where's da offas? Is we kno' dat sup'in happ'ned to 'em?"

"No Momma, dey jis' ain't here," Makita answers.

Just then the front door opens and in walks Poppa by himself, but before he could shut the door Abunda appeared followed by Jumba and Junta.

Cries of relief could be heard throughout the house. The heaviness that once consumed the dwelling was now gone. The entire family sat quietly, including Momma. They were so grateful that Abunda did not leave them.

Junna said, "Bunda, ya ain't go 'way. Ya gonna stay wit' us?"

Abunda picked up his little brother and held him so tight that it was hurting him. "Bunda, ouch." Abunda did not respond, but instead buried his head in his little brother's neck and started to weep.

"Don't cry, Abunda," Sha'myla says. "Please, don't cry."

No one knew that Abunda was crying because he was going to runaway, soon, and this would be his unofficial goodbye. Momma Basket took the child from Abunda's arms and held him tightly in hers. She was crying softly because her thoughts were still with Abunda's threats to runaway. She was attempting to fathom what she would do if it ever happened.

The two of them stood as statues for a long time and no one interrupted them. Poppa sat down and just watched the two. After a little while, some of the other children joined in what became a group hug. It was quite evident that Abunda's absence would create a huge strain on the family. Following the hug everyone sat down to dinner in total silence. Poppa Basket gave his usual blessing but was more thankful than before.

"God thank ya fo' what ya don' fo' us. Thank ya fo' dis family. Thank ya fo' keepin' us 'en our chil'len safe 'en to'gatha. Thank ya fo' our ancestors who is wit' ya now. I pray dat dey he'p us liv' a betta lif' den dey had. Amen."

The night ended with the family service and everyone going to bed. The night was unusually still with an eeriness that was creepy. The feeling was one of an invasion; like something from another world was about to destroy this world. Both Momma and Poppa tossed and turned. The little ones complained of not being able to sleep, also.

Abunda arose in the middle of the night when everyone else was sound asleep. He quietly moved about the room getting his shoes and clothes. Sneaking out of the room, he put on his shoes on the front porch and went to his hiding place where he put his belongings that he was to take with him. Since he had already planned to runaway, he had put the things away a while back. For a moment, as if suspended in space, Abunda sat on the front porch. He was careful not to arouse anyone or the animals around the estate that would thwart his runaway plans.

Tears now streaming down his face, he quickly walked into the darkness purposefully hoping not to be seen. Now a good distance from his house and the estate, Abunda breathed a sigh of relief that he made it off the grounds without drawing attention. Before joining the others, he had to make one very important stop.

Carefully approaching the back of another estate, Abunda made a noise similar to a bird call and after a few moments a figure was running towards him. For a moment, Abunda was afraid because the figure did not look like the person he was expecting. However, as the figure came closer he knew that it was the person he needed to see.

Once they both realized who each other was, they held each other gently, and protectively. Resting in each one another's embrace, only their breathing could be heard and the pounding of their hearts sounded like one heart. Slowly they raised their heads to face one another as he softly stroked her face and she responded by moving her face in the direction of his strokes. Their lips met and bliss overshadowed the hopelessness of the moment. After kissing, Abunda quietly said, "I'm leaving tonight but I had to see you. You're the most important person in my life and I promise I will be back to get you and we will be together."

Crying softly a voice responded, "I will always love you and wait for you until I die. Please be safe and make a way to tell me you're okay. Please promise me!"

"I promise and I will keep my promise," Abunda said now teary-eyed himself but wanting to be strong for her. "I have to go now." He kissed her gently, stroked her face again and walked off into the darkness. She stood, seemingly in shock, until his silhouette disappeared into the night.

On the way to the meeting place where the others would join him, he continually mulled over the plans for leaving the area. Still concerned about the number of people that would be traveling with him; his major thoughts were for his own safety. He purposed that he would never return to Annapolis Grove but he would find a way to see his family again. He did not know how he would see them but right now that was not his biggest hurdle to overcome, leaving Annapolis Grove safely was!

The others were waiting for Abunda in a wooded area just outside of Annapolis Grove. They too had left their places without being noticed and made it safely to the meeting spot. When the entire group was together, everyone was crying and no one spoke a word. The feeling of fear was gripping and everyone was now paying attention to that feeling.

Abunda broke the silence when he said, "We don' got dis far 'en dis da most 'portant part of da runaway. If we kin make headway 'fore mornin' den by da time we's missed we's be out dis area. 'Memba, when dey kno' dat we's gon', dey send da word out. Every estate ain't lik' ones we's come from. People's really mean 'en dey hurt us if we's ain't careful. We's gotta stay close to'gatha 'en y'all gotta list'n to me, ya hear?"

"We's y'eard ya Abunda. Ya's in charge 'en we's gonna do what ya say," responded Bela on behalf of the entire group.

The group was comprised of Abunda, his friend Bela and his brother Bakala, Ezkiel Bela's closet friend and his brother, Ezra. None of these boys knew where their families were, or for that matter, who they were. They had been with the estate owners every since they could remember.

Bela told Abunda, "Me 'en my brotha wanna git a good lif'. We's all we got 'en I want'em to kno' betta den me. All us feels dat way. We ain't got no family lik' ya, Abunda. We's jis' got each offa."

At that moment Abunda's sense of responsibility heightened. He knew that he was accountable for all of them getting to their destination.

The group pooled their resources and had $25 that they had saved over years. Some of it they stole from their estate owners and the rest they got when White folk threw coins at them for playing the role of a jester. They had little food, the clothes on their backs and maybe one other change of clothing.

Abunda had drawn up a route to runaway that would be the safest. Remember, he played ignorant and stupid at Annapolis Grove, but he was very smart and could read and write very well. The destination was far away, to a city called Settles Landing, where he heard Coloreds went to school and owned businesses just like the White people.

The beginning route took them around five estates where Abunda heard that the owners were extremely hateful towards Coloreds. These owners were evil to their workers and scared them with threats of separation and mutilation if they ever thought of running away or not doing what they were told. Coloreds did not have the same rights as White people. They knew the dangers of overstepping the race line and the vicious consequences.

"Abunda, 'en da rest y'all boys come git da water fo' da tub," called Momma Basket.

"Momma, Abunda ain't here," screamed Jumba as he was running into the other room. "He ain't here, Momma he gon'!"

"Boy don'cha play lik' dat, git ya brotha 'en com' in here. I ain't playin' wit' ya," demanded Momma.

Jumba, trembling cried out, "Momma, I ain't playin', he gon'."

Screaming to the top of her voice, Momma Basket starting calling, "Abunda! Abunda! Abunda!"

Poppa ran into the house when he heard the yelling, as he had taken his early morning walk. "Women, what ya hollerin' fo' lik' 'at?"

Hysterically, Momma cried, "Abunda, he gon'. He gon'. He don' runaway lik' he sade."

In unbelief Poppa responded, "He ain't gon', 'memba last night ya thought he was gon'? I go look fo' him outd'se. He roun' here som'where, ya see. Ya offa boys com' wit' me. When I find dat boy, I's gonna giv'em a good whippin'."

The rest of the family was in the all too familiar huddle that occurred just the night before but this time tragedy was imminent. Voices could be heard all around the Basket's house, "Abunda, Abunda, Abunda, Abunda." No response. Poppa Basket and the others returned to the house and everybody stood in silence.

"Y'all Baskets git out here on this truck for work," called a voice from outside.

No one was conscious of the time because of their concern for Abunda, who was gone. Poppa instructed the other boys to get to the truck before him so that he could console Momma, at least a little, before leaving. "He be al'right. I pray fo'em t'day 'en we's pray fo'em 'night soon we's git back from work," he encouraged Momma and went out to the truck with the others.

They were very quiet on the truck and made no mention of Abunda's absence until they were asked. "He sick 'day," answered Poppa Basket and the driver continued without further questioning.

60

Momma Basket knew that she needed to get to work and act as if everything was fine. She spent the day working very hard so that she would avoid conversation with any of the Rouses. Her total thoughts were centered on Abunda and the hope that he would be home when she returned.

The day seemed like it would never end, but finally Momma Basket was bidding the Rouses fair well for the evening. "Night," she said.

"Good night, Momma Basket," said Mrs. Rouse. "You've been very quiet today. We'll see you tomorrow."

Momma Basket hurried home to hear if there was any news about Abunda. The two older girls had started supper as usual, but were saddened to tell their mother, "Nobody said anything 'bout Abunda. We was listenin' to hear 'cause we know we can't ask, but we ain't hear nothin'. Momma we's sorry."

"Abunda better be working tomorrow if he knows what's good for him," a voice said from the truck that was dropping off Poppa and the other boys.

"Yes sir," Poppa said, "He's be here."

Rushing to the door, anticipating news of Abunda, Poppa and the boys entered the house. The looks on everybody's face and the somberness of the room told them that there was no news. Abunda was gone. He did runaway.

Poppa Basket strongly felt the need to protect the rest of his family and to assure them of their own safety and that Abunda was safe as well. Surprisingly to all, he said, "Let's pray. God thank ya fo' what ya don' fo' us. Thank ya fo' dis family. Thank ya fo' keepin' us 'en our chil'len safe 'en to'gatha. Thank ya fo' lookin' afta Abunda 'en keepin'em safe. Thank ya fo' our ancestors who is wit' ya now 'en is lookin' down on Abunda. I pray dat dey he'p us liv' a betta lif' den dey had 'en git Abunda to da place he's goin'. Dey a'ways sade ya got su'pin betta fo' us som'where. I's pray dat Abunda jis' do what I told him do, too Amen."

By the end of the prayer all the children were crying profusely, including the older boys. Poppa was also crying and the whole family sat together and mourned the loss of their loved one.

Abunda and the group traveled at night and rested during the day in secluded places. As they rested, Abunda slipped into a gentle sleep where he heard his name being called. "Abunda. Abunda. Abunda." The called startled him and he awakened only to find that it was a dream.

They had been traveling for sometime when one of the boys got separated from the group. His absence was not noticed until they stopped to rest. Everyone assumed that he was still with the group but was just slow and only a few feet out of eyesight. When they came to a rest and waited a few minutes for him to appear, they realized that he was not with them.

Bela said fearfully, "Where ya brotha?" to his friend Ezkiel. Ezkiel looked around frantically and replied, "Oh my God, where he at?"

They knew that they could not call out for him or even back track to find him, so they all sat and thought. "What if we jis' stay y'ere fo' a li'l bit, he git up wit' us," said one of the other boys.

"'Pose he don't find us?" said Bakala.

Ezkiel vehemently said, "I's gonna find my brotha."

"Wait. Wait. Ya's gonna git us all kil't if ya go runnin' off," said Abunda strongly. "We's gotta think what to do. Ain't none a us gonna git kil't 'en we's gonna git ya brotha. Jis' let me think fo' a spell."

All of a sudden the boys heard gun shots not too far off and they sounded like they were coming closer to them. Devastated by thoughts of the missing boy being killed and what would happen to them, the boys remained breathless. They each hid in the surrounding vegetation, some up the trees and others securely in the thickets. Day was dwindling and nightfall was entering. The boys were still entrenched in their hiding places but had heard no more gun shots since earlier in the day. There was still no sign of Ezra, the missing boy. Believing that they were all safe, the boys came from their respective hiding places.

Bakala emerged first from hiding and said, "Boy I sho' so scaked. 'Pose we gotta go back hom' leas' we's safe d'ere."

"Wait a minute," said Ezkiel. "We ain't goin' no where 'til I git my brotha back. Y'alls wanna com' 'en we's y'ere now. Lik' Abunda sade we's gotta stick to'gatha. Ya wan' som'body leave ya back if ya git lost from us? I's gonna git my brotha."

Abunda calmed the fears of the group by asserting his leadership abilities. "We gonna git ya brotha back 'fore we leave here 'en er'rybody gonna be al'right. We's gotta stick to'gatha. Don't go off by ya'self, see what don' happ'n?"

The group calmed themselves following Abunda's encouragement and waited to hear what was next. Overwhelmed by the situation, Abunda heard a voice from nowhere say, "Jis' do what I told ya." Trying desperately to interpret the meaning of the phrase that had captivated his father for so long, Abunda surmised one thing that he remembered. Poppa told him that his great grandmother told him that whenever he was in trouble to pray. Prayer was strange to Abunda because he had not put much stock in its validity. He concentrated more on his circumstances than the possibility of prayer helping to change them. But desperation now lurking at the door of his mind, prayer was the only thing he knew, just then, that would correct things.

Boldly, Abunda said to the group, "We's gonna pray!"

"Pray, fo' what?" asked Bakala.

"Fo' he'p 'en da Lawd ta show us what ta do," Abunda responded with confidence.

"What good dat is? I..."

Bela interrupted his brother's speaking. "Ain't we 'posa list'n ta Abunda? Jis' do what he don' told us?"

"God thank ya fo' what ya don' fo' us. Thank ya fo' my family. Thank ya fo' keepin' us safe 'en to'gatha. Thank ya fo' lookin' afta Ezkiel's brotha 'en keepin'em safe. Thank ya fo' our ancestors who's wit ya now 'en is lookin' down on Ezkiel's brotha. I pray dey he'p him find his way back wit us. 'En I pray dat we git to da place where we's goin'. Poppa always sade dat dey sade ya got sup'in betta fo' us som'where else. I pray dat ya care fo' my friend, ya kno' who. Amen." Everybody said Amen after Abunda finished the prayer.

The group sat around as if they were waiting for the answer to the prayer. Abunda reflected on the fact that he remembered Poppa Basket's prayer and what an impact it must have made on him. Tears began to well in his eyes as his family and being home raced through his mind. Immediately he wiped his tears so that the others would not see his vulnerability. He knew that he needed to be strong for everybody.

Feeling like hours had passed; the group began to discuss their plans for finding the missing boy. It was clear that going back was not an option, but they all agreed that finding him was. Stuck without an idea, they heard a rustling in the woods close to their hiding place. "Shhh," Abunda commanded. The movement seemed to be getting closer; faster than they could move to hid themselves from their unexpected visitors. The group looked like wax statues as they sat motionless. The footsteps were now close enough to the group to overtake them and they had nothing to defend themselves with. Abunda motioned for the boys to reach for big sticks that were lying close by and very quietly said, "Soon we see 'em, we gonna jump 'em, ok?" Everybody nodded their head in agreement.

The boys were watching the ground for the feet of their intruder. All of a sudden one foot appeared and before the other could surface, the boys tackled the intruder and was about to beat him until they realized that it was their lost friend, Ezra. Ezkiel hugged his brother and they both cried. Ezra was relieved that he found his group. After reuniting with joy, Ezkiel said sternly, "Don't ya' do dat no mo'. Ya scaked da wits out us."

"I sorry," a shaken Ezra muttered. "I jis' can't stay wit'ca 'en I ain't kno' how far 'way y'all was."

"It's ok," Abunda said. "But ya need to git in da midd'l if ya can't keep up 'en two offa boys kin git b'hind ya. Let's go."

Due to the circumstances and dangers of running away, Abunda was more cognizant than ever of the need for spiritual help. It was the only help they had and he knew somehow, within himself, that it worked. Even though Poppa was not very spiritual in their earlier years, of late, he began to embrace spirituality in a more significant way with Momma's help.

The group began to walk after Abunda took the lead. They stayed closer together and made sure that everyone, especially the last one was well within eye view. As they approached an open space, along a river bank, Abunda cautioned them to be very quiet and lay down on their stomachs to crawl so they would not be seen.

Unbeknown to the group, this particular estate owner had a reputation for torching Coloreds and making an example of any who thought they could be free and equal to the Whites. Rence Bartlett was the owner's name. His bitterness grew out of the loss of his family. His parents, wife and children were ambushed one night on the way home from a charity affair at another estate. Rence blamed the Coloreds but it was never proven that they had anything to do with it.

Abunda and the group were almost past the estate when they heard voices that were very close to them saying, "We hate Coloreds and today would be a good day to kill a nigger."

Ezra was so scared that he wet his pants and Bakala had to cough because the dirt had gotten into his throat. Quickly Bela put his hand over his mouth and muffled the sound of the cough.

"Let's go nigga huntin', perhaps some fool thinks he can get away. They probably would go down along the river bank, 'cause you know they smell so bad. You walk along this end close to the water and I'll start from the other end. We'll meet in the middle," barked Rence Bartlett.

The boys knew that they would be caught and killed for sure because they had no where to hid. Abunda had to think fast because he had taken responsibility for everyone's safety. Not being able to talk aloud, Abunda thought a prayer: "God, please he'p us. We's kno' dat ya is wit' us 'en we's need ya to he'p us now. Amen."

As Rence Bartlett's friend got close to the boys, almost enough to see them, he heard a gun shot from the other direction where Rence was. His friend starting running in that direction yelling, "Did you kill a nigga? Did you git one?"

When the man was out of sight, Abunda commanded the group to start running as fast as they could. He would be the last one. He wanted to make sure that everyone made it to safety. "Don't stop 'til ya git to some woods w'ere we kin hide. 'En don't worry 'bout me, jis' keep goin'," he commanded.

The boys did as they were told. When they came to a wooded area they stopped to wait for Abunda. They hid themselves to be safe and would appear only when they saw him. Some of the younger boys were very upset because they had no idea that running away would be so dangerous. They thought that they would be safe and free to make a new life for themselves immediately. "We can't ev'n go back now," Ezra mumbled. "We's gonna make it or die for sho'."

"We's ain't gonna die," Abunda said coming through the thicket. The group was so relieved to see him because they were afraid to think the worst: what could have happened to him and what would happen to them without him.

Abunda said to the group, "We's need to pray 'en thank God fo' hep'in us."

"We's ain't kno' how'ta pray," Bela replied.

"Well, we's need to 'cause it's all we's gonna have to git where we's goin','en it ain't hard. Jis' act lik' God y'ur Poppa 'en ya want'em to do sup'in fo' ya. 'En if he do it jis' tell'em thank ya lik' ya' tell y'ur Poppa," Abunda instructed.

"We's kin do dat," Bela responded for the group.

"Poppa God, thank ya fo' gittin' us outta trouble 'en gittin' us y'ere. Thank ya fo' lettin' us runnin' 'way. Thank ya fo' keepin' us to'gatha. Thank ya fo' gittin' us safely to our new home. Amen," prayed Ezra, the youngest in the group. Everybody hugged each other for encouragement and strength. Abunda walked away from the group seeing his family in their evening service.

"God thank ya fo' what ya don' fo' us. Thank ya fo' dis family. Thank ya fo' keepin' us 'en our chil'len safe 'en to'gatha. Thank ya fo' lookin' afta Abunda 'en keepin'em safe. Thank ya fo' our ancestors who is wit' ya now 'en is lookin' down on Abunda. 'En I pray dat he git to da place where he's goin'. Amen." Everybody said Amen after Poppa finished the prayer.

Momma Basket was sitting at the table, but she looked much older and had lost a lot of weight because of Abunda's running away. She had lost her spunk and optimistic outlook. "My baby don' gon'. Where? Why? God???"

"We's here, Momma. We's wit'cha," said Jayla as Junna crawled up onto Momma's lap and put himself in her arms. Instinctively she wrapped her arms around her son and held him with all her might. The room was quiet until singing could be heard as one of the girls started to sing. The mood in the room changed slightly but Abunda's absence was very strong. Poppa Basket told his family, "We's gotta go on. Som'how we's see Abunda 'gin 'en he be jis' fine."

As a hand touched Abunda on his shoulder it brought him back to reality. "Ya ok?" asked Bela, his friend.

"Yea, I's ok," Abunda answered.

"Destination, Settles Landing, our new home," Abunda thought. He learned of Settles Landing when he first over-heard some White people talking about what a shame it was that this city let Coloreds act like White people. Abunda was working close to the gardens one day, back in Annapolis Grove, when he over heard parts of this conversation. He stopped working and moved closer to the gardens so he could hear better.

"The place is an abomination to God. Who ever heard of niggers owning property and businesses? They need to burn the place to the ground," voiced one of the men with much consternation.

"Exactly where is this place located?" asked his fellow companion.

His angry friend continued sharply, "Someone told me that it's a lot of states from here and near the great water fall way up north."

Immediately when Abunda heard this he put the conver-sation in his mind, never to forget it. Settles Landing would be his new home and there he would continue his limited education and start his own business. He had not decided what his business would be, but he knew that he was tired of slaving for someone else while they got rich and he remained poor.

Abunda did not really know how to get to Settles Landing, but he had learned from Poppa to tell directions by the sun. He knew that when the sun was high in the sky that was north and this was the only direction he needed.

The group continued to travel by Abunda's directions and instructions. They passed by more than a dozen estates that reminded them of home. Each was so beautiful, yet the group only remembered the hardship and their reason for leaving.

The trip was becoming very tiresome as they walked for hours at a time and rested only a minimal amount of time. Abunda was in a hurry to get to his new home. He did not want to waste any time or risk the possibility of getting caught by some Whites who hated Colored people. His plan was to continue along the rivers mostly near swamps where the vegetation was grown and would provide a hiding place when needed. The group ate berries from trees, did some fishing with make shift fishing poles and whatever else they could find.

"How much long'r we gotta go?" asked one of the boys. "I's tawd."

"Yea, me is," added another boy. "Is ya sho' ya kno' where we's goin'? We's lost?"

Bela became very angry. "Why y'all com' den? Ya think it be easy run'way? I trust Abunda 'en if ya ain't wanna go, gon' back hom'. 'En I's ain't gonna y'ear anymo' dis kinda talkin'. Ya y'ear me?"

"We's gotta kno' where we is. Think we's gotta find a town 'en see where we is? Maybe we's kin git som' work 'en som' food 'en a place ta sleep. We's be walkin' fo' long time. 'Pose we's git pass da people who wanna kills us?" offered Bakala.

"Ok," Abunda agreed. "But I's gonna be da one to go find da town. Y'all gotta stay y'ere 'til I git back. If I ain't y'ere com' night fall, y'all jis' git goin' 'en I's git up wit'cha. Bela, jis' follow da moon by night 'en da sun by day if I can't git back."

"Ya's gonna git back, if ya ain't I's gonna do jis' what ya sade. I's really scaked but ya told me one thang dat's gonna he'p us," Bela informed Abunda.

"What's dat?" Abunda asked.

"Pray'r," answered Bela. "I's ain't na'va don' it 'fo now but I's be'leve it work."

"Me too, 'en I's gonna do it all da tim'. It lik' havin' a fatha I ain't na'va got," added Bela's brother.

The two embraced and promised not to tell the others of the plans. When questioned about Abunda's whereabouts, Bela would say that he just went ahead to make sure that everything was safe, and that he would meet them at a designated place.

Abunda left the group and as he was walking he came up on a small farm house that looked to be a part of a larger property. He hid, lying flat on his stomach, in a crop of trees. He heard some men talking about the horses and needing to get them ready for the riders. To Abunda the tone of the men's voices was not as evil as those he had heard at home and in their travels. "What if d'ese men don't hate Colored people 'en kin he'p us. How is I gonna kno' dat, 'en 'pose dey's bad men?" Abunda thought.

Abunda rested for a while and suddenly feel asleep. The journey and all the responsibility had taken a toll on him in this moment of vulnerability.

"Why are you laying on the ground? Are you hurt or sick?" asked a young boy who must have been eight or nine years old.

Abunda nearly had a heart attack because he did not hear anyone approaching and now he did not know what to do. He was caught! He knew that he could not hurt the little boy, but....

The little boy asked again, "Are you all right?"

"Yea, I's al'right. I's jis' restin' a bit." Abunda answered.

"Who are you? What's your name? Why are you out here? Where are you going?" The little boy asked question, after question, after question. Abunda was actually grateful for the questioning because it gave him time to think about his answers and, more importantly; to find out what kind of people owned this property. Would he be free or would he be hurt by these people? Would he hurt the little boy if he had too? As many questions bombarded his mind as those being asked by the little boy.

Abunda decided to respond with his own questions. "Ya liv' y'ere?"

"Yes, my family owns all this land!" responded the little boy.

"Where dis place?" Abunda asked.

Unsure the boy inquired, "What do you mean?"

Abunda now very anxious blurted, "What da name da town 'en ya e'va y'eard Settles Landin'?"

"The town is called Marata and I've never heard of Settles Landing. Why you ask?" questioned the little boy.

"Do ya' pe'ple lik' us Coloreds?" Abunda needed to know.

"Sure my folks like everybody. You should come with me so I can let you meet them. Are you looking for some food and work? Maybe my Dad can help you?"

Abunda was extremely apprehensive and took a minute to say a silent prayer, "God, Please let dis be good. Thank ya God! Amen."

Knowing that he should go with the little boy because if he did not the boy would surely tell of his existence, Abunda decided to trust the little boy and follow him. They emerged from Abunda's hiding place and began to walk across an open field towards the small farm house where the voices where coming from. The little boy yelled to someone that he recognized named Cliff, as they came running towards them. Fear gripped Abunda, but he managed to appear unshaken by the impending arrival of this stranger.

"Master Clark, what are you doing out here and who's your friend?" asked Cliff.

"I don't know his name, but he was resting out over the hill. I think he needs some food and maybe some rest. I don't know if he wants to stay here or not, he hasn't talked much since we met. I want him to meet Father and Mother. Do you think that will be all right?" he questioned.

"You know your folk is kind to all people and I'm sure they'd like to meet him," assured Cliff.

Abunda breathed a sigh of relief, but still did not know how he was going to tell them about the group that was waiting for him.

"Come on Master Clark, let's take your new friend to see your father. I believe he's in the study preparing for tomorrow."

The three walked up the hill and over the top was another exquisite estate but there was something very different about it. It had a sense of peace and tranquility that encouraged strangers to come. The atmosphere was one of 'we care and love is what we are all about'. The branches of the trees were like open arms waiting to embrace anyone. The layout of the landscape signaled inclusion not exclusion. There was an openness to the estate; it had no fences, not even further out. Strange place, but a peaceful place and Abunda felt it all, but remained silent.

"Father, father, meet my new friend. He was resting over the hill and I came upon him. He is hungry and needs some rest," little Clark yelled.

"Hold on young man and catch your breath. You're talking so fast and obviously you're excited," responded his father to his excitement.

"Oh, I am Father, I am."

The father reached his hand towards Abunda and said, "Hi, my name is Rev. Hope and it's nice to meet you."

Abunda was reluctant to shake his hand and Rev. Hope sensed his fear of touching a White man, so he took Abunda's hand.

"What's your name?"

"Abunda."

Rev. Hope still sensing Abunda's reluctance calmly asked, "Why are you shaking? I promise that no one will hurt you here."

Rev. Hope could feel the relief in Abunda's hand as he was making his statement of trust. When he finished, Abunda knew that he was telling the truth and that he could be trusted.

"Thank ya, sir. Thank ya. Me 'en som' friends is tryin' git ta Settles Landing so we's kin git a new life. We's don' run 'way from hom' 'en our family ta git d'ere. I's lookin' out fo' us but I's only kno' how follow da sun 'en da moon. We's hungry; en needs a place sleep. We's good workers 'en is willin' ta work hard."

"Slow down son, you're talking as fast as Clark. Where are your friends?" inquired Rev. Hope.

Abunda informed Rev Hope, "Out yonda. I's told'em wait 'til dark 'en if I's ain't back go wit'out me, sir."

Cliff was standing near, in another room and Rev. Hope called to him. When he entered the room Rev. Hope instructed him to follow Abunda to the group and bring them all back to the estate.

"Father, can I go, please, after all I found him? Please, father?" begged little Clark.

"Yes, but be careful and stay close to Cliff," instructed Rev. Hope.

Cliff obeyed and Abunda led him to the others. When the group heard the footsteps they hid, but Abunda called to them and they reappeared. Abunda explained what had happened and that they would now be safe. The group hugged each other with excitement, gathered the little things they had left and followed Cliff, little Clark and Abunda.

When they arrived back at the estate, Rev Hope was waiting for them as he said. By this time he had shared with his wife what had occurred and she too was with him. They saw the group coming from afar off and quickly went to meet them. They had instructed the cook to prepare a big meal for the group and told Cliff's assistant to make places for them to sleep in the farm house. When they met each other, Rev. and Mrs. Hope embraced the group. The boys were shocked that a White person touched them other than to do them harm. They received the embraces and followed the Hopes into the house for their meal. As they sat around the table everything was very quiet because the group was so hungry they did not have time to talk.

Mrs. Hope inquired, "Welcome to Maranatha. What are you young men doing out here and where are you going?"

Reluctant to answer, the group all looked to Abunda. "We's goin' to Settles Landing to git a new life," answered Abunda.

Rev. Hope added, "Well you can stay here for a while if you like. We have some work for you to do and we will feed you and provide a place for you to stay. We will even pay you a little something that you can save for your trip."

The group was ecstatic; everyone except the one who wanted to go back to Annapolis Grove earlier. He still seemed uncertain about the journey.

"My great great great grandfather founded Marata to help the slaves escape from the South. He would hide them in a hidden bunker over by the farm house; I'll show it to you later. He was a preacher like my father and he just wanted to help all God's people no matter what the color of their skin was. My parents are the same way and they will treat you good and help you to get where you want to go," shared Clark.

After the wonderful meal, Cliff was instructed to take the group to the farm house, introduce them to the others and found them places to sleep. The group left the house feeling safer than ever before as they headed to their new quarters.

Cliff introduced the others to the group and the farm hands were very friendly. The group was given space in the farmhouse to sleep; some had to make temporary bunks on the floor because the other spaces were taken. The group did not mind at all because they were finally safe and free.

After the group got settled and shared their adventure with the other farm hands, it was getting late so everyone went to bed because they had to rise early in the morning.

Chapter 3

The Blessing

The night around Annapolis Grove was quiet and still, but there was much activity at the Rouse Estate. Mr. Rouse returned late from his business trip and entered the house while everyone was asleep. He immediately went to each room to check on his family and the caretakers. Upon reaching Storm's room he heard the muffled sound and with much concern he entered the room without knocking. Shocked at what he saw, he stood speechless for what seemed like an hour. Regaining his composure, he said, "Storm what are you doing and what have you done? How long has this been going on? Does anybody else know about this? What are you thinking?"

Totally caught off guard with his father's entrance, Storm just stood lifeless. "Father, I can explain, it's not what you think?"

"Talk fast and I do mean fast."

"Father, I...," then the door flew open and Mrs. Rouse stood in its entrance. "Jet when did you get home? Honey, I'm so glad you're here."

Mr. Rouse rushed towards Mrs. Rouse because he did not want her to know what he had discovered in Storm's room. "I just got in and wanted to check everybody's room like I do when I'm here. I came to Storm's room first; you know he's my big man. I'm sorry that we woke you, so let me walk you back to our room."

Jet Rouse took his wife by the arm and together they went to their room. Storm closed his room door and took a big sigh of relief. Now he had time to get a story together that would get him out of trouble.

Mr. Rouse undressed, put on his pajamas and got in bed with his wife. Being affectionate now was not what he had in mind, as he was still thinking about Storm. He put his arms around Mrs. Rouse and kissed her gently. He held her until she fell asleep and then he quietly got out of the bed and hurried to Storm's room.

"All right young man, this had better be good. I'm listening."

To Storm's surprise his father had once again entered his room undetected.

"Father, I can explain. Please don't be mad with me."

Very disturbed, Jet Rouse paces the floor and tries to exhibit as much patience as he can while waiting for this much needed explanation.

"It's not mine, Father. Well it is, but it isn't."

"I am really running out of patience with you young man. I want the truth and I want it now."

"It really isn't what you think, father."

"I don't know what to think. I've never been confronted with a situation like this before. What is going on here and especially in our home," Jet Rouse exclaimed.

"I'm helping a desperate person to do something very special," Storm added while still wondering how to handle his dilemma.

"How can you be helping someone by breaking the law and endangering all of us, including that person?"

"I didn't think about it that way, Father, honestly I just wanted to help. Everyone sees me as such a heartless person.

Alyon gets all the attention because she is sweet and cute. I am a fine young man but no one seems to notice."

"You know that's not so, Storm. You are loved and cared for in this family as much as Alyon. Your mother and I don't discriminate with our love for you all. Now let me hear the explanation for this."

"I was out walking through the gardens one day and I heard this strange noise. I thought that it may be a little animal caught in the shrubbery. I continued to walk until the sound got louder and louder. I decided to ignore it thinking that it could rescue itself but the noise became even louder. I changed my direction and headed for the noise. I almost accidentally stepped into a basket that had this little baby in it. Oh, my God, a baby, I said loudly. This was the most beautiful precious baby I had ever seen. It had a round face, with big soft brown eyes, a head full of curly dark brown hair and inquisitive hands as they reached for my face. I bent down to get the basket when a voice said, "Please take care of my baby. Don't let him die. I have nothing to take care of him with." I was startled to see a beautiful young White girl standing before me in tears. I asked her what was your name and who she was and where she lived?"

"My God son, what did she say?"

"She didn't reveal her identity because she said that knowing it would bring great harm to both her and the baby. She begged me to make sure that her son got a proper upbringing and that he would never know the history of his birth or parents. She was so desperate I had to help her. The baby was crying so loud and hard, I didn't know what to do so I went to get something to feed him with. Now that I think about it I didn't know what I was going to get. When I returned, she was nursing him from her breast. It was a wonderful sight in the midst of a terrible situation. She also had prepared some bottles with milk and had diapers and clothing in the basket. Her nursing the baby was to be her last close moment with her son forever."

Mr. Rouse responded after hearing the shocking story, "I have so many questions, yet I am speechless. How long has the baby been here? How have you managed to keep him? What are you going to do with him?"

"Wait Father, I've asked myself all those questions, but right now I'm just taking it one day at a time."

The baby starts to fret a little because he is hungry. "Father, can I feed him he's hungry."

"Yes, sure son."

Jet Rouse watches with amazement at the sincerity and softness of his son as he cuddles and feeds this little baby. He realizes that somehow, not knowing how long, Storm has actually been taking good care of a precious life all by himself. At that moment he was so proud of his son.

While Storm was feeding the baby, Mr. Rouse said, "Son this is very noble of you but how are we going to keep this child? What will your mother say and what about the legal ramifications?"

"I don't know Father, but what else can I do I made a promise."

"Finish feeding the baby and both of you get some sleep. We will re-visit this in the morning. It's going to be a long night for me."

Jet Rouse returns to his room and quietly slips into bed next to his wife. He is exhausted from his trip but even more bewildered by this new situation.

"Good morning, honey, I'm so glad you're home. How was your trip?" inquired Mrs. Rouse with joy.

Still disoriented from the night and the heaviness of making an extremely serious decision, Jet Rouse says, "Oh, it was okay," with little of his usual enthusiasm.

"What's wrong? I know that you are tired from your trip but usually when you get home you seem to gather strength just by being back with us. Something is wrong. Jet, what is it? Are you sick? Is it your family? Honey, please tell me," Mrs. Rouse begged her husband.

Groping for words to say but coming up empty, Jet Rouse decided to take his wife to Storm's room and show her what was wrong. It was early morning, so Alyon was still resting.

"Let's take a walk," Jet said.

Mrs. Rouse now stricken with worry pleaded with her husband, "Honey, please tell me what's wrong and where are we going."

Firmly, Jet Rouse declared, "Just come with me."

Mrs. Rouse put on her robe and slippers in obedience to her husband's wishes. They started down the corridor from their bedroom and Mrs. Rouse became even more nervous. "Has something happened to one of the children? You were in Storm's room late last night, Jet please."

Jet takes his wife by the hand and holds it tightly to reassure her of his protection. She gives herself to the moment knowing that he would never let anything happen to her or their children. He has always been a great father and husband.

Approaching Storm's room, Jet gives his wife a look and proceeds to open the door. As they quietly entered the room, Storm and the baby were fast asleep on his bed. Upon seeing this, Mrs. Rouse becomes very limp, almost to a faint but Mr. Rouse catches her and supports her startled body.

"Jet, what is this? Whose baby is this? Oh, my God is this your child? What is going on?" rattled Mrs. Rouse.

"Honey, please, just a minute. No, it is not my baby; I would never do such a thing to you. I know that you're speaking from shock," Jet Rouse reassured his wife.

The commotion frightened the baby and caused him to cry. His crying woke up Storm, who was petty exhausted from the night's events. Storm reached to comfort the baby by patting him on his back, when he noticed that someone was in the room. As he turned towards the door there stood his parents; his mother in disbelief. Mrs. Rouse went to the bed and picked up the baby. She cradled him in her arms and immediately began to sing a lullaby. Her maternal instincts over rode her parental concerns. The men sat on the bed and watched her put the baby back to sleep.

The baby now sleeping, the three of them left Storm's room and went to their room. Storm was visibly shaking, not knowing what to expect. His father motioned for him to sit in the chair, while he and his wife sat on a chaise lounge.

Mrs. Rouse began to weep softly because she was completely overwhelmed by what she saw. Mr. Rouse gently took her in his arms and held her securely. When she regained composure, she looked at Storm and beckoned for him to come to her. When Storm was within reach, she took him into her arms and held him as if he was the little baby boy. Storm began to weep and so did Mr. Rouse, but softly and unnoticeably.

Jet Rouse began to explain the situation and Mrs. Rouse sighed the biggest sigh of relief. Concerned, Mrs. Rouse asked, "Storm, I'm so very proud of you my son, but what are we going to do with this baby? Jet?"

"Mother, I promised his mother that we would keep him and give him a proper home. I can't go back on my promise. Father, please?"

Jet Rouse said to his wife and son, "This is a very serious decision and much needs to be taken into consideration. Legally we need to know who the baby's parents are. By the way, what's his name?"

"I never thought to ask, I just didn't," Storm said.

"That's no problem, we can give him a name," Mrs. Rouse said with a happy sound.

"Okay, okay, back to the more serious issues. What are we going to do with this baby?" demanded Mr. Rouse.

"What's going on," Alyon wanted to know as she entered the room. "Daddy, I'm so glad you're home," she says as she rushes to embrace him. While in her father's embrace she notices that Storm is in their parents' room. She knows that only occurs when he is in real trouble. Releasing her embrace from her father, Alyon surveys the room and finds the baby on the bed.

"A baby. A beautiful baby. Can I hold it?"

Storm replies, "It's not an it, it's a boy and yes you can hold him but be careful."

"Why is Storm giving me instructions concerning this baby? No, it can't be his? Is this why you wouldn't let me in your room and why you've been so secretive lately? Boy are you in big trouble."

"See Father and Mother, she always thinks the worst of me."

"Let's stop this now," commanded Mr. Rouse. "Alyon, apologize to your brother. Just because he wants his privacy doesn't make him an immoral person and you need to think better of him."

"Yes, Daddy. But when I want to be with him he always pushes me away. I know that boys and girls don't always get along, but he is my only brother and it's just me and him. I'm sorry Storm."

"I'm sorry too Alyon, I really am. I will do better at being a brother to you."

Jet Rouse tells his family, "Now that we are all here, let's discuss this matter."

They informed Alyon of the baby's history and begin to evaluate the situation and consider decisions. The females and Storm quickly voice their desire to keep the baby. Their actions are more emotional than rational. Jet Rouse, seeing the joy and cohesiveness of his family, also begins to lean towards keeping the baby. But in the midst of his emotional moment, reality sits in and legal questions bombard his thinking.

He informs his family, "We'll keep the baby." Everybody shouts with excitement. "Wait a minute; I will need to investigate some things, so this is only a temporary decision. We must be sure of the mother's wishes. I need to find out who she is and speak with her, if I can. If not I'll have to pursue other avenues."

"But until then, Daddy, we can keep the baby?" asked Alyon bubbling over with excitement.

Storm interrupts, "Why are you so excited, it's my baby. See how you want to take away the only thing I have that's mine."

"Storm, it's not like that, I just want to help you and I want to make our baby a special part of our family," Alyon pleaded.

"I'm sorry, Alyon, that was not nice of me. I want our baby to be a special part of our family and make sure that he has a great life, too. That's going to take all of us to do that. Thanks for wanting to help make his mother's desire a reality; to all of you."

Mrs. Rouse and Alyon begin to discuss getting everything for the baby. They are planning to convert one of the guest rooms into the nursery and will have a decorator come to make the room special for their new baby. Storm advises them that he wants to be included in the decision making after all, it is his baby. Everyone is in total agreement.

While the rest of the family is engrossed in making plans, Jet Rouse begins to make some mental notes as to how best to proceed with the legalities of this matter. He is as excited as the other family members but realizes that he must also protect his family and their new baby.

"Mornin'," a call comes from Momma Basket as she enters the kitchen back door. "I's be gittin' breakfast to'gatha right 'way. Ya lik' any thang special, dis mornin'?"

The Rouses experience immediate anxiety as they collectively realize that they do not have an explanation for the baby. Storm asks the family, "What are we going to say about our baby?" Oh, ohs, could be heard around the room as no one had the answer.

Jet Rouse explains, "We are adopting the baby and that's really all anyone needs to know."

The family, a front of solidarity, proceeds to go to breakfast. Alyon is carrying the baby and nobody has remembered that the baby has no name. Upon entering the kitchen, Momma Basket has her back to the entrance but hears them. "Mornin', how's y'all dis fine mornin'?" she inquires, without turning to face the Rouses. She is focused on getting breakfast completed.

Alyon, full of excitement, says, "Oh, Momma Basket we are all great. All of us."

Suddenly a cooing sound is heard in the kitchen and Momma Basket is startled by the sound.

"I jis' y'eard a baby? I must be gittin real old 'en twad," she says turning to face the Rouses.

When she is facing them, she now sees that her age and fatigue are not at play, but that she really did hear a baby.

"My, God. My, God! It's a baby! What a beautiful child. Who baby dat is? Fo'giv me I ain't got no right ta meddle," Momma Basket says apologetically.

Mrs. Rouse interjects, "Momma you're not meddling, you're a part of this family and now so will this little baby be also. We are planning to adopt him."

"Mr. Storm y'use awfully 'cited 'bout havin' a baby brotha, ain't ya. Ya sound lik' ya is da fatha."

"What its name?" asked Momma Basket.

A hush comes over the room and Storm says, "We haven't picked a name for him, yet, but it's a boy."

Momma Basket was totally shocked that Storm answered her question and not Mrs. Rouse. Everyone chuckled.

"Thangs gon' be diff'ent 'round y'ere," said Momma Basket cheerfully while sharing in the Rouses' excitement.

Mrs. Rouse explained to Momma Basket that she needed her to convert one of the guest rooms into a nursery. Things had to be moved out because the baby things were going to be ordered. She also wanted Momma Basket to share in the caretaking of the new baby.

Momma Basket could not wait to get home to tell her family about the new baby at the Rouses. She was so excited as if she had just learned that she was pregnant.

On the following work day, Jet Rouse was about the business of identifying his baby's mother and her whereabouts. Wanting this situation to remain quiet, he secured some help from legal associates in another town. He explained the matter to them and agreed to wait to hear their results.

Momma Basket concerned with the events at her own house forgot to share the good news about the baby at the Rouses' home. Just before everyone was completely ready for bed, she shared the news. The Basket girls were especially excited about the news and offered to help Momma Basket watch and care for the baby.

The time had passed rapidly and things around Annapolis Grove were still pretty normal. All of the Baskets were still present. The Rouses were enjoying their new baby and had forgotten the legal issues that Jet Rouse was dealing with. Because of his obsession with protecting his family, all the time, Jet maintained quietness about the legal situation of the baby. He wanted his family to be free to enjoy their new happiness that had brought his family closer than ever. Storm was now a pleasant member of the family and still exhibiting father-like qualities toward the baby. The family, however, still had not given the baby a name.

Momma Basket entered the Rouses as usual and met Storm feeding the baby.

"When da baby gonna git a name?" asked Momma Basket.

"I guess we just forgot because we are so caught up in just loving him," Storm replied.

Storm rushes into the room where his mother is and blurts out, "When are we going to give our baby a name?"

"Storm you are so right," answers Mrs. Rouse. "How could we forget something as important as that? The Bible says that a good name is better than having money or other earthly possessions. Tonight, when Jet gets home we will give our baby a name and also make plans to have him blessed by our pastor."

"Thanks Mother," Storm said with great enthusiasm, as he walked away with his baby in his arms questioning what he wanted to name him.

Storm rushes to tell Alyon about the plans to name their baby. She was in the garden embracing the beauty of the flowers and shrubbery. It was one of her favorite places at their home. "Alyon, we're going to give our baby a name tonight!"

"Really Storm, how exciting, then he will be our baby for sure. What name do you have in mind? I've been thinking about what to call him since I first saw him," wondered Alyon bursting with curiosity.

"I don't know. I've been so busy being a father, I simple had not thought about it. When I talk to him, I call him son. I've been thinking hard since Mother said we would name him this evening but nothing pops up in my mind," informed Storm with authority.

The three members of the Rouse family are now thinking and pondering what to name this bundle of joy. They are giving no thought to the possibility that they may not be able to keep the baby. They are firmly convinced that the baby would remain theirs for life.

Momma Basket started preparing dinner in the Rouses' kitchen and she too is wondering what they will name the baby. She remembers the excitement of her and Poppa naming their own children. Poppa said that the name must mean something special, while Momma wanted the name to sound good.

The Rouses' kitchen had the most delicious smell around dinner time. Momma Basket was the best cook in the entire Grove. She took pride in her cooking and working for the Rouses because they were good to the Baskets.

"Boy, it smells great in here and I am very hungry," says Jet Rouse as he joyfully enters the kitchen. "Where is the rest of my wonderful family, Momma, and how are you doing today?"

"In da livin' room waitin' fo' ya, Sir, 'en I's good," answered Momma Basket.

Jet hurries into the living room where his family is waiting. This day they looked happier than usual with anticipation filling the room. "How's my family and what's going on? You all look so serious but not sad. Is there something that I should know about?"

"Yes, honey, there is," Mrs. Rouse responds without giving any clues. "Have a seat next to me, okay?"

Jet Rouse sat down as requested and waited anxiously to hear from his family.

"Father," Storm spoke first. "We need to name our baby."

"Is this what this is all about?"

"Yes, it's been a good while since we agreed to keep him and we haven't given him a name," Storm commented.

"I was so busy with the legal matters that I didn't even think about a name. And I guess that you all were so busy enjoying him that you didn't give it much thought either."

"Yes, Father" Alyon interjected. "Momma Basket asked Storm about our baby's name."

"Are we sure that we want to give him a name; after all, he isn't legally our son yet?" Jet Rouse interjected sheepishly.

The mood of the family slumped with despair at the thought of not keeping the baby.

"Oh, Jet, why do you have to bring that up now," said Mrs. Rouse, almost heartbroken.

"Because, I have some news about the legal matters," Jet Rouse informed his family.

You could hear a pin drop on cotton, as it appeared that everyone had stopped breathing. They wanted to hear, but did not want to hear and Jet Rouse gave no visible evidence of his findings. No one spoke for what seemed like forever. Then the baby started to coo and broke the silence. His coos were full of happiness as if he knew the results of the findings. The family embraced each other and the baby while awaiting the news.

"Please, Daddy, tell us you have good news," Alyon begged.

"Jet, don't keep us waiting like this," Mrs. Rouse pleaded.

Jet Rouse coughed and cleared his throat while his family sat breathless. "The lawyers that I hired sent me the papers to sign that would allow us to adopt our baby!"

Hollers, laughter and cries of relief could be heard in the kitchen as the family rejoiced that the baby was now legally going to be a legal member of the family.

"Well, what will we call him?" asked Jet Rouse matter-of-factly. "Storm since you found our baby what do you want to name him?"

Storm's face was flushed with redness at the thought of making such a major decision that he had not given much thought. He sat still for a good while and then said, "Joshua". It was what came to his mind when his father asked the question. The rest of the family agreed that it was a good name.

Jet Rouse pronounced ceremonial blessing as he prayed, "God thank you for our son, Joshua that was sent by you. We pray that no harm befalls him and that he will be a great man someday. We pray that you protect his mother in her unselfish act of love by giving him to us. We ask you to make us the best family possible for him and that he will have a great life. Amen."

"Momma Basket, come meet Joshua Rouse, our baby," called Alyon towards the kitchen. Momma wiped her hands on her apron and rushed into the living room. She reached for the baby and gently kissed him on his forehead saying, "Welcome Joshua, welcome."

"A celebration is in order. Momma pull out a bottle of wine so that we can toast our new son," instructed Jet Rouse.

Momma went to the wine parlor and got a good bottle. Jet Rouse taught her how to choose wine by the labels and the system he used for storing it. Momma came back with the bottle and sought Jet Rouse's approval. It was given. She then got four crystal stemmed wine glasses and filled two half full and the other two one third full. As she proceeded to the living room with the wine, she was overtaken with joy for the family she loved so much.

"Where's your glass, Momma, you are part of this family?" asked Mrs. Rouse. "Get yourself a glass and join us."

Storm offered the toast and everyone touched each other's glass. It was indeed a special and wonderful occasion.

Momma Basket served the Rouses, cleaned the kitchen and left for home. Walking through the gardens she was still engrossed with the happiness of the family. She was also glad for little Joshua who would now have a home and a family that loved him dearly. She also desperately wanted to see what her family would be like in the future.

Chapter 4

Safety

Abunda had mixed emotions; he was grateful for the Hopes and for the safety of the group. However, he missed his own family. He wrestled with sleep while everyone else was resting peacefully. Once he got to sleep he was in a strange place, his new home, and there was a large church in the background. Abunda was standing outside of himself looking in and he felt the presence of Poppa Basket. "Feels like Poppa is here." Abunda hears his voice saying, "Jis' do what I told ya do".

Abunda continues with the vision and now sees himself in the pulpit of the church talking to the congregation. He is not sure if he is the pastor or just a visitor. As he continues to wrestle, he sees Poppa in the very back of the church. A cloud fills the air and Poppa's silhouette is evident to Abunda.

"Is dat Poppa 'en what he doin' here?" Abunda thinks to himself.

"Abunda" Poppa says, as he sits straight up in his bed. "Abunda," he calls again.

Momma Basket awakes and says, "What wrong wit'cha? Ya ok?"

"I jis' saw Abunda talkin' wit' peoples in a big church. I's y'eard'em say his Poppa a'ways told'em, 'jis' do what I's told ya do' but he ain't kno' what dat meant."

"Poppa ya's dreamin'. Look we's in our room 'en Abunda ain't y'ere," informs Momma Basket.

Sorely disappointed, Poppa lies back on the bed. Momma caresses his forehead and tries to comfort him. He convinces Momma that he is okay and that she should go back to sleep. She agrees.

While lying there, Poppa remembers more of what happened to him in the cemetery and wonders about his dream of Abunda. He has not discussed much more of the events with his family since the first day and months have passed.

He remembers the Promise Store with the huge lock on it because nobody ever got what was promised to them. "How ya unlock dat do' 'en git what's yu'rs?" he thought. "Why I's 'memberin' dis now? If I can't git it fo' me, kin me chil'len git it; da promise? What's I been promised? Why's I dreamin' 'bout Abunda, now? I's miss'em, but I's kno' sup'in good gonna be out d'ere fo'em. I's wish I's could hug'em, 'cause I's na'va don' befo' 'en he was y'ere."

"Who touched me?" Abunda asked out loud. "I felt som'body or sup'in touch me 'en it felt lik' Poppa."

"God, I's feelin' Abunda. I's really touchin' 'em. He right y'ere wit' me. Thank ya, God," Poppa confessed joyfully.

"'Memba, jis' do what I told ya," he reminded Abunda.

"I 'memba, but what'd ya tell me ta do?" Abunda unconsciously answered his father.

"Da 'heritance, don't fo'git da 'heritance," Poppa speaks to Abunda.

"Da 'heritance," Abunda mutters. "Da 'heritance."

Abunda hears himself saying to this congregation that, "You have promises that you have yet to get. Don't give up on your future but keep working hard and one day what you want will be yours."

Puzzled by this, Abunda questions his surroundings. "Am I the pastor of this church? Why am I speaking here?" He did not sound like the Abunda he knew but more like a well educated Abunda; one who people looked up to.

"Pastor Abunda," someone called.

"Yes", Abunda responded. "Oh my goodness, I am a pastor. How did that happen? I don't know God that good!"

A voice says to Abunda, "But I know you real well. You have been calling out to me for a long time. You have adopted the prayers of your father and your ancestors. Do you really have to know me in order for me to know you? Should the created question the works of the Creator?"

"God? Is dat ya, God?" Abunda speaks as he wakes himself up.

He looked around to see where he was. Initially he did not recognize his surroundings but as he continued to look he remembered the farm house.

Abunda got up, went outside and looked up to the sky. He was really wondering if it was all a dream or some kind of spiritual visitation. His ancestors were always watching over them, could it have been a visit from them? Abunda sat on the ground and pondered "What did it all mean? Will I be a pastor? Am I going to make it to Settles Landing? A sign from God?"

The smell of country bacon, biscuits and coffee woke up the group. They were permitted to sleep a little longer, because Cliff was sympathetic to their travels.

"So' smells good out d'ere," Bela said aloud.

Cliff greeted the group, "Mornin', guys. You can wash up over there and put on some clean clothes and come get some breakfast."

"Boy dis here is great," responded Ezkiel.

"Sho' is," chimed in Ezra.

While they were eating Abunda's mind was back in Annapolis Grove. He was remembering the dream or spiritual visitation he had last night. It was so real that he surmised that it could not have been a dream. He actually felt the touch of his father. He felt a new connection to Poppa Basket; more different than before. His mind went to a higher level of consciousness and struggled to settle on the thought that 'there is something better for them, the Coloreds'.

"Abunda, ya okay?" Bela asked with much concern for his friend.

"Yea, I's ok," Abunda responded.

"Ya look lik' ya ain't wit' us," Bela pushed the issue.

"But I is," Abunda responded with conviction.

Cliff informed the boys of their chores on the farm. Two of the boys were taught to milk the cows. The other two were put on the detail of cleaning the stables and how to handle the horses. Abunda was given supervision over the boys as he was expected to learn what they were doing and especially working with Cliff on how to manage the estate. Cliff and Abunda quickly grew very close as did the others with the new workers.

Marantha was convincingly peaceful. It boggled the human mind that there could be such a place where everyone lived and worked in harmony. Everybody was their brother's keeper, as Rev. Hope often spoke. The Coloreds and the Whites worked side by side, hand in hand. The Hopes did not single themselves out but included all in their family. Once a month they held a family dinner in the main house and everyone dressed up and attended. They all went to church together and the Coloreds did not have to sit in the balcony like they did in Annapolis Grove. A special cloud hovered over Marantha, something that the boys had never experienced. Cliff and the other workers often talked about how special Marantha was and how the Hopes rescued him from the Whites who did not like other Whites because of their social standing or lack thereof.

Abunda and the group rapidly grew very fond of Marantha and came to accept it as their home. Many months had gone by, since arriving at Marantha, and they never discussed leaving, not even the boy who wanted to return to Annapolis Grove.

Rev. Hope, though he had no favorites among his workers, took a special liking to and care for Abunda. He sensed that there was something unique about him and wanted to cultivate what he believed was there. He was reluctant to speak to Abunda about this because he did not want to frighten him and the group away. But he knew that he had to do something before this young man left his presence.

Rev. Hope never discussed how long the group could stay or their travel plans. He did, however, pray and ask God what He wanted him to do for and with the group. This was when he sensed something special about Abunda. The group quickly learned their responsibilities and was eager to learn more. Most of the boys had not learned to read or write but they wanted to do so.

"'Pose Rev. Hope teach us read 'en write?" Bela asked his brother.

"I ain't kno' but I's wanna learn too."

"Me too," said Ezra. "I's tawd bein' treated lik' I's dumb. I betcha if I's learn read 'en write I's be smarta den lots White folks. I's git me a good job 'en git married 'en settle down."

Even though the boys were very comfortable with their surroundings, they still had some hesitation about approaching the subject of education. They had never met a White person who was willing to help them with anything, let alone education. They talked about it among themselves for a while trying to get rid of the fear of asking Rev. Hope or anyone else White for help. Finally at one of the monthly get togethers, Abunda's friend Bela spoke up, "Rev. Hope kin ya's he'p us read 'en write?"

There was a silence that stilled the entire room while fear ran rampant in the minds of the other boys. Did they make a mistake by asking such an important question that would give them a status equal to Whites; the ability to read and write with an education? They held their breath while waiting for the answer that seemed to take a long time coming. Finally, Rev. Hope responded, "It would be my pleasure to do so."

"What dat he sade?" inquired Ezra because he did not understand the formal reply.

Abunda replied, "He sade yea." The entire room roared with gaiety. The group started chanting, "We's gonna read 'en write. We's gonna read 'en write," while the others stood by amused.

"I wanna learn ta read 'en write, too," said one of the workers who had been at Marantha for over two years.

"Why didn't you tell me?" Cliff questioned.

"I was too ashamed," replied the worker.

The group was very amazed because they knew that every White person knew how to read and write. They never imagined that they would hear what they just heard. They looked at the worker strangely at first and then reached to shake his hand as a show of solidarity. The worker was over-whelmed with the response but chose to restrain his emotions. Abunda, however, was taken completely by surprise as his emotions became evident by the tears now streaming down his face. He was not even conscious of them until they had cascaded completely down and were dripping from his chin. Becoming conscious of this display he immediately wiped the tears away and excused himself from the room. He found the nearest room and cried with joy.

Rev. Hope prayed and thanked God for granting the desires of the group and his worker. He assured them that he would do everything in his power to see that they received the teachings they desired. He even stressed to them that he would assist in finding them work in another area after they finished learning to read and write, if they wanted to leave Marantha.

Disbelief engulfed the entire room and everyone that was present.

"Father, can I help teach them to read and write? You know I'm pretty good at it and I make good grades at school," asked Clark with a burst of energy.

"I can set up a classroom in the garden and we can set school hours that wouldn't interfere with their work. I don't want you all to be too tired to study," added Mrs. Hope.

"I'm glad to see that we have what we need and that everyone is so eager to assist. I will leave this part to Mrs. Hope because I know that she will do a great job. She has experience teaching others and, son, I'm sure your mother will be glad to have your assistance. Cliff will you design a work plan because I agree with Mrs. Hope I don't want the group to be too tired to learn, and we will still need the work done around here," instructed Rev. Hope.

"Rev. Hope, I's be glad take on more work, 'cause I's can read 'en write som'. I wanna learn mo; thangs, though," Abunda interjected.

"Of course Abunda, but I would like for Mrs. Hope to test you so that we can determine if you need additional help. I wouldn't want you to miss something as important as this. I'm so grateful for your willingness that shows how much you care for others," Rev. Hope stated.

The Marantha family concluded their dinner and everyone joined in cleaning the dishes, the kitchen and the dining room. The workers left the big house and walked back to the farm house. On the way back they were discussing what had just taken place.

Cliff started by saying, "When I came to the Hopes, I had no hope. I was treated badly by the last people I worked for 'cause I didn't have the kind of money they had. I didn't have a good education 'cause my family was sharecroppers and my father was an overseer. We never got the best of anything. My father drank a lot and my mother got tired of him beating her, so she left us. She didn't take any of us, her children, with here; just woke up one morning and she was gone. My daddy became like a mad man and we suffered 'cause of it. I am the oldest of the children so I had to work hard and look out for my sister and two brothers. We had to work the fields and do what my father was supposed to do with the other field workers. When we got old enough I took my sister and brothers and we left. I took them to the nearest town and left them at the orphanage. I hated to do that but it was best for them. I started traveling around from one job to another and one day I ended up here. I wasn't a religious man, but I thanked God for leading me to the Hopes. They really did give me hope and everything else I needed."

When the group returned to the farm house they sat around, quiet and very still. Everyone was still in awe of what had just taken place. The atmosphere was one of unbelief and they wondered when true reality would set in. Abunda's group knew that this was all too good to be true and was sure that by morning this dream would have been a nightmare. After a few hours of silence, the men started to get ready for bed. Cliff said, "We got a lot to do tomorrow, I'm gonna turn in, too. Good night."

Bela was lying on his bunk looking up wondering, "Is we's gonna git som' teachin' or is dey lie. I does really wanna learn read 'en write. God, if ya's still list'n lik' ya was when Abunda told us pray, please let dis be true. I's gonna work hard to learn 'en be my best, please?"

Tears began to stream down his face, first softly and then like an unannounced thunder shower, his face was drenched. Bela muffled his crying so that no one else would hear him. Unbeknown to him, others were crying as well at the thought of the next day. This day represented their emancipation, they hoped.

The next morning was no longer a dream but now a reality. Cliff informs the entire group that Rev. Hope wanted to see them at the big house. Everyone dressed and followed Cliff's instructions. On the way to the big house, they were met with delicious smells of different breakfast foods. Much to their surprise, when they arrived at the back door Mrs. Hope invited them in and the table was set. "Have a seat," Mrs. Hope suggested. "I wanted this to be a special day for you so I want us to break bread together first. Afterwards I will share with you my plans for our little school and Cliff will give you your work assignment."

Everyone took a seat and Rev. Hope shocked the group by asking Abunda, "Would you say a prayer for us?" Initially, Abunda was frightened but responded, "Yes, sa. God thank ya fo' what ya don' fo' us. Thank ya fo' my family. Thank ya' fo' keepin' us safe 'en to'gatha. Thank ya' fo' our ancestors dat's wit' ya now 'en is lookin' down on us. Poppa a'ways sade dat dey sade ya' had su'pin betta fo' us som'where else. Thank ya' fo' Rev. Hope 'en Mrs. Hope 'en little Clark 'en da offa workers here. I pray dat ya' cares fo' my friend, ya' kno' who. Amen."

The group said, "Amen".

"Abunda that was a lovely prayer. Who taught you to pray like that?" asked Mrs. Hope.

"My Poppa," Abunda answered.

The group ate and cleaned the area. "Follow me, will you please?" asked Mrs. Hope.

The group obeyed. She led them to an area in the garden just on the lawn where she had made a classroom. There were seats with notebooks on them, a table to the front that was her desk and to the side of it a smaller table with books on it. On her desk, she had pencils and a piece of slate that she would use as a blackboard.

"Please take a seat. This is how we will be conducting our school. The seat that you are sitting in will be your seat everyday. We will have school before work but not on Saturdays and Sundays. I will give everyone a notebook and two pencils. You are responsible for them. Please do not lose them. Today we will start class but you will not have to work. I know that you will be too excited to get any work done, so Rev. Hope has agreed to let you have the day off."

"We's na'va git a day off back hom'," exclaimed Bakala.

Chapter 5

Reassurance Completed

"I's could sho' use a day off from here," Momma Basket thought to herself while cooking in the Rouses' kitchen. "I's awfully tawd 'en needs rest."

Mrs. Rouse walked into the kitchen just as Momma Basket was sighing and asked, "What's wrong Momma? You sound so tired."

"I is, ma'am. I is tawd," replied Momma in a weak and strained voice.

"Take the rest of the day off, go home and get some rest. I can finish preparing the dinner. We will see you tomorrow," insisted Mrs. Rouse.

Momma Basket did not waste anytime getting out of her apron and out of the house. She was probably walking faster than she had ever walked in her life. Her body was so tired that she did not know if she could make it home without fainting. On the way, she slowed up and sat on a tree stump. She started to cry. She sat with her head in her hands just sobbing. Her mind traveled over time to the experiences her family endured and wondered what would happen to them next. "What's gonna happ'n if da Rouses leave Annapolis Grove 'en anuffa family toke ov'a? Is dey be as good as da Rouses? What's gonna happ'n to my chi'dren? Where's my baby, Abunda?" Momma Basket cried until she could not cry anymore. She cried until her emotions were drained. She sat still and hopeless.

Just at that moment, a little white bird sat on a piece of branch close to her. The bird began to chirp a beautiful melody that reminded Momma Basket of a song her grandmother used to hum when she was a little girl. That thought brought a sense of strength and hope to the gloominess that had consumed her.

After feeling like she had cleansed herself of the heaviness, Momma Basket wiped her face and continued to walk home. She put her hands in her pockets and realized that there was a piece of paper in one of the pockets. "Oh my goodness, dat's da paper I's took from da Rouse hous' long time ago. I's ain't look see what it was. I's wanna kno' why I's ain't kno' it t'was in y'ere. Guess when I's wear dis dress I's gotta apron on 'en I's jis' put my hands in da apron pockets. Anyway, I's wonda what dis tis?"

Momma Basket opened the piece of paper and realized that it was a deed. She was not sure because she had never seen one before, but at the top of the paper was the word DEED printed in bold letters. She had no idea what to do with it or who to show it to because she had taken it from the Rouses' house. Momma Basket refolded the paper and put it back in her pocket. Thinking to herself, "What is I gonna do wit' dis? I's ain't kno' what it mean or who could he'p me? I's ain't want troubl' fo' me 'en my family so I's betta keep it a li'l while longa. Maybe if we leaves y'ere I kin ask som'body."

Finally reaching home, she was greeted by her children with a big embrace that she needed. She held on to the girls for an unusually long time then took the littlest one and sat him on her lap. Sitting quietly she was thinking about Abunda but did not want the others to know. "I's jis' gotta rest a bit," she informed them. "Suppa ready, yit?"

"Yes, Momma, as soon as ya's ready 'en Poppa gits here," Makita replied.

"Poppa 'en da offas ain't here?"

"No ma'am."

"Dey kinda late, ain't dey?" Momma asked concerned.

"Dey be long shortly, I's sho', Momma. Ya jis' sit 'en rest; we's look afta da younga ones."

Momma Basket still distraught mumbled, "I's hope ain't nuffin wrong. I's hope ain't nuffin wrong."

"Everything's good," Makita assured her as she gave her mother a big kiss on her forehead.

The boys came in shortly after Momma's inquiry but Poppa Basket was not with them. This frightened Momma Basket who immediately rose to her feet in alarm. "Where Poppa? Where Poppa?" she asked franticly.

"He sade fo' us go 'en he com' shortly," answered Jumba.

"Why, what's wrong?" Insisted Momma more fearful than before.

"Nufin, he sade he wanna think," said Jumba as he searched for thoughts to comfort his mother.

Poppa Basket went back to the cemetery that used to be his favorite place to think. He was sitting on a head marker with his hands in his head when he felt a presence in front of him. Initially, he was too frightened to lookup because the presence was so strong, but it did not feel like a person. He remembered his ancestors telling him how they used to be visited by the ancestors who had been dead for a long time. He could not remember them saying how they felt about that experience, but just knew he remembered them telling him. Before he made a move he sat very still. "'Pose it go 'way if I's ain't move," Poppa thought to himself. But the presence lingered and it was now obvious to Poppa Basket that it was not going anywhere.

Poppa Basket finally looked up and saw Abunda. "Abunda, Abunda, ya's y'ere. I's so glad ya's hom'." As he went to embrace Abunda, he realized that it was not Abunda but someone who resembled Abunda.

"Jurann," the voice spoke. Poppa Basket was frozen in place when he heard the name. No one had called him that as far back as he could remember but his grandfather who died many years ago.

Poppa Basket did not respond. Concerned about losing his mind, he just sat very still.

"Now I's hearin' voices som' mo'. I's gotta stop comin' y'ere," he muttered.

"Jurann," the voice called again. "I's here ta he'p ya."

"I's need som' he'p, but who is ya 'en how's ya gonna he'p me?" questioned Poppa.

"I's ya granddaddy, Sambuka, ya momma's daddy," answered the voice authoritatively.

The voice did not sound like Poppa's grandfather but Poppa was sure that the presence was his. Poppa replied equally as authoritatively, "Ya's dead. How's ya gonna he'p me? Ya's don't kno' what we's need."

"Yea; I do. We's don' watchin' ya from da sky 'en we's see what's ya's doin' 'en ya family," Sambuka informed Poppa.

"Who's we?" a very disgruntled Poppa questioned.

Ignoring Poppa's attitude Sambuka continued, "Da ancestors. 'Memba ya ke'p hearin' jis' do what we told ya' but ya' ain't 'memba what we told ya, do ya?"

"Naw, I's ain't. I's be wonderin' what it all mean but I's git mad 'cause I's ain't kno'. I's kno' it he'p us 'cause I feels it inside," Poppa replied as his attitude began to adjust to a more calmer tone.

Wanting to calm Poppa's fears, Sambuka explained, "When da King com' from Africa he teach da spiritual rituals dat dey don' in Africa. He sade how 'potant dey was ta he'p us liv' in dis strange land. He ain't na'va want us fo'git 'em 'en make sure dat we's do'em ev'ryday. Da ancestors git pow'r ta he'p us from da' offa side, he told us. A pow'r dat we's can't git on our own or from dis side. But if we's ain't stay in touch we'd be scaked 'en he'pless on dis side. Ya fo'git da teachin's dat I don' wit' ya as a li'l boy? We git sep'rated when ya was li'l 'en I couldn't teach ya mo'. But I's here fo' ta he'p ya now."

"We's ain't do da thangs no mo'. Dey scaked da chil'len. I's kno' we's need som' he'p mo' den what we got. Abunda don' run'way. I's ain't fault 'em. We's jis' workin' hard fo' da others', ain't git nuffin fo' us. How kin ya he'p us?" Poppa urgently wanted to know.

Sambuka continued, "Da rituals was fo' giv' thanks, sing songs, giv' oblations (offerings,da po'ing water purify da air) 'en pray. Da King us'ta kill animals 'en sacrifice 'em. When we com' up dey teach us do da oblations instead. Our elders dance 'en wore African clothes. 'Cause we's on da plantation we can't do dat. Da 'potant thang dat ya lead ya family spiritually. Da powers of dis earth dey destroy ya 'en y'ur family if ya ain't got anuffa place ta git strength from."

Poppa agreed, "Ya's right. Momma Basket don' sade fo' me start prayin' a'gin 'en I is but Abunda still don' run'way. We's still workin' hard. 'En now I's scaked first tim' in my life as I kin kno'."

"Life scak'ry fo' Coloreds in dis country ain't got nuffin else fo' hold on to. We's ain't 'posa be y'ere but we's ain't got a choice. Da King, him was wise 'nuff kno' dat only da strong mak' it y'ere no matta what da Whites don'. Don't fo'git find da 'heritance. It got da answer ta lif', no matta what happ'ns," said Sambuka as he continued to enlighten Poppa.

"I's ain't kno' 'bout dat 'heritance. I's only y'eard one or two stories 'bout it. How ya find it?" questioned Poppa.

"B'gin lookin' in ya, not out ya. List'n ta y'ur self. What ya y'ear ya sayin' or thinkin'; y'ur mind thinkin'. Ya ain't crazy, ya jis' ain't kno' dat ya really got he'p 'en p'wer. 'Memba da tree of lif' in da li'l village?" asked his grandfather.

"How ya kno' 'bout dat?" Poppa Basket asked surprised.

"I's d'ere. Me 'en y'ur offa ancestors we watchin' 'en we's in da school, too. Soon ya seen da tree 'en y'eard what da li'l people sade 'bout it jis' bein', ya sade, why ain't us people jis' be lik' dat tree? It grows jis' 'cause it is." Ya's a man 'en nobody can take dat 'way from ya. Jis' be a man in ya mind. Jis' be. Jis' be." And the voice trailed into space.

"How's dat gonna he'p me 'en my family? Jis' be; what's dat? Do da spiritual thang? Is dis what I's tol'cha do? It ain't make sense. I's gonna ke'p on comin' here 'til I's gon' mad list'n ta dead people who say dey kin he'p me," Poppa recanted one more time.

Momma Basket gets really worried at the lateness of the hour and Poppa Basket is still not home. She has supper without him and gets the younger children ready for bed. The other children are preparing themselves and trying to comfort Momma by ensuring her that Poppa is all right and that nothing has happened to him.

The day slips slowly into twilight and Poppa is still not home. Momma tries to wait but falls asleep in her clothes. Poppa comes in shortly afterwards and sits at the kitchen table. Momma left his supper on the stove but he is so consumed with his thoughts that food is not a concern.

"How is ya 'pose ta jis' be? How?" Poppa questioned himself angrily. "How?"

Jumba awoke during the night to find Poppa still sitting at the table. At first he decided not to interrupt him but gave it a second thought. He too had many things on his mind especially since Abunda ran away. The family did not talk about Abunda much and only mentioned him when they had prayer sometimes, but Jumba missed his big brother and was finding it increasingly difficult to maintain silence about it.

"Poppa, why's ya sittin in da dark?" Jumba asked.

"I's can't sleep. Got much on my mind. What'cha doin' up?" Poppa answered.

Jumba replied to his father's question, "I's be thinkin' 'bout Abunda. Where him is 'en if him ok. I miss'em. I kno' we's ain't talk 'bout him much 'en I's 'fraid to say sup'in."

"Its ok, Jumba," Poppa said with assurance. "Ya's kin talk 'bout y'ur brotha."

"Why he runaway from us? We his family," Jumba asked gingerly.

Feeling Jumba's pain, Poppa Basket explained, "Abunda ain't don' run 'way from us, he wanna a betta lif'. I kno' he loves us 'en we's see 'em a'gin."

"Poppa, why's people don't lik' us. We ain't na'va don' nufin to them."

"I's don't kno'." "'Pose our ancestors be right, we needs dem he'p us from up 'bove," Poppa added feeling kind of helpless at this point.

"Poppa, I want us hav' a good lif' 'en ain't a'ways workin' fo' offa 'en ain't gitin' nufin fo' us. Maybe I do lik' Abunda 'en run'way, too."

Poppa, alarmed, let Jumba know, "Dat break Momma's heart. We's gonna do betta soon. I's list'n ta my granddaddy 'en I's gonna do what he sade. We's gonna do betta soon. Real soon. Please jis' us stay to'gatha."

Jumba went back to bed and Poppa followed shortly after thinking about what his grandfather said. He could not get the thought out of his mind: *How to be!*

Life was moving swiftly around Annapolis Grove. The Rouses were enjoying Joshua as he grew and became a permanent member of the family. Storm and Joshua were

bonding like brothers instead of the fatherly image that
Storm had in mind.

One day while Mrs. Rouse was hosting some ladies from
the Garden Club, Ms. Hautie one of the ladies, whispered to
Ms. Beatrice, "Joshua looks different now that he's a little
older doesn't he?"

Ms. Beatrice responded, "You know you're right. I guess
I never paid any attention because he really is so cute and
they love him so much."

"What are you all whispering about," asked Ms. Alvaria.
"You two are always up to something."

"Oh, nothing," Ms. Hautie, the instigator said. "It's really
nothing."

She lends back over to her cohort and whispers, "We'll
talk about this later at my house."

Her friend responded, "I can't wait. What do you think is
going on? You know they adopted him, don't you?"

"Et hum, please excuse us ladies," intrudes Ms. Alvaria.
"If you won't let us in on your secret, then please leave it
until later."

The activity did not bother Mrs. Rouse as she was busy
entertaining her guest. Joshua was the love of her life and she
could not see any wrong in him. He was receiving exactly
what his mother wanted, a family that loved him and he had
not just a good home but a great home.

Sha'myla, the Basket's second oldest girl, was at the
Rouse's helping Momma Basket with the garden party. She
overheard the two ladies talking about Joshua on their way
out of the house as she was assisting them in gathering up
their things. Sha'myla did not say anything to Momma just
then but went to find Joshua to take a good look at him. She
spent lots of time with him while babysitting and caring for
him on special occasions. Momma Basket needed Sha'myla's
help and was glad that the Rouses brought her into the big
house.

"Joshua, come here," Sha'myla called. "Let's play hide and seek."

Joshua came running from the other room as fast as he could. The sound of Sha'myla's voice was like his mother's would have been because they were so close. When he found her he had the biggest grin on his cute face and he ran right into Sha'myla's arms almost knocking her to the floor. She maintained her balance without both of them hitting the floor.

Cuddling and kissing him affectionately, she put her hands on his face and turned it directly to hers. They were both now looking each other straight in the eye. For a moment no one moved and then Joshua laughed and took his fingers and ran them over Sha'myla's face. She was so taken by the act of affection, that she momentarily forgot why she called him. But hearing Mrs. Rouse bid goodbye to her last guest jolted her memory. She took a careful look at Joshua's features, first his skin color, then his eyes, then his nose and his lips. She became immediately curious because Joshua's features were not like most White people she had ever seen. Not having been around much either, she realized the limitation of her travels and how small her world was before making a decision.

"Ya don't look lik' em," she said to Joshua quietly while holding him. "But I know dey ain't y'ur real kin folks anyhow. Wonder who y'ur real kin folks is 'en what dey look lik'? It don't matta to me, I love Joshua 'en Joshua loves me."

Poppa Basket came straight home from work because he wanted to talk to his family.

He was still feeling the affect of his talk with his grandfather. He knew that timing was important and that whatever he had to say now was the time to say it. This felt like something divine was occurring outside of the world he was living in. He felt that the ancestors may have troubled the heavenlies and made a way of escape for him and the family.

He was not sure of what was going on but he was sure that something was happening.

When everybody was home and supper was over, Poppa summoned everyone to his presence. He instructed them to sit wherever they could hear him and that they needed to listen carefully to what he was about to say. Everyone obeyed.

Poppa started telling about his day, "I's ke'p on havin' visits from da ancestors who's dead. I's ain't crazy fo' ya start thinkin' so. Since dat time Jumba, ya founded me in da cemetery, I's ain't stop thinkin' 'bout dat or what dey sade. My granddaddy com' ta see me da offa day when I's in da cemetery jis' thinkin'. I's scaked at first. 'Cause all I's y'eard was a voice but I's could feel som'body wit' me. Da voice called me Jurann 'en nobody called me dat since my granddaddy 'en y'all kno' he dead."

"What he want Poppa?" Jumba interrupted.

"He sade he wanna he'p us," Poppa answered.

"How?" Makita asked. "What kin dey do fo' us, dey's dead? Dey worse off den us."

Poppa Basket quickly responded, "Hold on boy 'en let me git don'. Ya ain't kno' e'rythang. Granddaddy sade a'gin jis' do what dey told me do 'en don't fo'git da spiritual traditions dat King Buswasla told us. He sade dey he'p us from da offa side 'cause we need pow'r 'en we ain't git it from dis side."

"Dat sounds spooky," Momma Basket interjected. "Sounds lik' we's talkin' 'bout ghosts."

"I's kno' dat woman," Poppa jumped in. "But I's kno' he's wanna tell me sup'in 'potant. We's workin' 'en gittin' no where. Ev'ryday da man com' git us 'en we jis' goes. Dey grow 'en we's git small. Our chil'lens runnin' 'way. We's stuck y'ere ain't got no hope. Granddaddy right, we needs he'p from anywhere."

Poppa went on to share the rest of the story. "I ain't tell y'all 'bout da big tree I's saw when Jumba found me. I's ain't kno' it a dream but it was sho' real. D'ese li'l peoples was carrying' me. We com' ta a big tree. I's na'va seen nufin lik' dat. I y'eard da li'l people sade da tree jis' bein' 'en growing' growing. I y'eard me sade why ain't we people be lik' dat tree? Jis' be 'en we grow. Granddaddy sade he com' back 'mind me of what I's said "bout da tree. Him want me kno' da he'p I need was jis' be. Don't worry, jis' be. He sade dat jis' bein' bring e'rythang ta me dat we's need. 'Cause it makes it do thangs fo' us on da offa side where da power is."

Jumba asked, "Poppa what is ya talkin' 'bout? How we jis' be lik' a tree? I's think dat tree fell on ya 'en mess up y'ur head." The whole family laughed.

"Y'alls kin laugh, but ya's gonna list'n ta me 'en do what I's tell ya do. I talk lik' me granddaddy, "Jis' do what I told ya do". We's gonna do da spiritual thangs er'ry night. We's all gonna do'em to'gatha. We's gonna go church Sunday wit' da Rouses; see how dey do spiritual thangs. Jumba 'en Makita, I's wan' cha git Momma's Bible 'en practice ya'll reading'. One y'all is gonna read ta us er'ry night. We's gonna pray ta our ancestors 'en God for pow'r. My great grandmamma sade fo' me a'ways pray. She learn 'bout pray'r ta God from da White peoples. She told me dat she 'memba King Buswasla teachin's she y'eard. She sade dat pray'r was talkin' ta som'body on da offa side dat could he'p ya. We's gonna be, by livin' lik' we's where we wanna be."

The Baskets began their daily rituals with more conviction as Poppa Basket instructed. Every night after supper they sang songs, had Bible readings and prayer. Now, they included some discussion about what they read from the Bible. The older children were becoming more curious about the religion of Jesus Christ and how it differed from the ancestors. On Sundays when they went to church with the Rouses, the pastor talked about Christianity and Jesus Christ but never about the ancestors. Poppa Basket explained that White people prayed to Jesus Christ and Colored people prayed to their ancestors. He also realized that some Colored people that attended the church were also praying to Jesus Christ. They were very serious about their religion of Jesus, and it puzzled Poppa Basket. He wondered who he could talk to about this, so he would understand the difference and if he was doing the right thing. He could not fathom praying to the White people's ancestors because they had always hurt Colored people.

One day, Poppa Basket asked Momma Basket to question Mrs. Rouse about his spiritual concerns. "Ask her 'bout prayin' ta dis Jesus Christ 'en who he is. Ask 'bout if he's somebody's ancestor 'en why all da White people pray ta 'em."

Momma Basket was a little reluctant but gave it some thought. "It good he wanna kno' 'bout mo' spiritual thangs. I's believe dat Missy Rouse be glad ta he'p me. I's ask her soon's I git a chance."

Momma Basket became excited over the prospect of learning more about spiritual things, so she questioned Mrs. Rouse as soon as she went to work. "Missy Rouse kin I's ask ya a question?"

"Sure, Momma," Mrs. Rouse responded.

"It 'bout God. Why's do y'all pray ta one man, Jesus? He all yawls God?"

With a pleasant response Mrs. Rouse said, "Yes, Momma, He is. Jesus loves everybody and wants to be their God."

"Do Jesus love us Coloreds? If He do, why we's treated so bad?" Momma Basket sincerely wanted to know.

Eager to help Momma Basket understand, Mrs. Rouse continued, "Yes, Jesus loves you all, too. Jesus doesn't treat you bad, its people that treat you bad."

Insisting, Momma Basket questioned Mrs. Rouse more, "Don't Jesus let it happen to us? Why He ain't stop it?"

"It's really hard to explain, so we need to sit and take some time to talk about it so that you will understand."

Relentless with her questioning, Momma Basket continued, "Why da preacha sade God told da slaves ta obey da mas'tas? Why's slaves hurt 'en kil't. Jesus love dat?"

"Oh Momma, I'm truly sorry for your hurt but I'm trying to explain it to you," said Mrs. Rouse as she continued to help Momma Basket through what appeared to be a difficult situation.

"I's wanna kno' now, if it's all right?" Momma Basket exclaimed as her patience was running low.

"Okay, we'll take a little time now. As I said God loves everybody and so does Jesus, who is His son. God wants everybody to be in His family but they have to accept Jesus His son first."

Still not understanding Momma Basket continue to ask, "Why, Missy Rouse?"

"Because Jesus died and became the sacrifice for everybody who had sin, which means to do something wrong or bad," Mrs. Rouse informed her. "God knew that people would not do right. So Jesus agreed to died so all people had to do was accept Him and be okay with God."

"Dat ain't mad' no sense. Why som'body die fo' me 'en I's ain't ev'n kno' 'em? I's told ya dat Colored peoples' treated real bad. Ain't n'body gonna die fo' us," Momma explained vehemently.

"God is not like a man. God is a spirit who looks after us. He wants us all to be okay and live a good life. I know that I'm not doing a good job of explaining this to you. I told you that it wasn't easy. But let me read this scripture to you from the Bible and maybe that will help. Its John 3:16, "For God so loved the world that He gave his only begotten son that whosoever believes on Him shall not perish but shall have everlasting life". It means that Jesus died for everybody: Coloreds and Whites. God does not hate anybody."

Really curious now, Momma Basket tried to explain her understanding, "We pray ta our ancestors 'en dey y'ears us. Is dat lik' y'all prayin' ta Jesus?"

"Sort of. But God also loves your ancestors," added Mrs. Rouse.

"Ya right, Missy Rouse, dis hard ta kno'. Maybe I's jis' stick wit' our ancestors 'en ain't kno' 'bout Jesus," Momma Basket conceded in a dejected voice.

Sensing Momma Basket's dejection, Mrs. Rouse wanted to help more by saying, "We'll talk more about this as I said, Momma Basket. When you come to church this Sunday listen to what the preacher is talking about and see if it will help you".

"Thank ya Missy Rouse," a weary Momma Basket responded.

Momma returned to her chores for the day thinking how she would relate this information to Poppa. She did not understand it and she knew for sure that he would not either. She did not want him to become discouraged in his new passion for spiritual things and somehow she knew that the spiritual things could and would help them.

Momma finished her day at the Rouses and journeyed home, still thinking how she would tell Poppa about God and Jesus. She repeated the explanation that she got from Mrs. Rouse: "God love all people; Colored 'en White. Jesus died fo' peoples he don't kno' so dey kin have a betta lif'. 'En God loves our ancestors, too!!" It was still too much for Momma Basket to understand. She just wanted to be able to explain it to Poppa Basket and afterwards he could draw his own conclusions. She purposed to wait until after supper and the evening service, so that she would not have to explain it to the children. She did not want anymore confusion than she already had. Much to her surprise, before she could start the conversation with Poppa he inquired of her. "Ya talk ta Missy Rouse t'day 'bout da spiritual thangs?"

"I's gonna talk 'bout it lata but yea, I's did," replied Momma sharply.

"What she sade?" Poppa insisted.

Irritated, Momma replies, "It hard ta say 'en we ain't don' talkin' yit."

Still insisting, Poppa continued, "Jis' tell me what she sade."

"She sade dat God loves er'rybody 'en Jesus His son. 'En dat Jesus died fo' er'rybody so's we's can be in God's family," Momma told Poppa so that he would stop pestering her.

Her efforts were futile, as Poppa commanded more, "How's God loves er'rybody 'en er'rybody treat us Coloreds real bad?"

"I's ask her dat. She sade it hard ta 'slain. She keep sayin' God loves er'rybody 'en it ain't God dat ain't lik' us Coloreds but man. She ain't told me why God ain't stop 'em from hating' 'en hurtin' us. She sade fo' me list'n ta da preacha Sunday 'cause maybe he say sup'in dat he'p me."

"What 'bout our ancestors?" Poppa demanded. "She ain't said much 'bout 'em she jis' keep sayin' it hard ta 'slain."

With finality to the conversation, Momma tells Poppa, "Well, we's jis' gonna ke'p on doin' our thang 'en list'n fo' what da preacha sides Sunday."

Sunday morning, as usual, the Baskets go to church and Momma and Poppa are eager to hear what the preacher has to say that will help them to understand God and Jesus. Upon arriving at church they go to the balcony where the Coloreds are allowed to sit. The service gets started with music and the Baskets join in because they like the rhythm. Momma and Poppa sit attentively waiting for the morning sermon. After the normal formalities, the pastor goes to the pulpit and begins his sermon. "Yes, God really does love you. He loves us all."

Momma and Poppa look at each other as if to say, "he y'eard us talkin'?" Stunned by the opening remarks, they did not speak to each other but gave even more attention to the pastor. "God gave His Son so that everybody could live and have everlasting life. It means that we will live after we die from this world and will go on to another world. In that world there will be no hatred or evil, just love and peace."

The Baskets could not believe what they were hearing. Poppa reached over and took Momma's hand and squeezed it gently. Momma understood that he was saying something to her through his gesture. She could not wait to leave church so they could talk about what the pastor had said. Neither of them heard the rest of the sermon as they were individually thinking about what had already been said. On the way home, Momma asked Poppa, "What ya think dat mean, 'em sayin' God love us lik' I sade ta ya Missy Rouse sade?"

"I ain't sho'. I's don't kno'. Maybe it's true, God do love us all."

"How we gonna kno' if He is?" Momma now insisting for answers.

"Woman, I ain't kno'. I's gotta think 'bout dis. I's gonna pray ta da ancestors fo' he'p. Dey tell me what ta do," Poppa remarked with assurance.

Even though the Baskets had gone to church that morning, Poppa still wanted to have his own service at home. He was more concerned than ever with the spiritual things of his ancestors and what he had heard in church about God. So, after supper, Poppa instructed the family to come together for service. "But we's gon' ta church dis mornin'," reminded one of the children.

"I's kno'. Don't sass me jis' do what I's sade," Poppa commanded.

"I's gittin' tawd dis church stuff. Maybe I's run 'way 'en find Abunda," thought Jumba to himself.

Poppa Basket changed the order of their little service by praying first. He needed to talk to his ancestors right away about his confusion. "God thank ya fo' what ya don' fo' us. Thank ya fo' dis family. Thank ya fo' keepin' us 'en ours chil'lens safe 'en to'gatha. Thank ya fo' lookin' afta Abunda 'en keepin' 'em safe. Thank ya fo' our ancestors who's wit' ya now 'en is lookin' down on Abunda. I pray dat dey he'p us live a good lif' den dey had 'en git Abunda ta da place he's goin'. Dey a'ways sade dat ya had sup'in betta fo' us in anuffa place. I's pray dat Abunda jis' do what I told 'em do, too. Grandmamma, I's need ya he'p me kno' 'bout da White man's God 'en Jesus. Dey ov'a d'ere wit y'all? Do I 'pose pray ta 'em 'en y'all too? Y'all talk ta each offa? Y'all told me ya he'p us 'en we's need he'p, now! Amen."

The room was filled with silence as everyone seemed to be pondering Poppa Basket's prayer and what it meant. A fear slipped into the room as a sadness welcomed itself behind the fear.

"Poppa, why's ya pray lik' dat? Ya's scaking' me," Sha'myla announced in a very fragile voice.

"I's ain't tryin' ta scak' ya child. I's need som' he'p wit' da spiritual thangs. Who we gonna ask? Our ancestors all we's got," Poppa explained.

"Ev'rythang is gittin' diff'rent. We's prayin' 'en doin' all d'ese spiritual thangs. Fo' what? I's ain't git it. How kin da ancestors he'p us?" Sha'myla asked sarcastically.

Momma Basket jumped in the conversation, "I's kno' dat we's 'en y'all fo' sho' is gonna git a betta lif'. Me 'en Poppa ain't got nufin fo' ta giv' y'all but what dey giv' us. We's ain't git da 'heritage yit, but 'pose dis spiritual thang be part of it. I's ain't gonna lose anuffa child lik' Abunda who don' run off 'en I's...." Momma starts to cry.

"Y'all go bed. I's sit wit' Momma," Poppa said.

Makita and Sha'myla took the younger children and got them ready for bed. After they were dressed, they returned them to Momma and Poppa to bid them goodnight. Momma squeezed them so hard that one of the children grunted in distress. Poppa removed her gripped from the child and the little one ran into the bedroom. The others came to say good-night and went off to bed.

Momma and Poppa sat quietly at the table, each seeming to be somewhere else. After sometime time had passed Poppa Basket said, "Com' on, let's git ta bed, we's gotta work in da mornin'."

He reached for Momma Basket's hand. Poppa was starting to be more affectionate toward Momma Basket after Abunda ran away and he also drew closer to the spiritual things. Momma Basket appreciated his new found affections, and needed them to cope with her changing life and the absence of her first born child.

In the middle of the night, Poppa Basket was awakened by a strange sound coming from the girl's room. He immediately got out of bed to see what was happening. As he approached the room, he heard Makita mumbling and could not distinguish whether she was crying or what. Putting his ear to the door he heard her saying, "God I know you are real. I know you love us. I've always known it. I never knew how but I know. I remember the night the first time my angel came to visit. I was scared to death, but something made me not be afraid. Every since then I know that you are with us. You have answered every prayer of mine and Poppa's. You are a God of love and I love you even though I don't understand you. Amen."

Makita was a quiet soften-spoken girl. Her round face and nickel size eyes with large black pupils made her standout in the midst of a crowd. With silky smooth ebony skin and thick curly hair, she could well have been a model. Slim built with robust breast and a flat stomach, her physical appearance could not tell of her life's experiences. She was determined to use her education to "have a good life" as she continually heard Poppa talk about lately. She anxiously awaited the day that she could speak with knowledge and accuracy as she heard others where she worked. She would speak that way within her own mind to assist herself with her hopes and preparation for her future. Quietly her mark would be made with excellence through her determination.

Poppa quietly returned to his room, got back in bed, and puts his arms across Momma as if to protect her. He never mentioned to Makita the next day that he heard her praying but it gave him a sense of peace that he needed. He was beginning to feel the weight of being responsible for his family much more than ever before.

Time seemed to pass quickly now that the Baskets had a sense of peace in the midst of their difficult life. Not much had changed at Annapolis Grove, in the natural, but the Baskets were believing that something had changed for them spiritually. They attended church regularly, on Sundays, and continued their evening services at home. Somehow the entire family had received the message that there is help from the other side, God and the ancestors, and that if they would just "be" help would come and free them from their bondage.

Momma Basket had a new sense of peace, even in Abunda's absence. She never acted like she was in bondage, because she felt that she had to remain strong for her family. She knew that Poppa was doing his best, but she also knew that he needed some help even though he never said so. But now Momma had a song in her eyes and a skip in her walk. She hummed around the Rouses' household while working. She was so joyful that it did not appear that she was working but rather that it was her home that she was caring for.

The Rouses were more pleased with Momma Basket than ever before. They never found fault with her but did see the new freshness in her. "Momma, I am so glad that you are happy. I know that things got bad when Abunda ran away, but you seem to be happier than ever before," said Mrs. Rouse, paying her a compliment.

"Thank ya Miss Rouse. I's kno' ya ain't want 'em catch Abunda. I's glad ya sees me now. I hope Missy Alyon, Mr. Storm 'en Mr. Joshua be good chi'dren ta ya. Dey's ain't gotta run'way from y'all 'en y'ere. Dey's got a good hom'. Ya kno', Missy Rouse, Joshua's gittin' bigga fast. Him's good lookin', ain't he?" Momma asked changing the subject just a bit to lighten the moment.

"He sure is and we are so lucky to have him as our son," said Mrs. Rouse beaming with joy.

Alyon, Storm and Joshua came into the kitchen and joined Mrs. Rouse and Momma Basket. "It always smells good in here when you're cooking Momma Basket," Alyon said. "I have to watch my figure because you know that I'll be going off to college in a little while."

Storm heckled his sister, "You know that the boys will be looking at you and you want them to."

"Oh, Storm".

A sweet little voice chimed in, "I don't want Ally to go. Don't leave me Ally."

Alyon, embracing Joshua reassured him, "I'm not going to leave you ever. You are my baby brother and I love you. I will be going to college, which is school, but you will always be with me."

"Okay, Ally. Okay," Joshua responses giggling.

Storm takes Joshua by the hand and they leave the kitchen for parts unknown. The ladies remain in the kitchen chatting while Momma Basket is finishing up dinner.

Storm and Joshua are now in his room and for some reason Storm takes a long look at Joshua. He sits Joshua on the bed and sits directly in front of him. His thoughts are his own, at this point, as he continues to stare at Joshua.

He gently touches Joshua's face and examines his eyes and hair. Not wanting to be intrusive, he looks at Joshua's nose mysteriously and then runs his fingers through Joshua's hair. Joshua is enjoying the attention of his brother as he chuckles while Storm continues his investigation. Now prepared to let the world in on his thoughts, Storm speaks, "Who are you really? What's your real name and who are you to be? I've not thought much any about your mother since the day she left you with me, but as you grow I wonder if I am fulfilling her wishes for you. I am so glad that you are my little brother and a major part of our family. I want the absolute best for your life. Maybe one day we can look for your real mother and show her how great you turned out." Storm takes Joshua in his arms and hugs him affirmingly.

"Joshua, Joshua," a familiar voice calls, and Joshua jumps out of Storm's arms and takes out running. At the bottom of the steps is Sha'myla calling for her little friend.

"Sha, Sha," Joshua responds as he runs and leaps into her almost knocking her to the floor, again. He seems to enjoy meeting her this way.

"Boy, ya's so big now. I ain't gonna be able pick ya up soon. How's my boy?" Sha'myla wanted to know.

"Fine. I glad to see you," Joshua answered.

"Let's go to the garden? Want too?"

"Yes, yes," Joshua responds enthusiastically as they both go running out the side door.

Sha'myla and Joshua have a favorite place just beyond the gardens down a little hill. The grass is so green and beautiful it looks like a huge carpet that can be seen for miles. While Joshua runs off to play, still in Sha'myla's eyesight, she sits and begins to ponder her life and more importantly her future.

Sha'myla is now a young lady who is ready for a relationship, marriage and a family. With the exception of Abunda, Poppa has managed to keep the family together. Knowing that he is particularly protective of his girls, Sha'myla ponders how she will leave Poppa and her family. Unlike Makita, the oldest girl, Sha'myla is like Abunda in that she has a free spirit. She knows that Annapolis Grove is not going to be her home for the rest of her life. She has not considered running away, like her brother, but she has considered other ways to leave Annapolis Grove. Sha'myla is quiet and no one really knows what she thinks. From time to time she will voice her opinion but not on a large scale. But now her thoughts are bombarding her on a daily basis and what to do is now a reality. "What will I do? Where will I go? I think about the inheritance but I never talk about it. Wonder if I can find it for our family?"

Still engrossed in her thoughts, Sha'myla remembers, "As a little girl, I overheard a story about some precious jewels from Africa being buried where King Buswala was when he was first brought to this country from Africa. The story was about a King from Africa who came to this country to buy some goods to take back to Africa. He was very rich and had brought many valuable stones: uncut diamonds, emeralds, and rubies. He also had hundreds of gold nuggets that his people had found on their land. He was coming to this country to buy some of his people back and to purchase some of the new inventions that were being made. This King paid a merchant who owned a ship to transport him and his group to this country. He came to buy back his daughters and sons that had been kidnapped and sold into slavery. This King had a good rapport with the merchants as he would often spend much of his jewels and gold purchasing things that they brought to Africa.

When this King learned that his children had been kidnapped, he was heartbroken and determined to get them back. After completing all the arrangements to make the trip to this country, he came along with some of his people. They had received information as to the whereabouts of his children. Amazingly enough the ship made it to this country without being attacked or robbed by pirates. The real trouble started when they got on the land. As I heard the rest of the story, they were warned by the merchants to bury their jewels and gold because they might be caught and taken into slavery. They did as the merchant suggested. They were also caught and taken to the plantation where our King Buswala and our family were enslaved. They told the story to King Buswala and they made something that looked like a map so that they would remember the spot where the jewels were buried. Shortly after they were captured, they were killed for trying to escape. Perhaps this is the inheritance! Wonder whatever happened to that map or piece of paper."

Realizing that it was getting a little late, Sha'myla called for Joshua so that they could return to the house. When they arrived at the house, Momma Basket had just finished cleaning the kitchen which meant that they would be leaving for home soon.

"Goodbye Joshua, see ya tomorrow," Sha'myla said as she was leaving.

"Bye, bye Sha Sha. I'll see you tomorrow, too," Joshua responded.

Chapter 6

Death Comes Creeping

Abunda is walking through the grounds of Marantha contemplating what tomorrow will bring for him and his new brothers. They had found a very safe home there, but he did not know how long they would stay or if the others wanted to continue to Settles Landing. The group was in school and Mrs. Hope was enjoying her school especially her new students. The group had done a marvelous job of learning their ABCs, addition, subtraction, multiplication and division. Enthusiasm exuded from them whenever they were asked to read. Reading had opened an entirely new world for the boys and the farm hand who was also a student. Mrs. Hope had given each student their own notebook and a reading book. When they completed their chores the guys would sit around the farm house and read to each other. Excitement permeated the atmosphere and for some time the guys forgot that they were Colored and that the rest of the world hated them.

Abunda's friend, Bela, appreciatively said to him, "Thanks for getting' us out. We gotta chance to be free. We kin have a good life now. Thanks Abunda."

Abunda was overwhelmed with Bela's sincerity and responded, "We always gotta thank God 'en our ancestors for makin' it happ'n. What you think 'bout us stayin' or leavin' here? Wonder if y'all ever wanna go to Settles Landing?"

"Why we wanna leave here?" Bela wondered out loud. "Its home, now. The peoples likes us, and they help us do betta. You wanna go, Abunda?"

"I don't kno'. I was jis' thinkin' 'bout y'all 'en what we was gonna do. I like it here, too," replied Abunda to Bela's concern.

Bela's concern caused Abunda to become more conscious of the need to have a very important conversation with Rev. Hope. He was feeling a special something internally but could not recognize it. He knew that every time he prayed something unique happened and he believed that God was speaking directly to him. Not knowing what the White people's religion was really all about, Abunda held on to his spiritual rituals from home. "Tomorrow I ask Rev. Hope if we's kin talk. I wanna kno' and I need he'p wit' som' thangs. Where I go from here," Abunda thought out loud.

"Mornin' Rev. Hope." Abunda greeted him. "Nice mornin' ain't it?"

"Yes, it is Abunda. Yes, it is," Rev. Hope replied.

"Rev. Hope can I's talk ta ya? I's need som' he'p. I's believes ya kin he'p me."

"Sure, Abunda. What is it?"

The two traveled a short distance, in silence, from where they were. Abunda was getting his thoughts together and Rev. Hope was wondering what could be wrong. He honestly cared for the group and wanted nothing negative to happen to them. He had taken them to church and into town when they needed more supplies. The community never treated them unfairly because of him, but he also knew that some folks would hurt the group if they had the chance. He had also considered whether the group should continue traveling away from the hatred even though he wanted them to stay.

"Rev. Hope, I's got su'pin in my head 'bout me 'en da boys. Y'alls been good to us. We's thank ya. We feel lik' we's livin' in anuffa world here 'cause ya 'en Mrs. Hope, little Clark, Cliff 'en da resta da people is so good ta us. We's wantin' ta kno' how long dis gonna be? Y'all not tellin' us go but...."

Rev. Hope interrupts, "Abunda, first I know that you are more educated and speak better than this and you shouldn't be afraid to speak properly when you're with me. Your maintaining this manner of speech let's me know that you still don't trust completely. We are your friends and we will never hurt you, so please be the man that I know you are."

"Thank you, Rev. Hope. I am so used to acting like I am dumb 'til it's hard not too. Again, I want to thank you and Mrs. Hope for what you have done and are doing for us. I never thought that such a world existed for us Coloreds and that anyone would care as much as you all have. You have truly lived up to your faith, and that's what I want to talk to you about."

"Go on, Abunda".

"So much is going through my mind about faith and where we will go from here," Abunda continued. "The boys have found a home, but is this the end for us? I don't know! Settles Landing is still in my mind but I wonder if I've found the place of freedom here? Marantha is a special place, but I don't think it is what I believe Settles Landing is like."

"Marata has its problems with Coloreds like so many other parts of the country," Rev. Hope explained to Abunda. "People have not yet learned to let everyone be and enjoy what God has blessed this entire country with. There is enough prosperity here for everyone, but greed has become the master of many. This makes it difficult for anyone who is not White to do anything good and great here. God never intended for this to be."

"I understand and I agree that there is plenty here for everybody. I will never understand why one group of people has to make others their slaves and servants against their will. I am sure to them they have a good reason. Yet, you have chosen not to be like them and you could. Why are you so different?" Abunda asked inquisitively.

"My parents taught me to love and respect everybody because we are all God's children," Rev. Hope informed Abunda in a loving manner.

Anxiously, Abunda asked, "Is your God White?"

"No," chuckled Rev. Hope. "My God, who is also your God, does not have a color."

"How can a person be without a color?" Abunda asked even more curious than before.

Trying to make Abunda understand, Rev. Hope explained, "God is not a person but a Spirit."

"Like a ghost?" Abunda asked now totally confused.

"Something like that but much more," said Rev. Hope not wanting to add more confusion to the conversation.

Abunda now engrossed in the conversation went on to tell Rev. Hope, "I want to know more about this God because every time we go to church and I do my spiritual rituals from home, something happens to me. I feel like I'm hearing voices and seeing things. It sounds like something is telling me to do things that I have never done before. Sometimes it scares me and other times I feel peace, not afraid. Do you know what I'm talking about?"

A huge smile covered Rev. Hope's face as he sat quietly.

"Daddy, something strange is happening to me. When I pray, mostly at night, I hear voices and I've been dreaming weird things. Every time we go to church I feel like the preacher is talking directly to me and I want to answer him. I'm being drawn to something that I can't explain but it won't let me go. It scares me. What is it and what am I suppose to do about it?"

"Son, don't be frightened. It is the hand of God," his father replied.

Unbeknown to Abunda, Rev. Hope was remembering when he had the same experience and how he went to his father asking similar questions. Lost in yesterday, Rev. Hope was brought back when he heard Abunda's voice.

"Rev. Hope?" Abunda asked concerned because it appeared that Rev. Hope had left the room but his body was still there.

"I'm sorry Abunda. I was lost in my thoughts," Rev. Hope said apologetically. "I was remembering the time when I experienced the same things that you ask about; and I went to my father. I was gripped by fear and had no idea what was going on with me. My Dad told me that it was the hand of God. He told me that God wanted me to become his servant, to take care of his people and do His Will. I still didn't know what that meant and I asked him to explain more. He summed it up in one sentence: God wants you to become a preacher!"

Abunda shocked by the moment asked, "A preacher, like you?"

"Yes, son, like me," Rev. Hope replied.

Continuing to make the moment clearer, Rev. Hope told Abunda, "I never dreamed of being a preacher, but I knew that my Dad was a great man and he was a preacher. I believe that God is calling you to be a preacher, Abunda."

Abunda is still. His thoughts racing, "I don't know about Rev. Hope's God. What about my ancestors? I'm Colored, the White man's God don't like us. He let's them hurt us. Maybe Rev. Hope is wrong. How can this be? Maybe this is a trick and we should leave Marantha. Why would Rev. Hope lie about this? He's been so good to us."

Never thinking about God as his God, Abunda acknowledged God because of his visiting church with the Hopes, and the Bible lessons they taught them. Now he was to engage on a personal level with God, about whom he had so many unanswered questions?

He believed as his father taught him, that the ancestors were protecting them from the other side. Abunda had never had a personal experience with the White man's God. But he prayed to God and his ancestors. He recalled Poppa telling him that his grandmother had come to believe in the White man's God. She believed that God had power over her ancestors but she included them in her prayers.

Still in total disbelief about this new information, Abunda gingerly replied, "Rev. Hope, I don't know what to say."

Abunda would not share his private thoughts because he did not want to hurt Rev. Hope. He did not share his dream of being a pastor, either. However, he wondered where he would get the answers that he needed so badly. He was so far from home and now wished that he could talk to Momma and Poppa Basket about this important turn of events in his life.

"Listen to what you are hearing, Abunda," Rev. Hope instructed. "Ask God the questions that are going through your mind. I had many and I know that you do also. Mrs. Hope and I will be praying for you to receive clear direction. I know that this is very strange to you because you have limited knowledge about our God. Why don't you pray to your ancestors and ask them to help you with this? They are your source of strength and trust. I know that somehow God, who is God of us all, will give you exactly what you need."

"You believe that it's all right for me to pray to my ancestors?" Abunda asked in surprise.

Now having a teachable moment, Rev. Hope wanted to clarify His God to Abunda. "I believe that God can use anyone, anything and anybody to fulfill His purposes, Abunda."

"Thank you Rev. Hope, that makes me feel so much safer. You are a kind and loving man, and perhaps I will be like you if I'm a preacher," shared Abunda endearingly.

The two shared a warm embrace for what seemed like a long time. When they separated, Abunda was crying because he missed Poppa at that moment and privately wished that the arms he was sharing was his own father's. Rev. Hope was also crying because he was grateful for the love of God that was forming in Abunda's life. He praised and thanked God for His continued goodness to his entire family that included everyone at Marantha.

When Abunda reached the farm house, he was very quiet. He decided not to share with anyone what had occurred between him and Rev. Hope. Sitting motionless on his bunk, he continued to ponder what had just taken place.

"Abunda, Abunda, you okay?" One of the farm hands inquired.

"I'm, okay. Everything is fine."

Noticing Abunda's new voice the farm hand inquired, "You sound different. You sound smart, talking like White folks."

Proudly, Abunda like a proud peacock replied, "I am smart and I recognize that I have a right to act like it. When you finish school you will be smart, too."

It was now time for supper and everyone gathered in the farm house for prayer to bless the food. Abunda was still motionless as he stood. When the prayer was completed, he left the farm house and went outside. No one paid him any attention, as he often separated from the group to be by himself. Someone did question if he was okay and the farm hand and informed them that he was.

Remembering Poppa's favorite place, the cemetery, Abunda wondered if the only place he could hear from the ancestors was in the cemetery. Marantha did not have one on the property, so how would he hear from the ancestors?

He began to walk the property, which was sprawling and beautiful. He walked for what seemed like miles until he felt his fatigue and looked for a place to rest. At the top of the hill, that Abunda unknowingly climbed, was a huge tree that overlooked the valley. The full moon was shining on the grass and each tree looked as if it had been hand planted in just the right place. Sitting under the tree, admiring the flaw-less night sky with the stars twinkling and dazzling, Abunda was in awe. The brilliance of the sky caught his attention as he wondered how it could be. The big dipper and the little dipper were clearly in view and the constellation contained an angelic format.

"Who is responsible for all of this?" Abunda thought.

The stars seemed to form some words as Abunda looked on. Little by little they moved into place and Abunda saw, "trust me". Rubbing his eyes to be certain of this experience, he looked again into the sky and saw the same two words, "trust me".

Immediately his thoughts were, "Who are you?" The stars stood firm and gave no indication of moving. The firm stance denoted a certainty in what they were saying.

"More and more strange things are occurring", Abunda thought. Nevertheless he sat still under the tree. This time he was not afraid but very much at peace.

After more time of quietness, Abunda made his way down the hill. The trip down was much faster than the one up. On his way, Abunda began to hum a song, something that he could not ever remember doing. He was not sure of the name of the song but the tune seemed very familiar. The song had such peaceful overtones that Abunda was no longer concerned about the name, but enjoyed its affects. Arriving at the farm house late, he found everyone resting. He quietly slipped out of his clothes and into his bunk contemplating tomorrow's events.

The sun rose early and it was another awesomely beautiful day at Marantha. All the hands were busy getting ready for the day's work and school. The breakfast call was given and all sat down to a great meal. Moving rapidly they all went in different directions to do their chores for the day.

Little Clark came down to the farm house, as he did when he had no school. He wanted to hangout with Abunda for the day. Abunda agreed. They headed for the north side of the estate and on the way Clark stooped to pick a four leaf clover. Suddenly Abunda heard a scream and ran the short distance back to little Clark. There he found him on the ground crying profusely and next to him Abunda heard a snake hissing. Abunda remained extremely still. He was thinking of how to kill the snake before it struck him or Clark again. The snake and Abunda was playing a cat and mouse game; who would move first? Slowly Abunda put his hand in his pocket and realized that he had been carrying the hammer to fix the post. Knowing that he had to be accurate on his first attempt, Abunda slowly withdraw the hammer from his pocket and hurled it at the snake. The hammer missed the snake but frightened it enough for it to leave quickly. With lightning speed, Abunda raced toward little Clark. He remembered that when he worked the fields at home sometimes they would encounter snakes and he was told that if anyone was bitten to suck the poison out immediately and spit it onto the ground.

Abunda gently lifted Clark into his arms and found the spot where the snake bit was. Clark was semi-conscious but gave a half smile as Abunda embraced him. Abunda put his mouth over the bite, inhaled deeply to get enough air, and sucked with all his might. He could feel a liquid substance in his mouth and immediately spat it to the ground. He did the same gesture once again, but this time there was very little substance. He also spat it on the ground. After this, he picked little Clark up and began to run as fast as he could towards the house, yelling all the way.

Some farm hands working close by heard the cry and ran to his aide. Abunda explained what had happened and the workers went ahead of him to get Rev. Hope. Rev. Hope met them just before they reached the house and took Clark from Abunda while Abunda was explaining what he had done. Rev. Hope was encouraged.

"It looks like you have just saved my son's life." Rev. Hope said with much gratitude. "I sent Cliff to town to get the doctor. In the meantime we'll put Clark to bed."

Mrs. Hope was extremely upset when told the news but she managed to contain her emotions by praying out loud as she paced the floor. "God this is the miracle child that you gave to us and we gave him back to you at his birth. We know that you have great things for him to do and we know that this is not unto death. Thank you for healing your child, Amen."

After Mrs. Hope finished praying she began to sing and seal her prayer with praises to God. She had such an assurance that everything was already all right that she went to Clark's bedside, kissed him gently on the forehead and headed back to what she had been doing. "Call me when the doctor gets here," she told her husband.

Rev. Hope awaited the doctor in Clark's bedroom. It appeared as though Clark was sleeping with such peace, and there was no indication of apparent harm from the snakebite. Abunda sat quietly in a corner of the room. No one noticed him.

"Rev. Hope, Rev. Hope, the doctor is here," called Cliff from a distance.

"We're in little Clark's bedroom, Cliff," Rev. Hope called back.

"Hello, Rev. Hope" the doctor spoke. "Cliff explained to me what happened on the way here. Please give me a little time to examine little Clark and then I can tell you how he is and what we need to do."

Cliff and Rev. Hope moved away from the bed and stood very quiet in the corner of the room. The doctor checked little Clark's vital signs and responded, "Humm". The majority of his examination consisted of grunts and groans that kept the two watching men on their toes. At times the non-verbal communication was encouraging and other times a little distressing. When the doctor would groan, Cliff's heart would skip a beat and he would hold his chest as if in pain. Rev. Hope would grip his hands tightly as if to absorb any pain that little Clark might be feeling.

"Rev. Hope, you can call Mrs. Hope back in the room now," the doctor instructed. "Who is the person that got the snake venom from little Clark's body?"

"It was Abunda, one of our workers," answered Rev. Hope.

"He saved your son's life. By removing the venom immediately very little of it was able to get into little Clark's blood stream thus it was unable to infect his entire body. He does not have a fever and that's good. Usually in snake-bites, a high fever is the first symptom of seriousness. Give him this medicine to counteract any poison that may have gotten in. Clark will be sleepy for a few hours and then he should be lucid. You will be able to talk to him and feed him something liquid like soup, broth or tea. He should rest for the remainder of the day and be fine by morning if no fever appears. If there is evidence of a fever, send Cliff for me immediately, but I honestly don't think that will be the case."

"Thank you, Doctor. I prayed for us and we believed that God would heal our son before you came," Mrs. Hope said with confidence. "Cliff will you see the doctor on his way while Rev. Hope and I sit with our son for a little while?"

"Yes, Mrs. Hope. I know that little Clark is going to be all right 'cause you all are such fine folks to everyone," Cliff encouraged.

The doctor and Cliff left the room and the Hopes thanked God for their son's healing. Each parent sitting on the opposite side of him, they remained quiet but unified.

Cliff saw the doctor out and returned to the room. "The doctor is on his way back to town, is there anything else I can do?" he asked.

"No thank you Cliff. Just continue your day as usual," said Rev. Hope. Cliff left the room.

Almost an hour had passed and little Clark was resting peacefully with his parents at his side. Every now and then he would moan a little, seemingly to inform them that he was okay. Continuing their vigilance, the Hopes remained encouraged. From time to time Mrs. Hope would touch her son's forehead for any trace of a fever. Each time her touch revealed no fever. The Hopes looked at each other and intuitively knew that they were ready to leave the room. Rising, almost simultaneously they reached for each other's hand across the bed and proceeded to leave the room.

"Oh my goodness! Abunda, wake up. We didn't even know that you were still here," Mrs. Hope exclaimed.

Abunda did not move.

"Abunda, Abunda, wake up," Mrs. Hope repeated with concern in her voice.

Abunda still did not move. Rev. Hope reached down to shake him by the shoulder but Abunda still did not move. Accidentally brushing Abunda's face, Rev. Hope was alarmed by heat. He immediately put his hand to Abunda's forehead and realized that he was burning with fever.

"Honey, pray. Abunda is sick. I believe that he is suffering from the venom of the snakebite."

"God this is your child, also. What you have done for our son you can now do for your son. We thank you for sparing Abunda's life, Amen." Mrs. Hope prayed.

Being concerned about the amount of time that had lapsed and the doctor now probably back in town, the Hopes hovered over Abunda. Rev. Hope yelled for Cliff as he was running towards the farmhouse.

"Abunda is sick. Go get the doctor, fast."

Abunda's group came running to the house into the bedroom. Rev. Hope was carrying Abunda from little Clark's room to another bedroom when they came. They took Abunda from Rev. Hope and followed his leading. The entire group was extremely frightened. They laid Abunda on the bed and moved to the walls of the room, all except his best friend Bela who refused to move from his side.

"What's wrong? What don' this to Abunda? He gonna die? What we gonna do wit' no Abunda?" Bela questioned frantically.

"My son, calm down. Abunda will be all right, I promise you. You know when little Clark got sick, Abunda saved his life by taking the poison from his body and in doing so he got sick from it. I have sent Cliff for the doctor and now all we can do is pray," answered Rev. Hope.

"Pray, okay. Y'all let's pray lik' Abunda told us to," Bela requested.

The others came together around the bed looking down at Abunda seemingly resting peacefully and looked to Rev. Hope to pray.

"Bela, you pray," Rev Hope suggested. "We all love Abunda but I know that you love him more than anybody in this room."

"Abunda prayed his Poppa's pray'r 'en its all I know," responded Bela.

"God thank you fo' what you's done' fo' us. Thank you fo' our family. Thank you fo' keepin' us safe 'en together.

Thank you fo' lookin' after my friend Abunda 'en makin' him ok. Thank you' fo' our ancestors who's wit' you now 'en is lookin' down on Abunda. I pray dat you help Abunda find his way back to us. En I pray dat we's git to the place where we's goin'. Poppa Basket a'ways sade dat they sade you got sup'in betta fo' us somewhere else. I pray dat you care fo' my friend, Abunda. Amen."

Sobs could be heard during and after the prayer. The group was so emotional with a sense of hopelessness now that Abunda was not with them. Their cries mimicked that of the mother of a herd whose children had been separated from her.

"What is we gonna do? We ain't got Abunda? Where's we goin'? Why dis don' to Abunda? Where da ancestors ain't lookin' out fo' him?" questioned Ezkiel with great despair.

Bela, in his own fear, reassured the group. "Abunda's gonna be okay. He told us to pray when we ain't kno' how to. He gonna be okay."

Cliff had not yet returned with the doctor and as Rev. Hope attended to Abunda it appeared that his condition was getting worse. Abunda was burning up with fever and Mrs. Hope worked diligently, along with the farm hands, to provide enough cold cloths for Abunda's body. The group began to fill tubs with water and put the cloths that were gathered into the tubs.

Mrs. Hope took her husband aside and suggested, "Let's put Abunda in a tub of water. The cloths are not working fast enough and I believe that it would be better if we could get more of his body cooled down."

"Bela, you and the group get the largest tub, even if it's the trough, and put it in the back of the house. Fill it with water so that we can put Abunda in it. Mrs. Hope and I believe that this will help to make Abunda feel better quicker."

Bela told the group to do as Rev. Hope instructed. "I'm gonna take my friend 'en put'em in the tub."

Everyone followed the plan. Bela picked Abunda up from the bed as Rev. Hope cautiously guided him down the stairs and through the house to the back where the trough was filled with water. It was used because it was the largest container that could hold enough water.

Bela slowly placed Abunda's limp body in the water, praying quietly to himself. At one point he placed Abunda's body in the water and then lifted him out. Again, he placed Abunda back in the water and lifted him out. Finally, he placed Abunda's body in the water and let it rest there.

The others were all gathered around the trough when Rev. Hope began to speak. "God, Abunda gave his life so that my son could live and now I am giving my life so that he can live. I promise you that I will be his father, in his father's absence. I will see to it that whatever you have planned for his life will be fulfilled. I will never leave him nor forsake him. I pledge this to you in the company of these witnesses. If I falter on this promise, I will suffer your consequences. I do not know why this is happening."

Chapter 7

Meeting of the Minds

Momma Basket paces the floor, crying profusely, "Why dis happ'n? Why my family so sick? We's been prayin' 'en doin' right. Why?"

Going from bed to bed, Momma Basket checks on her children who are very sick and lifeless. They are all hot with fever and dehydrated from the loss of water in their bodies. This has been going on for two days. It started when Sha'myla, came home complaining about not feeling well.

"Lay down child, you is hot 'en lookin' sick," Momma told Sha'myla.

"Yes, Momma, I's sho' tired 'en I feel sick."

Momma knew that something was seriously wrong because her children rarely got sick; especially Sha'myla who was one of the healthiest. However, Momma gave no more thought to that. She was busy getting supper ready because Sha'myla could not. Just about the time that Momma was finished preparing supper, Poppa and the three older boys were coming in early from work.

"Sup'in's da matta wit' two boys. Deys sick. We's gotta git back 'en don' workin' fo' we's could com' home," Poppa told Momma.

Momma rushed to check her two sons who were also hot and looking sick like Sha'myla. She checked them by feeling their foreheads and looking deep into their eyes. "Y'all is sick lik' ya sistah Sha'. What happ'n?"

Jumba, answered, "We's don't kno'. I's got sick yesta'day 'en Jassfa, too. Junta, he got it today."

"Go lay down, I's see ta ya shortly," Momma told the boys as they headed for the bed.

"Poppa, I's scaked! Sup'in's wrong. Why our chi'dren gittin' sick? Ya ain't look good na'va," Momma said in a frail tone of voice.

"We's gonna be okay, Momma. We 's gonna be okay," Poppa reassured her even though he had not told her how sick he was actually feeling.

He had been trying to rationalize the occurrences of the last two days when he woke up not feeling well. He did not want to trouble Momma because he was sure that this slight illness would soon dissipate.

"I's ain't hungry. I's gonna lay down," Poppa told Momma.

Sitting at the table now alone, wringing her hands, Momma attempted to make some sense of the situation, but to no avail.

The sickness spread through the Basket household like wild fires and no one had an idea why. Poppa managed to continue working but the boys were too ill to continue. It caused some consternation for Poppa, as the Overseer was very unhappy with the time the boys were missing from work.

Poppa Basket decided to take a special trip to his secret place. He wanted and needed to commune with his ancestors. He sorely needed some answers to this present dilemma. He traveled from the house to the cemetery tentatively as he was not feeling much better; but did not want to alarm Momma Basket and the children. On the way he stumbled a few times but managed to regain his composure while climbing the narrow incline that led to the cemetery. In his view was a huge weeping willow tree that looked as sad as Poppa Basket was feeling just now. He said to the tree, "I's understand how ya's feeling."

Arriving at his destination, Poppa Basket sat on the first available tombstone to rest. It was not his usual place but he was so winded and weak from the trip that he sought immediate rest. He sat with his head in his hands, sobbing gently but pitifully. Poppa Basket's behavior depicted someone trying to empty themselves by exercising the healing process of crying. He cried until his body was limp and his tear ducts were almost dry as Momma Basket had done.

"I's ain't gonna let me family sees me lik' dis," he lamented. "I's da man in dis family 'en I's gonna see 'bout us," he reassured himself.

Poppa continued his trip to his favorite spot, now feeling more rested and even energetic, despite his failing health.

"Well, I's back here 'gin. Looks like I's jis' ain't gonna git from y'all. I's been doin' what yawls don' told me, but now me family sick. Kin y'all talk ta God, seeing' yawls up d'ere to'gatha. I's gotta kno' if we's all gonna die? Where's our good lif'? Who gonna he'p us now?"

"Poppa, Poppa," a voice from afar called. "Poppa. Poppa."

"Dat sound lik' Abunda. Is dat ya, Abunda? I's don' lost my head. How's I's talkin' ta Abunda? I ain't even kno' where he at."

"Poppa, Poppa," the voice continues calling.

"My God what's goin' on? I's can't lose me head, I's gotta see afta me family."

"Poppa, Poppa," comes the call of the voice again.

"Jis' answer it," a new voice interjects.

Poppa Basket recognizes the new voice as one of the ancestors and immediately responds to the first voice. "Is 'at ya, Abunda?"

"Yea, Poppa it's me Abunda. I's gotta talk to you 'bout something powerful special."

"Abunda, where ya at? Ya all right? We's miss ya."

"I's sick Poppa. I got poison in me and it's goin' through my body. I feel like its done gone all the way back through our family; some kind of poison that done reached our whole family. I don't want us to die from this. I need your help, Poppa. I don't want to die. I want to see y'all again. Poppa, please help me!"

"Abunda, dat really ya, son? Ya's talkin' not lik' ya."

"Yea, Poppa, it's really me."

"Abunda, we all done got sick wit' sup'in, too. We's ain't kno' what. I's scaked sup'in gonna happ'n ta us. I's com' here fo' talk ta da ancestors 'en God. I's need dem he'p."

"Poppa, you believe in the White man's God, now?"

"Som', yea, som'. I's think God got mo' pow'r 'cause God mad' da ancestors. But I's still call on 'em, too."

"What we gonna do Poppa? What we gonna do?"

After a few minutes of silence between Poppa and Abunda, a huge wind swirled around Poppa, almost lifting him from the ground. The wind was full of whistling sounds that seemed to be a code of sorts. A short whistle, then two long whistles and then another short whistle. At one point the whistle was continuous with no interruptions.

"Ya feel 'at Abunda? Ya y'ear da wind?"

"No, Poppa. What wind and what noise?"

"A big wind jis' com' up. 'Most take me off da ground."

Though the experience was frightening, Poppa Basket felt no fear.

"I's 'memba when I's li'l, sup'in lik' 'at don' nearly git grandmamma when I's wit' her. She sade God was talkin' ta her by da wind."

"What she do, Poppa. What she do? I feel like I'm getting' sicker. I'm so hot and tired."

"Hold on Abunda. Hold on!" Suddenly Poppa lost contact with Abunda.

"Abunda! Abunda! Abunda! Where's ya? Talk ta me!"

Scared to death, Poppa fell to his knees sobbing out of control until he was prostrate on the ground.

"Poppa, Poppa, Poppa, talk to me," Abunda had mysteriously returned. There was no response from Poppa Basket though.

"God, please let me hear my father's voice and take this sickness from my family. I will do whatever you want and I promise not to let you or them down. I will tell everybody that you saved me and my family's life. I want to see them again, please God!"

"Jis' do what we told ya do. Jis' do it!" Those words resonated through the minds of Poppa Basket and Abunda. "We gave ya what ya need ta make it through dis life 'en ta giv' da next peoples. Don't fo'git da inheritance," the voice of grandmamma spoke. "It ain't nowhere near ov'a fo' y'all."

"Abunda, ya y'ere?" Poppa Basket asked.

The atmosphere was still with the silence from both worlds, yet a yearning was lingering that made it known that there was much more to look forward to. The atmosphere embraced the notion that in the face of adversity and disappointment success always triumphed. The silence modeled a peace that could not be understood by the human mind.

"Abunda, ya y'ere," Poppa Basket asked again, as his mind was still connected to Abunda's.

"Poppa, Poppa, please don't leave me. Don't leave me Poppa," Abunda cried out like a little child who had lost his father while they were on a journey together.

Sobbing, lost and frightened, Abunda felt as if all hope was gone. He knew that he and his family were doomed to death and there was nothing he could do. He cried out to God again, "Didn't you hear me? I'll do whatever you want even though I don't know you. I'm sorry for all the wrong things I've done and if you didn't like them. Nobody told me about you, just our ancestors. Do you hear me? Are you here?"

Immediately following Abunda's cry of desperation, he heard, "Abunda, ya y'ere son? I's lookin' fo' ya'. Abunda," Poppa called in despair.

"I'm here Poppa. I'm here," Abunda responded with glee in the midst of his pain.

"Poppa, I believe that everything is going to be okay. The family will not be sick anymore and I am going to live. I don't know what this all means but I am going to trust what you taught me through our ancestors and this new God. I know that I'll see you all long before anybody dies. Give Momma and the children my love. As you would say, we's gonna be jis' fine."

In a matter of minutes, the same swirling wind left the area where Poppa Basket was so that he was awakened from his catatonic state. The awesomeness of the experience caused Poppa Basket to remain lifeless. His mind yet reviewing the experience, he began to wonder what it all meant. There was nobody that he could share this with and he did not want to burden Momma Basket by saying that he and Abunda had been talking.

"I's da man of me family 'en I's gonna take care us," Poppa reassured himself.

Now fully conscious, Poppa headed for home. Everyone seemed to be resting peacefully so Poppa quietly took off his clothes and slipped into bed along side Momma Basket. Once again, he put his arms around her and quietly whispered, so as not to awake her, "Er'rythang gonna be jis' fine".

The next morning Momma Basket arose earlier than usual to check on her sick children. She went to each one of them and touched their foreheads for fever but there was none. Slowly the children began to wake up with much more vigor than the night before.

"Poppa, Poppa, da chi'dren ain't sick no mo'. Dey's all betta," Momma yelled out and went into a crying wail.

"Why's ya crying?" Poppa asked with concern.

"I's jis' happy our chi'dren ain't gonna die. I's was scaked."

"We's gonna be jis' fine. I's gonna take care me family, I promise y'all," Poppa insisted.

The children remained at home while Momma and Poppa went off to work. Poppa explained that the boys were sick and would be back to work in the morning. Poppa had gained favor with the overseer.

"Mornin', Missy Rouse," Momma said as she greeted her.

"Good morning Momma Basket," Mrs. Rouse replied.

With a big shout, a voice yelled from the other room, "Good morning, Momma Basket".

"Mornin' Master Joshua. Boy ya's jis' gittin" bigga 'en bigga. Ya's good lookin, too. Soon ya's git grown da ladies is gonna be afta ya."

"Oh, Momma Basket, I don't even like girls," Joshua replied in a timid voice.

"Jis' wait, we's gonna see," Momma said jokingly.

Joshua went outside to play and two strange men were approaching the front of the house. Joshua ran to meet them. "Hi there, my name is Joshua."

"Where's you mammy," one of the strangers asked.

"What's a mammy?" Joshua wanted to know.

"The cook your mammy, boy?"

"No, sir."

Mrs. Rouse had come to look for Joshua and saw the two men talking with him, "Good morning gentlemen may I help you? Joshua go to your room and play. I'll be with you as soon as I attend to these gentlemen."

Joshua goes in the house to the kitchen and asked Momma Basket, "What's a mammy?"

"Who sade dat?"

"Some men outside talking to Mother."

"Dey sade dat ta her?"

"No, I was playing before Mother came to get me and they asked for my mammy. What is that?"

"Don't worry 'bout it."

Joshua went off to his room and Momma Basket pondered, "Why som'body ask Joshua fo' his mammy?"

Momma Basket began to take note of the Rouse's home like she had never done before. She looked around the large kitchen where she spent so much of her time. Her mind traveled to the parlor, the formal living and dining rooms, Mr. Rouse's study and the wonderful sitting area that Mrs. Rouse designed for her quiet time. Mentally walking the stairs, Momma Basket perused the bedrooms that were elegantly adorned with matching bedspreads, pillows and curtains. The aristocratic furniture remained in her thinking for more than a few moments. "Where ya git dis kin'a stuff," she questioned herself? "How's we ever gonna git dis? It gonna take mo' den som' ancestors ta do dis. Maybe it jis' ain't fo' us Coloreds? We ain't na'va git nu' fin."

A somber feeling was now flooding Momma Basket who earlier was so grateful for the healing of her family. Confusion covered her mind like a tsunami. "I's thankful ta God fo' saving' my chi'dren. I's jis' ain't kno' what ta do now. Poppa is gittin' old 'en I's kno' he twad 'en tryin' kno' what ta do fo' us. How's we gonna git up from y'ere 'en do betta? I's jis' don't kno'."

Just when Momma Basket was feeling that all was doomed for her family, she received some surprising news when she arrived home from work. Makita was home from work early.

"Makita, ya al'right? Why ya hom', now? What's wrong wit' ya?" Momma bombarded her with questions.

"I'm all right, Momma, but I need to tell you sup'in", Makita replied mysteriously. "I need to tell you first 'en you can tell Poppa 'cause I'm scared to."

"Is ya sick child?"

"No, ma'am, I'm all right. I'm gittin' married, Momma."

Momma Basket fell into the nearest chair and gasped for breath. Mumbling under her breath, she was awestruck by the news. She didn't even know that Makita had been seeing anyone.

Momma asked, "Who he is, da man? How ya kno' em? Where's ya meet 'em? How com' we ain't na'va saw 'em?"

"Wait, Momma, not so many questions. I tell ya 'bout 'em but please don't let us not get married."

"Answer me, first."

"I met 'em a good while back at my Missy's house where I work. He keeps her place up. I was pickin' some flowers for the table when I saw him. He was lookin' at me but I got the flowers and ran to the house. He didn't say nuf'in, then. One other day, he was out there and I saw him lookin' at the house. I think he's lookin' to see me, but I didn't let him see me. And so, when I was pickin' more flowers he come up back of me and scared me to death. He laughed. I was mad but I laughed, too. Then we started meetin' in the garden. He asked me my name and said he liked me. We meet at lunch and after work and jis' talk."

"So how y'all git ta be married?"

"He's a fine man Momma and I love him and he love me. Oh, Momma, I kno' he make a good man like Poppa and take care of me, too. I want you to meet him, please Momma?"

"I's ain't gonna do it wit'out Poppa. You kno' how he loves ya."

"Momma, jis' meet 'em first and see, then we tell Poppa. Please, Momma?"

"Okay, but I's gonna tell Poppa right away."

"Good, I bring him to ya work, tomorrow. Thank ya, Momma."

Makita left Momma with her heart racing about tomorrow, and knowing that she had finally shared her secret. She did not want to keep it from Momma for that long but so much had been going on with the family.

Momma was in a quandary because so much was going on with the family. Seemed like one thing after another was taking place and she hardly had time to catch her breath. Her children were growing up faster than she had realized. She never thought about the day that any would leave her let along Annapolis Grove. Abunda's running away shook her family's foundation, but they had managed to move on and draw closer together.

Poppa became stronger and more committed to his family then ever before when Abunda left.

Makita arouse early in the morning with so much anticipation that she could not eat her breakfast. She went through the house singing and laughing unlike her usual subdued morning behavior. Dressing in some special clothes really drew attention to her from the family.

"Why's ya so dressed up?" Jumba asked. "'En where's ya goin'?"

Laughing, Makita said, "Betcha wanna kno, uh?"

Junna looked at Makita and said, "Ya is sho' pretty, Kita."

"Thank ya, Junna. Gotta go now. I need to git to work. See y'all later."

Makita went bouncing out the door as if propelled by some invisible force. The family laughed and went about the business of getting ready for their day.

"Pss, pss," a voice familiar to Makita whispered. Her heart leaped as she knew that it was her man coming for them to meet Momma. Makita ran out the back door to see him but he was not in sight.

"Gotcha," he said touching her on the back.

"Ja'cin, you gonna cause me to have a heart attack."

"Naw, then we can't get married."

"I told Momma 'bout us and we is goin' to see her now."

Ja'cin was so ecstatic he reached out and picked Makita off the ground, and swung her around a few times until she was almost dizzy. They embraced for a while and then headed for the Rouses to see Momma Basket.

Momma Basket was busier than usual because she needed something to keep her mind off the impending meeting with Makita and her man. Still, no one knew of this situation and Momma Basket certainly did not want to carry this secret any longer than she had to.

Makita and Ja'cin arrived at the kitchen door of the Rouses and tapped lightly. Initially, Momma Basket jumped from her fragile nerves, but looked up and saw Makita. She went to the door and opened it for them to come in.

"Momma, this is Ja'cin Bongera, the man I'm gonna marry. If it's okay wit' you and Poppa, I mean. Ja'cin this is Momma, her name is Ms. Martha."

Ja'cin extended his hand to Momma and said, "Good to meet you, Ms. Martha."

For what seemed like an eternal to both Ja'cin and Makita, Momma said nothing. She looked Ja'cin up and down as if he was a side of beef. Making guttural sounds she continued her inspection then finally she broke her silence.

"So ya's da man wanna take my girl, uh?"

With excitement and obvious happiness Ja'cin replied, "Yes, ma'am, Ms. Martha. I love Makita and I want her to be my wife."

Momma Basket inundated Ja'cin with questions: "Where's ya from? Where's ya peoples? How ya gonna take care my baby? Where's ya gonna live? What ya do fo' work?"

"Momma," Makita interrupted. "Let 'em answer you."

"I don't know my people. I was taken from my family when I was a little boy but I've been with these people for a long time. They treat me good and gave me my papers so that I could be safe. They showed me how to do the gardens and flowers and keep the land pretty. They taught me to read and write. I work for people doing that. I work hard cause I am a good man. I hid my money for when I meet somebody like Makita and we can get married. I want to go away and start a good life where Coloreds ain't treated so bad," Ja'cin answered proudly.

"Ya gonna take my baby, 'way?" Momma Basket reeked.

"Please don't be upset, Momma. Ja'cin want us to have a good life like our ancestors said we would. Momma, I stay in touch wit' cha, I promise," Makita said almost crying.

"I ain't gonna lose anuffa child. I ain't," Momma cried reaching for Makita.

Standing in the kitchen crying in each others arms, Makita and Momma forgot Ja'cin's presence. Ja'cin remained quiet realizing the importance of this moment.

"Ya promise me, ya be good ta my baby. Ya ain't, I tell our ancestors 'en ya git in troubl'," Momma said to Ja'cin as she and Makita released their embrace.

Makita grabbed hold of Ja'cin's hand and squeezed it tight and he responded.

"I be good to Makita, Ms. Martha. I promise. We try to git back here to see y'all, too," Ja'cin assured Momma.

"Git now, and call me Momma. I's gotta finish gittin' suppa ready. Makita, bring Ja'cin hom' 'night 'en we tell Poppa."

Momma Basket hurried her chores and requested to leave a little early. Mrs. Rouse granted her request.

Hustling through the estate, Momma wanted to be home and prepared when Poppa arrived. She wanted to tell him before telling the family, because she was not sure what his reaction would be. Hoping that he would consent to the marriage, she mentally prepared her persuasive speech. She was so nervous; one would think that she was getting married.

Momma cooked a special supper and made sure that the two youngest ones were not in the way. She had not given them much attention since Abunda's absence so they were used to playing alone outside or in another room. From time to time she would give them a special hug and kiss to let them know that they were good children.

The house again smelled wonderful with Momma's great cooking. The atmosphere was one of excitement and peace that had not been since Abunda ran away. It mirrored the dawn of a new day, as the words of the ancestors may be actually taking life in the family. It means that another child will be absent from the family but this one will be leaving with her parent's blessings, hopefully. Momma has committed herself to seeing that this will be a reality.

Sha'myla is the first to come in from work. Poppa and the boys follow shortly behind her. Everyone is excited yet puzzled about the special supper and wondering what the reason is. Makita would be home a little later, as she had to serve a dinner party at her work place.

"Sho' smells good in here," Jassfa remarks.

"Sho does." Jumba echoes.

"I's wanna eat," Junna announces.

"We's gonna eat in a minute but I's gotta talk ta Poppa first," Momma informs the family.

"Woman, why's ya wanna make us wait when we's don' smelled da food?"

"It's 'portant, Poppa, real 'portant. I gotta talk wit'cha in da room."

Grumbling, Poppa consented to Momma's wishes. "Dis betta be good 'en fast."

After they entered the room Poppa sat on the bed and Momma wasted no time. "Poppa, Makita is gonna git married 'en go 'way wit' her husband," Momma said real fast and all in one breath.

"Wha'cha say? Dis ain't true! Who da man? 'En how long ya kno' 'bout 'em?"

"Makita told me yistaday 'en I's met 'em t'day. Her really love 'em 'en he love her, too. Him a good hard workin' man. Dey wanna talk wit'cha but I's wanna tell ya fo' dem. 'Pose dis da new lif' da ancestors talk 'bout? 'Pose da chi'dren git it if-in we's ain't?"

Poppa remained speechless. His demeanor was that of a father who had been informed that his child was missing or dead. He sat with his head in his hands; motionless. Momma was afraid to interrupt, so she waited for him to make the first move.

"Momma, we's hungry!" yelled one of the children.

She did not answer, but stood quietly waiting for Poppa's response. "Poppa, say sup'in," Momma urged. Still nothing.

Finally, Poppa arose from the bed and took a few steps, breathing methodically so as not to appear angry. "Whys our chil'len wantin' leav' us? Ain't we's good ta 'em?" Poppa questioned Momma.

"Yea, we's good ta 'em but dey's gotta grow up 'en do lik' we's did. Dey's got a chance ta git 'way from y'ere 'en do betta den us."

"Momma, is ya sho' 'bout dis man? Is ya?"

"Yea, Poppa, I's sho'."

"When dey comin' fo' me ta see 'em?"

"Dey's comin' soon, fo' suppa."

In the next room new voices were added to the others, Makita and Ja'cin had arrived. The family was tickled with meeting Ja'cin and teased Makita about her new boyfriend.

"Poppa gonna git ya seein' a man wit'out 'em sayin' so," Sha'myla commented.

"Ya's gonna git it," the others teased in unison.

"Don't listen to 'em, Ja'cin. They's wantin' to scare ya," Makita added.

"They's doin' a good job. I's scared," Ja'cin nervously remarked.

"Leav' 'dat boy alone, ya'," Poppa's voice announced, as he and Momma made their way into the kitchen.

"Evenin', sir. I'm Ja'cin."

"Evenin'. Ya sit so we's kin eat. God, thank ya fo' dis food, Amen."

The quietness of the room was overshadowed by the good food that everyone was now consuming. Makita and Ja'cin ate very little, but the others dined for them. When supper was over, Sha'myla started to clean the dishes and the kitchen. The other children stood around to hear what was about to be said to Makita and her new friend. However, Momma sent them to their rooms as they waited for Sha'myla to finish in the kitchen. She went to her room when she was done in the kitchen.

Poppa spoke frankly to Ja'cin, "Ya wanna marry my girl 'en take her 'way ta anuffa place 'en live?"

"Yes, sir. I love Makita and I will be a good husband to her, just like you are to Ms. Martha. I have money put away for us."

"Ya a learn't man, son? Ya talk lik' White peoples?"

"Yes, sir," Ja'cin replied speedily. "I learned to read and write and was able to learn a lot of other things. I want a good life for me and my family so I keep learning more and more. It's hard not to let the evil White people know that I can read and write. They still want to hurt us. But I know that we can go somewhere else and I won't have to act dumb. I will teach Makita so much more than she knows now. She is a smart lady already."

Poppa was relieved at what he heard. Constantly remembering the words of the ancestors, 'a better life', he was gratified to see that it was actually going to take place for his daughter. A teardrop trickled down his face as he embraced his thoughts.

"Looks lik' we's gonna have a weddin'," Poppa said with jubilance.

Ja'cin grabbed Makita and hurled her around and around while Momma stood crying in unbelief. She had expected Poppa to resist the marriage. The entire foursome was now embraced in a group hug with laughter and tears. It was now time to inform the rest of the family who was already eager to know what was going on.

Momma Basket summoned the others, "Y'all com' y'ere, right now! The others came running from their respective rooms in answer to the call."

"Maikta gittin' married ta dis man, Ja'cin," Momma blurted out.

Sha'myla hollered, "Oh, my God!"

The others trapped Makita and hugged her with giant bear hugs. Ja'cin was just watching the gaiety that was taking place and knew that he had made the right decision.

He would not only be getting a wife but the family that was taken from him as a little boy, as well.

Jumba approached Ja'cin and said, "Sorry we ain't mean fo'git ya, but we happy fo' Makita. En ya too. I betcha make her a good man."

"Thanks, I'm sorry I don't know your name."

"My name is Jumba. I'm the next older boy. My older brother, Abunda, ran away for a betta life."

"Makita told me about Abunda. I'm sure one day he'll return to see his family," Ja'cin said encouragingly.

"We got a weddin' to plan," Sha'myla shouted with more happiness than she had ever displayed in her life. "I want it to be beautiful fo' Makita 'en maybe one day I'll have one too."

Makita turned to Sha'myla with a big smile, "Thanks for that. I know one day you'll be as happy as I am. What kind of wedding dress should I git? Will you be in it with me? We can git you a pretty dress, too."

"Momma, can I please, please?"

"We's gotta git su'pin ta make da dresses," Momma declared. "I's ask Missy Rouse if she git su'pin. I's cook a great suppa 'en we kin have a party afta da wedding. We's gotta git som'body marry 'em, ain't we? 'Pose Mr. Rouse kin, him a lawyer 'en Poppa kin' stand up wit' 'em 'en say som' words, too?"

Poppa responded rather harshly, "We's ain't need no White man marryin' my girl. I's kin' do it."

"Poppa, da Rouses been good ta us 'en I's want dis marriage be real in da White man's eye," Momma added. "Jis' let me ask Missy Rouse?"

"All right, but I's gonna say su'pin. I's her Poppa."

The rest of the family was busy meeting their new brother-in-law, Ja'cin. The boys were particularly interested in him because he was an educated Colored man and they had not met anyone like him before. They asked him a myriad of questions and he did his best to answer them all. Finally he had to excuse himself from the boys and get with Makita, because the hour was getting late.

"Makita, I'm glad for us," Ja'cin said with overwhelming joy. "Your family will be my family. I want to take care of you like your Poppa takes care of his family. I need to be leaving now, but I will see you tomorrow and you can tell me all about our wedding. I love you so much."

The couple walked to the front door and onto the porch where they shared an intimate embrace. Knowing that their lives were about to take a traumatic change, they held on to each other in silence. After their embrace, they looked up at the dear sky overhead and saw a shouting-star falling through the sky. Each made a secret wish.

Momma could not wait to get to work so that she could share her news with Mrs. Rouse and ask for her help. Before opening the kitchen door Momma started talking, "Mornin' Missy Rouse," before she even saw her.

"Momma Basket, is that you?" Mrs. Rouse asked. "Why are you talking to me from outside?"

"Makita's gittin' married. Ain't dat good?"

"That's wonderful. When did all this happen?"

"Dey asked us last night 'en Poppa sade yea. Kin' ya he'p me git som' cloths ta make da dresses? Oh, Sha'myla gonna be wit' Makita. Kin' Mr. Rouse married 'em wit' Poppa? I's want dat marriage be right in da law."

"My goodness, Momma, you have so many things going on in your mind. Sit with me and we can discuss them. Let's have a cup of tea while we talk, okay?"

"Yes, Missy Rouse."

Mrs. Rouse told Momma that she would be more than happy to help with the wedding and that she would provide whatever was needed. She also said that she would ask Mr. Rouse about Momma's concerns and if he wanted to participate in the wedding. Mrs. Rouse was excited for Momma and her family as she had always wanted good for them.

In her excitement, Mrs. Rouse went to her bedroom closet and pulled out a chest that was filled with fine cloth and other nice things; some of which she was saving for Alyon's big wedding day. She had more than enough and was very eager to help Momma Basket with Makita's wedding. She chooses two separate pieces of cloth, one for Makita and the other for Sha'myla.

One piece of cloth was a soft mint green with sparkling silver outlining miniature leaves that were scattered throughout. The border was a mixture of green and silver with silver threading traveling the background. It was a silky cloth that flowed by itself and spoke of its own elegance.

The other piece of cloth was a royal purple silk that denoted status and wealth. It needed no accessories because of the depth of the intricate brocade weaving in the cloth which could be seen by the naked eye. So rich it was that it would force a potential customer to buy it.

Mrs. Rouse rushed to the kitchen to show Momma and get her opinion. "Look, Momma. What do you think?"

Losing all her composure at seeing the beautiful pieces of cloth, Momma was crying with joy. She was so moved that she could not control herself. Mrs. Rouse realizing that she was overwhelmed comforted her by putting her arms around Momma Basket.

"Missy Rouse, I's ain't seen nuf'in so pretty. Thank ya, ma'am. Thank ya. My girls is gonna be so pretty 'en so happy. I's git ta makin' da dresses t'night."

"Mr. Rouse and the rest of the family will be glad to attend the wedding. I also want to give you all the food for the celebration after the wedding, Momma Basket. You have been so special to our family and have helped us through many different times. It is my pleasure to help you and your family."

The day could not go fast enough for Momma. She wanted to get home to show the girls what Mrs. Rouse had given for the wedding. Things had been so difficult since Abunda left that Momma was determined to make this wedding a celebration that would replace their hurt with three times as much joy. Rushing in the door carrying the bundle of cloths, Momma yelled,

"Y'all com' y'ere," and the children obeyed.

Sha'myla said, "Momma what's wrong, why ya hollering like 'at." The two youngest and Makita were with her. They had looks of amazement on their faces.

"Look, look, at what Missy Rouse don' give us fo' y'ur wedding Makita, look," Momma declared as she took the purple piece of clothe from the bag.

Makita feel on the nearest chair in shear disbelief as she stared at the gorgeous cloth Momma was holding.

Sha'myla shook Makita, "Girl look, look at what Momma got. I ain't seen nuffin this pretty in my life. You gonna have a good wedding and you is gonna be so beautiful Makita."

Sha'myla embraced her sister with two arms full of love and expectancy for her. She wanted Makita to know that her happiness was one of the most important things in her life. She and Makita shared so much together, being the two oldest girls, and having to comfort one another over a lifetime. Now they would be separated by miles but never by love.

Soon a weak, shaky voice was speaking, "Momma, oh Momma. I don't know what to say. It's soooooooooo beeeeeeautiful. I never thought I'd have anything like it in my life. Missy Rouse is good to give us this. I gotta thank her."

Interrupting Makita, Momma said, "Wait look at dis," She pulled the mint green piece of clothe from the bag. "Dis fo' ya Sha'myla!"

Jumping up and down and running around the room, Sha'myla's demonstration displayed her feelings about the surprise. "I's gonna be real beautiful," she declared in a very ethnic way. "It's a good thing you the bride, Makita, or else you betta watch out for me," she added jokingly.

The house was filled and bursting at the seams with so much laughter, happiness and joy. Even the younger boys were happy for their two sisters. Momma stood back and drank the moment taking little sips at a time, as if drinking a fine wine. Her aged but defined face recorded this moment and cataloged it in her mental archives. "D'ere *is* mo' fo' us," she thought vehemently. The determination of her statement negated many others that had been filtering through her mind since Abunda left. This would indeed be the greatest thing that had happened to the Basket family. Still thinking to herself, Momma remembered, "I's got sup'in special fo' Makita. I's ain't told n'body 'bout it." Then she smirked and rejoined the activity in the room.

Junna said, "Makita, what ya dress gonna be like?"

"I don't know, Junna. I want something long with points at the bottom, a head piece and, this is funny and Momma might not let me do this, but I want one side to have a long sleeve and the other no sleeve. What do you think? I saw it in a book at my work place."

"It pretty. Momma gonna let you git it," Jayla said convincingly.

Momma overhearing the conversation began to think how to construct the dress that Makita had described. She was also preoccupied with how Sha'myla's dress would look, in her mind. Momma and the girls had spent years sewing and they had done a pretty good job, but now she wanted it to be perfect, excellent. She wanted to show off both her girls.

The girls said almost at the same time, "Momma we can help ya make our dresses." Then they both started laughing.

"No I's gonna do dis fo' y'all. I's gonna surprise y'all, jis' ya see."

Folding the cloth carefully and neatly, Momma begins to envision where to start making them and how the dresses would look. She has every confidence that they will be perfect and will make her daughters look like the queens she already knows they are.

Poppa and the older boys entered the house while the laughter and gaiety was still going on. "Why ya'll so happy? It ain't matta, its good to hear, anyway," Poppa says.

"Momma, Momma, please show Poppa the beautiful cloth for our dresses," Sha'myla pleaded.

Momma fulfills Sha'myla's request by taking the cloth out of the sack. She holds it up while waiting for his remarks. Poppa says nothing. He simply looks and mumbles, "Hmmm."

Momma Basket is getting a little agitated with Poppa's lack of response, but does not want to spoil the family's mood with her displeasure. Still Poppa says nothing. Everyone in the house is now waiting for his response. The older boys who are just arriving home with him are waiting as well. Surprisingly, they are not anxious to eat supper, as they usually are when they get home. Finally, a tear drops from Poppa's face and Makita was the first to see it. "Poppa, don't cry. Oh, Poppa it's been a long time since we seen ya cry."

Overwhelmed with emotion, Poppa timidly says, "I's ain't seen nu'fin dis pretty in a long time. I's kin jis' see y'all bein' so pretty. I's kno' d'ere's sup'in betta fo' us, lik' our ancestors always sade."

Reaching to Momma and taking a piece of the cloth from her hand, Poppa says, "Momma, where's ya git dis from?"

Momma was a little afraid to answer because she knew how Poppa felt about the Rouses giving to them. Poppa is a very proud man and prides himself on taking care of his own family.

"Missy Rouse don' give it ta us fo' da' weddin'. She sade, too, Mr. Rouse kin' he'p ya wit' da weddin' 'en dey all wanna com'," she added and held her breath awaiting Poppa's response. The tension in the room was thick enough to cover the entire room. The children were all still and quiet. It was so quiet in the house that all you could hear was breathing.

"Dat's mighty nice a Missy Rouse. I's happy dey wanna com'. 'En Mr. Rouse kin' he'p me so I's git it right fo' our girl."

Again, the house was alive with laughter and happiness that just kept growing more than before. Poppa's new attitude made everything all right. The entire family was now in agreement.

When Momma Basket went to work and told Mrs. Rouse the good news, and gave her everybody's sentiments of thanks, she received yet another surprise from Mrs. Rouse.

"Momma Basket, how would you like to have the wedding right here on Annapolis Estate. We can decorate the garden area and even have the reception there as well. I want to help make this the happiest occasion of your life. I can't wait to do this for Alyon, but marriage is so far from her at this point. Mr. Rouse said that he, too, would be happy to help Poppa with the wedding and make sure that everything is right according to the law."

Tears streaming down her face, again, Momma struggles for a response. "Missy Rouse, I's ain't kno' what ta say. Thank ya, ma'am. I's sho' my family be happy dat ya be y'ere fo' da wedding."

Momma hugs Mrs. Rouse and they both cry with happiness.

Momma Basket finished the dresses the day before the wedding and had the girls try them on. They were perfect, as she had wanted them to be. She put them away so nobody else would see them.

The big day is here and the first wedding in the Basket family is about to take place. In an environment of love and caring, the Baskets will share this special day with family and friends from around Annapolis Grove. All the Coloreds are excited to come to Annapolis Estates; nothing like this has ever happened in Annapolis Grove.

Mrs. Rouse took complete charge of making the arrangements for the wedding and the reception. She had an archway constructed on a small knoll that was covered with flowers and greenery. In the middle of the archway was an altar, which was a little table with a Bible on it. In front of the table was a broom decorated with green, purple and white ribbon. Floral arrangements of green and white tiger lilies, lilac roses, majestic white lilies sprayed with silver, with baby breaths and greenery were placed around the area. White chairs in two sections were available for guest seating.

Fried chicken, greens, macaroni and cheese, cornbread, mashed potatoes, okra, green beans, potato salad, ham, ribs, biscuits, sweet potato pies, cakes, and all kinds of drinks were waiting for consumption following the wedding. Mrs. Rouse had everything catered and prepared in a beautiful white tent that was surrounded on the outside by flowers that came from the garden. There was so much food and drinks that it looked like she was trying to feed the whole town. Momma Basket had no idea what Mrs. Rouse would do when she agreed to let her do it.

The guests began to arrive at Annapolis Estate. Most were Coloreds. A few Whites who were invited by Mrs. Rouse came to share in the festive time. For the first time that most Coloreds knew of, they were allowed to sit on the front chairs and not in the back. The Rouses sat on the front row with Momma Basket and the rest of the Basket family. No one there had ever seen Momma Basket look so beautiful. She wore a multi-colored African dress that was purple, mint green and silver. Her head was covered with a wrap that stood high. Poppa Basket could not keep his eyes off of her nor could everyone else. Momma Basket could not remember looking or feeling this good since her grandmother gave her the dress many years ago.

All the guests sat together with no regard for who was next to them. Soft music was being played as the guest gathered. Mr. Rouse and Poppa Basket were standing between the archway. Poppa was dressed in a three-piece African attire; an outfit that he had only worn three times before. He looked like a king with his kufie atop his head. He beamed with enthusiasm and honor.

Sha'myla's empire-neck dress draped over her with a wide band that started from her shoulder. It trailed down to her waist and wrapped around in layers, tied and sleekly rested in two pieces at her side. Her head was covered with a headpiece made of the same cloth wrapped in layers like a crown. Even though the cloth had a very European look to it, Momma Basket gave it an African style. Ja'cin's best friend, the escort, was dressed in an African suit with a long tunic top, with pants and a kufie to match. Sha'myla and her escort came in towards the altar from different sides and stood in front of the guests. The two were so stunning that they looked like they could have been the ones getting married. Sha'myla was so beautiful that when Joshua Rouse realized who she was he yelled, "Sha, Sha!" Mrs. Rouse immediately put her hand over his mouth and everyone else laughed. Sha'myla gave Joshua a wink.

African music now filled the air and everyone looked to the back where Makita and Ja'cin, handsomely outfitted in an African outfit like his best friend, were now walking towards the altar. Makita's dress was royal purple and Momma Basket made it just as she asked. It had one long sleeve on the right side that was adorned with silver ribbon around the wrist. The bodice was cut on an angle from the sleeve to the other side and the top was covered with silver ribbon. It was pointed all around the bottom with little silver bells at the end of each point. A thin piece of cloth rested gently on Makita's left shoulder and fell down her arm. Her headpiece was tied from two pieces of cloth; one gold and the other silver to form a Nefertiti look. She was indeed the queen for the day.

When the couple reached the altar, Poppa Basket spoke first, "Ja'cin, ya's take good care of my girl, ya y'ear? Make her happy. 'En I wants som' grandchil'len. She a good woman. Our ancestors sade we'd gonna git a betta lif' 'en dis y'ere's da start. Ya gotta pray 'en git 'em ta he'p ya, Makita kno' what ta say. Work hard 'en do right; right com' back ta ya. Makita, hear 'em, he da man. Be a good wife lik' ya Momma. 'En a good Momma, too. Com' back ta see us," "Poppa Basket's voice broke as he fought to hold back the tears.

Jet Rouse realized what was happening and stepped in, "Ja'cin do you take this woman Makita to be your lawfully wedded wife. To love, honor and cherish? Will you take care of her in sickness and in health and always be there for her? Will you make her feel safe at all times and promise never to leave her until death parts you?"

Ja'cin stood speechless for what seemed like an hour. Jet Rouse said, "If you do, say I do."

Ja'cin, smiled at Makita and said, "I sure do."

"Makita, will you take this man to be your lawfully wedded husband; to love honor and cherish? Will you take care of him in sickness and in health and always be there for him? Will you make him feel safe at all times and promise never to leave him until death parts you?"

"I do and I will." Makita responded with beams glowing from her eyes to Ja'cin's eyes.

Poppa Basket, now composed, says, "Y'all gonna jump da broom 'en ya's gonna be married 'den."

Sha'myla and her escort took the broom from in front of the altar and placed it behind the bride and groom. They turned and now stood in front of the broom.

Poppa said, "When I's say jump, ya jump."

"Jump." And they obeyed as the guests joined in with laughter.

Now on the other side of the broom, Jet Rouse says, "You are now man and wife."

"She y'urs now," Poppa tells Ja'cin. "Y'all kin' kiss."

And they did gladly!!

The reception was full of food and fun. Poppa and Momma stood a distance away just inhaling the cheerfulness of the day, after having endured much hardship in their marriage. The Rouses were as proud as the Baskets to have been a part of this happy occasion. Everyone ate and danced long into the evening.

The couple moved into Ja'cin's place. His boss told him of a friend who needed someone to work for him and encouraged Ja'cin to go. Ja'cin decided to try the new adventure. He and his new wife would soon be leaving Annapolis Grove.

Makita pays a visit to Momma Basket and tells her, "We'll be leaving soon and I want you to know now. I'm gonna miss y'all, Momma," as she starts crying. "I've never been away from my family and I love ya'll so much. Oh, Momma...."

Momma takes Makita in her arms with a firm embrace. "Y'all is gonna be al'right. We's gonna miss ya'll, too. I kno' one day ya'll git back see us wit' 'dem babies. 'Memba, I's sade I's got sup'in fo' ta give ya?"

Momma rushes off to her room and comes back just as quickly. She gives Makita a piece of paper. "I's got 'dis a time ago from 'neath da bed at Missy Rouse. I's ain't read it but I's kno' it's sup'in good. I's want ya have it. Might be sup'in 'bout da 'heritance? Y'all look at it when ya gon'. Y'all com' to suppa 'fo ya go. I's gonna miss ya..." and now Momma is crying.

Ja'cin and Makita came for supper a few days later and the encounter was very emotional.

"Makita, we gonna miss ya su'pin terribl'," said Jumba, struggling to hold back his tears as he reaches for his sister.

"Ain't got n'body tuck me in 'en tell me stories no mo'," little Junna added.

Sha'myla was very quiet; as if in shock. Her pupils did not move as she stared across the room. Her heart was racing and her palms were sweaty. Finally she stood up and proceeded toward Makita with her arms stretched open. Makita immediately ran into her arms and together they wept giving no thought for anyone else. Understanding that Sha'myla would be feeling quite alone, Makita wanted to assure her that they would always be together, regardless of distance. She gave Sha'myla a keepsake that was special to her. She said, "This means that we are always together and that our love can never be destroyed by distance or time. You are my sister and I will never forget you. When we get settled we'll find a way for you to come to visit us, okay?"

Wiping the tears from her eyes, Sha'myla motioned with her head in agreement. In a weakened voice she whispered to Makita, "I love you. I'm gonna miss you," and ran from the room.

"What 'bout me Sha? I ya sistah, ain't I?" Jayla asked with her face covered with tears.

Makita rushes to her little sister and picks her up in her arms. "Of course you my little sister. I'll never forgit you. I love ya and you can come to visit me with Sha'myla; ya hear?"

The most difficult time was about to take place as Momma and Poppa were next to say their good-byes. Bravely, together while on opposite sides of Ja'cin and Makita, Poppa prayed, "God thank you fo' what ya's done fo' us. Thank ya fo' my family. Thank ya fo' keepin' us safe 'en to'gava. Thank ya fo' lookin' afta Makita 'en Ja'cin 'en keepin' dem safe. Thank ya fo' our ancestors who is wit' ya now 'en is lookin' down on our family. I pray dey he'p Makita 'en Ja'cin git back ta us. 'En I pray dey git ta da place where dey's goin'. Y'all a'ways say dat sup'in betta fo' us som'where else. I pray ya care fo' my chil'len. Amen."

Momma squeezed Makita's hand in agreement and took her in her arms. At the same time Poppa did something that was so uncharacteristic for him, he turned and took Ja'cin and held him in his arms. The rest of the family was looking on.

As the evening drew to a close, Makita and Ja'cin left the house hand in hand walking across the estate. The family stood in the door and watch until their silhouettes faded into the night. Quietly, Poppa closed the door and everyone, except Momma, went to bed without saying a word. Momma sat alone and thought, "Dis what's happ'n is a good thing."

Chapter 8

A Place of Hope

R ev Hope rests by Abunda's side still asking, "Why would this happen to Abunda?" He gently strokes Abunda's hand as if to transfer life from himself. Abunda's group remains in the room quietly. Bela is sitting on the other side of Abunda looking for some sign of hope and life in his friend. It's been almost a whole day since the snakebite and all concerns have left little Clark and are now focused on Abunda when a little voice says, "Father, I'm hungry!" Rev. Hope looked up and there stood little Clark. Mrs. Hope ran and scooped little Clark up in her arms. He was much too big for her to be lifting but she was ecstatic to see that her child was safe and apparently well.

"Mother, may I have something to eat?" Clark asked.

"Sure honey, you sure can. I will get you something from the kitchen."

Little Clark looks around, sees Abunda in the bed and notices the sadness on everybody's face. He goes to the bed and touches Abunda. "Ouch he's hot. Is Abunda sick, Father?"

"Yes, son. He is very sick. He saved your life and now he is sick."

Little Clark walks to Abunda's bedside and whispers in his ear, "Wake up Abunda I need you. Thank you for saving my life, now come back to me."

In a weakened state, little Clark stumbles while backing away from the bed when Rev. Hope reaches out and catches him. He starts to take him to his own room, but little Clark requests that he stay with everyone else in Abunda's room.

Rev. Hope tells Clark, "If you feel sick let me know and I'll take you to your room and sit with you there, okay son?"

"Yes, father."

Mrs. Hope returns with some soup for her son.

Night is falling and still no signs of Cliff and the doctor. As Mrs. Hope checks Abunda's forehead, for fever, she indicates that it is still very high and that she believes his condition is getting worse.

Everyone has grown tired of the wait. Some of the group has fallen off to sleep at the foot of Abunda's bed. Even the Hopes are having difficulty staying alert because of the strenuous events of the day. Nevertheless, no one left Abunda's room. Even the farmhands that had been with the Hopes for a long time stayed. It is evident that this group of people see themselves as a family, regardless of race.

"Abunda, Abunda kin ya y'ear me? Please say su'pin, Abunda. I gotta talk ta ya. Da chil'len ain't sick no mo'. Dey's ain't sick, Abunda. God, please don't kill Abunda! Abunda..." Poppa's voice trailed off in despair when there was no answer. Poppa Basket was heartbroken. He had no connection with his son since he ran away and now when there was a connection; it appears that it is announcing Abunda's death.

As the wrestling took place in Abunda's mind, he remembered telling Poppa that everything would be all right but now he found himself traveling backward in time. "Did I speak to Poppa or was it all a dream? I must be all right so that my family can be saved and safe. I must get away from this place and go back to those who love me."

A piercing light invaded Abunda's room. It awakened everybody that had dozed off to sleep. They all covered their eyes to protect themselves from the strength of the light. Some of them were unable to stand; and as they attempted to do so, they fell back to the floor. It was something that no one in the room had ever experienced. Abunda's group was most frightened, including Bela, but he had to remain strong for the others in Abunda's absence.

When Mrs. Hope was able to gain her composure, she realized that it was the morning sun gushing through the curtains in the bedroom window and she immediately closed them.

"My that was interesting, almost angelic," Rev. Hope commented.

"Yes, it was dear. Yes, it was," responded Mrs. Hope.

Bela had been holding Abunda's hand throughout the ordeal but felt no signs of life. Heat was the only feeling that was evident. As he went to change positions on the bed, a strange coolness introduced itself to his hand. Bela looked shocked and reached to touch Abunda with his other hand. The same coolness was there.

"Abunda, ain't sick no more," he yelled to everyone. "He ain't sick."

Rev. Hope asked, "Bela, how do you know?"

"His hand ain't hot no more. It's cold."

"Oh no," Rev. Hope thought. "Abunda didn't die! He can't be dead."

Rev. Hope had no idea of how he would tell the group that Abunda was dead and that his cold hands meant just that.

"Honey, would you come with me outside the door for a minute?" he asked Mrs. Hope.

Mrs. Hope agreed.

"Dear, I'm afraid that Abunda is dead because of the coldness of his body and I don't know how to tell the group, nor do I want to believe that it is true. We prayed and asked God to save him. What are we going to do?"

"If it was God's will to take him, there is nothing that we can do, dear. We will have to get the strength and courage to tell everyone and assure them that they can remain with us."

The Hopes made their way back to the room to give the distressing news of Abunda's death. As they pushed the door ajar, they heard crying and they knew that the group had learned of the situation. Feeling relieved that they did not have to break the news, the Hopes felt a little better.

"Come," said Bela. "Please, come. Look Abunda ain't sick no more! His eyes are open! Look! Look!"

Rev. Hope looked across the room at Abunda who was still lying in the same position, but now with his eyes open.

"Abunda, can you hear me? Can you see me?" Rev. Hope asked with utter excitement.

In an extremely weak voice, he answered, "Yes, sir. I can hear you and I can see you."

Now the Hopes had joined the others in tears of joy. Little Clark was so happy that he almost fainted from the excitement. "Abunda, is okay. He is going to live and always be my friend," he cried out.

Abunda drifted off into a peaceful sleep while the others went back to their respective duties. It was settled with everyone that he would be okay even though the doctor and Cliff had yet to return.

Bela said, "I stay with Abunda 'case he want somethin', okay Rev. Hope?"

"Sure Bela and we'll be back to check on you both."

Cliff finally arrived back at Marnatha but he was alone and very tired. He went to the house to find out about Abunda and to tell Rev. Hope that the doctor was not available. Cliff knocked on the back kitchen door and Mrs. Hope opened it.

"Cliff, you look so tired. Where is the doctor?" she asked concerned.

"I'm sorry Mrs. Hope but they told me that Doc was called away on another emergency and that he would be back in a few hours so I waited and waited. Then somebody else said that Doc wouldn't be back for days so I came back to tell you the news and see about Abunda. What do you want to do? Is there another doctor we can git?"

"No, Cliff, that won't be necessary. Abunda is going to be just fine. God answered our prayers."

Cliff was so excited that he stumbled over his words, "Can, can I see him?"

"Of course, you can. Bela is with him in the upstairs bedroom."

Cliff climbed the steps three at a time not wanting to waste anytime seeing his friend and brother, Abunda.

Cliff burst into the room, but composed himself when he saw that Abunda was sleeping. He was a little concerned seeing him lying there like he left him, but he instantly remembered that Mrs. Hope said that he was going to be okay. When Bela saw Cliff, he leaped from the bed into Cliff's arms to share the good news. They hugged and cried together and then sat quietly by Abunda's side waiting for him to awake.

A few more hours passed and Abunda opened his eyes again. Both Bela and Cliff were nodding when they heard, "Wake up, I'm the sick one," with a slight chuckle from Abunda.

Abunda's recovery was slow but sure. The doctor never did make it to Marnatha but as Mrs. Hope said, "God did heal Abunda."

When he was able to get up and move around the first thing he did was to have a talk with Rev. Hope and tell him of his visitation by his father and the promise he had made to God. "Rev. Hope, I don't know anything about your White God, but I told Him that if He saved my family I would do whatever He wanted me to. I didn't want my family to die and I don't want to go back on my promise. How am I going to keep this promise and I don't know what God wants. I know what you said about me being a preacher, but how am I going to do that?"

"Abunda, we prayed that God would not let you die. I told God that I would do whatever I could to help you be what you are to be. And I will. I don't have all the answers, only a few, but I believe that as we spend time together things will become more clearer to both of us."

"So where do we start?" Abunda asked in a very feeble voice.

"First, you must regain all your strength and I will pray about what to do."

Sunday morning came and everyone at Marnatha went to church to give thanks for Abunda's recovery. Unlike the other churches, the Coloreds did not have to sit in the balcony but most Whites did sit together away from the Coloreds. Rev. Hope was not a proponent of this behavior and tried to discourage it.

After praying about Abunda, Rev. Hope felt that he should teach him how to be a preacher and make him an assistant at his church. He knew that this would draw much controversy but was sure that this was what he needed to do. He and his family were no strangers to controversy.

Abunda's tutelage began with evening classes between him and Rev. Hope 2-3 days a week. Biblical books and literature became his closest friends. He spent countless hours absorbing what was on the pages. This experience opened a whole new world of learning to Abunda. Not only was the Biblical information astounding and fascinating to him, but he was also introduced to scholarly information as well.

"Abunda, you have exceptional intelligence," Rev. Hope complimented. "You have accomplished so much more in a short period of time than others I know. I want to enroll you in a mail order course for preachers. I will take care of your registration and will continue to tutor you, if you need me. I'm more than sure that you will do extremely well with this and perhaps we will move on to other courses. What do you think?"

"I don't know how to thank you for your support, Rev. Hope. I want to do all of this and more. Maybe this is what our ancestors meant when they told Poppa that there is a better life for us? I need to have a talk with the group because we haven't been spending much time together. I want to explain to them what I, I mean, we are doing."

"That's fine, Abunda," Rev. Hope added in agreement.

Rev. Hope had relieved Abunda of his duties so that he could give all his attention to learning. The group was ecstatic about Abunda's news and wanted to do everything they could to help him.

Bela asked, "Is we gonna stay here forever? Is we goin' to Settles Landing?"

"I don't know," Abunda answered. "Maybe when you all feel stronger in your learning you can go without me? I just don't know right now. You can talk it over with each other and let me know what you come up with. I will be with you whatever you decide to do. Rev. Hope will help you, I'm sure."

A sadness engulfed the group but Bela spoke up, "We ain't gon' nowhere yet. Let's don't git sad now; we's still to'gatha."

This broke the sadness and restored a lightness to the group.

Learning and studying consumed Abunda. In record time he completed the mail order course and Rev. Hope was in a quandary as to what to do with him now. Abunda's thirst for knowledge caused Rev. Hope to evaluate his current surroundings. He surveyed his church and realized that he was doing 98% of the work including services. Wanting to do more for the community, Rev. Hope knew that he needed assistance, but was positive that Whites would not receive what he had in mind. He wanted to make Abunda his assistant because his desire was to help the Coloreds improve their living and educational conditions.

"Abunda, I have an idea that I think will please you. How would you like to be my assistant at the church? You can help me with the daily operations and meeting the needs of the people. I know that it will be difficult, at first, but I believe that everyone will welcome you when they see your sincerity and enthusiasm. I especially want to help the Colored people who need to improve their quality of life. What do you think?"

"I don't know what to think, Rev. Hope. White people don't like us Coloreds and they don't want us telling them what to do. They sure don't need our help. I would really like to help my people, though. I have an even better idea. What if I start a church for my people that will be separate from yours? Your church can help by giving us what we need, like clothing, money, books, furniture, you know?"

Rev. Hope was full of hope listening to Abunda's idea. "That's an excellent idea!! Your church will become our mission field. We can help you get started and I think I know just where a building is that you can use. I know the owner and he is a good man. The building is empty now but it needs some work. Everyone can pitch in and fix it up. This is going to be great. I will ask the owner about donating the building, and my members about assisting with fixing it up. I can't wait to get started."

Rev. Hope called a church meeting to discuss his ideas for Abunda. He informed the congregation that it would be an excellent opportunity for missions right at home.

Unfortunately, the meeting did not go as well as he had hoped. Many members were reluctant to support a Colored church, because they knew that much of the surrounding community had very negative feelings towards Colored people.

"We are not like those other people. Can't we be an example of good and not be frightened off by the evil?" Rev. Hope questioned.

"Rev. Hope, we all know that you are a good man and would like to help everybody. We would like to do that too, but what if there is a backlash and our families are put in jeopardy?" asked one parishioner.

From the rear of the church someone yelled, "Maybe we should put this to a secret vote and let that be our decision?" The rest of the congregation was in total agreement with that idea.

"Everyone write yes or no on a piece of paper and we will pass the collection plate to gather the votes. I pray that you all will be prayerful about your decision and consider what God would want and not be afraid of man," Rev. Hope instructed.

The votes were counted and the decision was to support the mission project. Many expressed their continued fear but took to heart what Rev. Hope had instructed.

With overwhelming enthusiasm, Rev. Hope shared, "We will continue making the plans and you will be informed of when we will start the actual project. Those who are unable to assist physically can donate money and supplies."

Rushing home to give Mrs. Hope and Abunda the news, Rev. Hope could not get there fast enough. This effort of support encouraged his faith and he knew that God would be pleased.

"Honey," he said bursting through the door. "The church has agreed to take on the project of building a church for the Colored people and Abunda will be the pastor. Many said that they are afraid of repercussions but voted to support the project anyway. This is one of the greatest things that have ever happened in Marantha. See, even though everybody does not dislike the Colored people; some people do have a genuine relationship with God. Abunda will be so pleased when he hears this. I'm going to the farmhouse to let him know right now."

Running across the estate, Rev. Hope almost falls while trying to get to Abunda as fast as he can. "Abunda, come quick!" he yells.

Abunda is startled by the call, so he does just what Rev. Hope says and moves very quickly. "What is it Rev. Hope? Is everything all right?"

"Yes, Abunda, it is better than all right. The church members have agreed to take on your new church as our mission. Initially, they were afraid of others who still have a hatred for Coloreds, but they decided to trust God and do the right thing. We need to start working on our plans immediately, before they have a change of heart. Tomorrow I will go to see Mr. Witherspoon to ask him for the building. I am confident that he will say yes."

"Rev. Hope, I don't know what to say, again. You have always been so good to all of us since we arrived and I never thought that anything like this would happen to me. But, Poppa always said that our ancestors told him that there was a better life for us. It looks like they were right. I'm going to tell the others the great news. Thanks again, Rev. Hope for giving me hope."

Abunda heads back to the farmhouse where the group is gathered. He walks in the door with a newness to his body as he pranced with confidence. Going to the middle of the room, he beckoned for everyone to come close to him. "I have something very special to tell you. I hope that it will make you very happy. I am going to be a preacher like Rev. Hope. I only hope that I can be as great as he is. We are going to start a little church for the Colored people here in

Marantha where we can do what we want to in our church. Don't you think that's a great idea?"

Bela was shocked by the news. "Is we gonna go to the other place we started out fo'?"

Abunda responds, "Bela, you've been a great friend. I know that we are supposed to be on our way to Settles Landing but I have to do this for now. Remember, we talked about the rest of you all going on without me whenever you wanted to. I am sure that Rev. Hope will help you get there and I will do whatever I can."

"We not going without you. It's been good fo' us here. We don't wanna be without you," Bela replies sadly.

"I believe that something special is going to happen to all of us if we stay here in Marantha. I don't know what the rest of the world is like out there, but I do know what life is like here. I want all of you to finish your learning and get a good trade, something that you can do anywhere you go. That's why me and Rev. Hope want to open the church so that we can help our people learn to read and write. We, Coloreds, aren't dumb people, we just never had the chance to learn and prove ourselves. Look how we keep up property, land, animals, planting and harvesting food, taking care of children, cooking and so much more. We need to learn now how to do it for ourselves. We can become our own boss. Yes, we can!"

Abunda experienced an exhilaration that he had never encountered before. The sound and force of his words made his statements a truth and a reality. He was assured that his people could and would do whatever they desired, as long as they were given the opportunity. Abunda looked upward to the heavens, past the roof of the farmhouse, to his ancestors who he felt agreed with his thoughts. The group mumbled in agreement and a new vigor was cultivated among them. They too wanted to be more than they had ever been. They wanted that better life!

Early the next morning Rev. Hope left for Mr. Witherspoon's place. He was very anxious to discuss the matter with him and get on developing the plans with Abunda. He also wanted to take a look at the place to ascertain what improvements needed to be done.

Arriving at the Witherspoon's, Rev. Hope met Mrs. Witherspoon in the front of the huge house. "Good morning, Mrs. Witherspoon. How are you today? It's been a while since I've seen you!"

"Good morning, Rev. Hope. It's good to see you. I've been a little under the weather so I haven't been to church in a while."

"You look very well. I'm glad to see that you must be doing much better. Is Mr. Witherspoon around? I would like to talk with him."

"Yes, he's right inside. Come with me."

"Mr. Witherspoon, good morning."

"Hello there, Rev. Hope. This is a surprise. Come in and have a seat while the Misses get us something to drink. Would you like coffee?"

"That would be very kind of you."

"What can I do for you Rev. Hope?"

"I don't know if you heard but the church voted to adopt a mission that would help to start a Colored church right here in Marantha."

"No, I hadn't heard that. I think it's a good idea, though. Most people in Marantha are good honest folk and don't mind helping the Coloreds."

"I'm glad you feel that way, because I want to know if you will donate your old building at the edge of town for their church. Our church has agreed to do whatever repairs are needed as part of the mission."

Mr. Witherspoon got up from his seat and stood with his back to Rev. Hope while he looked out of the window. He turned to face Rev. Hope and said, "You mean the old raggedy building on the open lot with all the weeds up around it?"

"Yes, sir. That's the one."

The suspense made Rev. Hope very nervous. He was sure that since Mr. Witherspoon thought the mission project was such a good idea, that he would readily give the old building for the church.

"Son, I've spent years building a good reputation in Marantha. My folks were some of the first people to settle this little town. We have always done right by everybody, but you know that there are some mean people that hate the Coloreds. Personally, I disagree with them but they are mean-spirited. They have been known to kill Coloreds for no reason. Are you sure that everybody has thought this through, especially the reality of serious trouble?"

"We have Mr. Witherspoon. We believe that God will be pleased with our decision to help our fellowman."

"Well, in that case, you can have the building. I will have the papers drawn up so that you will own it legally and no one can take it from you. Oh by the way, who is going to be the pastor?"

"I have a young man; name Abunda Basket that has been with us for a good while now. He is Colored and very intelligent. I told him that I wanted to make him my assistant so that we could help the Coloreds but he came up with the idea of them having their own church. We both came up with the idea of our church supporting them as a mission project. He is an exceptional person."

"Seems like you have everything taken care of. If you need me for anything else just let me know. You have always been good for our town and this will help to make it even better."

"Thank you so much Mr. Witherspoon. Thank you."

All the way home plans and ideas were rolling through Rev. Hope's mind. Life had not been so exciting since the group arrived at Marnatha. He now had a sense that he still had much more to give and that Little Clark, who was not so little anymore, would have a legacy of humanitarianism to be the foundation for his life.

Mr. Witherspoon did exactly as he said and had the legal papers sent directly to Rev. Hope. In the meantime, Abunda, Cliff and Rev. Hope had gone over the building and recorded all repairs that were needed. The church was informed of the repairs and the need for supplies and help. The outpour of support was overwhelming. No one complained and not a negative word was heard. The community worked day and night to complete the project and now it was the big day: the opening of the church.

The word had spread throughout the Colored community in Marantha about the new church and especially about the new young Colored pastor. Because Marantha was so much different than other communities that detested Colored people, all the Colored people were allowed to attend church. They all came from far and near to see this wonder that was taking place.

The old tattered building was now bright with fresh gray paint, red and blue stained glass windows, a three-step entrance with an oak bar to support the elderly, and a sign that read, 'Welcome to the Place of Hope Church'. The inside of the church had twenty rows of pews on each side. In the pulpit was a wooden stand where the church Bible rested along with water glasses for the pastor. There were three chairs behind the pulpit; one for the pastor and the other for guest preachers. Like in African worship, pieces of consecrated wood, rock and statuettes representing objects to be worshipped were included to remind the church of their country.

Rev. and Mrs. Hope, along with some of his members, attended the first service at the new church to demonstrate their continued support. Rev. Hope sat in the pulpit. Abunda introduced Rev. Hope and shared with the congregation the great things he had done for him and his group. He asked Rev. Hope to say something to the church and was surprised at what happened. Rev. Hope had instructed Bela and the group to come to the front of the church. They were all dressed in nice clothes that Mrs. Hope provided. Little Clark, Cliff, the other farmhands, Mrs. Hope and Mr. Witherspoon were also asked to join the others at the front.

"Abunda, would you please join the others?" Rev. Hope asked. Not knowing what was to take place, Abunda obeyed. He had unlimited trust in Rev. Hope.

"This morning is a historical moment in Marantha. We have opened our first church for Colored people which they can operate by themselves. Our community has come together and put aside differences to help our fellow man improve their quality of life. We have given unselfishly of time, money, supplies, equipment and whatever was needed to make this day a reality. Mr. Witherspoon gave the building without any reservation at all. Today it gives me an enormous amount of pleasure and pride to ordain Abunda Basket as the preacher of this church. Let us pray, God you know all things and this is your doing. We all lay our hands on this man and ask you to empower him to do your will. We agree in your presence to stand by and assist him in this endeavor. From this day on, you will be known as Rev. Abunda Basket, Amen.

Abunda, we know that you would have liked for your real family to be with you and I'm sure that they are. But we stand with you today in their place as your family: Bela, the group, Mrs. Hope, Clark, Cliff and the farmhands. We hope that you will continue to accept us as family and request our help whenever needed."

Rev. Abunda was soaked with tears. Bela was the first to embrace him with a huge brotherly hug, and the others followed. Mrs. Hope cried, just like Momma Basket would have done, as she held him in her arms. Clark asked him to bend over and whispered, "You are my big brother and best friend in the whole world. I love you, Abunda. I mean Rev. Abunda."

They were pleased with the service and found it interesting how emotional the Coloreds were about their faith. Many of the songs were in an African language and the rest were from the White church. Because many of the Coloreds could not read or write the words were read aloud first and then the congregation would sing afterwards. This came to be known as lining a hymn.

Abunda greeted his new congregation with a message of love and hope. "This is our church; our Place of Hope. It will represent the freedom that we will all experience one day. Here we will honor our ancestors and the White man's God. No one will be excluded from our worship experience or from learning. In this Place we will build together. Cry together. Hope together. Provide correction together. Establish a Place that no one will be able to take from us. When we have come out of the fields, we will find a place of peace here. Whatever is done here will be done for the good of us all. No one person or group will have control over the destiny of our church. We will never allow outsiders to shatter or take over what we have established. Everyone is welcomed, but those who helped in building this Place of Hope will be respected and will be with us as long as they wish. If anyone violates our understanding, they will be corrected and shall remain apart of us as long as they wish.

We have been through much as a people and I believe that the best is yet to come. We have made this country great and rich with our blood and labor. Families have been destroyed, our men castrated, and our women raped, but yet we live on. I know that we will succeed beyond our wildest dreams and will not let our ancestors down by giving up.

Education will become our main priority; and everyone *will* learn to read and write!"

The congregation went up in an uproar. It was more like a motivational speech than a sermon. When service was over, everyone congratulated and thanked Abunda for doing such a splendid job. The visitors expressed their support and gratitude for him wanting to help his people.

Being flabbergasted by the turn-out and reception of the people, Abunda remained at his church long after everyone else had left. He sat still in his chair behind the pulpit mulling over the events of the day. Astonishment clouded his thinking as to what had just taken place. "What am I doing and where am I taking these people," this sobering thought invaded his mind.

Suddenly, a feeling of hopelessness overtook Abunda as he thought of his new mission. Since leaving Annapolis Grove he was thrust in the middle of caring for others; something he had not done in the past. Poppa was always there for him, his brothers and the family. Unfamiliarity gripped him as he pondered the "White man's God", whom he told that he would do whatever he wanted for saving his family. "Who is this God and how do I come to know Him? What am I suppose to do with my ancestors who have been our God since I can remember? Poppa's grandmother told him that she learned about the White man's God while on the plantation. She convinced Poppa that this God was real and was a friend to Coloreds even though they were in slavery."

There was so much for Abunda to think about and seek understanding. All the pictures of God were White! How would he convince his parishioners that this God loved them and wanted the best for them? His personal evidence was being healed from the poison of the snake bite and the spiritual experience he had with Poppa. Perhaps if he shared that with his church they too would begin to believe in this new God.

The Place of Hope Church was becoming a historical event in Marantha and the news of its success was traveling throughout the land. Abunda had started reading classes after Sunday morning services. During the week, services were held late because his congregation worked late in the fields and homes. They did not mind the lateness of the hour because they realized the significance of what was taking place. Many who had never hoped to read were now able to pronounce and read small words. This opened up a whole new world for them.

Rev. Hope and his congregation stood by their word. They were faithful in contributing money, supplies and their time to assist Abunda with his huge responsibility. The people of Marantha gained a new sense of pride in giving to help the development of others in their community. It brought the town much closer together.

As the news spread abroad, other Coloreds wanted to hear Abunda and learn what he was teaching. They would come as far as 20-30 miles on foot just to attend service. Many were caught on the way and assaulted even though they were free to travel.

One particular Sunday, a family entered the church and two young boys were carrying a man. It turns out that the man was their father. They told that as they were traveling to church, some men jumped them. Their father told them all to run and hide in the bushes with the women in the group. He did not want any of the women to be raped, as had happened in the past. The boys did as their father instructed, but the men caught him and gave him a brutal beating. They left him for dead. When they were gone the others came out of hiding and quickly attended to their father.

"You wanna go back home, Daddy?" one of the boys asked.

Needing serious medical attention, the father said, "No, we're goin' to church."

The boys and the women lifted him from the ground, and literally dragged him the rest of the way to the church. When they opened the church door everyone looked to the rear and immediately jumped to assist them.

"Bring him to the front," Pastor Abunda told them. "We know that this was a senseless act of brutality and we will never be able to do anything about the people who did this. But we have a great hope and it has kept our ancestors alive through horrible things. We will come together as one, a big family, and we will overcome these difficult times. For sure, our children will know what true freedom is and they will enjoy the fruit of this land even though it is not ours. We made it rich, yet we are without. We made it strong, yet we appear to be weak. We gave our blood, yet we have no rights. Nevertheless, we have a history of survival and this too shall pass."

The members of the congregation shouted in agreement and some took the beaten man into another room to clean him up and to attend to his wounds.

After that incident, Abunda began to think of how he could travel and meet with people where they lived. He reasoned that it would be easier for him to travel with a few men, than to have women and children threatened with brutality. He decided to have a talk with Rev. Hope to get some wisdom as to what to do. A meeting was arranged and they met at Abunda's church.

"Rev. Hope, I'm really concerned about my people being beaten on their way to church. I know that we can't do anything about it, but I was thinking about me traveling to them. I could go to different places during the month and teach and preach to them right where they are. How does that sound?"

"Abunda, I think that it is a very selfless act on your part. But I would be as concerned for your safety as you are for the others. Some people are just mean and evil with no thought for harming anyone. I don't want you to get hurt, and possibly killed while you are traveling. This is a difficult decision but yet I understand your heart for your people. I did promise to help!"

"I feel such a need to help my people that I can't rest knowing that they are getting hurt because they want to come to church. You can give me papers, as your assistant, so that I can travel. I must do this, regardless!"

"Where will you go, Abunda? Will you travel alone?"

"I will ask my people at our next service and see who is traveling a far distance. I will also ask if they know of a place where I can come to them and help them there. I have studied your God and learned that He cares for all people and that He is a God of love and not hate. I know that He wants us all to have the best, but I also know that He lets man do whatever he wants to. I am going to continue to learn more and know this God, so that I can help my people. Maybe when I'm sure, they will come to know Him and have a hope like we do in our ancestors. I will ask the group if any of them would like to travel with me. Perhaps we could alternate people and that way if harm comes, we all won't be hurt or destroyed."

"Abunda, I'm still concerned about your safety, but I do understand your burden. Your plan sounds like a good one. When will you ask the group?"

"When they come in from work today. I am going to do this even if nobody goes with me."

"I will continue to pray, and you have my absolute support. I am so proud of you, Abunda. I wish your family was here to see this!"

"Thank you Rev. Hope. But as you said, you and the group are now my family and especially my congregation, wherever they may be."

"Let's go home, Abunda."

Abunda could not wait for the group to return to the farmhouse. He wanted to start making his plans immediately. This new responsibility, that is much more like a burden, would not go away from him. He constantly had dreams and often daydreams as to how he could help his people against such great odds. The majority of his prayers were still to his ancestors, but gradually he was praying to his new God. Looking for a reality in his new God has him on a quest that was so different but necessary.

Ancestor worship was his family heritage and they put great confidence in it. The ancestors were patriarchs that included the eldest male who was very spiritual and was the only one that could communicate with God through prayer. The clergy consisted of priests, prophets, and elders who conducted the worship experience. Sacrifices were made to recognize the power of a deity to remove sin by consecration of a sacrifice thereby purifying both the sinner and his community offerings included: domestic animals, non animal objects, beer and other drinks. All substances in someway symbolized the nature of the person for whom the sacrifice was made and the force to which it was offered. The ancestors controlled all the material wealth and built temples to worship in. The temples had statuettes, wood and rock that symbolized nature.

All African religions included a belief in a creator-deity, or High God, omnipotent, everlasting and possessed of many attributes, each of which is reflected in a particular name which arises on appropriate occasions.

Abunda was told and learned that this form of worship was all they knew in Africa, but when they came to this new country, the White people introduced this new God to them. It sounded something like the ancestors, but their God was suppose to be of love and caring like the ancestors, yet the Colored people were still treated so bad. This Abunda had to find a way to understand for himself, and then convince his people to follow this God.

The group finally came in from working. They were very tired because they had an exceptionally long day. The estate was growing in every area and they had to put in extra time in addition to doing their studies. After dinner, Abunda summoned the group together in a corner of the farmhouse.

Abunda started by saying, "I want to ask you all something that is very important. You need to take your time and think about it. You also may want to pray about it and tell me your answer tomorrow."

Everyone was very curious about what Abunda was saying. They listened conscientiously to his instructions.

"I want to go to our people in other parts of town and the surrounding areas. I don't want them to be beaten for wanting to come to church. I feel that I must do something to help them. If I go to them they will not be in danger."

"But you will, Abunda, or do we have to call you Pastor Abunda, here?" Ezra asked.

"No you don't have to call me Pastor here, and I know that I will be in danger but something must be done. I also want to ask if any of you would like to travel with me when I go."

Immediately Bela spoke up, "You know I will, Abunda."

The room remained silent after Bela answered. Anxiety was on the face of the others who knew the pending danger. Remembering their travels to Marantha, their faces looked like little children who had just experienced a recurring nightmare. Marantha was a place of safety and they had never ventured far from it.

"Thank you, Bela," Abunda said. "The rest of you, if you want, can let me know tomorrow. I don't want you to go if you don't want to and I won't be mad with you. You can stay back here and take care of the others in our church while we're gone."

It was time for church and people continued to travel from near and far. The violence subsided a little, because Rev. Hope placed an article in the local paper about the hatred that was being done to the Coloreds for traveling to church.

Pastor Abunda stood in front of the pulpit to address the waiting congregation. "I want to know how far some of you travel to get here."

A voice from the side said, "We's walk pass two big houses 'en land."

Another, "We's walk pass three big houses."

"We's come by four houses," adds another.

"Four houses?" Pastor Abunda reacts in unbelief.

Each house, as the people call them, are estates with at least 25-50 acres of land. The travel time would be about two hours or more for each one.

"I's said sup'in wrong, Pasa?" one of the congregants asked in concern.

"No. No. I'm just amazed to know that you all walk that far to get here. I'm truly grateful."

"We's need ya. Ya's all we's got, Pasa."

Moved by this statement of trust, Pastor Abunda, composes himself to share his idea with his congregation. "I want to come to where you all live, so that you won't have to travel so far to get here."

Everyone in the church displayed thunderous sounds of joy. Shouts of 'thank ya's echoed through the building. "Ya's gonna com' see us, Pasa?" asked a teenage boy with an unbelievable look on his face. "I's wanna be lik' ya. I's wanna learn 'en be smart, lik' ya."

Again Pastor Abunda was moved. "I'm going to bring the church to you all. We will have services and teachings at different times. I need to know where you live and how to get there, so the rest of this service we will get that information from you."

The rest of the service was used together the information. A schedule would have to be made and places to be found where services could be held. Pastor Abunda would need Rev. Hope's help with this because he had a good rapport with most of the people in the area.

Abunda approached Rev. Hope with the information and Rev. Hope immediately began to work on it. He contacted many people and told them of Abunda's desire, and was met with many positive responses. Only a few were hesitant about the idea but none were outright hostile.

Rev. Hope completed the plan and gave it to Abunda. Seven owners had agreed to have services and teachings held at their places. Abunda was astounded by the response and wanted to begin immediately. The plan included his traveling two days a week to other places and doing two days in Marantha.

The day was rapidly approaching for Pastor Abunda to make his first trip. He had received reassurance from Rev. Hope that everything was ready for his arrival and that someone would meet him. Bela was the only one of the group that consented to travel, so he and Abunda left. The journey took about an hour. They came upon an old barn where a Colored man was standing outside.

"Pastor Abunda?"

"Yes, sir."

"Hello, my name is Ja'cin Bongera. Welcome to Crusidea. We are excited about you being here with us."

"Thank you, Mr...."

"Just call me Ja'cin, Pastor."

Abunda noticed something different about this man. "Excuse me, but you seem to be an educated man. Why are you here?"

"I'm here, my wife and I, to help you in anyway we can. We moved here a short while ago and heard about your church. We have not been able to get there, so we were excited to here that you were coming here. The people who allowed me to be educated had me since I was a little boy. I believe that I was taken from my family. The people that I lived with treated me very well, educated me and gave me my papers. They also taught me a trade and that's why I'm here in Crusidea."

"Thank you, again, Ja'cin. It looks like we'll be doing much together and I can't wait to meet your lovely wife. Let's go inside."

There were about 15 people gathered in the barn eagerly waiting for Pastor Abunda to begin his teachings. The teenage boy that spoke about wanting to be like Abunda was sitting in the front of the group. He looked determined to soak up everything that was coming and was prepared for more. His vigor gave a sense of hope and perseverance to the group. Abunda decided to name this group Courage Well.

After meeting the people, Abunda began to teach the people of Courage Well how to read and identify the alphabets. He and Bela had now become experts at this because of their work in the Place of Hope Church. Mrs. Hope had provided some books to be used in the teachings. The teaching lasted for about an hour and everyone in attendance was sorry to see the time end.

"Pastor, we don't know how to thank you for what you are doing. We know that your life is in danger and we pray that you and Bela will be safe as you travel," Ja'cin adds.

The teenage boy runs to Pastor Abunda and says, "Pastor, I's gonna learn all da thangs ya's got, so I's kin be lik' ya. I's gonna work hard 'en ya see. Thank ya fo' he'pin' us?"

"What's your name, son?"

"Esa."

"Please to meet you Esa. I'm sure you're going to be my best student and thank you."

Bela and Abunda headed for home with another new and exhilarating feeling of accomplishment. Their lives had changed dramatically since leaving Annapolis Grove. The words of the ancestors were becoming a reality: here is a better life for you all.

As they journeyed home almost in complete silence they came to a very dark place and heard loud voices. The voices sounded like men who were drunk. Being concerned for their safety, they agreed to stop and hide in the thicket until they could locate the place where the voices were coming from. As they hid, the voices got closer and closer until they were just upon them. Abunda and Bela knew that if they moved they would be spotted, so they remained deadly still.

"Be a good night to lynch some Coloreds," one drunken man yelled.

Another replied, "Ain't no Coloreds out here and we wouldn't be able to see them in this darkness, anyway."

The others laughed. They walked right pass Abunda and Bela.

When they were a safe distance off, Abunda and Bela came from out of the thicket and quickly headed for home. Neither spoke, but great fear could be sensed among them. The reality of the mission was more real than ever before.

Arriving at Maranatha safely, the two men quietly entered the farmhouse and went directly to bed. Abunda could not sleep as he was recanting the events of his day; a day that was filled with excitement, yet with much fear. Wondering to himself, "How will I cope with the potential of danger and possibly death? How did our ancestors survive the brutality?"

"We giv' our lives dat da resta ya git a betta lif'" a voice from nowhere said. "We git beat, burn, cut up 'en kil't, we's na'va giv' up hope. Only da strong last, 'en y'alls livin' t'day. Ya git what ya need ta do mo' den we don'. Y'all mak' it."

Tears streaming down Abunda's face he vowed, "We will make it and I won't let you all down."

He drifted off to sleep.

Abunda's notoriety was covering Marantha and surrounding areas near and far. He was beginning to be known as a savior to his people. Colored people were learning to read and write in record numbers. Many started their own businesses that gained them a level of respect that they would never have imagined. As The Place of Hope Church grew, they started a school that was also supported by Rev. Hope's congregation. Life was great! Rev. Hope could not have been more proud of Abunda's accomplishments.

"Abunda, you have become a magnificent orator and educator," Rev. Hope said while beginning to share his good news with him. "Your name has been mentioned among some of the more prominent leaders in our church movement. They want you to come and share with them sometime. We are eager to learn how to replicate what you have done at your church in other places. It is not easy to do this everywhere because of the feeling toward Colored people by others, but there are those who really want to try. Would you like to travel with me to a major meeting of church leaders? They would like for you to come and speak to them."

"Rev. Hope, I would love to, but who will look after my church. I don't want to let them down by leaving."

"We will work all that out. This will be a great opportunity for you to help more Colored people than you would be able to reach from here. I will talk with Mrs. Hope and some of our church members who have helped in the past. We will only be gone for a short while and I know they will be more willing to help out. Bela will remain here. He knows the work very well because of your teachings."

Abunda's anticipation was staggering. He could not believe that all this was taking place and now he would get to leave Marantha and travel with Rev. Hope. Meeting others from the church community would be an event that he would never forget, but the idea of speaking to White preachers at a convention was too much for him to handle.

Awe clouded his mind as to what to say, and how to act. "Will they like me?" The ancestors were surely right about there being a better life for them. He deliberated as to whether the inheritance would be a part of this better life. Closer to home, he needed to make plans for Bela and the others to take over in his absence.

Abunda approached Bela, "Rev. Hope wants me to go to a meeting of church leaders so I can tell them about what we do. We won't be gone long and I need you to take over the church while I'm gone. What do you think?"

"I don't kno', Abunda," Bela responded hesitantly. "That's a big job. I might do it wrong."

"I trust you, Bela. I know that you love me and what we do, so I know you can do this. Rev. Hope is going to ask Mrs. Hope and some others to help you. This is important. I will be able to talk to other people to help our people. Maybe we can open some other schools in different places."

"Are we goin' to leave Marantha?" Bela seemed anxious to know.

"No, but we can do some good work in other places. It will be all right, I promise you. I won't leave you and the others. But sometimes I will need to travel to help others have a good life. You want that for them, don't you?"

"Yes, Abunda. Yes, I do. I do my best when you gon'."

"I know you will, Bela. I believe that one day you will be traveling to different places with me. Thank you for being my friend."

"Thank you, Abunda for stayin' our friend."

Rev. Hope meets with Mrs. Hope and others who agree to assist Bela in Abunda's absence. Plans are made for the teachings and services that also include Bela traveling to other churches as Abunda had done.

Abunda is very excited about his new opportunities and meeting new people. He is in awe of the notoriety that he has received from his people and from the White church community, especially the leaders. Rev. Hope continues to share with him the good reports that he has heard concerning his work and success with helping his people.

As Abunda bathes in this glory, he is ever more conscious of his burden to continue the awesome task of getting his people out of their present state and into the 'better life' that the ancestors spoke of. Not wanting to be over confident, he consistently looks for help from the ancestors and the White man's God that he is growing closer to daily.

The plans for the trip to the Faith Convention are now completed and Rev. Hope and Abunda will be leaving the next day. Abunda has rehearsed his speech countless numbers of times alone and before the workers in the farmhouse. He has sought their opinions and received astounding compliments. But his concern is that they are his friends and family and they would say good things even if they did not like the speech. He could not find a sense of peace. Fear and nervousness crippled his desire to believe his friends. He considered, "What will I do? How will it be with complete strangers?" A need to separate from the group came across Abunda's mind and he decided to take a walk in the cool night air.

"Can't rest either?" came Rev. Hope's voice surprisingly.

"No. I'm nervous and afraid about our trip and what will happen. I've been safe here at Maranatha for some time and even the townsfolk have been kind to us. This trip is taking me out of my comfort zone and into unfamiliar surroundings. Terrible things have happened to my people and many of my church folk by Whites who say they love your God. Now I'm going to walk in the midst of these people in a strange town and share with them what we're doing. Wouldn't that frighten you?"

"Yes, Abunda it certainly would. I'm kind of on a limb here myself by constantly reminding my fellow clergy of their shortcomings and now bringing you, the evidence; right in their face. Everybody has not received this idea well and they have expressed their feelings to me. Some are very hostile but I promised to help you in every way I can and I know that this is God's will for me. We will conquer this together!"

"Thanks, again, for your support and love, Rev. Hope. You are an example to me of what your God is even though our people have not seen it in many. I look forward to our trip and to not being a disappointment to you or the Convention."

"Good night, Abunda. I'll see you in the morning."

"Good night, Rev. Hope."

The two men went their separate ways to their respective quarters. Now Abunda had the peace to rest and the confidence in what he would face.

Chapter 9

Opportunity Knocks

The Faith Convention was held in a big city called Valentine. It had a population of about 10,000 with large buildings in the downtown area. The surrounding city was quaint with neighborhoods sprawling with stylish houses lined in rows but not connected. Many of the houses had manicured lawns, beautiful shrubbery and variations of flowers.

The streets were immaculate and there was a park in the very center of the town square. It looked like a picture postcard. Rev. Hope and Abunda would be staying at the largest hotel, The Dover. It was known for its elegance and elite status. Everybody that was anybody stayed at The Dover, but not Colored people.

As Rev. Hope and Abunda entered the main door they were stopped by the doorman. "Excuse me, sir," speaking to Rev. Hope. "He can't come in this door. He has to go to the back where the Coloreds go, if he's with you."

Rev. Hope replied, "I'm sorry sir, but this is the guest speaker for the large church Convention that's going to be held here over the next few days."

"I'm sorry, sir, but he still has to go to the back door."

"May we at least go in and speak with the manager about this, I am sure there's some misunderstanding?" Rev. Hope asked.

"Wait here and I will see."

The doorman returned and informed Rev. Hope that the manager would see him at the front desk and that Abunda could come in with him.

"Greetings, my name is Rev. Hope and this is Pastor Abunda Basket our guest speaker for the church convention. I understand that there is a problem with him staying at your facility. I had no problems making the reservations and if you check, you will see that he is listed."

"Greetings, Rev. Hope you are right," the manager informed him. Pastor Basket is registered but you didn't inform us that he was Colored. Had you done that we would have advised you that no Coloreds are allowed to stay in the main section of the hotel. They are housed in the back quarters with no exceptions."

"I am appalled by such action. Is there someone else that I can take my concern to?"

"The only person is the owner and he is not in the hotel. I have the authority to operate the hotel, as I've done for years," the manager stated vehemently.

The incident was becoming disturbing to others who were waiting to complete their registration at the desk. Affluent Whites were whispering among themselves about Abunda's presence in the lobby. Over hearing some of the conversation and gathering that he was not a bellman, they wondered how he had managed to get into the hotel. Abunda was just a little behind Rev. Hope and kept his head slightly down towards the floor. He was a little nervous and scared because he had not been directly involved in racial matters since coming to Marantha.

Suddenly, a White woman who was waiting to register expressed her concern over the matter to the manager." Sir, what harm would it do if this gentlemen where to stay in your quarters. He is a refined gentleman by his looks and has not acted unseemly while this issue is being discussed."

The manager now concerned that the hotel guests were getting involved reassured the lady. "Ma'am, I'm sorry that you feel you've been drawn into this matter, but I assure you that we will take care of it expeditiously."

"I just don't want it to be taken care of, I want this man to be treated with some dignity," she insisted.

As they continued to discuss the matter, Abunda remained quiet and still, but something began to disturb him. It was the woman's voice. It sounded like someone he knew from Annapolis Grove. He knew better than to look up especially into the woman's face, but he needed to identify her. Slowly moving toward her, making sure that no one noticed him advancing, Abunda managed to get to an angle where he could see the side of her face. Her identity was still not clear to him. Just as he was about to inch a little closer, the woman turned abruptly in disgust with the matter at hand. Moving rapidly to excuse herself from the registration desk, she inadvertently bumped into Abunda.

"Please excuse me sir," she said before looking directly at him.

When their eyes met for a split second they each recognized one another, but were unable to speak. They also knew that they could not continue to look directly at one another.

"That's all right, ma'am," Abunda replied. "Are you okay?"

She answered with a quiver in her voice, "Thank you, I am all right!"

Lost in space and time they did not move until a rather harsh voice interrupted their miraculous meeting.

"Are Colored people staying here now or what?" demanded an irate guest.

The harshness broke their concentration on one another, but they knew that they had to meet somewhere to talk. The woman taking the lead motioned to an area on the other side of the hotel behind a curtain. She held up five fingers, and moved her lips slowly to tell him to meet her there at 5:00 o'clock. He nodded in agreement and she went briskly on her way.

Abunda was in shock after the chance meeting. He gave little or no thought to where he would stay, but was only concerned about his meeting later that evening with his new found friend from home.

The ruckus finally settled down at the registration desk and much to everyone's amazement, he was permitted to stay at the hotel. However, his room would be in an isolated area where the probability of others seeing him would be nil. Rev. Hope looked around to found Abunda and tell him the good news, but he could not be seen in the crowd. Previously he was standing directly behind Rev. Hope but now he was not. Rev. Hope moved from within the crowd to look for him and found him at the end of the circle of people.

"Abunda, thank God, you can stay in the hotel. However, your room will be in a different location from mine but it is a miracle that you are staying here."

He did not respond and Rev. Hope noticed the distant look on his face.

"Is something the matter? Do you mind being in a different part of the hotel? All the rooms here are nice, but if you mind I will argue some more with the manager."

Again, Abunda did not respond.

"Abunda, Abunda." Rev. Hope called to him with concern.

Finally, Abunda came to his senses and realized that Rev. Hope had been talking with him and he had not heard a word because his mind was totally on seeing his friend and their subsequent meeting that night.

"Rev. Hope, I'm sorry. My thoughts were a hundred miles away. Please forgive me. What were you saying?"

"You will be permitted to stay at this hotel, but in a different part. I said that all the rooms here are nice, but if you mind I will argue some more with the manager. That young lady was a very big help."

"That's fine. I honestly didn't believe that they would let me stay here. This is a miracle."

"Yes, Abunda. God is on our side. The bellman will be showing me to my room and I will show you to yours. They told me where it is. I want to make sure that your accommodations are suitable. We can rest until later and then meet for dinner."

Rev. Hope and Abunda followed the bellman through the plush hotel with huge paintings on the walls and chandeliers made of crystal and brass. Abunda had never seen anything like it before and could hardly believe that he would be a part of it. He walked a few steps behind them so as not to bring more attention to himself. His distance gave the impression that he was a hired servant and not a hotel guest. Walking with his head hung slightly toward the floor, he was still able to see the beauty of the walkways and perfunctory areas.

"This is your room, sir," the bellman said to Rev. Hope while giving him the keys.

Rev. Hope responded, "This is just fine. I will take my things into my room then I will show my friend to his room." He reached into his pocket and gave the bellman a tip.

"Thank you, sir. I hope you have a good stay."

As they entered the room, Abunda breathed a sigh of relief at what had occurred. "Why are people so hateful? My people were forced to come to this country, beaten, killed, our families destroyed and they still hate us? Why? I thought that other parts of this country were different and that we could live and be treated with respect, I was wrong. It appears that the whole country just hates us. I'm beginning to be sorry that I made this trip but it has allowed me to see what the real world is like."

"I'm so sorry, Abunda. I can't answer your questions, I can only be to you who I am and help you to become who you are. I've had the same questions, but even God hasn't changed the behavior of some people. Please don't view the trip as a total loss; I know that you have a divine purpose for being here. I will try to make it as pleasant as possible. Let's get you to your room."

The two men walked down the corridor in silence. Although they had an excellent relationship, an eeriness surrounded them in this strange place. The peace that was evident at Marantha was nowhere to be found. A heaviness of isolation and differences was most prevalent.

Continuing down the corridor, the pathway took an abrupt almost dead-end into an alcove under a stairway. The journey took the two into an area of the hotel that was truly isolated. It was still arrayed in splendor, but no one was in this section. Abunda would be there alone. This particular section had been used for hired servants of wealthy people who frequented the hotel. It had its own sense of sadness and despair in the midst of the splendor and awe.

Room 980 was Abunda's room. Rev. Hope put the key in the door, opened it and entered for his inspection. It was quite a nice room. They brought Abunda's luggage into the room and placed it on the bed.

"Again, I'm sorry Abunda," Rev. Hope expressed with much sadness. "I will see you for dinner. We've been invited to a clergy's home."

"I'm not sure that I'm up to it. I want to get some rest and I will contact you shortly as to my plans," he informed Rev. Hope as he was leaving the room.

Abunda entered his room and sat on the bed as his thoughts traveled back to his meeting with his friend from home. As he glanced at the clock on the night stand; it was

3:00 p.m., and he knew that the next two hours would seem like an eternity. He decided to rest by stretching across the bed, hoping to take a nap.

Rev. Hope went back to his room with much concern for his friend, who was more like a son. Not wanting the trip to be devastating for Abunda, he prayed as he walked that God would somehow make this a special time in spite of what had already taken place. Reaching his room he, too, decided to take a nap until dinner. Neither of them knew what time to meet for dinner as they had not discussed it.

Now both of them peacefully resting, they had allowed time to have control over their plans and concerns. They had been through disturbing times before and had seen the faithfulness of God fix their situations. They had no reason to believe that this would be any different.

Abunda began to awake from his rest. He was glad that he was able to rest because the trip had been long and tiresome. Looking around, he had almost forgotten where he was and what had taken place. Now focusing his thoughts, he hurriedly remembered his 5:00 p.m. meeting. He looked at the clock which now said 4:30 p.m. He jumped to his feet and rushed to get the basin of water to refresh himself. He changed his shirt and jacket and looked in the mirror, making sure that he was pleased with his appearance. Now came the hardest task, getting to the meeting place without being noticed or stopped.

Aware that the area where he was staying was isolated, Abunda strolled the corridor without concern until he reached the sharp curve that would lead him to the main part of the hotel. He saw a flight of stairs that looked to be headed away from the main hotel and he decided to see where it would take him. On the way, he passed some Colored workers who he asked how to reach his destination. Armed with the information, he continued until he was behind the area where he was to meet his friend. It was too risky for them to meet in the hotel lobby, even though the area was semi-secluded. Abunda thought how he could get close enough to whisper to his friend.

Now in place, he waited for her to appear and she did in a short amount of time. He did as he had planned and whispered as she stood waiting and looking for him to appear.

"Pss. Pss. Here. I'm behind you," Abunda informed his friend.

She turned to the sound of the voice and upon seeing his face motioned for him to meet her outside. He followed her instructions and they both left and met outside of the hotel. Both knew that they had to be very careful and find a place where they could be alone and not bring attention to themselves. After all she was White and he was Colored.

They walked swiftly around the backside of the hotel toward some lovely gardens that were void of guests but surreptitiously available for them. The gardens were almost covered with weeping willow trees that served as cover for privacy. Finally reaching a place where they felt safe, the two stopped and turned towards each other. Their empty arms were now filled with each other and their heartbeats could be felt as one. The embrace took the place of words that would be so inadequate at a time like this. The woman rested her head on Abunda's chest as tears trickled down her face. Above her head, his face was likewise wet with tears.

Quietly speaking, Abunda asked, "What are you doing here, Serenity?"

"I came to the church convention. What are you doing here?" she asked.

"I'm the guest speaker for the convention."

"Oh, my God," she gasped forgetting the enormous weight of his previous statement. "Abunda, I've missed you terribly. My love for you grew more and more while we were separated. I felt at times that I was going to die if I never saw you again."

"Serenity, my love, I never told anyone about us. When I left Annapolis Grove you were the last person that I saw. I didn't want to run the risk of you getting hurt for being involved with a Colored man. My life is so much different now and I have much to tell you."

"So do I as well, Abunda. But can we just enjoy this little time together first? What I have to say will make a huge difference in our lives. There has to be a place where we can go and spend time together before we leave."

"I will find us a place. I have to meet Rev. Hope for dinner but can you meet me here tomorrow and I will have a place for us to go."

"Of course. I've waited all this time to see you again and I thought this would never happen. Tomorrow will seem so far away."

The two closed their time with a tender kiss and headed back towards the front of the hotel. He allowed Serenity to go ahead of him as he returned the way he came out. As he reached the curve in the corridor again, Rev. Hope was approaching.

"Abunda, have you been, out?"

"Yes, I decided to take a walk. I saw some of the workers in the hotel and asked them which was the safest way for me to leave and they told me. What time are we going to dinner?"

"I was just about to get you. I received a message from our host and they will be sending a carriage for us. There will be no problem with us traveling together because they know that you are a Colored person. These people are different anyway. They care about people because God made us all, so I'd like to think that they are much like me and Mrs. Hope. Let's hurry. We will go down the front way."

The two men left immediately and rushed through the hotel lobby. They could sense the looks of some of the hotel guests but it did not bother them anymore. When they reached the front door, the bellman opened the door and they both went out swiftly.

There was a very fine carriage enclosed with velvet cushions and pillows and a crest on the side. The crest was shaped like a heart with a background that was red velvet. It had a gold cross in the middle with embossed lettering. The Colored driver, dressed in a stately uniform containing the same colors and emblems of the carriage, opened the door for the two men and they both entered the carriage. They sat across from one another and took in the breathtaking countryside as they journeyed to their destination. Neither said a word.

In less time than they realized they were approaching a huge wrought-iron gate with the same crest as the carriage. The ride through the estate took them down a long winding road beautifully scalloped with trees and shrubbery. Sitting at the entrance of the main house were several men dressed in clergy clothes. When the carriage came to a stop, the driver opened the door and Rev. Hope and Abunda stepped out.

"Rev. Hope, welcome to our home. We are pleased that you could join us," said one of the clergy who was in front of the group.

"Thank you Rev. Pitaron. This is Rev. Abunda Basket," replied Rev. Hope.

"It's my pleasure," Rev. Pitaron said, while extending his hand to shake Abunda's.

Abunda graciously replied, "Thank you, sir for inviting me to your lovely home."

One by one, Rev. Pitaron introduce Abunda to his guest. Each was warm and friendly and seemingly eager to talk with him. The group went into the house where Mrs. Pitaron and some other ladies met them. They were introduced and informed that dinner would be served shortly. Prior to dinner they enjoyed hors d'oeuvres and interesting conversation with Abunda being the center of attention.

The majority of the conversation was directed at Abunda's work and his future plans. Obvious amazement was evident at his intellect and his masterful command of the English language. So in awe were some that they merely stood and listened without asking a single question. As the evening began to draw to an end, Rev. Pitaron suggested that the group pray for the success of the convention. Everyone joined together as he made his petition to God on behalf of the group. Agreement with the prayer was felt and no one had anything to add.

Rev. Pitaron walked Abunda and Rev. Hope to the carriage and bided them farewell, acknowledging that he looked forward to seeing them in the morning. The feeling was mutual.

Again, Abunda and Rev. Hope traveled in silence. By now it was dusk and the landscape was fading into the night. Before they arrived at the hotel, Rev. Hope asked, "What do you think of the group and did you enjoy dinner?"

"I enjoyed dinner and was pleasantly surprised by the warm reception I received. It was as if I was in another town; nothing like my arrival at The Dover Hotel. I think that the group was very interesting. They reacted towards me as a strange creature. It's apparent that they have had no interaction with an educated Colored man. But they were quite gracious."

"I'm glad that you enjoyed yourself under the circumstances. I don't know if I could have done as well as you. The Convention starts tomorrow and you will be speaking at the main session. The group would also like to know if you will be available to meet privately with some who are hesitant to meet with you publicly. I will certainly understand if you elect not to."

"I will meet with them. I don't understand their reluctance but.... What time will I be free?"

"Around 4:30 p.m., just before the dinner hour. The Convention will be hosting everyone that attends with a sit down dinner around 6:30 p.m."

The carriage arrived in front of the hotel. Once again the doorman opened the door for Rev. Hope who held it open for Abunda. They went through the lobby to their respective rooms.

Morning could not come fast enough for Abunda so that he could meet Serenity again; but he knew that more preparation was needed for his speech. This was a great opportunity to help his people by telling others of their need. He wanted to let them know that Colored people were human beings created by God, but he did not want to alienate them with guilt. This was a very sensitive time and diplomacy was of the utmost importance.

Seated at the desk in his room, Abunda read the speech that he had prepared. However, after arriving and encountering intolerance, he wondered if he should rewrite it. While attempting to make this decision, he was constantly interrupted with his thoughts of Serenity and their meeting tomorrow. He knew what he wanted to share with her, but he also wondered what she had to share with him. Surely she would tell of home and how everything was in Annapolis Grove, he surmised. Even the possibility of her having gone away to school could be part of the news. There was much to talk about because he had been gone for a good while and had no contact with Serenity.

At last, Abunda had revamped his speech to his liking. He was sure that few, if any, would be offended by it and that his people would be proud of it. Leaving it on the desk, he undressed and went to bed purposing to have good dreams because of the awesomeness tomorrow held.

Morning came as fast as Abunda had hoped. He arose, dressed quickly and waited for Rev. Hope. A knock came on the door and he opened it. Standing there was Serenity, not

Rev. Hope. She had a pleasant look on her face and rushed into Abunda's room.

"Serenity, we can't be seen like this and you can't be in my room. You know what will happen to me if anyone sees you here. I can't wait for later either, but we must. How did you find me?"

"I couldn't wait until later, I had to see you now," she said quickly as she hurried into his arms. "I asked the Colored help where you were and someone led me here. I know they won't tell anyone."

"Serenity, this is the most important time in my life. I have an opportunity to help my people and bridge the evil between the Coloreds and the Whites. I must be focused on what I am going to say. Please understand. I know that we have been apart for a long time, but waiting until later is much shorter than the time that we've been apart. Hurry you must go."

Even though saying that she had to leave, Abunda was holding her tightly in his arms not wanting her to leave. She responded to his embrace, but he slowly began to separate them. "I will see you to the corridor."

They left his room and just as Serenity went in the opposite direction, Rev. Hope was approaching Abunda's room. Abunda saw him and hurried back to meet him. He could not get in his room before Rev. Hope.

"Abunda, good morning. Have you been out?"

"Yes, I took a walk. I'm really nervous and I wanted to talk with my ancestors and God before facing all those people."

"Everything will be fine. Let's go."

The corridors were full with men who would be attending the Convention. Little attention was paid to Abunda as everyone was busy trying to get breakfast before the Convention began. Rev. Pitaron had arranged for Abunda and Rev. Hope to have a private breakfast with him in one of the small dining rooms. Rev. Hope had not shared this with Abunda but led him to the private room.

"Good morning, gentlemen," Rev. Pitaron spoke with a pleasantness as bright as the sunshine of the morning. "I'm so glad you could join me Pastor Abunda. I want everything to be as pleasant as possible for you. Do you mind if I call you Pastor Abunda?"

"Not at all and thank you Rev. Pitaron; your hospitality is most appreciated."

"Ditto," Rev. Hope added.

"After breakfast I will be escorting you into the main ballroom. We will wait for everyone to be seated. Is that all right with you Pastor Abunda?" Rev. Pitaron asked with excitement.

"It is, sir."

Breakfast now over and the lobby relatively quiet, Rev. Pitaron led the two men into the meeting with Pastor Abunda directly behind him and Rev. Hope following. As they entered and were recognized, the room became very quiet. They made their way to the platform where others were seated and Rev. Pitaron motioned for Abunda to have a seat in the center chair. Mumbling could be heard in the room. Rev. Pitaron opened the meeting and introduced the platform guests. After completing the program preliminaries, Rev. Hope was asked to introduce Abunda and he did with such elegance that left a thickness of anticipation in the air.

"I now present to you, Pastor Abunda Basket."

Abunda rose to his feet in the midst of a thunderous applause. As he made his way to the podium his heart nearly stopped and he hesitated for a few seconds. When he reached the podium, that seemed a thousand miles away from his seat, he rested his arms to support himself. While waiting for the applause to die down, he looked around the massive ballroom at the hundreds of clergymen that had gathered for this Convention. Rev. Hope told Abunda that this was to be the largest number in attendance for many years and it was because he would be speaking. Even with that piece of knowledge, he never imagined that so many people would come just to hear him speak. This increased his fear, but at the same time expressed to him the urgency of making an impact for his people.

Now fully erect with a confident posture, Abunda began, "Good morning to you all. Thank you for inviting me to be a part of your Convention. It is indeed an honor for me to be here and one that I do not take lightly. I know that I am the first Colored person to be your keynote speaker and that in itself has made me just a little nervous. After all I am just a little person in this big world that has a heart and desire to help all people. I believe that it is the will of God for us to be 'our brother's keepers and that command has no barriers.

I must give honor to Rev. Hope and those who are responsible for my being here. Rev. Hope has been more to me than I could ever imagine. He has been a pastor, a father, a friend, a tutor and above all he and his family have been loyal to me and to my people. He took us in when we had no place to go and treated us with respect and decency. When I knew that something was happening to me on a spiritual level, I went to him immediately and he said that he would pray about it. I was not that familiar with your God, you see because we pray to and rely on our ancestors for strength and help. They keep us encouraged from beyond the grave, so your God was foreign to me. Rev. Hope helped me to see that your God, who is now my God also, loves us all and Rev. Hope is an example of that love. Publicly, I thank you Rev. Hope, Mrs. Hope and Clark for what you have done in my life."

His speech was interrupted with a resounding round of applause. The climate was now conducive for him to give the speech that he had prepared with no reservations.

Abunda continued, "There are so many that I am grateful to, mentioning them would take too much time. I do however want to express my gratitude and love to my family. My Momma and Poppa did an exceptional job rearing us under our life situation. I also give thanks to my friends, the group back in Marantha, who risked their lives for a better life. Now to my reason for being here.

Would you please indulge me by traveling with me on a journey through time? I would like for you to be the person that is in need of some assistance. You were borne into abject poverty. You have no education. You have no resources. You have been alienated from your love ones. Your family has been separated and destroyed; yet you have something inside of you that yearns for more. You can't even put your finger on the more but it haunts you day and night. You are prepared to do whatever is necessary to get, if you will, 'the more'. You constantly tell yourself that you are a good person and that if you had just one small chance you would prove it to the world. Just one small chance. Perhaps the opportunity to learn to read and write. Just one small chance. Perhaps the opportunity to learn a trade that you could work. Just one small chance. To see people who are like you actually having, 'the more' that you so long for. Just one small chance. To be recognized as a worthy vessel that God placed on this earth. Just one small chance. To help someone who is in the same boat as you. Just one small chance!

That's what we are asking for, just one small chance. God has blessed me to learn to read and write. My parents saw to it that I learned, but I had to act stupid for fear of retribution from those who hated us without cause. My parents also instilled in me that there is a 'better life' that today I identify as 'the more' in this speech. My parents taught me the importance of faith in our ancestors who they said were watching over us and, if you will, interceding for us. They told us that God loved our ancestors like he loved everyone else.

It is God that gave me the ability to and desire to help my people; not just those in Marata, but everywhere. Through the guidance, instruction, and tutelage of Rev. Hope and his church, we started our church, The Place of Hope. Rev. Hope's church recognizes our church as their mission field. They have assisted us in every area needed. Because of his unselfishness and love for God, our people are learning to read, write and yes, undertake new trades.

We have taken our program to other Coloreds who were beaten on the way to our church and established schools in their areas so that they would be safe. We have trained instructors and those interested in the ministry. We have collaborated with estate owners to get permission for their workers to engage in our programs, with much success. We have taught our people to love God and our ancestors. We have given our people hope, encouragement and the practical training/education that they need to succeed. 'The more' is for us all.

We, as Colored people, will make a major contribution to this country because we love and respect it. All we ask is just a chance!!! Thank you."

Sobbing could be heard in the ballroom by the end of the speech along with the warmth of the applause. Abunda took his seat and held his head down because he too was now entrenched in tears. For more than five minutes no one said a word because everyone was spellbound by Abunda's speech. Finally, Rev. Pitaron rose to give remarks and close the session. His voice cracked as he attempted to share what he was feeling. Realizing that he could not give remarks, he simply said that the meeting was over.

Clergymen from everywhere rushed to the rostrum where Abunda was still seated. They waited patiently for him to rise from his seat so that they could speak with him. Unaware of the response and waiting group, he remained seated until Rev. Hope whispered something in his ear. Abunda looked up and was astonished at the waiting numbers. He was greeted with handshakes, and surprisingly, by others who wanted to embrace him. He responded graciously to each one.

Comments could be heard throughout the ballroom about the content of Abunda's speech. One clergymen said, "I had no idea that Colored people even wanted to learn to read and write."

His companion responded, "I was so moved by the correlation between his ancestors and our God. I always thought of ancestor worship as heathenism and never related it to family as Pastor Abunda so eloquently shared!"

Another comment coming from another direction stated, "I am amazed at the level of commitment and education Pastor Abunda has acquired in such a short period of time."

Yet another interjected, "He has such a big heart and determination to help his people who are in dire need of everything. Some of our people still hate Colored people and would rather see them dead than to help them. I feel convicted to do more than we have been doing at our church and in our community."

Rev. Hope and Abunda were moving through the crowd with Rev. Pitaron to go back to their rooms. However, Rev. Pitaron invited them to his room. "Please come to my suite with me before you return to your rooms. Abunda, you will be a guest in my room. There are some key people in this Convention who would like to speak with you privately concerning some matters they want to undertake to help your people. Would you be so kind as to grace us with your presence?"

"Will Rev. Hope be joining us?"

"Of course. Please forgive me, I thought that was understood."

"Again, I would be honored," Abunda replied.

It was about mid afternoon when the group convened in Rev. Pitaron's suite. Once again, Abunda was the center of attention but this time he was bombarded with questions. The concerns were how they could be of help to his church and the Colored people in their church communities. Discussions focused on education, fair wages, housing and violence against the Colored people. There was talk of providing money to assist in the areas that were discussed. Abunda was asked to develop a master plan that could be replicated throughout the churches involved in the convention. This was a dream come true for him but how to accomplish it was escaping him just now. He was sure that he would be able to provide what was requested because he wanted to help his people.

The meeting ended with plans to gather at another time. Rev. Hope assured the group that he would be in their area before Abunda's return and that he would bring the plans to the group for their approval. This met with everyone's approval.

Abunda and Rev. Hope left Rev Pitaron's room and headed for their own. Abunda was exhausted as was Rev. Hope so they agreed not to meet for dinner but to see each other in the morning. Rev. Hope informed Abunda that he would have some food sent to his room so that he could rest.

Abunda rushed to his room and fell on the bed. He cried profusely. Unbelief was trying to torment his mind. It was as if the entire day was a dream and reality was a far distance away. But to bring himself back to reality, he recanted the day and realized that it did happen. He also looked at the proposal he was given to develop and he knew for sure that it was not a dream.

"Our ancestors said that there was 'a better life' for us. It looks like they were right but we had to fight so hard to get it. We're going to have to fight even harder to go farther than we already have, but we can make it. Our ancestors and our new God together will be a powerful force in helping us. I can't wait to tell Bela and the others what has happened."

Abunda dozed off to sleep and was awaken by a knock on his door. He arose to open it and there stood a pretty young Colored girl with his dinner tray. She came in and sat it on the table and left without saying a word. He thanked her as she was leaving.

As he sat down to eat, he forgot about his meeting with Serenity until he happened to glance at the clock. It was 4:55 p.m. He left his food and went as fast as he could to meet her. When he arrived at the meeting spot he did not see her and was afraid that she had left. He waited around. Serenity was the love of his life that he had not seen in such a long time. Now it looked as if he would not see her again and his heart was as sorrowful as it was glad earlier. Still he waited. Just about to give up hope, Abunda started to walk towards the hotel when he heard footsteps. It was Serenity.

Right away he took her to the spot he had found so they could be alone. There was a huge tree stump that was large enough for them to sit on in the midst of a crop of trees. No one could see them.

"I love you with all my heart. I thought that I would never see you again. I knew that it was impossible for us to be together but I always believed that somehow we would. I have never loved anyone the way I love you and it feels like we have never been apart," Abunda softly spoke while holding Serenity in his arms.

"Abunda, I love you and there has never been anyone that I have loved more. I wanted to be with you and to be your wife but we both had no idea how that would happen. Nonetheless, it didn't stop our love from growing and being real. Please tell me what happened to get you here," Serenity inquired.

"So much has happened since I ran away from Annapolis Grove. We met Rev. Hope and he took us in; Bela and three others. They taught them how to read and write. We live on their estate and they treat us like family. Rev. Hope realized that I was educated; so he asked me to trust him by speaking properly and not acting like I was illiterate. Serenity, there is too much to tell and I don't want to take all our time with me. As you can see I am doing far better than I would have had I stayed in Annapolis Grove. I do regret leaving you there and not being able to get back to you. Believe me, I never stopped loving you and it was always my plans to come back for you once I was settled and could give you a good life."

"Abunda, I know your love for me and mine for you but there are some things that I have to tell you and I don't know where to start. First, because you were gone so long and I never heard from you, l went off to school. My parents wanted me to leave Annapolis Grove because they thought that I was involved with someone; but they never knew who. While I was away at school, I met a very nice man who was a little older than me. He was patient with me because he knew there was someone else in my heart. By the time we graduated, I had some feelings for him but nothing like what I still have for you. You will always be my love."

"So what happened to him?"

"I married him! I'm so sorry Abunda I didn't think that I would ever see you again."

Abunda's head dropped to his knees and he sat silently as if he was in shock. Serenity raised his head to meet hers as she looked deep into his eyes. Tears were dropping from her face as she experienced her pain and that of the man she still loved. Taking his head in her hands, she kissed him gently on the forehead. She wiped his face with her hand and laid his head on her breast. Both devastated, Serenity spoke first, "Abunda, there's more. We have a son. I gave him to a family in Annapolis Grove. I couldn't keep him because we both know that my family would never let that happen."

"A son?"

"Yes. When I left for school I was pregnant but no one knew. I went on to school as planned and found a friend that I confided in. Our plan was for me to send her letters and she would mail them home, for me, to my parents. This would help to alleviate any suspicion they might have had concerning my lack of corresponding. Afterwards, I went to a home for unwed mothers. After the baby was born and I held him in my arms I couldn't bear to give him away. I continued the pretense of being in school and became a mother to my child. I was scheduled to go home from school but I didn't know what to do about our son. I arrived in Annapolis Grove earlier than my parents expected with the baby. Instead of going directly home I saw this estate and, I took our baby and left him in the gardens of this beautiful estate. Before I could leave a young boy saw me and I asked him if he would give my son a home. He promised me that he would."

"Where was this estate?"

"It's near the edge of the city. It's a very beautiful place with rolling hills and grass that looks like a carpet. The young boy was very nice."

Serenity began to cry frenziedly. Abunda put his arms around her and they both wept once again but this time neither could comfort the other.

"I'm sorry Abunda but I didn't know what to do. I had no one to talk to and no one to help me. I panicked."

"It's all right Serenity. I understand. Do you know the name of the people you left him with?"

"No. All I know is the boy's name was Storm."

"Storm! Storm Rouse. You gave my son to the Rouses; the people who my mother work for?"

"Abunda, what if your mother has been taken care of her grandson all this time? What are we going to do?"

"I have to think about this. I don't know what to do. You are married and I am a pastor. We'd better go back to the hotel. We can meet here tomorrow after we've given this some thought. I am very sorry that you had to experience that all alone. I know it must have been extremely difficult for you. I love you even more. I will meet you here at the same time tomorrow. Please know that I don't blame you for any of this. Serenity, you are a very brave woman and you deserve every happiness."

"Thank you, Abunda. I have tried to imagine all these years what you would say or how you would react. I should have known that our love would survive anything."

The two walked together as far as they could without being seen and then went their own way. Each was in a quandary. Each wanted to be with the other but realized that it was now impossible. But both wanted to see what tomorrow would bring.

Rev. Hope and Abunda were scheduled to leave Valentine in two days. However, he needed more time to be with Serenity so that they could work out their predicament.

"Should I tell Rev. Hope about this?" Abunda thought to himself. "I can't leave her again. But she's married and I'm a well-known pastor. Can I pray about something like this? I did wrong before I knew about God. If the Convention hears about this they will not help my people. What will we do?"

Abunda walked swiftly to his room and sat on the bed staring down at the floor pondering and wondering what to do. Sleep is eluding him now. Serious consideration has to be given to the matters at hand.

"Do I put myself over my burden for my people? Or how can I integrate the two? Is there a possibility of me and Serenity ever being together with our son? What will my people think of me marrying a White woman when we are in such dire straits? Will she leave her husband? Is this where I need to make a tremendous sacrifice and lose the only woman I've ever loved and the son I never knew I had?" The questions were like fire crackers blasting off in his mind. Clearly, he was in a position that he never thought he would be in and had not the faintest idea as to what to do.

Abunda laid starring at the ceiling for most of the night, but somehow he drifted off to sleep and was awaken by the morning sun piercing through the window. He quickly got up and prepared himself for the day. He was to meet with Rev. Hope for breakfast and then would be free for the rest of the day. Rev. Hope would be attending the closing sessions of the Convention. Still in a quandary as to what to do, Abunda was open to suggestions from anywhere in the spirit realm: his ancestors or his new God. Surely they would have the answers to his dilemma.

"Abunda," called Rev. Hope while knocking on the door. "Are you ready for breakfast?"

He opened the door and responded, "Yes, I'm just about ready."

"We've been invited to brunch at another clergy's home and I hope you don't mind that I took the liberty of accepting for you."

"No, I don't mind, but what about the session?"

"I will be attending the closing session today, but this is someone I want you to meet and get to know personally. He has a true heart for helping and has done much philanthropically for Colored people. He wanted to meet you personally."

"I have made some plans for the day, but if this won't take too much time it will be all right with me. I wanted to see just a little more of the city. Since my speech, many of the locals seem to know me and don't mind my frequenting their establishments."

"Let's be on our way so we can both get to the rest of our day. Before we know it, it will be time to leave for home."

Again, a carriage came to the hotel to pick them up. This one was rather conservative, but costly. This estate was not as far out as Rev. Pitaron's but the ride was equally as enjoyable. Abunda was extremely quiet, but Rev. Hope had no problem with that because their last trip occurred in silence. He surmised that Abunda was merely enjoying the view as he was.

As the carriage approached the front of the main house, a man was standing at the entrance. When the carriage came to a halt, he came down to meet the men as the driver opened the carriage door. With a warm smile, he extended his hand to Rev. Hope with a greeting that was as warm as his smile.

"Rev. Hope, it is good to see you again. Pastor Basket, I am honored that you took the time to accept our invitation. There is so much that I want to discuss with you and I know that your time is scarce. I'm sorry, Pastor Basket, my name is Hais Bishop."

"Thanks for having us, Hais, it is good to see you again," Rev. Hope added.

The three men headed into the house that was richly adorned with original oil paintings, which included family portraits, still-life's and garden scenes. The main entrance took them through the living room and into a parlor of two gathering rooms that ended in a huge dining hall. The table in the hall could seat up to 25 people with its elegant cherry wood table set that included cherry wood chairs covered in off-white satin cushions. A sterling silver tea set adorned a teacart that could not be missed off to the left of the table. Two vases of imported fresh flowers were placed toward each end of the table.

Abunda's eyes, once again, could not believe what they were seeing.

Hais Bishop informed Rev. Hope and Abunda, "Gentlemen, we will be meeting in the room just off this area where we will have complete privacy. I want to take full advantage of the little time we have together. Others will be joining us for brunch when we have completed our business."

As Mr. Bishop instructed, the three men went into the room and he closed the door behind them. "Pastor Basket, I am fascinated with what I've heard about your history and your work from Rev. Hope. I want desperately to be of help to you. Please tell me of your plans for helping your people."

"Thank you Mr. Bishop for having me," Abunda replied with a sense of gratitude. "I am humbled by your kindness and concern. Rev. Hope has spoken of your generosity in helping others regardless of their color; that tells me that you have a sincerity that makes you quite different from others. To answer you, my plans are to build schools and housing for my people in my congregation. I am also planning to start other churches, in addition to those we have, in and around our area so that my people will not have to travel long distances and become victims of beatings and killings on their way to church. Please don't be offended, but there are still many, many Whites who hate us and want to do us harm."

"I'm not offended, Pastor Basket. I believe that all people should be treated equally and that is why I have dedicated my wealth to helping those who don't have. Please, continue."

Abunda continued, "I would like to have the Faith Convention adopt some of our plans so that others can be reached that are not in my area. Rev. Hope has opened a door for us through the Convention and I believe that there are others that are also interested in helping. It is not my intention to consider anyone's motives less than honorable, so we are soliciting the help of others as well. Of course, we are in need of financial assistance that will aid in purchasing supplies, equipment, and developing areas for housing."

Impressed, Hais Bishop commented, "Your plans are quite lofty."

"Yes they are, only because my people are in such need," now comfortable with the meeting Abunda responds.

"Have you investigated how to handle the physical violence, Pastor Basket? I know that it is an enormous problem."

"I'm hoping and praying that some laws will be adopted that protect us and that others like you will stand with us in our struggles. My ancestors often spoke about 'a better life for us' and my Poppa told us about an inheritance that we would get if we could find it. Perhaps this is a part of what they both spoke of?"

"This is tremendous. I want very much to be a part of your mission and maybe a part of your inheritance. I have written my desires and will be providing them to you before you leave. Let me know what you think and we can continue from there. Again, thanks for taking the time. Let's join the others. My wife has invited a few close friends that she would like to meet you," said Hais Bishop as he concluded the meeting.

The men left the office and headed towards the dining room where voices of other people could be heard. Abunda is mentally concerned because he is not quite up to this social gathering. He would actually rather be in his room contemplating the meeting with Serenity this evening.

"Good day, everyone," Mr. Bishop said jovially. "Permit me to introduce Rev. Hope and our special guest Pastor Abunda Basket. Some of you heard him at the Convention and others of you have heard of him because of his speech at the Convention. Where is my wife?"

A friendly woman responded, "She said that she will be right in, she wanted to give the cook some additional instructions."

"Okay, why don't we all sit?"

Suddenly Mrs. Bishop rushes into the room, not taking thought for her surroundings. "Please forgive me."

"We got your message, dear. Please meet Pastor Abunda Basket. Pastor Basket this is my lovely wife, Serenity Bishop!"

Serenity loses her balance and her husband catches her. "Are you all right, dear. You look as if you've seen a ghost!"

"I'm so sorry," Serenity said apologetically. "I rushed in from the kitchen and must have…. Forgive me, it's my pleasure to meet you, Pastor Basket."

"Likewise, Mrs. Bishop. Thank you for having me in your lovely home!" Abunda responded with no glimpse of surprise.

Everyone was now seated and lunch was being served. Rev. Hope sat between Abunda and Serenity. Unbeknown to him that created a much needed space so that the two would be unable to look directly at one another.

Brunch now over, the Bishops walked their guests to the waiting carriage and waved them farewell. Serenity rushed back into the house and went to her room explaining that she really was not feeling well. Hais understood.

When Abunda and Rev. Hope arrived back at the hotel, Abunda went immediately to his room, also. He was not sure how many more surprises he could take on this one trip. His decision was just to wait until later when he was to meet Serenity. Thinking aloud, "Will she still come? I hope so."

The hour grew closer to the meeting time and Abunda left the hotel via his usual route. This time he would be early because he wanted to give Serenity no cause to think that he would not come. Reaching his destination about twenty minutes early, Abunda paced up and down. "How could this situation become even more complicated," he thought. "My darling Serenity, how is she bearing up under all this?"

It would not be long before he would find out as he heard her weak voice say, "Abunda?" Again she lost her balance and Abunda caught her.

Never imagining that their circumstances would heighten with despair, the two were really speechless. Words that were so necessary needed to come from a source higher than them both. Wisdom had to call out from their inner being to aid them in making the greatest decisions of their lives. The silence was broken by Abunda saying, "Serenity, I had no idea!"

She interrupted him, "I know. What would be the odds of such an occurrence taking place? It seems that we have been innocent, if I can use that word, but sorrow and guilt have emaciated our innocence. Our relationship could have never been with so much against us anyway. I honestly believed that love could survive the worst of anything, but this is too much even for love."

"Our love was innocent. We were both victims of time and cultural differences. It amazes me that God made us because of His love, but we have no love for one another because of race, economics, and whatever differences man wants to interject. I was very comfortable with my ancestors who always encouraged us towards better but this White-man's God, I'm having some serious challenges accepting."

"Abunda, don't blame God for what people do."

"But again, as I've said to Rev. Hope, He (God) allows people to do it and I still don't understand. Why couldn't we love one another and celebrate our happiness. Because of differences, we have lost our son and were never able to openly share our honest love. That makes me angry and sad at the same time."

"What are we going to do?" Serenity seriously needed to know. "Things are so much different now that my husband is in the picture. You all will probably be seeing more of each other if you accept his proposal to help with your work."

"There is so much at stake here, Serenity. Having an affair with you would have been an extremely difficult decision for me to make, with all the circumstances. My heart breaks for you to have lost our son and what you went through alone. My greatest sorrow was learning about our son, who we won't get to share as his parents. I believe that the best thing for us to do is to go on with our lives and make the best of them. You will always be in my heart and our son also. Time may present a new set of circumstances to us. Your husband is a fine man and it appears to me that he loves you deeply. Having lost you lets me know what he would feel if he ever lost you and I will not be a party to his sorrow."

"I see why you are a pastor. We never knew that this would be your fate, but even with our indiscretion I knew that you were a fine man. Our relationship was not lustful, but honest. Neither of us was at fault for being from different races. Maybe one day we will get to see our son. I'm sure that the Rouses are rearing him to be a fine man. I pray that he will never be victimized for being a Colored man's son; not because I'm ashamed of you but because I know how cruel my people are."

"I will try to meet your husband other than at your home; that way it will not be awkward for any of us. You will always be in my prayers along with our son."

"I hope that you meet a woman who will love you as I have and give you a son that you both can be proud of. I know that the both of them will be special to you. Abunda Basket there isn't a man on this earth that is greater than you. I look forward to hearing wonderful things about your accomplishments and will proudly smile in my heart every time I hear or see your name."

"Serenity, may God bless you with other children and a life full of love, happiness and joy for both you and your husband."

The two shared their last gentle embrace and with respect for one another separated without looking back. Their heartbeats sounded like footsteps fading in the distance as tears became the stream following along side their paths.

The Faith Convention was now over and it was time to return home to Marantha. Rev. Hope and Abunda both realized that there was much to do when they got home because of the overwhelming success of Abunda's speech. There were some that rejected him, but they were in the minority and those in the majority gave him great hope.

Chapter 10

Birthing The Vision

"Father, father," Clark yelled as he raced across the lawn with his mother.

Bela and the others were racing as well to greet Abunda. Everyone was excited to see them and to inquire about their trip. Abunda was equally excited and wanted to hear how the churches' activities were faring in his absence. He also wanted to share about the promises of help he received.

Mrs. Hope had arranged a special homecoming dinner that everyone shared in the main house. Questions were flying around the table from all directions. In amusement, Abunda and Rev. Hope tried to catch all the questions and answer them. It was a delightful homecoming.

Abunda could not wait to attend church and tell of the good things that happened while he was gone. Much to his amazement, good things had happened in Marantha during his absence. The Place of Hope Church was now at full capacity and the church at Crusidea was growing equally as fast. After meeting with Bela and Mrs. Hope to receive the report from his absence, Abunda planned to go to Crusidea soon. He wanted to meet the new people and see the growth there.

"Bela, we will be traveling to Crusidea. I'm anxious to meet my new people. Thanks again for doing such a great job while I was gone. I want to talk with you about getting more education for you. Perhaps even the mail order course that Rev. Hope got for me, if you like!"

"Thanks Abunda, but I don't think I wanna be a preacher like you and Rev. Hope. I love workin' with our people though. Maybe I can get som' learnin' in something else."

"That's fine Bela, if you don't want to be a preacher. You have made such great progress with your education I would like to see you continue. We can discuss this later after you've thought about what you would like to study. We will be leaving for Crusidea tomorrow."

The two men sat out for Crusidea at midday so that they would arrive shortly before the workday was over. They wanted to do some preparations at the Church before the people came. Abunda was overwhelmed at the consistent participation of the members and others who had begun to attend. Now, he desperately needed something to take his mind off of Serenity and the news of his son. Fresh ideas had come to him about his work while he was away, and he wanted to implement some of them.

"Hello, Pastor Abunda, it is great to have you back," a voice spoke from the direction behind Abunda. He turned to see who was speaking and it was Ja'cin.

"Remember me? My name is Ja'cin and we met before you went on your trip. How was your trip? Bela, Mrs. Hope and the other helpers did a great job while you were gone. Our group has become bigger and more people are still coming."

"I had a wonderful trip," Ja'cin thanks for asking. "Thanks also for being such a big help around here. Bela told me of your dedication to what we are doing."

"I'm glad that I can help. The people will be coming soon. They will rush today because they heard that you were back. Esa has been talking about you every since you left. He has been working very hard learning to read and write better. He wants you to be so proud of him and I know you will be."

"Ja'cin, Bela and I are going to be doing some fixing up before the group comes. We could sure use your help."

"Sure, Pastor."

The men got busy rearranging the church so that it looked more like a classroom. Some furniture had been sent from supporters at the Convention and Abunda was ecstatic about them keeping their word.

Little by little the members began to trickle in and take their seats. They immediately began to sing and give thanks for Pastor Abunda's homecoming. Eagerly waiting to hear his message, they sat attentively like new sponges in fresh water. Pastor Abunda participated in the singing and quietly gave thanks for their trip and safe journey home. After Ja'cin welcomed him home the members gave an applause to let Abunda know of their care for him.

"Thank you all so much. It is good to be home and even better to see all of you. Many of you I know but thank God for the new faces. Welcome to our place of love and hope: The Courage Well. I have so much to share with you about my trip and the new things that will be taking place. My trip was a great success and I was embraced by the White pastors in the Faith Convention. Many of them want to help us with our work and are willing to give money, supplies and furniture. They also want to start doing what we are doing in their church communities for the Colored people. You see, they sent this new furniture to us while I was still in Valentine City and that makes me glad to know that they will keep their word. There is so much more to...." Pastor Abunda stopped in the middle of his message when he looked up and saw someone he thought he knew slip in the back of the church.

"Excuse me church, but that lady who just came in would you look this way please?"

"Abunda!" the lady yelled out and burst into tears.

Abunda ran from the pulpit and rushed toward the lady. He grabbed her up off the floor and into his arms. "What are you doing here? How long have you been in Crusidea? How did you get here?"

The lady responded, "Are you going to put me down and let me answer any of your questions or are you going to just keep asking them?"

"I'm sorry, but I am shocked to see you here, Makita."

The church was quiet and everyone was just looking and listening to Pastor and Makita.

"Please forgive me, church, but this is my sister Makita. I've not seen her since I ran away from home a long time ago."

Again, he turned to Makita and said, "What are you doing here?"

"She's with me," Ja'cin answered.

"With you?"

"Yes, Pastor. She's my wife! Remember I told you about her when we first met but she didn't come to church that night. Makita told me that her brother had runaway a long time ago; she mentioned the name Abunda but I never put it with you. I had no idea. I guess that I was so busy telling her of this great work this new pastor wanted to do, that I didn't mention your name."

All of a sudden the church members began to cheer and clap with happiness for Abunda and his sister. Each member started to get up from his or her seat and hugged Abunda and Makita. It was a time of celebration, love and a sense of unity among the entire group, even the new ones.

"Let's get back to the lesson for tonight. My sister and I will have plenty of time to get together. I've been away and I don't want to misuse my time with you."

Everybody returned to their seats. When church was over Abunda, Bela, Ja'cin and Makita stayed behind. Abunda introduced Bela to Makita. Ja'cin invited them to their home for the night so that Abunda could spend time with Makita. They accepted. When they arrived at the house, Ja'cin and Bela left Abunda and Makita alone.

"How are Momma and Poppa and the children? How long have you been married? How....?"

"Please, let me answer you Abunda," Makita pleaded. "Momma, Poppa and the children are fine. They've been very sad since you left. Poppa knew you would be all right and that you left to find what our ancestors said we'd have, 'a better life'. Momma always cried for you. Why did you runaway?"

"Poppa was right, Makita. I was dying in Annapolis Grove and I couldn't see anyway we would ever get out of there. I didn't mean to hurt anybody, but I had to leave. I promised myself that I would go back but time just kept going. We came to Marantha and Rev. Hope took us in. He is the nicest White man I've ever met."

"Abunda, you sound so smart and you are very different. How did that happen?"

"Rev. Hope and his wife took us in; me, Bela and the group of boys that ran away with me. We live on their estate. They taught the others to read and write better and Rev. Hope recognized that I was not an ignorant person. He wanted me to trust him by being the person that he knew I was. He helped me to get more education and to become a pastor. To me he represents what the White man's God is supposed to be about. Tell me about you and Ja'cin."

"I met him at my work place; he was the gardener. I was seeing him for a while but didn't tell Momma or Poppa. Then Ja'cin asked me to marry him because he was going to leave Annapolis Grove and wanted me to be with him. When he was a little boy he was taken from his family and the people who had him taught him how to read and write. They taught him how to keep the lawn and the flowers and gave him papers. They told him about a friend who needed someone to keep their estate and told him to go. They were so good to him, just like Rev. Hope is to you. I told Momma first and she told Poppa. Ja'cin is a good man, Abunda, and he loves me."

They hugged each other and cried together. It seemed that loved ones showing up unexpectedly in Abunda's life was becoming the norm. But this chance meeting was one of joy and hopefully not sorrows as had been his ending with Serenity.

Ja'cin and Bela joined Abunda and Makita. They all sat around and caught up on their progress and where they wanted to go in the future. It was a night full of hope and encouragement. A part of Abunda's real family was now with him and it made him happy and more determined. Makita could identify with his suffering and his anxiousness to have 'the better life'. Perhaps now she could even be a part of making that life a reality not only for Abunda and herself but for other Colored people as well.

Abunda and Bela left early in the morning to get back to Annapolis Grove so that Rev. Hope would not be worried. They arrived safely and in record time. Bela went directly to the farmhouse to report to Cliff for work and Abunda had to see Rev. Hope to tell him of his good news. He proceeded to the main house where the Hopes were having breakfast. He knocked for entrance and was greeted by Mrs. Hope who invited him in. He told them of his meeting with his sister and they were excited with and for him. In spite of the situation with Serenity, Makita's presence gave Abunda a new sense of urgency. He wanted his sister to see what he was doing and to become a part of the work.

Abunda immersed himself into his work, but a constant battle was waging within him: his ancestors and the White man's God. He knew that somehow he had to have an under-standing that would merge the two or delete one or the other. A systematic study of the White man's God, Christianity, would be possible and assist him in gaining more knowl-edge. He completed his biblical studies but was yet to estab-lish a 'relationship' with this God. Hinging his beliefs on the example of Rev. Hope, it was now time for him to make a decision that could alter the spiritual foundation of his back-ground. Abunda decided to do an in depth study into the life of Jesus Christ. Not many of the White preachers were preaching about Jesus Christ rather, their focus was on God only. Some even used God to validate slavery and to keep the Colored people in a subservient state.

Months of study brought Abunda to several questions: Was Jesus Christ real? If yes, why would He die such a horrid death to save anyone? Abunda's answer came as he drew a correlation between Jesus Christ and the struggles of his ancestors. His ancestors gave their lives so that future generations would 'have a better life'. Jesus gave his life so that future generations would be free from sin that would give them 'a better life'. The ancestors were always pointing out that you must do the right thing, which to Abunda equaled not to sin. Sin was doing wrong and disobeying your elders. Again, inquiries flooded Abunda's mind: why didn't my people serve this God? Is this God bigger and better than the ancestors? How can this God let such bad things happen? Why did this God let my people be enslaved? These ques-tions were not easy to answer and most could not be answered directly from any book. God had to become something real to Abunda, something that he could feel innately.

Being a proponent of prayer, Abunda offered his concerns to God and his ancestors. A feeling of assurance that he would get the answers to what he was seeking consumed him. Not abandoning his ancestors was paramount to Abunda, but his spiritual dilemma had to be clarified. He wanted to teach his people the truth as he had received it for himself.

The final decision came when Abunda decided to go on with his work and let the answers come to him. He decided to 'just be". Not being privy to Poppa's revelation of 'just being' it had now become a part of Abunda's foundation. He was sure that something greater than he had protected him and made things 'better for him'. Now he wanted to know to whom the credit would go; this was to be who he would present to his members.

The word of his work continued to spread throughout the region and was now moving into areas outside of the region. He had opened several churches complete with schools. People were learning to read and write in these areas. A little trouble was being experienced as some Whites would not permit their workers to participate in Abunda's programs but overall success could be seen.

On his next trip to Crusidea he decided to talk with Makita and Ja'cin about some different ideas he had. He knew that they loved him and would support his efforts.

After service he told Makita and Ja'cin that he would like to visit with them at their home. Of course they gladly accepted since Makita had not seen him, just to visit, as much as she would like.

Excited by Abunda's request, Ja'cin responded, "Abunda we're so glad you're here. Makita has cooked up some special food that you used to have at home. It is just good for you to be here with us. Where is Bela?"

"He went back with the others. I knew that I wanted to spend some time here with just you and Makita."

Makita comes from the kitchen, clad in her apron just like Momma. It brought back memories to Abunda and the look on his face was one of sadness.

"You look just like Momma coming out of the kitchen," Abunda said looking like he had just lost his best friend.

"I miss her so much. We must plan to make a trip home soon. I want to see the family and I want them to know what I'm doing. I also want to ask their forgiveness for running away. I don't want Momma or Poppa to die before I get back there."

"We will plan to do it soon because I want to tell them something," Makita yells, "I'm gonna have a baby!"

Abunda jumped up and hugged Makita and Ja'cin. "You all will make great parents and I'm gonna be an uncle." They all laughed together.

In the midst of the joy, Abunda interjected, "I'm here because I want to tell you all something special and get your advice."

"You getting married, Abunda?" Makita said smiling.

"No, Makita, that's not it. There are other Colored preachers who want to meet with me who have been trying desperately to do what we are doing. I know these preachers don't have resources but they want us to come together and unite our efforts in some form. I am as honored and over-whelmed by these inquires as I was with the invitation from the Faith Convention. I want to consult Rev. Hope for some wisdom. It would be an awesome thing to have our people working together for our good. What do you think?"

Ja'cin leaped to his feet saying, "Pastor Abunda what a great opportunity for you. I will be honored to help in anyway possible. You have been an inspiration to us all and our people, here, are improving because you care enough to help. I'm sure that all around this country our people need what you have to give. Maybe this is the way to what your ancestors talked about, 'the better life'. Makita told me how Poppa always reminded you all about that and the inheritance. Could this be a part of the inheritance, as well?"

Makita was crying and now was very emotional. "Abunda, we can go home and help our own family. What if we could bring them all here? I'm glad that Momma forced us to learn to read and write even though we had to act stupid for the White people. Yes, Abunda you need to do this."

"I will need you all by my side. It won't be easy because many Whites still don't want us to have anything. There might even be some danger involved," Abunda replied as his mood turned to somber with the reality.

"We are with you, Pastor Abunda," Ja'cin added strongly.

"Ja'cin, please call me Abunda."

With great pride and honor, Ja'cin responded smiling, "Thank you, I will."

Abunda gave his life to building the church and caring for those in need whether near or far. He taught the doctrines of Christianity and reminded his members about the ancestors who had given their lives for them to be free and have better. All of Abunda's resources went into his work. He received monies from the supporters in the Faith Convention and a substantial amount from Hais Bishop. The Place of Hope Church became the nucleus for the Colored churches throughout the region. Schools were established in each church, not only for the people, but also for the preachers and those desiring to be preachers.

When the opportune time presented itself, Abunda had his conversation with Rev. Hope. "Rev. Hope, things are going very well for us, and there are other Colored preachers who want to meet with me like I did with those at the Faith Convention. I know these preachers don't have resources but they want us to come together and unite in some form. What do you think?"

"Abunda, I think it's a great idea. The more support you have the more you all can get done for your people. I have heard some wonderful news about other Colored preachers who are doing what you are doing. A few have met with strong resistance from the White community who don't want them to progress. Some have even been brutally beaten, their churches burned down but they continue the work wherever they can. Perhaps there is a way that they can all come to Maranatha to discuss their concerns. This is how we started our first Convention. It would be an excellent idea if the Colored Churches had their own Convention."

"Do you think it is possible?" Abunda asked with great expectations. "It is such a big undertaking and I'm not sure that I am ready for all this. We have been doing so much traveling and working in this region I hardly gave any thought to those in other places."

"Mrs. Hope and I will be glad to accommodate your guests."

"Thank you again, Rev. Hope. You are truly an exceptional man. I will let you know what I've decided to do."

Abunda ponders, prays and deliberates over this new yet awesome work that is to be undertaken. Considering all the ramifications of the effort, he wants to be certain that the work will be established and completed. The forces against him are enormous and it would take Divine intervention to make it successful. Yet, Abunda feels this heavy burden and tug in his heart that he can not explain; somewhat like when he was sick and knew that there was something for him to do for his people.

Abunda decided to take a walk around the estate that he loved so much. It was spring and everything was in full bloom. Beauty was the backdrop of the estate with ecstasy as the curtain. As he looked up into the skies it looked like an ocean of blue water. Amazed at the splendor of his surroundings, he began to sprint across the knolls of the estate like a little child. His arms were waving rhythmatically as if he was a symphony conductor. For these few moments he is lost in unconcern. He continues to run until he reaches a place on the estate that was unfamiliar, yet familiar to him. He felt as if he had been here before but had no conscious memory.

The feeling grew stronger and stronger, pulling him into a lost place.

Abunda looks up and sees a silhouette in the distance. Unable to determine the identity, he continues to approach the figure. Even though he could not recognize the figure, he felt no fear, for he was sure that it was someone from the estate. Each traveled toward the other. Finally they met but to his surprise it was a total stranger, yet someone he felt he had known before.

"Hello," greeted the stranger.

"Great day to you," Abunda replied. "Do I know you?"

"I don't believe we've had the pleasure. My name is Deston and yours?"

"I'm Abunda Basket. My pleasure."

"It looks like you're really enjoying the day. Is something special happening today for you?" Deston inquired.

"Funny you should ask that, sir."

"Please call me Deston."

"Call me Abunda. Yes, something special is happening today that will affect the rest of my life and many, many other people. I have to make a major decision and I'm seeking help from my ancestors and God."

"What do you need to help you make such an important decision?" Deston asked out of concern.

"I don't know; and that's an interesting question you raised. My Daddy, when he had something on his mind, would go to his favorite place which was a secret to us. He would stay there sometimes for hours talking to our ancestors trying to get help for our present circumstances...."

"Regardless of the circumstances, there is a better life to be had," the stranger injected.

"Wait a minute, that's what my Daddy said the ancestors would always tell him. He would always remind us, too."

"We really don't have control over our circumstances or anything, we're just suppose to live and know that..."

Abunda interrupts, "How do we live without control-ling our lives? Colored people have no control because the Whites refuse to let us have dignity and purpose. We are treated worse than cattle. They prefer their cattle over us."

Abunda is feeling a sense of rage that he has not expe-rienced since coming to Marantha. He realizes that some of his old issues have not been resolved within himself. Deston notices the change in his demeanor.

"Are you all right, Abunda? Your face is looking sad. Did I say something wrong? If I did please forgive me."

Apologetically Abunda continued to explain his present demeanor. "It wasn't what you said, but it reminded me of who I am and how my people are regarded. I thought that I was over the negative feelings but...."

"Some things take a lifetime to resolve and others never get resolved," added Deston with a voice of wisdom. "Those that never get resolved we leave to someone greater than us. But back to your special day here."

"I wish my Daddy were here with us, he could tell me what to do. We didn't talk much when I was home but I've come to understand his ways and wisdom since we've been apart."

"I would be glad to listen, if it's okay with you?" Deston was now encouraging Abunda to share his intimate feelings.

"I don't know you but yet I feel like I do. I feel safe to talk to you."

Abunda begins to share his life's story with Deston. Every emotion imaginable occurs during the conversation because he has never done this before. Deston sits quietly and listens intently. Out of Abunda's entire life story, Deston is quite intrigued with the mystery and the inheritance.

"Has anyone solved the mystery or found the inheritance yet?" Deston wanted to know.

"No, but almost daily without conscious thought I feel like I'm getting closer and closer to finding them both. Poppa said that whoever finds them will have the key to living the better life. He made it sound like you could control your own life?"

"The ability to control lays within us, Abunda. Control is an internal function that results in an external demonstration. The most important thing to remember is that control is not in the hands of others, but again within us. How you respond to situations and circumstances demonstrates your level of control. If you react negatively, you are not in control. If you react positively, you are in control and have the power over the situation and circumstances. It was my pleasure to meet you."

Deston left Abunda in a state of awe as he pondered what was just said. He wonders, "How does this help me in making my decision? What does control have to do with this? Who was that strange man?"

Life had been great since Abunda and the group arrived in Marantha. The Hopes were incredible people and the town had grown to love and respect Abunda. In his wildest dreams, he never envisioned what was taking place in his life. He now saw himself somewhere else.

Abunda was meeting with Bela and two other preachers to discuss the possibility of forming a Colored convention that any Colored church could be a part of. "As you all know this has been on my mind for quite some time and I want you all to help me make the decision. It wouldn't be my decision but ours. Much is at stake here?"

Bela speaks up and says slowly with fear, "Abunda this is a great thing that you want to do. I want to help you but what will the Whites do to us when they hear what we is doing?"

Pastor Titus, the preacher whose church was burned down chimes in, "It's a wonderful idea. I'm not so afraid of the Whites because this helps me to see our future. I have something new to look at and that gives me hope."

Abunda smiles at the remark. The other preacher is still silent. The look on his face can not be interpreted. So, a stillness rests over the group. The gentlemen sat in stillness for almost fifteen minutes. The unspoken intention was that no one should be rushed or coerced into the idea but respond voluntarily.

"This is cause for great thought. It's not something that should be entered into quickly or emotionally. True, there is much at stake and we will be on the front lines," the quiet preacher finally interjects. "It's as if you're asking us, Abunda, to save thousands of our people from what has been occurring for years. What we have been a part of ourselves; first as victims and now as saviors. This is a life changing decision with no turning back?"

"It is," Abunda replies. "And that's why I wanted to speak with you all because there is wisdom in a multitude of counselors."

"How will this be done on a large scale?" the first preacher asked.

"First we must agree to be the nucleus and that we will be honest and open with one another. I'm going to ask my sister, Makita and her husband, Ja'cin, to be a part of this foundation group. They have been very supportive of our work in Cruisdea. I want us to take a few days to pray and think about this undertaking, and then we will meet again with Ja'cin and Makita. When the foundation group is in place, we will gather others who you will recommend to be a part of the second level group. The foundation group is extremely important because we are the ones who will actually be lying down our lives for this undertaking. During my trip to the Faith Convention, I received many promises of help, and we can depend on it, too. We do have a good starting point and can proceed after the formation of the second level group is securely in tact. How does that sound?" Abunda asked.

By now the three men had very impressive looks on their faces. Almost in unison they responded, "Sounds like a good plan."

"I forgot to mention Rev. Hope. He absolutely must be a part of the foundational group. I would not be where I am today if it were not for his love and continuous support. I know that he is White," Abunda chuckled.

The others agreed.

They departed, Abunda and Bela going in one direction and the other two preachers in the other. Bela is bubbling with excitement while still expressing his fear. He has always been with Abunda and desperately wants to assist him however he can.

As they approached the farmhouse, Abunda says, "Bela, I'm going to talk with Rev. Hope, see you later."

He continues to the main house and knocks on the back door. Mrs. Hope comes to the door and greets him pleasantly.

"How are you, Mrs. Hope? Is Rev. Hope in?"

"Abunda, I'm just fine. We haven't seen much of you lately. Are things well with you, the church and all?" inquired Mrs. Hope.

"All is very well Mrs. Hope. Forgive me for not stopping by, but I have been extremely busy since our return from the Convention."

"That's okay. I'm glad to hear that things are well with you. Excuse me, Abunda, let me get Rev. Hope for you." Mrs. Hope left the room and shortly thereafter Rev. Hope appeared alone.

"Hello, Abunda, it is so good to see you. Please come over and have a seat. We've not talked in a while and I've been wondering about our last conversation; the Colored Convention."

"That's why I'm here. I ask you to forgive me; also, for not stopping by, things are happening so fast!"

"Come, tell me about them," Rev. Hope suggested.

"I met with Bela and other preachers about the Colored Convention. I shared my vision and asked their wisdom. Acknowledging the roadblocks up ahead, everyone was in agreement and wants to proceed. I suggested that we form a foundational group first to be the nucleus which will lay down our lives if need be, and then a second level group who will agree to help make the vision come to pass. I would like for you to be on our foundational group, I am who I am because of you. It would be an honor for you to serve with us."

"Do you think this is a wise idea, Abunda? You know I'm White." They both let out a robust laugh.

"Seriously, Abunda, I would be honored. Yes, I am willing to lay down my life for you and your vision. What is the next step?"

"I've asked the others to pray about this and we will meet soon. When will you be available?"

"I'll be around for the next few days; perhaps day after tomorrow?"

"That sounds fine. I will let the others know?"

"Can we please meet here? I will have Mrs. Hope to make a nice lunch for us."

He replies with gratitude, "Thank you so much Rev. Hope. It will be our pleasure."

Abunda leaves the main house to return to the farmhouse. Walking along in deep thought, reflecting on the day, he is unaware of the shadow behind him. As he continues to walk, so does the shadow, now appearing to come closer to his back. As he goes through a crop of trees, the shadow grabs him from behind and wrestles him to the ground striking him in the head over and over with a heavy object.

"No Colored is gonna take over this town," the shadow repeated as it was hitting him. "You Coloreds need to stay in your place, the field."

Bela was becoming concerned that Abunda had not returned to the farmhouse, so he went out to look for him. Heading in the direction of the main house, he decided not to go through the crop of trees but something convinced him to take that direction, anyway. Hurrying along, wanting to get through the trees, he heard something. Because of his fear he moved even faster. Again, he heard something but could not distinguish what it was. Now almost in a full gallop, Bela rushed to get out of the trees. Just as he was almost out, he heard a moan and then nothing. Again, unsure of himself, he hurried and in doing so tripped and fell over something. When he realized that it was a man he became paralyzed with fear. However, instantly a calming feeling overtook him and he looked to see who it was he had tripped over.

"Oh God its Abunda," he screamed. Immediately he began shaking Abunda trying to wake him. He checked his breathing and was glad that he was still alive. Abunda was demonstrating no other signs of life at this point.

"What happened? Who did this?" Bela questioned Abunda as if he could hear him.

Finally, he managed to get Abunda up and into his arms and hurried across the estate. It was a long walk and now it seemed even longer to him because of the urgency. Instead of going to the farmhouse, he took him to the main house and repeatedly kicked the back door with his feet. When he did not get a timely response he started to yell. "Rev. Hope! Rev. Hope! Rev Hope!" as loud as he could.

A light came on upstairs and Bela was relieved. Soon he could see Rev. Hope approaching the door. Tears streamed down his face in relief and for fear of what might happen to Abunda.

Rev. Hope opened the door and saw Abunda in Bela's arms. Immediately he assisted him in getting Abunda upstairs to the same room where he had taken ill before. They placed him gently on the bed and Rev. Hope asked, "What happened Bela? What happened?"

Bela replied quite disturbed and noticeably distraught, "I don't know. I don't know."

He began to weep openly and Rev. Hope took a few minutes to console him, still being mindful that Abunda also needed immediate attention.

Bela continued telling what had happened after Rev. Hope comforted him. "I was worried that Abunda was late comin' home to the farmhouse. After our meetin' with the preachers, he said he was goin' to see you and come home. When it started gittin' late, like I said, I was worried so I decided I walk toward the main house to see if he was comin' and was okay. Somethin' told me to go through the bunch of trees; the one I'm scared of. I didn't want to do it but I felt like I really should. I thought I heard a voice when I was walkin' so I started runnin' and tripped over somethin'. I was almost laying on him. I was scared to look at him but again somethin' pushed me so I looked. That's when I saw it was Abunda. I tried to wake him up but he didn't move. So I picked him up in my arms and ran for here as fast as I could."

By this time Mrs. Hope was awake and standing in the doorway. "My God, what has happened?" she asked with great concern.

"Honey, we don't know. Bela was just telling me that he found Abunda in the trees like this."

Rev. Hope begins to examine Abunda, sees the blood and finds bruises on his head. Mrs. Hope leaves and returns with some cloths and water in a basin.

Very angry, like no one had seen him before, Rev. Hope demanded, "Who would do such a thing and why?" intimating that someone, not something, had done this.

Mrs. Hope cleaned the bruises but found a deep gash in the back of Abunda's head. Chagrin consumes her face. Rev. Hope and Bela see the look on her face and are now more concerned. She tells the two men, "There is a deep gash right here and maybe that's why Abunda is unconscious. What are we going to do? Is there time to go way to town and get the doctor?" She, too, begins to weep openly and was comforted by her husband.

Rev. Hope instructs those present, "Let's clean the bruises good with an antiseptic. Remember when little Clark ran into a branch from the tree stomp and gashed his leg open? Let's use the medicine that Doc put on his gash to heal it. And we will pray."

They sat around the bed, again, all three separately remembering when they had to do this before while waiting for some signs of improvement from Abunda. Unlike the last experience, in about thirty minutes, Abunda began to moan. His loved ones were overjoyed with relief. Abunda's first act was to raise his hand to his head but he realized that there was not enough strength to complete the act. His hand falls, almost useless, to his side. The others were not sure if he could see them because his eyes were half-open and then they slowly closed.

"Abunda, Abunda," Bela cried. "Can you hear me? Please answer me, do somethin'."

"Abunda, it's me and Mrs. Hope can you hear us?" Rev. Hope pleaded.

They all stood motionless, waiting for some sign of hope. After what seemed like an eternity, but actually only five minutes, Abunda opened his eyes all the way. They could tell that he was struggling to focus because he opened and closed his eyes several times.

"What happened?" he asked again as he attempted to raise his hand to his head, and this time was successful.

Bela exclaimed, "Abunda you all right? I was so scared you would die."

"How are you feeling?" the Hopes inquired.

"My head hurts real bad and my left arm is numb. What happened, did I have a fall?"

"We don't know," Rev. Hope replied hoping that they would get some clarification from Abunda. "Bela found you in the trees like this. He brought you to the house and we cleaned your wounds. We've been waiting for you to wake up so you could tell us what happened. It looks like you're going to be fine but we won't know for sure right now. Do you remember anything?"

"I was walking back to the farmhouse after my talk with you. I was so excited that I decided to take the short cut through the crop of trees. I was in a hurry to tell Bela about our conversation and your support for us. And all I remember was something hitting me in my head."

Bela wanted to know from Abunda, "Did you see or hear anybody?"

"No, Bela. I was really engrossed in my thoughts. Why would you ask that anyway?"

"You rest now Abunda. Bela and I will take a look around the trees in the morning to see if we can find anything. You rest now. Thank God you're alive. We'll see you in the morning. If you need something just yell out and we'll be right here. We can hear you from our bedroom," Rev. Hope concluded.

Mrs. Hope leaned over and kissed Abunda gently on the forehead, "Good night dear."

Bela refused to leave and the Hopes allowed him to stay.

The sun rose over the estate from the east as beautifully as ever. It looked like a big yellow ball had rested in the sky. The birds were chirping loudly adding gaiety to the day. There was a soft wind just whistling through the trees that added a symphonic background to the bird's chirping.

The sunlight was so bright in the room that it caused Bela to wake up. Getting his bearings, Bela, for a split second wondered where he was. In another split second, he remembered last night and got up to check on Abunda who was still asleep. He put his hand on Abunda's heart. It was still beating and he was relieved. A soft knock came on the door and he opened it. It was the Hopes.

"Good morning Bela. Is Abunda awake?" Rev. Hope asked as they came into the room.

"No, he isn't, but he's alive and breathin' all right," Bela responded. "Good morning, Rev. Hope and Mrs. Hope."

The Hopes walked to the bed, one on each side. Mrs. Hope checked Abunda's pulse and concluded that it was fine. She really did not want to awake him, but she needed to check his injuries so she gently whispered his name in his ear, "Abunda. Can you hear me?"

Not moving his head, he opened his eyes and looked in Mrs. Hope's direction without saying a word.

Mrs. Hope asked, "How do you feel?" hoping for him to respond.

"My head hurts," came a ginger response from Abunda.

Everyone was glad that he was getting better, even though he was still in a significant amount of pain.

"Would you like something to eat or drink, Abunda?" Mrs. Hope inquired.

"Just something to drink, thank you."

Mrs. Hope left immediately to fulfill his request while the others remained. Rev. Hope informed Abunda that he and Bela were going immediately to checkout the area around the trees to see if there was anything that would help them to understand what happened. In the meantime, Mrs. Hope returns with some hot tea for Abunda while Rev. Hope and

Bela departed to investigate the trees. As they approached the trees this eerie feeling begins to attack Bela and Rev. Hope notices his discomfort. "What's wrong, Bela?" Rev. Hope asks very concerned.

"I don't know, I just don't feel right. I'm scared of this place. It's the only place on the whole estate that makes me scared. It feels like, strange, like evil."

"Bela," Rev. Hope queries with unbelief at what was just said. "I've never heard you say anything like that about our home since you've been here. The trees may be frightening to you, but evil...."

As they got closer to the trees Bela starts trembling and walking a little distance behind Rev. Hope. Rev. Hope stops to reassure him but he is not easily convinced. Soon they are in the crop of trees looking around with Bela making it a point to stay in Rev. Hope's sight. He shows Rev. Hope where he tripped over Abunda and they begin to concentrate on that particular area. Bela sees a rock with a sharp edge and picks it up but soon drops it. He is now sharking noticeably and can hardly speak. Precisely at that moment Rev. Hope turns to speak to him and observes his behavior. With the utmost concern Rev. Hope says, "Bela, Bela what's wrong? Why are you shaking? Have you found something?"

He tried to reply but could not. Rev. Hope came closer to him and looked around. He, too, noticed the rock on the ground. He reached down to pick it up and Bela screamed, "No. No, don't touch it. It will hurt you!"

"Bela, it's only a rock and it looks like it could have been used to hit Abunda. Look, there is blood on this side. Why would anyone want to hurt Abunda and right here at our home?"

Shaking frantically and crying audibly, he pleads with Rev. Hope to get rid of the rock. "Rev. Hope, its evil, please throw it away. Please."

"Okay, Bela I will and everything will be all right. I want to look around some more but if you want to go back to the house its okay."

He elected to return to the house and instead of throwing the rock away, Rev. Hope put it in his pocket without Bela seeing him.

"Dere's danga here fo' Abunda," Bela heard as he was walking along. "Som' people's gonna hurt 'em 'en e'vn try ta kill 'em." Bela put his hands over his ears to stop the thoughts from coming. He was more scared than ever because he was alone. "Ya ain't gotta be scaked, we's wit'cha. We's protect ya."

"Who you?" Bela shouted unaware of the volume of his voice.

"We y'ur ancestors, Bela."

"How you know my name? I don't have any ancestors only Abunda do?"

"We's da ancestors fo' our people. We's care 'bout y'all jis' lik' Abunda 'en we protect all 'em dat list'n 'en trust us. We's y'ere wit' ya now 'cause we's need ya he'p Abunda be safe. Som' White people ain't wanna Abunda do good wit' he'pin' our peoples. Dey feels dat Coloreds kin jis' be good slaves 'en nu'fin mo'."

"What you want me to do?" Bela asked while sobbing in fear. He was experiencing that feeling that made him go into the trees while looking for Abunda. A feeling that he could not explain but was compelled to obey.

"Git Ja'cin 'en Makita. Tell'em what happ'n wit' Abunda. 'en dey com' wit'cha. Dey 'en Abunda gotta do a trip ta Annapolis Grove 'fo too long. Ya kin stay wit' Rev. Hope," the ancestors instructed Bela.

Bela was really more afraid than ever and did not want to make a trip to Cruiseda alone. He was always fearful of what might happen when he traveled with Abunda, but he draw from Abunda's strength and faith. Now he had to stand on his own strength and faith; both of which were still some-what foreign to him. Bela was more acquainted with God than the ancestors because he sat with and was taught by Mrs. Hope about their Christian faith. But this experience, with the ancestors, was new to him and he recognized it as something spiritual. He remembered the stories that Abunda told the group about the ancestors but before now he never encountered them. However, that compulsion stayed with him to obey what he was hearing and he remembered that his previous obedience saved Abunda's live.

Bela reaches the main house, knocks on the door and Mrs. Hope lets him in. He speaks abruptly and in a rush heads for Abunda's room. He bursts into the room exclaiming, "Abunda, they talk to me. They told me some things. I'm so afraid."

In a frail voice, Abunda speaks, "Slow down Bela. Who are they and what did they say?"

Breathing rapidly and talking equally as fast, he replies, "The ancestors. The ancestors. They talk to me when I was comin' back here by myself. I left Rev. Hope in the trees 'cause I was scared. I feel evil there. Rev. Hope told me I could come back to you. Abunda they say you in danger. They said somebody wanna kill you 'cause they don't want you help our people. They said Whites say Coloreds is only good to be slaves."

Bela was now very disturbed and crying hysterically. "I don't want you to die, Abunda. What will we do if you die?"

"I'm not going to die," Abunda reassured Bela. "There are too many things that I must do and I have not found our family's mystery or inheritance, yet."

"What did the ancestors mean when they said....?"

Abunda interrupted Bela, "You said they told you that someone wanted to kill me. That was a warning. The ancestors are there to protect us, Bela."

"They never talk to me befo'. Why they talking to me now?"

"I believe because it is now time for you to develop your own faith and trust in our ancestors and in God. You know more about God than you do about our ancestors because of what Mrs. Hope taught you and the others. What you learned and heard about our ancestors you received from me, but our ancestors are for all our people, not just me and my family!"

"That's what they said," Bela chimed in.

"What else did they say?" Abunda was curious to know.

"Go tell Ja'cin and Makita what happened and they will come back with me. They said y'all gotta make a trip home to Annapolis Grove." As if to anticipate Abunda's next question, Bela continued, "They ain't say why."

Bela asked Abunda, "Why we have the ancestors and God? Mrs. Hope says that God loves everybody and protects us too."

"I'm not sure yet Bela, but when I get a real understanding I will tell you first. I believe in their God but I don't understand some of His ways."

"I gotta go git Ja'cin and tell them what happened. I'm scaked, Abunda. What if somethin' git me on the way?"

"Nothing will harm you. Take one of the other boys from the farmhouse with you; they're not boys anymore, huh? You all will be fine. Thanks Bela, you've been a very good friend."

"Now I know you'll be all right I leave right away." He leaves to go to the farmhouse to get his traveling companion.

Rev. Hope concludes his investigation of the tree area and returns to the house. He is extremely concerned about his suspicions. When he reaches the house he stops to have a cup of tea and to think. "God what is going on? We've never had any trouble here." Finishing his tea, he precedes to check on Abunda while still wondering about the situation and how he will share his concerns with him.

"Knock, Knock," he says as he slowly opens the door to Abunda's room, hoping not to disturb him if he's asleep.

Abunda replies in a stronger voice than before, "Come in." Rev. Hope enters the room.

"Good morning Abunda, how are you feeling?"

"Good morning Rev. Hope. I'm feeling much better thank you but my head is still throbbing."

"I would imagine so. You have quite a gash up there. Abunda, I need to tell you something. Bela and I went to the trees where he found you to see if we could find any clues as to what happened to you. I found this rock and it has fresh blood on it. It was near the area where Bela found you. I can't fathom why someone would want to attack you like this, but it looks like that's what happened. Do you remember anything?"

"No, sir, I don't."

"I will be traveling to town tomorrow on business and I will tell the authorities what has happened. I'm sure they won't find who did this, but they will know that someone wants to harm you. You rest now and get your strength back. Mrs. Hope will look after you while I'm gone. I will tell Cliff what has happened and he will look after you, Mrs. Hope and the estate more closely."

Abunda mulls over what is happening to him. Why is his life being threatened and who hates him enough to do it? He begins to consider his undertaking a lot more serious than before and he concludes that someone else has also. Living in a world where Coloreds had no respect, he wondered what made him think that he could go against what half an entire country stood for.

"Death might be imminent," he considered. "My ancestors died some horrendous deaths to make a better life for us. This situation that was meant for evil, however, it may produce more good than my perpetrator could ever dream possible. I must count the cost for this and decide if I'm really willing to pay it."

Chapter 11

The Convention

"Ja'cin, will we have enough money to pay for our baby?" Makita asked. "I want our baby to have the best of everything. I know you work hard for us and I love you for it."

"Don't worry Makita; you and our child will have the best."

"I've been thinking about what Abunda is going to do and it scares me. People are cruel Ja'cin and they don't want us to have anything good. What if something happens to Abunda while he's trying to do this great thing for our people? Something's just not right, I feel it. Poppa used to say when I felt like this that the ancestors were trying to warn me about something. Maybe we should go to see Abunda. I would like for us to plan a trip to go home to see Momma and Poppa and the family. Wouldn't it be great if I could have the baby at home?"

"Hold on Makita. Wait a minute. First of all Abunda is fine and I think a trip home is a great idea. I don't know about having the baby there, though. We'll talk to Abunda about the trip when he returns here."

"Thanks Ja'cin. I love you so much and you are so good to me. Momma and Poppa will be very happy to know that.

Ja'cin I have something to show you. Momma gave it to me before I left home and told me to hide it in a safe place. You heard me talk about our family mystery and inheritance? Well this might be the answer to it or part of it. Wait just a minute."

Makita leaves the room and returns with a piece of paper that she hands to Ja'cin.

"Open it and read it," she instructs.

Ja'cin quietly reads the paper and exclaims, "Makita, this is a deed to somebody's property. Where did Momma Basket get this from and does anybody else know that she had it?"

"She told me she found it under a mattress at Mrs. Rouse's house a long time ago. She thought it might be our inheritance and wanted me to have it. She gave it to me before we got married. I never read it. I just hide it like she told me. But now I feel like we need to do something about it. I want to show it to Abunda when we get together if that's okay with you? Ja'cin what if it is our family inheritance? We can move all of our family from Annapolis Grove here with us and that would make me so happy."

"My wife. My wife. Please don't get so excited and don't get your hopes up to high. First we have to find out about this deed, and I don't know anyone that I trust to help us. I don't want it falling into the wrong hands and we get blamed for stealing it."

"Mr. Rouse can help us, Ja'cin," Makita screams abruptly! "He a lawyer and we trust him. Momma been with him for years."

"Yes, but he's in Annapolis Grove."

"That's why we going home, you think? I feel the ancestors are telling me something, Ja'cin."

"Let's wait for Abunda," he encourages Makita. "He will help us to think about this and give us some good advice."

He succeeded in calming Makita down and she started to prepare dinner. He sat in serious thought about what had just transpired. Before he knew it, Makita was calling him for dinner. While they were eating, a knock came on the door and Ja'cin got up to answer it.

"Bela, what are you doing here and where is Abunda?"

In a very excited and nervous tone Bela replied, "Abunda been hurt. You need to come back with me."

"Oh, my God," Makita screamed. "Is he alive? How is he? What happened?"

Ja'cin calms Makita and invites Bela and his companion to enter the house while holding Makita in his arm.

"What are you talking about Bela?" he insisted.

As they all sat, Bela told them what had happened. He also told them about his experience with the ancestors and that he really believed that something was wrong and that Abunda was in danger.

"The ancestors never talk to me befo'. Why they tell me now?" Bela questioned.

Ja'cin interrupted, "Let me get you and your friend something to eat and drink and we can talk about this some more. I will have to get someone to take over for me before we can leave; people depend on me, you know."

Bela and his companion took a seat and had a quiet supper with Ja'cin and Makita. The quietness was unnerving and could be felt all around the table. Makita breaks the silence, "Ja'cin when can we leave to go to Abunda? I want to go now!"

"Makita, this is not good for you and the baby. Everything will be fine. We will leave as soon as I can get someone to take care of our business. I know you want to see your brother and so do I, but I must handle my business first. It will not take long. We should be able to leave tomorrow or the day after." He embraces his wife tenderly and she responds by allowing her body language to receive his tenderness. He knows that she is okay because there is no tenseness in the embrace.

Ja'cin does as he has promised and immediately takes care of his business. Because of Makita's pregnancy, he got a horse for her to ride on. He did not want her walking that distance and risking her health. By midday the foursome are on their way to see Abunda. Everyone is excited but nervous as well. The conversation centers on Abunda's health and the news of the Colored Convention. Excitement is looming over the possibility of helping their people to 'have a better life'. Bela is quietly reflecting on his experience with the ancestors and wants someone to explain to him what it all means.

Bela breaks the silence by asking, "Please tell me about the ancestors. Why they talk to me? Abunda said 'cause I have to know them for me and not by him. But he's the strong one. He got us from Annapolis Grove to Rev. Hope. We didn't get hurt 'cause he was with us and he know what to do. Are they gonna say something to me again?"

"I don't know," Ja'cin answered. "The ancestors are our people who have died and are still looking out for us from heaven. It's like when you feel something but you don't know what it is."

"That's what happened to me in the trees," Bela shouted hysterically. "Somethin' told me to go in there but I was scaked to. But I went anyway 'cause I wouldn't found Abunda if I didn't."

"It's hard to explain, Bela, but you have experienced the ancestor's protection and guidance. I believe that they work for and with God; you already know the White's man God."

"How? The White man don't like us, they wanna kill us. How can our ancestors work with they God?"

"Bela, it's not God that does bad things, but people. God wants us all to be safe but too many people don't listen to

God. They think they know what's best. Like the person who hurt Abunda. Whoever it is thinks that they have done the right thing. They probably don't want Abunda to teach our people how to have a better life, but God wants him to."

"This is hard to know," Bela asserts. "Why don't God just make everybody to do right and what He wants?"

"It is hard, Bela, but the more experiences you have with God and the ancestors, the more you will understand."

"I hope so," Bela says as he seems to have accepted the explanation and slips into silence.

"Makita, how are you doing?" Ja'cin asks.

"I'm just fine. I just want us to hurry and get to Abunda. We don't know how he is and I'm worried."

"We'll be there soon. Try not to worry," Ja'cin encourages.

Before they knew it, they were in sight of what Ja'cin believed was the Hope's estate. They saw the beautiful mani-cured lawns with trees placed perfectly as if in a picture. Ja'cin had not been to the Hopes before but his love for landscaping was heightened with this new experience. He marveled at what he was seeing.

He thought, "There must be almost 50 variations of flowers and additional greenery and shrubbery. Someone must have paid a lot of money to get this done. One day I will do something like this for someone or maybe even my own home."

His thoughts were interrupted with Makita's yelp, "Look, is that where Abunda is?"

Bela responded, "Yes, it is. Welcome to Marantha, the Hope's Estate. This is where we live."

"Oh, Ja'cin, this reminds me of home, the Rouse's Estate. It makes me so homesick for Momma, Poppa and the chil-dren. Ja'cin when can we go home? Ja'cin please...."

"Makita, please calm down. We will work everything out when we see Abunda. Please calm down?"

Bela was showing them to the back door of the main house while his traveling companion took the horse and went on to the farmhouse. Cliff was approaching them. Bela was so glad to be home. "Hey, Cliff. This is Abunda's sister, Makita, and her husband, Ja'cin."

"Nice to meet y'all. I'm sorry to hear about what happened to Abunda. We never had this happen here before."

"Thank you for your kindness, sir. Abunda has told us what good people you've been to them every since they came here," Ja'cin shared while shaking Cliff's hand.

"Yes, sir," Makita added. "We are very grateful."

"Please call me Cliff. I know you want to see Abunda so let's go."

As they approached the back door, Cliff knocks and Mrs. Hope comes to the door. When she opens it she immediately knows that this is Abunda's family and greets them warmly. "Welcome, I am Mrs. Hope. Please come in. I know that you are anxious to see Abunda."

"How is he?" Makita asked in a nervous tone.

"He's doing very well. We are pleased with his progress and he's going to be just fine in a short while. He needs to rest more, though, so that his wounds can heal."

"Oh, thank God," Makita replied as she slumped onto Ja'cin for strength. My name is Makita, I'm Abunda's sister and this is Ja'cin, my husband. Can we see him now, please?"

"Sure, follow me. I hope he's not asleep?" Mrs. Hope wondered. She knocked softly on the door, not wanting to disturb Abunda if he was sleeping.

"Come in," was Abunda's response to the knock.

Makita almost knocked the others over rushing into the room. She was crying for joy and glad that her brother was all right. "Abunda!" she yelled, as she reached out and grabbed him forgetting about his injuries.

"Makita," Abunda replied, wincing in a little pain from her grip that caused his voice to quiver.

"I'm sorry Abunda. Did I hurt you? I didn't mean to. I'm just so glad to see you and to know you are all right. Bela told us what happened."

"Hi, Ja'cin," Abunda acknowledges peeping over Makita's body that has blocked his view from everyone else.

"Hi, Abunda," Ja'cin responds with a smirk.

"I am fine, just need to rest and heal," Abunda reassured everyone.

"Do you know anymore about what happened?" Ja'cin questioned.

Abunda concerned about their tiredness from the trip replied, "Not really but we can talk later after you all have rested. Makita needs to rest her and the baby."

"Of course," interjected Mrs. Hope. "You can stay in our guests' quarters, I'll show you there. Rev. Hope will return shortly. He went to town on business."

"Before you leave, Ja'cin and Bela, can I talk to you for a minute?"

"Of course, Abunda," they replied.

Makita in a solemn tone said, "I want to stay, too."

"You need your rest," Abunda said compassionately. "I will talk to you later, just you and me, okay?"

Mrs. Hope told Ja'cin how to find the guests quarters. She and Makita left the room while the others remained as Abunda had requested. It was clear that Abunda wanted to speak with them alone and what he had to share he did not want to disclose to Makita.

"About what happened, Rev. Hope did find a rock in the trees with fresh blood on it. He said that he didn't think we would ever find out who did this but that he would tell the authorities when he went to town. He is so hurt and concerned about this incident," Abunda told the guys.

"Me, too," Bela stated forcefully.

Ja'cin wondered aloud, "What does this mean Abunda? Is somebody trying to stop you from helping our people?"

"They gonna kill you, Abunda?" Bela asked in fear. "I saw the rock in the trees but dropped it 'cause it was evil. I know somethin' was wrong. We gonna be treated just like the other Coloreds. Where we going now from here?" Bela rambled on until Ja'cin stopped him.

"Hold on, Bela. Everything is going to be all right."

Abunda agreed, "Everything is going to be all right. I know that all Whites don't like us Coloreds and that some don't want us to be here. We have to look at what happened as a warning and be careful about our goings and comings. We will have to decide what to tell the others who will be part of the Colored Convention. One preacher has already been beaten and his church burned but he is still willing to participate. Most other Coloreds have not had the advantages that we've had here or that you had at home, Ja'cin. When I am better, we will have a meeting and tell the others about this; we must make plans quickly. I'll ask Rev. Hope to inform the supporters in the Faith Convention of our situation. I want to see if they will help to provide some protection for our people who are on their grounds. This may be dangerous for them as well."

"That sounds good to me," Ja'cin added. "By the way, Abunda, Makita wants us to take a trip home."

Bela was excited at the thought of getting away now and replied, "Yes, we can go soon."

"I've been thinking a lot about Momma and Poppa and the children lately. I want to go home to see them too, but I must take care of this matter and get the Convention together before we leave," Abunda added.

"How long that take?" Bela asked in disgust.

"Don't be upset Bela. It won't take long, I promise," Abunda told him in a calming voice.

Abunda looked at Ja'cin and their eyes connected in unity with an understanding that this situation would be resolved for the best.

Bela and Ja'cin left Abunda. Bela went to the farmhouse and Ja'cin went to found the guests quarters. On his way, he took full advantage of the opportunity to enjoy the landscaping, again. When he arrived at the guests' quarters, Makita was sleeping, so he slipped in quietly and laid beside her. Soon he was asleep.

Abunda was resting peacefully from his wounds, but now his mind was centered on his assault, how to release the information and where to go with starting the Convention. As he drifted, he was hoping that some answers would come to assist him in making decisions that would affect so many people.

"What are you going to do about this?" Abunda heard the voice of Deston ask.

"Deston is that you?" Abunda replied. "Where are you?"

"I'm in your heart," Deston answered. "Abunda what is your heart saying to you. It is important for you to listen to your heart not your mind. Your mind will tell you to do what is safe for you. It operates logically. What you have been charged to do has to be dealt with by faith first and then the logic will appear."

"I'm not sure what you mean," Abunda retorts.

"How do you think your ancestors made it through such difficult times? If they had listened to the voice of reason from their mind, they would never have attempted to escape from the plantation. They would never have considered that a better life ever existed for Coloreds. They were used to being treated as slaves with no respect, dignity or hope of a future, yet they found a way or something to let them know that they were better than how they had been treated. The only way many heard of a future was through the storytelling of your ancestors. They started with everything and were stripped to nothing."

"I never thought of it that way. I heard about our people from Poppa and it was a long time before he told us the stories of King Buswala, his, great, great, great, grandfather who was a King in Africa," Abunda added.

"Someone always has to sacrifice for the good of the others," Deston instructed.

"I see," said Abunda. "But what about...."

Abunda realized at that point that Deston was no longer with him. He returned to the words that Deston spoke and concentrated on them until he fell into a deep sleep.

While Abunda was resting, Makita had awakened from her rest and was anxious to talk with Ja'cin about his meeting with Abunda. She was also in a hurry to see Abunda and make plans for their trip home.

Makita nudged Ja'cin who was still asleep next to her, "Wake up Ja'cin. Wake up."

Ja'cin awoke still half-sleep, "Yes, Makita?"

"We need to talk. I want to know what Abunda told you and Bela and I want to see him right away."

"We talked about the Convention and I told him about your wanting to go home to see the family?"

"What else did you talk about? What about what happened to him? Did he say anything about that?"

"Makita, you know that we Coloreds are not liked by many Whites. But you also know that there are many Whites who like us. Someone wanted to scare Abunda from doing what he does to help our people. We must realize that this is a dangerous work and plan how to do it," Ja'cin informed Makita.

Makita begins to cry softly for she knows that reality has found its way into their lives. For a while she sits in silence wondering. "Why are people this way?" Intermittently she wipes the tears from her face and retreats inward.

She was never very outspoken and lived most of her life introspectively.

Ja'cin broke the silence, "What are you thinking, Makita? You know that me and especially Abunda would not let anything happen to you and our child. We will find a way to do what we have to and be safe. I will give my life for you, our child and your other family members."

"I know Ja'cin. I know," Makita says in a hopeless voice. "Can I go see Abunda now?"

"Yes," Ja'cin concedes. "I will walk you there and come back for you later. I don't want it to be too late. I know you will probably want to stay with him all day and night if you could."

Ja'cin, always looking for the opportunity to view the landscaping, walked Makita the long way around to the main house. They stood holding hands as if it they were at home. Neither mentioned the time the walk took but they just enjoyed the view. They were now knocking at the back door of the main house.

"Hi," Mrs. Hope greeted them. "Please come in."

Makita entered and Ja'cin kissed her on the cheek as he left to return to the guests' quarters.

"Abunda is doing much better and I know he will be glad to see you," she informed Makita as they headed towards his room.

Mrs. Hope knocked on the door and Abunda responded, "Come in."

Mrs. Hope asked him, "Would you like something to eat or drink?"

"Yes, that would be fine," he replied.

Makita entered the room and Mrs. Hope went back downstairs. She immediately headed for Abunda's bedside and sat very close to him on the bed. He took her by the hand and held it tight as if he were talking to her.

Makita expressed her concern to him, "What's going to happen to you? Will they kill you, Abunda?"

"Makita I have much to do for our people. I can't think of what will happen to me but I must think of what will happen to them if I don't at least try to continue doing what I have started. Our ancestors gave their lives so that we could have a better life. Who am I not to if this is my destiny? Our people need to be free, like Poppa told us about our inheritance. We need to find it so we can be free forever and no one can enslave us again."

"I know, Abunda, but I'm scared for you and especially our men. I want us to be alive to enjoy our progress without danger. You know I will help anyway I can."

"I just want you to give me a healthy niece or nephew and take good care of yourself. Please try not to worry. Let's change the subject and talk about going home," he knew that this would excite Makita.

"Oh, Abunda, let's go home to see our family before Momma or Poppa dies, please," Makita pleads.

"We will go soon Makita, as soon as I get the Convention started. It won't take long. I already have some key people in place that can carry on while I'm gone. This is very important because Bela and Ja'cin will also be going home with us and they are who I really depend on."

"How long do you think it will take?" Makita urgently wanted to know.

"Not long at all. As I told the guys as soon as I'm out of this bed, which should be in a few days we will get started on the Convention. Rev. Hope has offered to let us meet here. I will need to get the word to the others and we will probably meet next week."

"That'll be great, Abunda. I have something that I need to show you. Momma gave it to me before my wedding and told me to hold on to it. She acted like it was something very special, maybe our inheritance. I showed it to Ja'cin, for the first time before we left home. I want you to read it and tell us what we should do."

Makita handed the paper to Abunda and he begins to read it. His initial exclamation was just like Ja'cin's. "Makita, this is a deed to somebody's property. Where did Momma get this from and whose is it?"

"You sound just like Ja'cin. I don't know, Abunda. Momma said she found it under the mattress at the Rouse's and stuck it in her apron pocket. She forgot it was there. Like I said, she gave it to me before my wedding. She never read it. Ja'cin says that we need a lawyer and he don't want it to fall into the wrong hands 'cause they might think we stole it."

"He's right, Makita. This is serious. The only lawyer we know is Mr. Rouse. Maybe that's why we're going home?"

"That's what I said to Ja'cin. Maybe the ancestors are leading us back home for something."

"I don't know what this all means but please hide this carefully as you have done all this time. Put it in a place where it can't be found or bring danger to you all, Makita. When we get to Annapolis Grove we will go see Mr. Rouse right away."

Abunda's thoughts drifted from Makita to the Rouse estate where his son was living as their child. He wondered how he would react to seeing Joshua for the first time. Would he be able to maintain his composure and hold onto his secret? He thought about having Serenity at his side so that they could see their son together.

"Abunda, Abunda, what are you thinking?" Makita said almost in a yell. "You left me and went off somewhere; it must have been mighty special. You were deep in thought."

"I was just thinking about how good it will be at home with all the family."

Mrs. Hope returned with food for Abunda and Makita. The two talked on and on and reminisced about the past.

They talked about how separate they were growing up and how different they had become since leaving home. They always thought that Sha'myla would be the first to leave home or get married. Makita was always the quiet shy one.

Before long, Ja'cin was back to get Makita. He stayed for a short while and the three talked more. There was excitement in the air around the baby and going home, that for the moment overshadowed the impending danger of Abunda's life.

Abunda's recovery was as speedy as he had hoped. He began making plans for the meeting at Rev. Hope's because he knew that Ja'cin needed to return home and prepare for their trip to Annapolis Grove. He predicted that they would be gone for at least a month, maybe two.

THE MEETING OF THE CONVENTION

The day of the meeting was at hand. Everyone invited was present at the Hope Estate. Mrs. Hope had engaged a local caterer for the event. She knew how special this day was for her husband and Abunda so she wanted it to be special as well. The meeting was to be held in the gardens directly behind the main house. This is where Mrs. Hope held her special personal functions. There was a large white tent next to the gardens that held the most scrumptious foods and deserts for their guests.

Just like Makita's wedding reception, they had fried chicken, greens, macaroni and cheese, cornbread, okra, green beans, potato salad, ham, ribs, biscuits, sweet potato pie, cake, and drinks. The foods that Colored people loved and cooked so well.

Abunda called the meeting to order as his guests were busy appreciating the surroundings.

"Good day to everyone. I'm so glad that you could make it. This is a very special day for us. First I would like to thank Rev. and Mrs. Hope for inviting us to meet here."

"You're quite welcome," Rev. Hope replies. "When the meeting is over Mrs. Hope has prepared a wonderful food feast for us so please stay." Murmurs went around as this was a first for many of those present. "Rev. Hope would you lead us with a prayer, please," Abunda requested.

Rev. Hope agreed "Dear God, thank you for this special day that you have brought us together; men of different colors who love and want to do your will. Thank you for these brave men who have put their lives on the line to help their people. Thank you for my people who have given generously to help others in need. We thank you for the hearts and desires of those in the Faith Convention who have stood by their promises of assistance to Abunda.

Now God, this is the day that you have made. You called this day to be in the beginning of time. I ask you to bless the labor, desires and outcomes of this gathering for a Colored Convention. I ask that it be a witness to your awesomeness as our God for all people regardless of race. I ask that you do exceedingly abundantly above what we can think or even ask. Let my Colored brothers know beyond a shadow of a doubt that you are their God also and that you are no respecter of persons. Thank you for my faithful wife and those here at our home that have worked so hard to demonstrate your love. In Jesus name I pray, Amen.

It was a moving prayer because a White man was asking God to help, protect and enable Coloreds. All present could tell that it came from Rev. Hope's heart and that he really meant it.

Abunda explained to the group what happened to him in the trees. Some of them had heard but many had not. He reassured them that he was still going to continue his work and to do what he intended by expanding into the Convention. A few expressed their concerns but most had become used to the way of life.

Abunda shared his vision and mission for the group, informing everyone of his trip to the Convention and the positive reception he received especially from Hais Bishop. In spite of the looming danger, everyone present was pleased to hear of the financial as well as motivational support for Abunda and his undertakings.

Addressing the group as to the legal formation of the Convention, Abunda asked, "We need to see how we are going to setup the Convention and who will head it?"

A response from within the group said, "You will head it, Abunda. It's your dream and we just want to be a part of it."

Everyone agreed with, "Yes, that's right."

"Please don't feel like I have to head it. I need everyone's input and ideas. This is going to affect our people all over. Many of you have been here so much longer than I have and you know what is needed and probably the best way to start any plan."

"We understand, Abunda. But you are the only one that has moved out into bigger things. Rev. Hope has really helped you and we are willing to follow you," Pastor Titus added.

"All right," Abunda conceded. "But please remember that this could be very dangerous. Our lives may be lost for this cause but many others will reap the benefits of our efforts. I know that our ancestors are with us and I'm learning more that God is not just God of the White people, but God of us all. I believe that God is passing on to us what our ancestors worked for but never received. Through the schooling that Rev. Hope provided to me, I've learned how to put things together in an orderly fashion. That's how our efforts have been successful so far, but now we are going to expand even greater. That means that we will have to duplicate what we've done here in many other places."

Again, as an act of reassurance someone said, "Abunda, just tell us what to do and what we don't know, teach us first and we'll teach our people."

"Can I ask Rev. Hope to help us with this? He is a member of the Faith Convention and perhaps he can tell us how best to get started. I want what we do to be legal and accountable."

Again, the entire group agreed.

Rev. Hope stood in front of the group but he could hardly compose himself for he was honored and moved by their actions to include him. Almost tearful, he began to thank the group, "I am overwhelmed by your faith in me and your decision to allow me to be a part of this special history making occasion. I will do my best to live up to your expectations of me and I ask you to hold me accountable to you."

The group all stood and gave him a roaring applause.

Rev. Hope shared the legal requirements and a proposed structure for the Convention that would be similar to that of the Faith Convention. He explained the necessity of having strong leadership so that the organization would grow beyond its beginnings. Much of his presentation was very technical but he took the time to answer any questions and concerns as they were raised. He offered to help with getting an attorney to draw up the organizing documents that would make the Convention official. Most of those present were in awe because they had never been involved in anything on this level. Ja'cin knew of legalities because he owned his own business but many of the preachers were still working on estates.

By the time the meeting was concluded the group had chosen officers and provided suggestions for expanding the areas that Abunda had already started. All agreed that those present would be the first to learn and then their people. The majority of the preachers were of the Christian faith and had been allowed to attend services with the Whites; however, they still had to sit in the balcony. Somehow they had a spiritual experience with "the White man's God" that impacted their life to the point that they gained hope and faith.

Everything that transpired during the meeting was written done by Ja'cin. He was careful to document all comments, suggestions and recommendations. Rev. Hope had provided him with handouts of the structure of the Faith Convention for him to include. It was agreed upon that the foundation group would review the materials from Rev. Hope, the information that Ja'cin had recorded and structure the Colored Convention. The group would meet again and the foundation group would share their recommendations that, if accepted by all, would formalize the Convention. When the meeting was over, Rev. Hope requested that everyone follow him to the tent for the feast. The group was in shock when they saw the spread that Mrs. Hope had prepared for them. They mixed, mingled, talked and ate until it was time to return home. Some lived a distance away and needed to be leaving before nightfall when traveling became even more dangerous.

After everyone was gone, Abunda, Bela, Ja'cin and Rev. Hope sat reflecting on the happenings. Mrs. Hope and Makita entered to hear what had taken place.

Mrs. Hope started, "How did your meeting go?"

"It was astounding," Rev. Hope replied.

Bela bursting with excitement shared, "All the preachers want Abunda to do for them like he's doing for us. Helping our people learn to read and write and other things he teached to us. They want to learn first, if they don't know, and then tell their people. I feel like I'm special."

"I will never forget this day," Ja'cin added. "I used to dream of our people being free to do whatever we wanted to. I knew that we could learn if someone just took the time to teach us. When I was taken from my family, as a little boy, I was so scared because I didn't know what would happen to me. I had no idea that I would end up with people, White people, who really cared about me and would teach me how to read and write and learn a trade. What a privilege it will be to help others like I was helped. I will do whatever I can to help?"

"Wait a minute Ja'cin, don't forget about our child," Makita speaks up while rubbing her stomach. "We need you too," she chuckled.

"Don't worry, Makita, I'm doing this for all of us," he reassured her as he grabbed and held her hand.

The foundation group met within days of the initial meeting and unanimously developed the structure and plan for the Convention. They were anxious to share it with the rest of the group for approval.

The plan was very detailed and explicit. It contained geographical breakdowns to cover the immediate area and areas that were a distance away. Initially, the Convention would begin and continue where Abunda had begun but pastors would be prepared first through a group of trainings that mirrored those Abunda had completed with Rev. Hope.

Pastoral training would take place on-site once a week and those who could read and write well enough would participant in the correspondence course like Abunda had done. Rev. Hope was very instrumental in securing the materials for the course because of his connection with the Faith Convention. Since Abunda's speech many of the attendees to the Faith Convention were more than willing to accommodate the needs of beginning and sustaining the Colored Convention.

Since the Convention was such a huge task, the foundation group gave serious consideration as to how best serve the many in need. Abunda was responsible for the allocation of the funds and materials that would be received from the Faith Convention. He wanted to make sure that he was honest and fair in the distribution of these resources.

As they expected the remaining members of the group listened to the plan and gave their approval. They wanted to get busy working within the Convention. Abunda informed the group that he would have to be out of town but wanted them to continue in his absence. He told them that he would provide information to cover his absence. The group selected, Pastor Titus, from within themselves, to be in charge during Abunda's absence. Rev. Hope would be available for any assistance needed.

Afterwards Makita, Ja'cin, Abunda, and Bela met to discuss the plans for going home to Annapolis Grove. Ja'cin reminded them that he would have to return to Crusidea first to check on his business and then return to Maranatha to travel home. Makita was so excited she could hardly wait to go home. She and Ja'cin went home to Crusidea.

Abunda now had time to reflect on all that occurred: his attack and recovery, the deed Makita showed him, the meetings and the actual beginnings of the Convention. It all happened so fast that it caused him to consider what was going on.

Spending hours agonizing over how best to accomplish the mission of the Convention, Abunda was besieged by issues of morality, integrity, fairness, faith (the White man's God or the ancestors), the denial of his personal life, giving everything he possessed and more. He no longer had a life, but was totally dedicated to assuring the success, not only of the Convention as an entity, but to see that the people were not overlooked or lost in the excitement of organizing and maintaining this new venture. This was all very new to Abunda. He watched in awe and inquisitiveness as to how the Faith Convention managed and operated. Hundreds of people, pastors, their families and leaders gathered in one place with no evidence of discord. Wondering how to do it all now consumed Abunda. "Will I be able to do this? Can I lead such a large mass of people? Our issues are much different from the Faith Convention because safety is a major concern for my people. I thought that I had really thought this through, but the looming reality makes me wonder more."

Quickly needing to put things into motion, Abunda wanted to be an integral part of the beginnings of the Convention. While waiting for Ja'cin and Makita to conclude their business at home and return to Marantha, he began to instruct the preachers on what he was doing with the people. He demonstrated lessons to them and ascertained the educational level of each of them. Most needed to be taught but still had the tenacity and fortitude to lead their people. It was amazing that with so little education they were able to amass a following. These preachers were very successful in instilling hope in their people of 'a better life'; now the practical opportunity had presented itself. They were more than willing to do whatever was necessary for their people and themselves.

Abunda continued to have his meetings with his people and others who had started attending before the Convention. Some of these people he used to facilitate sessions with others.

The Convention group was bubbling with enthusiasm, excitement and more hope than any of them had ever imagined. At times it was very difficult for some of the people to travel because of the danger and beatings that took place, but many found a way to get to Abunda. Rev. Hope did as Abunda asked and held a meeting with some estate owners to encourage them to help protect their people who wanted to be a part of Abunda's program. Many were conciliatory but others were not and wanted no part of Rev. Hope's vision for the Coloreds. Rev. Hope informed Abunda of the decisions of the estate owners and they decided to devise a plan whereby everyone could participate in the Convention activities.

Ja'cin and Maktia had finally returned to Marantha in anticipation of their trip home to Annapolis Grove. Abunda had everything in place with Rev. Hope and the others carrying on in his absence. The excitement of going home was overwhelming to all, Bela included. Bela was not sure where his family was now but Abunda assured him that he could stay with him because he was his family.

Chapter 12

Miracles for Real?

S ha'myla was sitting on the porch thinking about her family. She missed Makita something terribly and could hardly bring herself to think about Abunda. He had been gone for so long she was afraid that something awful probably happened to him. She was more aware of the attitudes of Whites toward Coloreds and felt that Abunda had not gotten far without being accosted by them. Her life had not changed much since Makita's marriage and departure. She was still a slave to the unkind White family. Her joy in the midst of all of this was her relationship with Joshua that had developed over the years. They were the best of friends and Joshua loved and respected Sha, Sha, as he called her. Joshua taught Sha, Sha things that he learned from school and encouraged her to explore more of the world through books. He would supply her with another book whenever she finished reading. There was still something about Joshua that puzzled Sha'myla but she could never put her finger on it.

"Sha'myla," Momma Basket called. "Com' eat, we's all y'ere but ya."

"I'm comin' Momma," she responded and leaped to her feet and ran the short distance to the front door. She loved Momma's cooking as did everybody.

The Basket family was seated for dinner; all except Makita and Abunda. The children were all growing up and the family was blessed to still be together.

Poppa said, "Let's pray. God thank ya fo' what ya don' fo' us. Thank ya fo' my family. Thank ya fo' keepin' us safe 'en to'gava. Thank ya fo' our ancestors who's wit' ya now 'en lookin' down on us. I pray dey he'p Abunda find his way back to us. 'En I pray dat we git ta da place where we's goin'. Da ancestors a'ways sade ya had su'pin betta fo' us som'where. I pray dat ya care fo' my Makita 'en Ja'cin. Amen."

Just before dinner was over, there was a knock on the door. "Who dat?" Poppa questioned as he arose to answer the door. Everyone else was very still and quiet. It was not often that anyone came to their house except to get them to go to the fields.

Poppa proceeded towards the door and upon approaching it he placed his hand slowly on the doorknob wondering what was on the other side. Gingerly turning the knob, thoughts went through his mind as to what he would do if danger lurked. He knew that he could not have a weapon but he knew that he had to do something to protect his family. Not having the time to alert the family, what he could do alone that would draw all the attention to him thereby sparing his family was in his thoughts. Poppa concluded that he would step outside to meet with whoever was there and that he would re-enter when all was well. He reasoned that the older boys would know that something was wrong if he did not come back into the house.

Beads of perspiration were dripping from Poppa's face; to him it felt like a flood. He did not bother to wipe the sweat because his concentration was on what would happen next:

opening the door. Inner tremblings invaded his body but he managed to mentally still the earthquake that was occurring within. The moment of reckoning was at hand and Poppa knew that he had to open the door to who knows what. With one swift twist of his wrist he yanked open the door and when he saw what was on the other side he nearly collapsed.

"Poppa, you all right?" Makita asked.

Yelling and screaming was heard throughout the house by everyone when they heard Makita's voice.

Momma said in a tone of unbelief, "Dat ain't Makita is it? Oh my God my chi'dren' com' hom'."

Momma rushed to the door to see for herself. Poppa had not yet composed himself enough to share the good news of the visitors.

"Momma, Momma!" Makita screamed as she lunged into her mother's arms crying like a hungry baby.

The rest of the family rushed to greet Makita. There were many questions being asked all at once and everyone forgot about Poppa who was still outside the house.

"Where is Ja'cin?" Sha'mlya asked.

"I'm right here," he answered as he made his way into the house.

Momma was now concerned about Poppa's whereabouts. "Where Poppa?"

"I's right y'ere," Poppa replied as he came into the house holding Abunda's hand.

Pure pandemonium broke out! Some family members had fallen to the floor sobbing hysterically. Others stood in complete shock as if they had seen a ghost. Momma was paralyzed. An uncanny atmosphere of serenity filled the house; a peace that the family had not known since Abunda's separation. Years of tension were washed from everyone's face and hope now filled their eyes. Unbelief was subtly replaced with assurance. An unexpressed finality was reached that the ancestors did hear their prayers.

Abunda stood crying openly as he looked around at his family that he thought he would never see again. His body, too, was trembling from internal emotions. He beheld his Momma still paralyzed in her spot. He saw the years of age on her face and knew that some of them were as a result of his leaving. This was a moment that he would cherish for the rest of his life.

"Momma," Abunda finally spoke. "Momma." He slowly moved toward her. He put his arms around her tenderly and drew her close to him. Gently stroking her face with his fingers, he planted a kiss on her right cheek. He then took her face and cupped it in his two hands and peered into her eyes. The nonverbal communication between them spoke of missing each other and a love that survived a separation.

Momma Basket received Abunda's affection by resting her head on his shoulder, still in silence. She did not want to disturb this moment. For as long as she could, she would savor this moment and paint a mental picture that would be hers forever.

"Abunda, ya com' hom'," Momma Basket manages to utter. "Ya hom'."

"Yes, Momma, I'm home," Abunda assures her.

Again, Momma, repeats as if this was not happening, "Ya hom'."

"I'm here. Yes, Momma, I'm here," Abunda repeats.

The entire family then rushes Abunda as they had done Makita. All of them wanted to know the whats, whens, wheres, and hows of his life since he left home. There was no order to the discussion yet no one seemed to mind.

Poppa Basket finally takes control, "Jis' a minute. Y'all sit down. We's gonna y'ear Abunda 'en Makita talk."

No one even noticed Bela until Abunda introduced him to the family. Bela was so pleased to be a part of this loving event. It made him wonder about his family that he was separated from at a young age. It was now just him and his brother who was back in Marantha.

The reunion went on late into the night. The family was entertained by Abunda's storytelling of his travels with the group from Annapolis Grove to Maranatha. Amazement was evident of Abunda's accomplishments and his honored position among the White people in Marantha and the Faith Convention. Abunda could not give enough praise and thanksgiving for Rev. and Mrs. Hope.

Bela spoke up, "Thanks for letting me be a part of y'alls family. Abunda's been a brotha to us who left with him. Poppa and Momma y'all done a good job raising him up. He's a smart man."

Momma and Poppa Basket were beaming with pride and thanksgiving.

Abunda felt an urgency to address his family. "Before we go to bed, Momma and Poppa I am sorry for all the pain I caused by running away. I wasn't running away from you all, but from the life that offered no chance of 'a better life' as the ancestors told you, Poppa. You wouldn't believe what the rest of the world is like. It's not always easy or perfect but there are places where Coloreds have a real chance at 'a better life'. I wish that I could get all of you away from here and bring you to where I am. I'm going to make a way for that to happen."

Poppa responded, "We kno' Abunda. Ya was 'pose ta be betta. We's jis' glad ya com' hom' see us 'fo we die. I's want us all be to'gava. It late now, we's need go bed. E'rybody jis' git som'where sleep."

And they all did. The boys went into one room and the girls into the other. Some slept on the bed and some on pallets on the floor. They were so excited to be together that nobody cared where they slept.

The odor of Momma's good cooking had filled the house. She was humming and singing as she prepared her family's favorites: grits, eggs, sausage, and toast. There was always food at Momma's because the Rouses' shared with her. One by one the family started to emerge from the rooms and prepared themselves for breakfast. After everyone was up, they all sat around to eat.

Poppa started with his prayer, "God thank ya fo' what ya don' fo' us. Thank ya fo' my family. Thank ya fo' keepin' us safe 'en to'gava. Thank ya fo' bringin' my chil'len back safe. Thank ya fo' our ancestors who wit' ya now 'en lookin' down on us. Amen."

Poppa begins to cry. The family embraces one another in an atmosphere of gratitude and love. For a short while they clung to each other in complete silence.

"Da food's gittin' cold," Momma announced and broke the stillness in the room. Everyone rushed to get their food and enjoyed the scrumptious meal together.

"What y'all gonna do t'day?" Momma asked. "Glad it ain't a work day. How long ya be y'ere?"

Abunda responded, "Maybe a month, Momma." Momma smiled at the thought.

Ja'cin rose to his feet and requested order. "I have something to tell you. Me and Makita is going to have a baby!"

Once again there was pure pandemonium in the house. Sha'myla almost knocked her brothers down getting to Makita. They hugged and danced around in the small spot where they stood. Momma cried. Poppa shook Ja'cin's hand and gave him a bear hug embrace. The youngest children that Makita cared for forced themselves between her and Sha'myla to hug their big sister. The air was so full of hope and encouragement, what more could the Baskets want?

"Back to your question, Momma, I want to visit town and also see Mr. Rouse. I am a free man now and can go wherever I want," Abunda informed those present with pride.

"Ya still gotta be car'ful," Poppa added. "Dey still killin' Coloreds."

Momma asked Abunda, "Why ya wanna see Mr. Jet?"

"I want him to look at something for me. I'll tell you about it later." Abunda replied.

"I go wit' cha," Momma Basket volunteered.

"No, Momma. I'll go alone. I still know how to get there."

The rest of the family spent the time catching up on more news, this time about Makita and Ja'cin. They wanted to know all the details about their new life. They wanted to know when the baby would be born and if they would come back so they could see the baby. After everyone got the answers to their questions, the women separated to talk more. Bela and the boys continued to talk especially about how they ran away from Annapolis Grove.

Abunda takes a leisurely stroll to the Rouse Estate; his first time as a man not controlled by anyone in Annapolis Grove. He was, however, wise enough to take a safe route that would not bring attention to him. He walked across the estate that reminded him so much of Maranatha. His thoughts floated to days when he worked and lived here as a different person. He was amazed, himself, at how far he had come and what he had accomplished. As he got closer to the house, it came across his mind about the deed he was to show Mr. Rouse. He, also, remembered Poppa telling them the story about King Buswala and a deed.

"That's ridiculous. That was so long ago, there's no way." Abunda dismissed the idea from his thoughts.

Before he knew it, he was approaching the back door to the Rouse Estate. He proceeded to knock on the door and a young man appeared. Abunda was astonished because he thought this could not be his Joshua.

The young man spoke, "Good day, can I help you?"

Abunda was speechless and the moment became very uncomfortable for them both.

Again Joshua said, "Good day, can I help you?"

Rushing to collect himself, Abunda hurriedly replied, "Yes. I mean good day to you. My name is Abunda. I'm Momma Basket's son. I came to see Mr. Jet if that's possible."

"Momma Basket's son, yes, come in. It is so nice to meet you. We love your Mother very much. She is so special to us. I'll see if my father is available. I'll be right back." Joshua darted off to look for his father.

Abunda was still very much unnerved by the experience. How would he ever divulge to this young man that he was his father? Would the day ever come when they might be friends or acquaintances? What had he done by running away leaving Serenity to make the decision to give up their child? Thoughts. Thoughts. Thoughts.

"Please come," a soft voice spoke, but once again Abunda did not respond because he was lost inside himself.

"Excuse me," the voice reiterated.

"I'm so sorry. I just seem to be in a different space today. Please forgive me," Abunda spoke to the lady who was standing before him. "Mrs. Rouse?"

"Yes, I am." She stopped for a moment realizing that there was something familiar about this stranger in her midst. "You told my son that you're Momma Basket's son. My goodness you're Abunda. I know Momma Basket must be ecstatic about you being home. She's been heartbroken since you left. How are you? Come, please come in. Joshua didn't know who you were. I think you had gone shortly before he came to us."

"Yes, ma'am. I hated the idea of hurting my family," Abunda shared with Mrs. Rouse.

"You're so...," Mrs. Rouse searched for the tact to complete her sentence. "Grown up?" Abunda said trying to assist with her struggle.

"It's much more than that. You're educated and sophisticated. Pardon my saying this, but you don't seem like the

Coloreds; you seem like a man of means. I don't mean to be flippant …," and once again she groped for words.

"Thank you, Mrs. Rouse. I understand and appreciate what you're saying. Life's been good to me since I left. I've been able to get more schooling than I ever imagined. There are other Whites like you and Mr. Rouse who believe that Coloreds should have a chance to better themselves and they help to make it possible."

"I know your family is so proud of you. Let me not take all your time, Mr. Rouse is waiting for you. I'll take you to him. It is a pleasure to have this conversation with you. Perhaps before you leave we can hear more?"

Mrs. Rouse takes Abunda to the parlor where Mr. Rouse is waiting. "Honey, this is Abunda, Momma Basket's son."

"My pleasure. Please have a seat," Jet Rouse replies.

"Thank you sir for meeting with me. I have something that I would like for you to look at. Momma gave it to my sister and she had no idea what it was. Momma said that she found it," Abunda informs Mr. Rouse.

"All right, let's have a look," Mr. Rouse replies.

Abunda hands the folded paper to Mr. Rouse. The paper is very old and fragile but the writing is still legible enough to read. Because the paper was under the bed it was shielded from aging. When Abunda shows Jet Rouse the paper, he is shocked because he remembers his father giving him the paper and asking him to put it in a safe place for him. This was at the beginning of his career when he first graduated from law school. He did not want to put it with his business papers so he carried it in his briefcase. One day he realized when he was at home in his room, what was now he and his wife's bedroom, while cleaning out the old briefcase to exchange it for a new one, the paper was still there. He slipped the paper under the bed as a temporary solution but forgot about it. He can not let Abunda know that he recognizes the paper because his father told him that it was something he should not know about.

Still trying to maintain his composure, Mr. Rouse speaks, "This is a deed to an old plantation. It is a very large piece of property that belonged to the Magnolia Family. The story told was Mr. Magnolia's grandfather killed another plantation owner and put it on a slave. His grandfather took the papers from the plantation owner and hid them for safe keeping so that years down the road he would claim the property. The dead plantation owner's family had lots and lots of money; folks even thought some was buried on the land. Mr. Magnolia and a kin to the dead plantation owner planned to take over the plantation years later. And what irony, because now it's in the hands of.... I'm sorry I didn't mean it like that, I was just looking at the recompense that may be about to take place."

"I accept your apology, Mr. Rouse. What do we do with this?"

"This is truly amazing to me because I heard just the other day that what's left of the property, and it's a good bit, is being sold at an auction. But if this deed is true the holder of the deed will own the property and stop the auction."

"Do you mean that this could be Momma's property?"

"Could be, she found the deed."

"Who's going to let a Colored own that amount of property? I'm sure that somebody will try to kill my whole family when they learn that Momma has the deed. They will probably justify killing us by saying that we stole it. This could be what our ancestors say is our inheritance and 'a better life' for us but it could also mean our death."

"I agree with you. How long will you be home? I will need a few days to investigate this and determine what will be the best course of action to take. God knows I would like nothing better than to see your family with this property.

Momma has been so good to my family. Would you trust me to hold on to this until we meet again?"

"Of course. Your family has always been good to us for White people. I don't mean any harm by that but it's true."

"I understand, Abunda. Would you come back in a few days and I will have an answer for you."

The men shook hands and Abunda left whistling on the way home. Could this really be the inheritance? It would surely be a way to 'the better life'. He decided that he would not say anything about what Mr. Rouse had said until he returned and got the final verification from him.

When he arrived home, he was bombarded by Makita, "What'd he say? Tell me what'd he say?"

"Trust me Makita, I'll tell you soon enough. Mr. Rouse has to look into it first and I have to go back to see him in a few days," he advised her.

The few days seemed like a lifetime to Abunda. He busied himself with the family doing some thinking about the Convention while Poppa and the others were in the fields. Mr. Rouse sent word home by Momma Basket that he wanted to see him.

"Why Mr. Jet wanna see ya fo'? Is ya in troubl'?" Momma asked.

"No Momma," Abunda laughed. "It's a business matter and Mr. Jet is the only lawyer I trust and it's all because of you." He gives Momma a big hug and kiss on the cheek.

"Okay. He sade com' by to'mrow."

The night was too long and Abunda could hardly sleep because he was filled with great expectation for his family. Maybe now they could really leave Annapolis Grove and come to Marantha with him and Makita like they had hoped. Maybe this was 'the better life'.

Morning finally peeped over the horizon, and Abunda arose before anybody. He soon realized that it was too early to go to the Rouse's, so he went outside and found a nice place to meditate. For a brief moment he thought of the Hopes and what was now his home. He missed being there very much.

Once again, Momma's cooking was waking up everybody in the house. One by one the boys came out to wash themselves for breakfast before going to the field. Momma started them doing this when they were little boys. She always wanted her family to be a family in spite of the circumstances. She taught them that if they rise early enough they could eat and not be hungry in the fields. They worked long hours and it was very hard work. Poppa still says his usual prayer and the family partakes of Momma's good cooking.

The truck comes to gather the men, Sha'myla leaves walking and Momma is on her way to the Rouses. She still manages to take the two youngest with her so they can continue to learn to read and write while helping her at the Rouses.

Finally, it is time for Abunda to meet Mr. Rouse. Once again, perhaps for the last time, he travels the estate on foot. He has decided not to entertain any mental anguish by guessing what might or might not be. "I will just wait to hear what Mr. Rouse has to say," he thought out loud.

This time he was greeted at the back door by Momma. "C'mon in. I tell Mr. Jet ya y'ere. He got som'body wit'em, too. But he sade bring ya in soons ya com'."

Momma knocks gently on the parlor door and Mr. Rouse answers, "Yes, Momma?"

"Abunda's here fo' ta see ya, sir."

"Send him in."

He enters the room to find Mr. Rouse and another gentleman, whose back is to him.

"Come in. I want you to meet a dear friend of mine who may have an interest in this matter."

As Mr. Rouse begins to make the introduction the gentleman turned to face Abunda, the two responded to each other, "Mr. Hais Bishop."

"Abunda?" Hais Bishop said with shock and happiness. Instantly they embraced one another while Mr. Rouse was looking very puzzled.

"You two obviously know each other?"

Mr. Bishop responds, "We sure do. He was our keynote speaker at the Faith Convention. I was so impressed that I wanted to help him with his endeavors. He has done an outstanding job teaching his people how to read and write and learn skills. He is an astonishing man. What are you doing here in Annapolis Grove?"

"This is my home. I came home to visit my family."

Abunda did not want to divulge his business to Mr. Bishop so he did not tell him of the matter at hand. He did, however, wonder if Serenity was with her husband, back in Annapolis Grove. "How is Mrs. Bishop?" he asked as the beat of his heart became more rapid.

"She's fine. Thanks for asking. She's here with me. We came to visit her family and I stopped by to see my old friend, Jet. I will tell her that you are here and that you asked of her. She thinks so highly of you, as do I."

Immediately, Abunda's entire thoughts shifted to the possibility of seeing Serenity and them seeing their son together. So entrenched in his thoughts, he did not hear what Mr. Rouse was saying to him.

"Abunda?" Mr. Rouse asked.

"I'm sorry sir, I was lost in thought."

"I believe that I have some great news for you and your family. The deed is authentic so the property cannot be auctioned. It has to be given to whoever has the deed, and you have it."

Abunda was overwhelmed, but he wondered why Mr. Rouse was sharing his business in front of Mr. Bishop even though they were best friends. The look on his face must have prompted Mr. Rouse to explain.

"Forgive me," Mr. Rouse asked. "Hais was in town and he came to visit because we had not seen each other in years. I hope you don't mind but I was sharing with him about this situation and asked for advice as to how best to proceed. The law states that Coloreds can't just walk into the property office and say I have a deed to property. They will be jailed or even killed for stealing. Hais has an excellent suggestion, he proposes to buy the deed and then the property will belong to him. I told him that the people who had the deed were special to our family and that they were Coloreds. That gave him more incentive because he has a heart to help the Coloreds and now I see why. What do you think?"

Abunda was dumbfounded! He thought if only Hais Bishop knew about Serenity, his wife, and his history. He felt like he was a thief or cheat even though his relationship with Serenity happened so many years ago. What would happen if they told Hais Bishop the truth about them? How could they tell him about Joshua? He had only recently found out about his son, himself.

"Abunda," Mr. Rouse mused. "Are you in shock?"

"Yes, sir, I am." He had so many questions. "Why would you want to do this Mr. Bishop? What legal actions have to be taken to get this done? How much property is the plantation? What is it worth? How will my family get the money?"

"Wait a minute," Mr. Rouse petitioned. "There are many details that have to be worked out but Hais and I don't foresee a problem. We will do what is best for your family in terms of getting the money to you. The property is very valuable. However, because it has been empty for years there are back taxes that must be paid. They will be paid out of the proceeds of the plantation. We're talking about approximately 250 acres of prime land. I would like to purchase it myself but.... Anyway Hais and I will draw up the papers so that he will have proof that the deed is his; you leave that to us. I will have to find out about Marantha's banking system so that we can get the money to your family. Do you think the family will leave Annapolis Grove after this? We will hate to see you go, but we have always wanted what was best for you all. We will help you leave in safety if you plan to go."

"This is more than I ever imagined" Abunda spoke in awe. "Our ancestors are always telling us that there is 'a better life' for us but we never knew what or how. Exactly what does this all mean?"

Hais Bishop responds this time, "You and your family can live wherever you want and do whatever you want. There are many Coloreds in the north who are living very prosperous lives and are leading citizens in the community. You have amassed a great following and your name is honored in the church community."

"But I'm still Colored," Abunda responds disgruntled.

"I can connect you with some very affluent Coloreds who are openly living in safety. They have developed communities, just like the Whites. It will require some changes on your family's part but it is workable," Mr. Bishop advised.

Mr. Rouse adds, "Let me and Hais complete the arrangements first. The auction is scheduled for a few days from now, so I have to contact the proper authorities and advise them of the deed. I don't foresee any problems because of Hais' reputation. The deed will officially be turned over to him and he will pay you for the property. No one will ever know that you had ownership of the deed so your family won't be in any danger."

"I don't know what to say or how to thank you both for this gesture of kindness," Abunda told the men. "My family and I will be eternally grateful for this. Mr. Rouse would you please let Momma know when you want me to come back? Mr. Bishop, as always, it is my pleasure. We will make plans to discuss what I'm doing with the people back home. Perhaps now we won't need you to support us financially?"

"Of course I will continue," Hais Bishop insisted. "This money will be for your family. Your sisters and brothers can be educated. Your parents can purchase property and live very comfortably. I am a man of my word and I intend to keep it."

They all shook hands and Abunda headed for home. He concluded that he would not tell the family until everything was final. His thoughts now shifted to Serenity and Joshua. He longed for them to see their son together. Was it possible? Could another miracle take place, like the deed?

At home the family was excited about the new baby and wanted to do something for Makita and Ja'cin before they went back home.

Sha'myla thought to herself, "Maybe we'll have one of Momma's good suppers and everybody can make something special for the baby. I don't know what the boys can do, but we can think of something."

She approached Momma with the idea and she instantly agreed. "Yea, dat a good thang, Sha'mlya," she said wondering what she could make for the baby. "We's don't kno' if it a boy or girl. So what is we gonna make?"

"I don't kno'. We can all think of sup'in they can take back home. It gotta fit in their suitcases, though."

The family was approached with the idea later that day and all agreed that it was a good one. They figured that they could make something as a family; even let Makita help so that she would not be suspicious. The boys wanted to make some carvings out of wood like little statutes while Momma, Sha'myla and Jayla could do something girly.

Celebration was in the air! The whole family had done something for the baby and now it was time to share it with Makita and Ja'cin. Momma had cooked one of her scrumptious suppers under the guise that she wanted to treat them royally while they were home. They were none the wiser.

Ja'cin and Makita had been away from the house for the day and was now returning. Jumba spotted them coming from a distance and yelled to everyone that they were on the way. When they entered the house, everyone was sitting around as usual.

Ja'cin says, "Momma, it sure smells good in here."

"Yea baby. I's cookin' sup'in good fo' ya 'en my baby. Y'all be leavin' soon 'en I's wan' ya 'memba bein' back hom'." A sadness overtook Momma but she regained her composure. "It be time eat soon."

Momma nodded to the rest of the family and they scattered; each going somewhere in the other room or outside.

Makita wanted to know, "Where y'all going?"

"Nowhere," Jayla told her. "We just playing a new game we made up. We be right back."

That answer seemed to satisfy Makita so she and Ja'cin remained seated in each other's embrace.

Momma dropped a big pot on the floor that made a loud noise and everyone came running to see if she was all right. When they all got in the kitchen, everybody was carrying something. Ja'cin and Makita paid no attention to the others because they were so concerned about Momma's safety.

"Momma, you all right?" Ja'cin asked in a serious voice of concern.

"I's fine. I jis' drop dis on da flo'," she said with fun in her tone.

Then the entire family displayed what they had made for Ja'cin, Makita and the baby while yelling, "We love y'all."

The females of the house had made a blanket for the baby, a shawl for Makita and had given her some of their personal things to remember them by. The men had made carvings: one little bird that was named 'our baby'; there was a carving that looked like Poppa; some blocks and a little house that looked like the family house.

Sha'myla started the festivities by announcing, "We wanna do something for y'all and the baby. You won't be here when the baby is born so we wanted to be with you." She starts to cry. "Take these and our love with you so y'all know how much we all love y'all. We gonna miss y'all, too."

The whole household is now in tears embracing one another. Each has expressed their sentiments and given a gift; it was a another moment never to be forgotten.

Momma calls, "Let's eat," and everyone rushes toward her. Poppa asks Abunda to say the prayer this time.

He prays, "Dear God and the ancestors, it looks like our better life is happening now. Poppa always said that they said you had something better for us somewhere else. God thank you for what you have done for us. Thank you for our family. Thank you for keeping us safe and together. Thank you for our ancestors who is with you now and is looking down on us. And thank you for Poppa who taught us this prayer. Amen."

Poppa was surprised and honored that Abunda remembered the words to his prayer. They embraced each other after the prayer with mutual respect. Ja'cin thanked the family. Makita was too emotional to utter a word. The feast was on!!! A great time was had by all and nobody really got any sleep, again.

The next day Momma returns from the Rouses' and informs Abunda that Mr. Rouse would like to see him in the morning. This time she does not inquire as to why.

When Abunda returned to the Rouse's, Mrs. Rouse was hosting her annual mother and daughter tea. Alyon was away at school, but Mrs. Rouse continued the event. While being escorted to meet with Mr. Rouse, he sees Serenity with an older woman who he assumes is her mother. She was so beautiful wearing a soft blue dress with lace at the bodice and around the bottom. Her wide light blue bonnet with a spray of artificial flowers around the front was a perfect match to her dress. These chance meetings were getting to be more than he could contain. He has experienced every emotion possible in a confined place and has had to restrain himself. Abunda follows the servant to the parlor quietly so as not to disturb the gathering.

A small knock on the door provided him entrance to the room.

"Hello, do come in," Jet Rouse expressed with warmth. "How are you and the family?"

"Everyone is fine, sir. Thanks for inquiring," Abunda responded.

"Well, let's get down to business. We have much to talk over."

Hais Bishop's absence was obviously noted by Abunda and he wondered if something may be wrong. "Is Mr. Bishop joining us today?" He inquired of Mr. Rouse.

"No he isn't. I feel that this portion of our business needs to be discussed between you and me. I want to make sure that there is no indication of collusion between Hais and me. My job and my wish are to make sure that you and your family gets the best deal possible. Hais agrees."

"I understand and appreciate that, Mr. Rouse."

"Abunda, you and your family are soon to be very wealthy people. The plantation is 250 acres and very little has been damaged. It was literally abandoned when the war was getting too close and for whatever reason no one returned. I've had the deed put in Hais' name and he has signed a document saying that the deed was originally yours and that he is acting in your stead. This is to protect you if something were to go wrong. At first he was going to buy the property but I have learned that some investors want to pay

more than Hais was willing. The property is valued at one
million dollars."

Abunda loses his balance and tilts in his chair.

"Are you okay?" Mr. Rouse asked with great concern.

"I am, but I never imagined anything like this!"

After gathering himself, Jet Rouse inquired, "May I
continue?"

"Of course," Abunda responded with anticipation that he
had never felt in his life.

"This is the document that Hais has signed to protect
your family. Before the sale if anything happens to either
of us make sure this is in a safe place and maybe in a few
more years you can redeem it. I'm sure that nothing is going
to happen to either of us in the next few days; that's when
the sale will take place. The investors in Annapolis Grove
want to close the deal quickly. They have plans to develop
the land. The moneys that will come out of the deal are for
back taxes, re-recording the deed and a few other small legal
matters. It is my pleasure to do this for your family with
no charge. So, there should be at least $900,000 left. Any
questions?"

The ability to think and reason had distanced itself from
Abunda just now. This recurring phrase kept going through
his mind, "A better life, a better life." The ancestors were
right. Again Mr. Rouse had to request Abunda's response.

"Please, please forgive me. I don't know what to say. Oh,
thank you Mr. Rouse. Thank you. On behalf of my family I
can't thank you enough. Thank you."

"As I said, the sale will be final in a few days. We need
to think of how to handle the money. We cannot put it in the
bank in your name, here. It will raise all kinds of suspicions.
What about Marantha?"

"I am well respected there, but still how does a Colored
person explain having that much money. I didn't tell you this
but I was attacked on the property where I live. Someone

or some people don't want me to expand the work with my people. We couldn't find who did it but Rev. Hope reported it to the authorities. So, I don't think that Marantha will be a good idea, either."

In his first solemn mood during the entire exchange, Jet Rouse says, "What good is money if you can't use it? How will you have a better life then?"

Abunda assured him that God and the ancestors already had the answer because they had made the money available to his family. "We will know what to do, Mr. Rouse. Don't be upset. It will all workout."

"Thank you for your courage, but we need a place to put the money right after the sale."

"I have an idea. Mr. Hais has promised to finance my work at home and around. I've been receiving from him, in small increments, for a while. We have just begun our Colored Convention that includes people from everywhere; in and outside of the state. We will need more money to operate our Convention. I have not informed Mr. Hais of the expansion as it just took place shortly before I left home. Those that I left in charge are setting things in place and when I return we will begin a great work. Perhaps Mr. Hais can funnel our money through the Colored Convention by directing some to me and others to the Convention. I can also ask Rev. Hope, with whom I will share some of our good fortune, if he can deposit some in his church or personal account. He is an upstanding citizen and has been there for many many years."

"Abunda, I believe that God and the ancestors are both talking to you now. Those are great ideas. I'm glad you have people that you can trust. This is a lot of money we're talking about here. I don't personally know of any Colored family that has that kind of wealth in this day and time. I will discuss this with Hais and all plans will be finalized in the next few days. You can tell your family now because I'm sure you all have some plans to make. I will let Momma Basket tell Mrs. Rouse that she will be leaving. We're all going to miss her something terrible. We will help you all to get away safely. Perhaps my family could make a trip to Marantha and you all could accompany us as our help and that way no one would question you? We could journey on to visit with Hais for a while. I need a trip. I've been doing nothing but work and I'm sure that Mrs. Rouse and Josh would love the idea. Storm and Alyon are away at school and we could return before they come home. Sounds good to me."

"Mr. Rouse I don't know how to thank you enough. If there is ever anything that we can do for you, please tell me. Please."

The gentlemen ended the meeting and Abunda leaves to tell the family of their upcoming 'better life'.

The tea party is still in progress but Serenity's mind is miles away. Her thoughts are focused on her son who is close by, in the very house she's in, and the love of her life happens to be in the same city. Her husband told her that he met Abunda at the Rouses and that he was in town visiting his family. Serenity's only desire was to meet Abunda so that they could plan to meet their son, together. How? How could this possibly happen, she wondered. She decided that she would ask Mrs. Rouse to have Hais, Abunda and herself over for a personal gathering. Mrs. Rouse had just recently learned about the friendship between Abunda and Hais, so Serenity, surmised that they could all meet and hear of Abunda's accomplishments.

During the tea, Serenity, slips next to Mrs. Rouse. She does not want her mother to be aware of her plans or she will want to be included. "Mrs. Rouse, may I have a word with you in private for a minute?" Serenity requested.

"Yes, dear," Mrs. Rouse graciously responded. The guests were so busy enjoying one another's company that they never missed her departure from the room.

Serenity followed her to another small parlor nicely furnished with oak wood reading chairs and oak wood bookcases. The room possessed a peace that was striking upon entering. Mrs. Rouse starts the dialogue "What is it, Serenity? Are you enjoying the tea and your visit home?"

"I certainly am and thanks again for inviting me and Mother. I know that I was not a frequent visitor while growing up in Annapolis Grove, but my mother has spoken very highly of you over the years. I would like to ask a favor of you."

"Yes, how can I help?" Mrs. Rouse inquired.

"Would it be presumptuous of me to ask if you would arrange a small gathering for me, my husband, you, Mr. Rouse and Abunda Basket?" Serenity requested. "My husband has been impressed with Abunda Basket since meeting him at the Faith Convention but they have not had much time together. He wants to support Abunda's endeavors and I believe that you and Mr. Rouse would enjoy hearing about his accomplishments since he left Annapolis Grove. I was thoroughly impressed with Abunda's presentation at the Faith Convention and would welcome the opportunity to hear more of his plans. I hope you don't think this is too forward of me. I can't invite him to our home here, because of my family's attitude toward Colored people. Would you give this some consideration, please?"

"Well Serenity, I think this gesture is so thoughtful of you," Mrs. Rouse agreed. "I will be glad to but let me check with Mr. Rouse first. I will let you know after conferring with him. As a matter of fact let me try and do it before you leave today while he is still meeting with your husband. I would love to hear more about Abunda's accomplishments. Let me see if I can interrupt their meeting for just a minute and ask him about this. I'll be right back. I don't want to be away from my guests for too long."

Serenity's insides were bubbling with joy at the possibility of being in Abunda's company. She was more determined than ever to make sure that they would meet their son together. Now daydreaming about what could be, she allowed her mind to float to an intimate encounter with Abunda. Dreaming that she was married to him and sharing their love together, was in the front of her mind. Her thoughts were diverted by Mrs. Rouse's re-entrance to the parlor.

"Serenity, I have great news. Both my husband and your husband thinks it's a great idea. We will be meeting here in a few days. I will tell Momma Basket to let Abunda know about our plans. I hope that he will be able to join us."

"He will," Serenity assured herself mentally as the ladies returned to join the others.

Once again Momma Basket informed Abunda that he was wanted at the Rouse's place. Again, she asked no questions. Abunda assumed that it was about the property and never bothered to question the request. By the next meeting, the Baskets would have what they needed to 'have a better life'.

It was now evening at the Baskets and everyone was at home. They were waiting, as usual, for Momma's delicious food and did not care what it was. She was such a great cook, everything she made was good.

The family gathered around for prayer and supper. Because of working for the Rouses', Momma was always given food to take home. Sometimes she would take home the leftovers from parties that included all kinds of delicacies; things the Baskets would never have eaten on their own.

Supper was over and Abunda spoke up, "Everybody come here, I have something important to tell you."

In surprise everyone obeyed and found a place in the room. Bela drifted to the back but Abunda demanded that he be in the midst with the family. He came closer and sat quietly.

"The ancestors have been true to us. Poppa always told us that they said there was 'a better life' for us somewhere and there is. I am going to tell you something very special and you cannot tell anyone, I mean anyone. As a matter of fact, I want the youngest children to go into another room and find something to do. We will call you when we're finished."

They complained, "Oh, please Abunda we won't tell. Please let us stay."

"I will tell you soon enough but just do this for me now, okay?" He requested. They immediately left the room.

"Back to where I was. Momma, you remember the piece of paper you gave to Makita? Well, she gave it to me while we were back in Marantha. I took it to Mr. Jet and asked him to check it out for me. He did. It was a deed to an estate over 250 acres that was to be auctioned off, until Mr. Jet showed the deed. The deed is real. We now own the deed and the land. Mr. Jet is going to sell the land for us and we will get $900,000."

Poppa fell to the floor gasping for breath.

Momma yelled and cried, "Thank ya God!"

Poppa had not moved and the others were so busy trying to understand the news that they paid no attention to his inactivity. Poppa finally let out a huge sigh that got everybody's attention except Momma who was still crying. The other boys ran to Poppa's side to make sure that he was all right.

Jumba lifted Poppa's head in his hands and said, "Poppa you all right? Poppa talk to me. Poppa. Poppa."

In a vulnerable tone, Poppa speaks, "I's okay. I's dreamin' 'cause Abunda sade we's got lots a money."

Abunda answers, "No Poppa you're not dreaming. Our 'better life' is here. We're all leaving Annapolis Grove together."

All members of the family had gone into their own worlds, no one speaking to the other. Each was now dreaming of what this 'better life' would be for them. Thoughts of school, marriage, a new home, different friends, living in freedom, bombarded each mind. Makita wondered about Ja'cin expanding his business and about having more children, now. Sha'myla knew that she was about to be the woman that she had always wanted to be. She would meet good people and do the things she had seen in magazines. The sky, now, was the limit for her.

Momma finally speaks, "How, Abunda? How's we gonna....?"

Before she finished he assured her, "Momma, everything is worked out. Trust me. But we need to decide what to take and what to leave. We'll have enough money to buy anything so we don't have to take any old stuff from here. Everybody get your special stuff so we can start packing."

"Were we's goin' Abunda?" Poppa demanded. "How's we gittin' d'ere? We's could be kil't."

"No Poppa. The ancestors wouldn't give us the money and then not make a way for us to enjoy it. I'm working everything out. You just trust me and make sure the family gets packed. We may be leaving in a few days."

"A few days," Momma yelped. "What da Rouses gonna do?"

"They're going to help us get away from here, Momma," Abunda replied sternly insisting that the family understood his instructions.

Abunda took Makita, Sha'myla, Bela and Ja'cin aside to talk with them privately. "I need your help so that we can move quickly. As I said, everything is in place except for our traveling arrangements. I realize the danger we might face so I have to make a good plan. A large group of Coloreds together is going to bring attention to us if there are no Whites. I will talk with Mr. Jet about this but I need you all to get the family together so when I say we're leaving everything will be ready. Any questions?"

Sha'myla questioned, "Are ya sure 'bout this Abunda? I want to leave here, but I'm scared su'pin'll happen to us. I've never been away from Annapolis Grove."

Makita answered instead, "We'll be okay Sha. Me and Ja'cin didn't have no trouble 'cause we acted like servants to White people. Nobody bothered us. Abunda will figure it out. Y'all don't know this Abunda like we do. He's a great man."

Ja'cin added, "She's right Sha'myla. Your brother is a pastor now and many many people count on him. So I know that he will make sure that our family is safe."

Bela's reaction was, "Oh, my God Abunda. Ya ancestors is real and did make a 'betta life' fo' your family. I hope you ain't gonna leave us now?"

"No Bela, and you are my family, too. This is for you just like it's for us," he assured his old friend, who was now his brother.

Immediately, the family started to make decisions as to what would go and what would stay. They forgot about the young children who finally surfaced and wanted to know what was going on. One of the older brothers told them, "We's leaving Annapolis Grove with Abunda and going to 'a better life'.

The children ran straight to Momma to get confirmation of what they were just told. Momma confirmed it and instructed them to get their special things together for packing.

The day had actually arrived when the Baskets would be leaving Annapolis Grove for the 'better life' that was promised to them by the ancestors. Anticipation, anxiety, enthusiasm, hopes and fears infiltrated the atmosphere of the house. Over each head was a different symbol that quietly but powerfully announced their internal thoughts. A dark cloud with a bright cloud beginning to eclipse, was looming over Poppa's head. The dark cloud of yesterday, years of bondage that adversely affected his mental stability from time to time, was about to disappear by the on coming bright cloud. Times when Poppa did not know whether his family would stay together. Times when Poppa was so afraid, but as the man he could not tell any one. Times when Poppa wanted to runaway by himself to escape his dreadful life. Times when he wanted to destroy himself and the family to relieve them of the life of Colored people. Now, times will be different and freedom of the mind and body will actually be a reality. Can this be so?

A family portrait with Momma and Poppa centered around the children whimsically dangled over Momma's head. It danced like a little girl learning a pirouette for a ballet class. Each time the young dancer would position herself, she would falter slightly and have to start again. So was Momma's picture! When her camera was about to take the picture, one of the children would move. Abunda ran away. Makita got married. Poppa was nervous. Sha'myla was anxious to leave. Would this picture ever come together, Momma always wondered? Now she will have the picture of a lifetime because tomorrow will erase all the yester-days. This picture will be a still life permanently recorded in time.

Of all the children, Sha'myla was the most affected. Abunda had his taste of freedom. Makita had her dream: a husband and a child on the way. But Sha'myla, the most progressive in the family had no way to actualize and though she dreamed of today, her environment made the possible impossible. She had more than one symbol, hanging over her head but they were all in the same genre: English punc-tuations. They were question marks, exclamation marks, periods, commas, and colons; each representing the over-whelming possibilities now racing through her mind. The question marks represented uncertainty: is this too good to be true? The exclamation marks throw her into a windfall of possibilities: schooling, career, marriage, etc. The period, commas and colons housed the complex sentences that were forming in her mind. Run-on sentences fought to occupy space in the thought process, but because Sha'myla's nature and temperament was one of a perfectionist, she utilized the necessary punctuations to make her internal thoughts reflect her external habits. Her conclusion was: we will see!

With everyone busy getting their things together to leave; Abunda was to make yet another trip to the Rouse's. He was sure that this would be his last before taking his family to freedom. He quietly left home and went to the Rouse's his mind traveling faster than his footsteps.

"When will we really leave this place?" he wondered. "A place that can not be relegated to home because of its disdain for human life. A place where animals were treated better than a Colored person. A place that denied and stripped dignity and hopes from the hearts of God's people? A place of frustration. A place that birthed bitterness in innocent people: Colored people. A place that destroyed the most precious thing on earth, the family as a whole."

Soon he was knocking yet again on the Rouse's back door and he was glad because his thoughts were becoming traumatic. Composing himself before entering was an absolute necessity, due to the rage that wanted to stand in place of his peace.

Mrs. Rouse greeted him, "Abunda, please come in. You could have used the front door. The others are waiting."

Abunda had no response as he was stilling the rage within. He quietly followed Mrs. Rouse. Arriving in the parlor and expecting to meet with Mr. Rouse and possibly Hais Bishop, he was stunned to see Serenity among the others.

"Why hello, Abunda," Serenity spoke without hesitation. "It is wonderful to see you again. My husband told me that you were here and I am glad that we could spend sometime together before we return home."

"Abunda, as always it's my pleasure," joined Hais Bishop. "Serenity suggested this meeting and I'm glad she did. We want to hear about your work. Are there any new developments? Forgive me, my wife and I have taken complete charge of the evening."

Jet Rouse interjected, "No need for forgiveness, please continue. I didn't have the pleasure of knowing Abunda when he was here but I'm certainly glad for this opportunity now. Abunda would you like something to drink? Let's be seated and get comfortable. I feel like this will be a great encounter. We will be having dinner shortly."

Abunda was indeed the center of attention, again. Question after question was poised to him by everyone present. The difficulty of the situation, Serenity being present, did not hamper his ability to field and answer the questions succinctly, intelligently and in some cases boastfully. Hais Bishop was delighted to learn of the new Colored Convention that Abunda had recently formed. Again, he pledged his support for the cause. The Rouses' were astonished to learn of Abunda's accomplishments and though they respected Momma Basket, they gave no credence to the possibility of any of her family members being more than she was: a servant, their polite word for....

Because Serenity had personally asked Mrs. Rouse to host this gathering, Mrs. Rouse wanted to prepare the meal herself. She loved to cook and saw serving as an act of respect to the person served. Momma Basket did assist her, but was not required to return to serve the guests.

"Shall we move to the dining room?" Mrs. Rouse asked rhetorically.

Everyone followed Mr. and Mrs. Rouse to the dining room. There was no particular seating arrangement because of the intimacy of the group so Serenity insisted that Abunda sit next to her. "Abunda would you do me the honor of sitting next to me? Mr. Bishop won't mind, I'm always with him," she requested while chuckling and winking at her husband.

"Please do so," Hais Bishop encouraged. "And if it's all right with Jet, I'll sit next to Mrs. Rouse."

"That's fine," Jet Rouse agreed. "It won't be so awkward for me now sitting at the head and not being next to my wife."

The table was beautifully adorned with complete settings of Blue and White Wedgwood China, crystal stem wine and water glasses, a handmade linen table cloth with a pattern of intricate diamond shapes outlined in a blue that matched the china, the silverware was polished to a glitter, and the center piece was a spread of fresh cut red, yellow and pink roses surrounded by small twigs of baby's breathe.

Abunda had yet to respond to Serenity's request but rather stood speechless, lost in time, once again. Wondering exactly what was occurring, he was waiting to be sure that this moment was real. In the company of the woman he has loved for so long, in the very house where his son lives, and being accepted and respected as a Colored among affluent Whites was mind-boggling to him. He had to reassure himself that this was not a dream, so he waited for the request to happen a second time.

This time Mr. Rouse spoke up, "Abunda, please be seated next to Mrs. Bishop."

Nervously he compiled, like a gentleman, by pulling the chair out for Serenity to be seated and then took his seat. His hand brushed lightly, but mistakenly, against Serenity's hand causing her to take a deep breath.

Mrs. Rouse had prepared a wonderful meal of roasted lamb with mint jelly, baked chicken with rosemary and basil, roasted red potatoes with butter sprinkled with parsley, spinach and a fresh salad of, romaine lettuce, cherry tomatoes, green onions, mushrooms, and orange bits with a light balsamic dressing. The deserts were homemade ladyfingers and apple pie that could be had a la mode if desired.

Once everyone was seated Mr. Rouse blessed the food and there was no noticeable shyness as all partook generously of the delicious meal. The conversation around the table was as rich as the meal until it was interrupted.

"Excuse me, please. Mother may I...," her son proceeded to speak but Mrs. Rouse halted his words by introducing him to their guests.

"Joshua, this is Mr. and Mrs. Hais Bishop and Abunda Basket. I'm sorry, Pastor Abunda Basket. Everyone this is our son Joshua."

Under the table Serenity had rested her foot against Abunda's leg signifying unity as they met their son together for the first time. She had no knowledge that he had already met Joshua. This moment was another freeze point for Abunda, but instead he responded in a timely manner by moving his leg in acknowledgment to Serenity's gesture. Not wanting to be obvious, he tried to look at Serenity and as he did he saw a small teardrop well in her eye.

"Hello," Joshua bided to everyone. "It's nice to meet you. Pastor Abunda you were here a few days ago, weren't you?"

"Yes, I had some business to conduct with your father. I'm glad you remember me."

Serenity, now dabbing her eyes gently, remarked, "My you're a handsome young man. I was thinking about what it will be like when Mr. Bishop and I have our children and I got a little teary eyed."

"If I were next to you I would grab your hand," Hais Bishop informed his wife. "But since I'm not, Abunda would you do me the honor."

Abunda could not believe his ears, but he gladly obliged and held Serenity's hand for a precious moment. She unbelievingly responded to his tender touch. It was as if God had prepared and sanctioned this moment for them.

Joshua finished his request to his mother and left the room. The others completed their dinner, but the remaining time was quite awkward for Abunda because he knew that he and Serenity had to see each other, but how? Now he was not so sure that he could honor their agreement of not having an affair if the opportunity presented itself like before. Touching Serenity had awakened something that was dead to him, something that he refused to acknowledge: his longing for love and Serenity.

Jet Rouse's invitation for the men to follow him to his study brought reality to Abunda's thoughts. "Abunda and Hais, let's go to my study. I have something that I need to discuss with you all; it won't take long."

The men followed as requested and Jet Rouse informed them of his plans to take a trip to the Bishop's in order to aid the Baskets safe passage from Annapolis Grove. He continued by saying, "Abunda, Hais lives in a progressive area where Coloreds have rights and their safety is not threatened. This is why I thought of us taking this trip so that your family can travel as our servants and no one will question why such a large contingent of Colored people are traveling alone. I will try to get good accommodations for you all; the best I can. My concern is that you reach your destination safe so that you can enjoy as you say, 'a better life'. Do you have an idea where you want to go?"

"Yes," Abunda answered. "When I ran away I wanted to go to a place called Settles Landing. They say it's like what you are talking about with progressive Colored people living like White people. I want to take my family there. Have you heard of this place? Do you know anything about it?"

Hais Bishop replied, "I've heard of it, Abunda. Its a little distance but not too far from our home. I think Jet has a great idea, and I too am concerned about you and your family's safety. If we all travel together, it won't look suspicious having such a large group for two families. Jet, will the Mrs. and Joshua be coming with you?"

"By all means," Jet said jovially. "They will be glad to get away. I've been working long hours for quite a while. They'll just love it."

"I don't know what to say," Abunda added. "Rev. Hope always tells me that God has people here to help you regardless of whether you're Colored or White. He says that God loves us all. And once again it looks like God certainly has some White people looking out for me."

As the evening was drawing to a close, Serenity thanked Mrs. Rouse for being such a gracious hostess as she and Hais were leaving. It had been a perfect evening; Serenity was with the three men she loved most: her husband, the father of her child, and her son. But she was not satisfied because she also wanted to spend some time with Abunda alone, but how?

Abunda also thanked the Rouses and departed for home. Walking through the manicured and sculptured grounds, thinking what was next, he realized that so much had taken place in such a short span of time. His focus had to be on getting his family to Settles Landing.

The family had all done as instructed; gathered those few things that were very precious to them each. They did not have much to choose from because life in Annapolis Grove was utilitarian for them. But over the years a few things had become meaningful to each of them. Jayla and Junna took the coverings from their beds that were made by their sisters. Jumba, Junta and Jassafa, the older boys, took their rock collection. Sha'myla had much difficulty deciding what to take. She had amassed some things that were very special and that she wanted to keep for her very special day. She had a collection of magazines that she got from her job. They became her imaginary world. She had made some pieces of clothing that were to be placed in her hope chest. Her books were the most special of all and they were many. While cleaning, both at her job and the Rouses' when helping Momma, she would gather all the books that were being discarded. After much consideration and pain, Sha'myla made her choices. She would take some of everything. Momma had an old Bible that her grandmother gave her and she was determined that where she went it would go also. Some of the small art pieces that Mrs. Rouse gave her through the years would accompany her to their new home. Poppa got what was special to him, 'a better life'. He was too anxious to think of what to take so he left everything. He wished to take his secret place but knew that was impossible. But the memories from this place would forever be with him wherever he went.

Poppa gathered the family for one last time in Annapolis Grove. Despite the excitement of going to 'a better life' there was sadness in the air. The Basket family had been through so much and had fought to keep themselves together. Momma and Poppa were determined to let their children know that life had much more to offer than what they were experiencing. They had no idea of how 'a better life' would come about but they knew that they as the leaders must keep the possibility alive in their children. Poppa's resurgence of strength through his ancestors gave him the fortitude to continue regardless of the circumstances. He now had someone to encourage him and make him accountable.

The entire family was now gathered in the house and Poppa spoke from his heart. "I almost ain't b'leve dis day was com'. I kno' da ancestors sade it would but…." He starts to choke with emotions. "It b'en hard fo' us y'ere. We's got sick. Abunda run 'way. Momma heart break. We's work hard in da fields. B'en treat lik' animals. Da old family token 'way. But we don' mad' it. We's gonna say da las' pray'r

315

in dis place. 'En den we's gonna thank God fo' where we's goin'."

A silence covered the house that lingered for a while. No one said anything. Heaviness attempted to invade the silence, but a joy was dancing so rhythmatically that it over-shadowed the heaviness.

"God thank ya fo' what ya don' fo' us. Thank ya fo' dis family. Thank ya fo' keepin' us 'en our chil'len safe 'en to'gatha. Thank ya fo' our ancestors who is wit' ya now. I pray dat dey he'p us liv' a betta lif' den dey had. God thank ya fo' where ya's takin' us. Thank ya fo' our new hom'. Thank ya fo' da peoples dat don' he'p us go d'ere. Amen." When Poppa finished praying, the family had a group hug and then individually hugged each other. Most of them were crying. With their special possessions in hand they were ready to make the journey to Settles Landing.

As Jet Rouse had supposed, the trip from Annapolis Grove was peaceful and safe for all. The entire trip was a blessing especially to Serenity who had the opportunity to spend time with her son as they traveled. Carefully surveying his facial features, she noticed how much he looked like his father, Abunda. His skin color was not as White as others but contained a slight pigmentation making him look permanently tan. This was a concern to Serenity because she wondered if anyone else had noticed this distinction. Nevertheless, they talked about his life growing up with the Rouses and what he wanted to do in the future. Joshua said that he wanted to become a lawyer like his father. Serenity sighed within. She was glad that Joshua had such a good father in Jet Rouse who was a loving and caring man. Would the day ever come when she could tell him the truth about his special father?

Jet had arranged for some pretty good accommodations for the Baskets since he was able to pay the cost associated with upgraded quarters for Colored servants. The property had been sold and three accounts were established with the

Rouses, the Hopes and of course, the Bishops. This way neither of these families would have to justify having such a large amount of money.

The Basket family was in awe as they traveled far from the only place they ever knew to be home. Each face beamed as they passed a new town or saw many things that were different to them. Abunda had planned to stop at Marantha and tell the Hopes of their good fortune and introduce his family. It would also be the perfect opportunity for Jet Rouse to take care of some financial matters. He was to make a deposit into the Hopes' account and open another account for the Colored Convention with Rev. Hope as the overseer. He also thought that Bela might want to remain there as he continued traveling to Settles Landing with his family. Ja'cin and Makita would travel a little further with the group to go home to Crusidea which was on the way. Makita wanted desperately to travel on with her family but Ja'cin needed to check on his business affairs.

Jet Rouse had done as Abunda requested. He opened the account by explaining to the banker that the money was for the new church program but the banker informed him that Rev. Hope needed to come and sign some papers. Jet also made arrangements for a deposit into the Hopes' personal account, but it too was pending the Hopes' approval.

Mr. Rouse was dutifully handling business but also managed to make arrangements for everyone's stay in Marantha for a short time before continuing their travels. When they arrived in Marantha, everyone got settled then Abunda and Bela went to the Hopes.

Chapter 13

Betrayal

Clark Hope saw them coming from a distance and began running to meet them yelling their names, "Abunda, Bela you're home. I'm so glad to see you. I missed you and was afraid you wouldn't come back."

Clark was much too big for them to grab up off the ground like they had done so many times before, but they all did a group hug. When they separated they hugged Clark individually to further show their care for one another.

"Mother and Father will be so glad to see you. We've been talking about you every since you left," Clark informed them both. "Let's go to the house now." The three moved swiftly to the main house to see the Hopes. Both Abunda and Bela had also missed them tremendously and were very eager to see them.

"Mother, Father, look whose here, come quick," Clark yelled with such excitement and enthusiasm. "Come quick!"

The Hopes were concerned about Clark's yelling and what would cause this kind of reaction from him, so they hurriedly rushed to find out. From a short distance, they saw Clark with two men coming quickly toward them and suddenly they realized that it was Abunda and Bela. They too started running toward them.

The homecoming was a picturesque moment! It could not have been more real than what happened at Annapolis Grove when Abunda returned to his family but it was high in the rankings. Mrs. Hope was crying. Rev. Hope was containing his emotions. Bela cried at receiving such love and now he knew that this was truly his home.

"Welcome home. It is good to see you both. I thank God that you're safe. We've been praying for you every since you left," Rev. Hope told them.

Mrs. Hope added, "I am so glad to have you back home. We've missed you terribly. I was afraid that you might not come back but I would have understood."

Rev. Hope asked, "How is your family? All is well with them I hope?"

Abunda could not wait to tell them the good news, but first he wanted to go to the farmhouse with Bela to see the others. He wanted them to know that he was back so he and Bela visited with the others first who were also glad that they had returned.

Abunda was about to leave for the main house when he asked Bela, "Do you want to go back to the main house with me to talk to the Hopes?"

"No. I want to stay here with my brothers. You go and tell your good news," Bela answered.

Abunda went to the main house and told the Hopes what had happened in Annapolis Grove. They were informed that a deposit had been made into their personal account and that a new bank account was opened for the Colored Convention with Rev. Hope as the manager of the funds. This account would have a portion of the money for the Colored Convention and the other belonged to the Basket family. Abunda told Rev. Hope that he needed to go to the bank and sign the papers. They could not express enough their happiness for Abunda, his family and his generosity. Now, however, they were really concerned as to whether or not he would leave them.

"Does this mean that you'll be leaving us for good, Abunda?" Rev. Hope needed to know.

"I need to make sure that my family is properly settled. I ran away from them before but I will not leave them like that again," was Abunda's reply to Rev. Hope's question. "I know that you and I have so much to discuss about my work and the Convention. I have not forgotten what I started."

"Take your time and do whatever you need to, as always we will support you," Rev. Hope assured Abunda.

"Rev. and Mrs. Hope, I want you to meet my family, if that's all right with you? You have been my family for so long and I want my two families to know each other. They are staying in Marantha for a short while but will be traveling on soon."

Mrs. Hope was beaming with excitement and responded, "Oh, but of course Abunda, we would love to meet your family."

Clark wanted to know, "Can I meet them too?"

"Of course," was Abunda's reply to him.

Rev. Hope agreed with the rest of his family.

"Will they come here, Abunda? Shall I prepare supper?" Mrs. Hope asked anxiously.

"If it's not too much trouble, Mrs. Hope, I would really appreciate it. We are traveling with the Rouses and the Bishops and I would like for them to join us as well."

"Hais Bishop?" Rev Hope exclaimed.

"Yes, Rev. Hope, Hais Bishop," Abunda retorted. "Mrs. Hope there will be 17 people all together and here we would have privacy; no one will question the Coloreds having supper with the Whites."

Mrs. Hope, like Mrs. Rouse had done before, got busy making preparations for the gathering. She wanted everything to be perfect for her guests. Meeting Abunda's family would be like meeting an extension of her own family, she thought, regardless of their skin color.

Arrangements were made with the caterer, who would bring the food but not stay to serve it. Everything would be buffet style so that the evening would be as stress free as possible. There would be no worry for the group that non-understanding Whites would start a rumor about the Hopes entertaining Colored people in the same fashion of entertaining White people. Mrs. Hope wanted to host the best party she had done in years.

Abunda left the Hopes to their planning and went to be with his family and friends back in town. He took them to see his church and the building they used for the school. His family, the Rouses and the Bishops were in awe of his accomplishments. No one in the town gave notice to the Whites with him because they were used to him and his work. He informed his family and the others about the gathering to be held at the Hopes'. More excitement filled almost every space of the Baskets' air. Unbelief was now commonplace to them.

The Basket women received a special surprise when Serenity gave them all new dresses for the party that she had purchased. She had also talked her husband into purchasing suits for the Basket men. Serenity desired that Abunda's family look like prosperous people when they met the Hopes. She wanted Abunda to be proud of them as well.

The time had come for the gathering. Abunda hardly knew his family when he saw them so arrayed in their new clothing. He now had a great picture of what they would look like in their new homeland.

The entourage was being introduced to the Hopes and the farm hands that were also included in the festivities. "Rev. and Mrs. Hope, this is my mother and father who we call Momma and Poppa. These are my sisters and brothers; as you can see it's a lot of us." Abunda chuckled at the thought as he introduced his siblings.

"It is our pleasure to meet all of you. Abunda has been like a son to us and we are so proud of him as we're sure you are. He is a fine man," Rev. Hope informed the family.

"Hais Bishop, what a surprise," Rev. Hope continued as he interacted with his guests. "It is great to see you and Mrs. Bishop."

"This is my best friend, Jet Rouse and his wife. We've been friends since college and while my wife Serenity was visiting her family in Annapolis Grove, Abunda's home-town, I decided to visit my old friend that I'd not seen in a good while. I had no idea that Abunda was even there," Hais Bishop shared with the Hopes. "We are so glad that we can help him and his family get settled in a new place."

All the introductions were completed and everyone was milling around the grounds when Mrs. Hope announced that it was time to eat. The Basket children had not seen anything like this since Makita's wedding. They were very excited.

Fried fish, grits, pork chops, rice, green beans, macaroni and cheese, flatbread, okra, kale, white potato pies, and ice tea. Mrs. Hope had everything outside in the garden. Rev. Hope asked Abunda to bless the occasion and the food.

"God thank you for what you have done for us. Thank you for my family. Thank you for keeping us safe and together. Thank you for our ancestors who are with you now and looking down on us. I pray that we get to the place where we are going. Poppa always said that they said you had some-thing better for us somewhere else. Thank you for the people you sent to help us: the Hopes, the Rouses, the Bishops, and the farm hands here. I pray that you bless them and the food that has been prepared for us. Amen."

A tear formed in the corner of Poppa's eyes as he recog-nized his prayer. Abunda looked in his direction when he finished the prayer to let Poppa know that he was not ashamed of their prayer and that it was a permanent part of him.

The food was now the center of attention as everyone was busy heaping their plates with all kinds of goodies. Freedom was in the air as the Baskets went about celebrating and receiving the kindnesses that were bestowed upon them. Some of the Basket boys were about the same age as Joshua and Clark, so they all enjoyed one another's company.

The wonderful affair was drawing to a close and a somber atmosphere swept over the garden. Soon it would be time to depart this fantasy to enter reality, again. Whites were used to these events, it was normal to them, but to Coloreds this was a dream. Yes, Coloreds celebrated, in their own way, but were not allowed to participate with the White people; let alone be treated with dignity. Surely the host of this affair and their kind could not imagine what was being assessed in the minds of their guests. Their reality was somebody else's fantasy.

The entourage was now back in town getting ready to depart early the next day. Before leaving, Abunda wanted to meet briefly with those he left in charge during his absence. Once his family was settled in their quarters, he made his way to the church. While approaching the church, he saw some people gathered outside and he was glad to see the activity. As he reached the steps, a stranger greeted him, "Hello 'en welcome to Place of Hope Church. Kin' I he'p you?"

Abunda decided not to identify himself, but responded instead, "Thank you for the welcome, I would like to see the person in charge. Is he here?"

"Yes, com' in. I git'em." The stranger showed him to a seat in the back and rushed off to get the person in charge.

From a room off to the right of the church, that Abunda knew was his office, a man appeared and headed for him. He did not recognize this person and was a little alarmed.

"Hello, can I help you?" the man replied, as he extended his hand to Abunda.

"Yes you can. Where is Pastor Titus?" Abunda inquired.

"He's not here no more. I'm in his place," the stranger advised.

Consternation consumed Abunda. "What does this mean?" he thought. "Had something happened to Pastor Titus while he was away?"

"Where is he?" he demanded to know. "What happened to him?"

"The Convention had a meeting and they put me in his place."

"Who did this and how? They cannot just get rid of people like that," he demanded while being livid about this news. His anger was visible now; however, it confused the stranger. He had never met Abunda and had no idea what was causing this negative behavior.

"I'm sorry but is there something I can do for you since Pastor Titus is no longer here?" the stranger asked attempting to comfort this stranger to him.

"Please forgive me. Can you tell me how you got here and where Pastor Titus is now?" asking in a more controlled tone.

"Pastor Titus is back at his church. People in the Colored Convention felt like he was more loyal to the founder not to the mission. They wanted to do some things differently and Pastor Titus didn't want to. Other people wanted to join the Convention, but Pastor Titus said we had to follow the rules and wait awhile."

"Who were the others and was Rev. Hope aware of this?" Abunda insisted.

The stranger, now thoroughly confused, paid notice to the fact that he did not know this man. His behavior was beginning to be very disturbing and frightening.

"Who are you?" the stranger sought to know politely.

Abunda could not wait to reply, "I am Pastor Abunda Basket, the founder of this Convention. I have been away on business and Pastor Titus was left to take care of things in my absence."

"Pastor Basket, it's good to meet you. I've heard wonderful things about you. Let's sit and talk a minute."

The stranger informed Abunda of some startling changes that were instituted in his absence. The new people thought that it would be good to implement them so they approached Rev. Hope and he agreed. There was a consensus among the group, but again, the stranger reiterated that Pastor Titus continued to disagree. To help resolve the issues, Pastor Titus asked Rev. Hope to meet with the group and explain the rules and regulations of the Convention. Rev. Hope did as he was asked, but the new members told him that they needed to slow down the scope of work rather than the aggressive plans that were instituted. Rev. Hope gave considerable thought to the recommendation and concluded that it was a great idea.

Abunda was speechless. His mind was racing, "How could Rev. Hope circumvent my authority? There must be an awfully good explanation for this. And why didn't Rev. Hope tell me of this important news when we were together? I must get some answers now."

"Thank you for your kindness," Abunda apologetically said to the stranger. "I must speak with Rev. Hope and others about this."

For the first time in their relationship, he felt betrayed by Rev. Hope. Knowing that there had to be a good explanation; he did not want to assume the worst. He always knew that Rev. Hope had his best interest at heart, but this was....

Abunda forgot about his plans to leave again to take his family to Settles Landing. How could he possibly leave now with this turn of events? Caught between the two most important things in his life, he needed to take the time to contemplate about this matter.

With all this on his mind, he decided to return to the Hopes and possibly talk to Rev. Hope before leaving Marantha. As he was walking away from the church, deeply entrenched in thought, he was unaware the he was being followed. He continued to head for home but decided to take a different route. Once he had cleared the town the person following increased their steps. Abunda now heard the steps and became alarmed. He then increased his steps. This did not stop the person following him. He quickly hid to allow the follower to pass him, but as the person went by he realized that it was Serenity. Seeing her made his current issues dissipate because he had quietly hoped for this moment.

"Serenity, I'm sorry. I was captured by my thoughts. Where are you going?"

She replied, "I was just out for some fresh air when I saw you leaving the church. I had to see you. I knew that tomorrow we would be traveling for a long time and I wanted to enjoy this stop before we left. I so enjoyed the gathering today and especially being with Joshua. Abunda, he is such a fine boy, just like his father. I was happy that we were together at the Rouses when he came in. I hoped that he would be there."

Serenity began to walk away but beckoned for him to follow her. He responded, but when they got out of sight he began to lead her to a safe place that he knew of where they could continue talking. Abunda had no idea that there was another shadow following them. When they stopped, the shadow stopped to watch and hear as they proceeded with their rendezvous. The two were so engrossed with one another that they had no idea they were being followed and watched.

"Abunda," she said softly and affectionately. "What are we going to do?" Just then she leaned over and kissed him gently. He responded to her kiss and amorously planted his kiss on her lips. This was the kiss that made up for the lifetime of their separation.

"Serenity, we decided not to do this because of your husband and my position. My heart has longed for you even more since I found you at the Faith Convention, but I've tried to put away what I know I can't have."

Reaching for her hand to hold, instead he took her into his arms and they stood in a passionate embrace for moments without speaking.

"Is it possible to love two people?" Serenity struggled to comprehend. "I love Hais but I never stopped loving you. I don't know how I'm going to do this, now seeing you. I will be seeing more of you but what will I do? Hais is a good man and a great husband."

"Had you thought about having children? Maybe that will help you to stay focused on your marriage. The Rouses have done a great job rearing Joshua and we wouldn't want to do anything to damage their relationship. Serenity, so much has happened and I need time to think about everything. Let me walk you back and I'll be going home. We'll be together tomorrow."

"What else could happen?" Abunda thought as he traveled home. Our 'better life' is ahead of us, yet today seems like devastation; first my church and then Serenity. What will they do when I leave to take my family to Settles Landing?"

Returning to the Hopes, he surveyed the avenues of his mind to gain some perspective on his present situation. Since being at Marantha, and the Hopes, he had dedicated his life to God, the ancestors and helping his people. He had denied himself of having his personal family, a wife and children, because the needs of others were so great. Thinking that his mission would be the sum total of his life and that perhaps one day it would reward him, now he begins to speculate again: "Why am I doing this at such a great cost." The situation at the Colored Convention left him stymied: how could they redirect what he had so painstakingly put in place? What regard had they for his sacrifice? He never asked anything for himself only the people, yet his first major action was undermined by those he assisted. They listening to strangers, instead of evaluating his faithfulness, was a painful thought that he honestly did not want to address just now. And, even more, the thought of Rev. Hope being in agreement with them was insufferable.

Because of the hour he reached home, he knew that he would not be able to speak with Rev. Hope. He did not want the meeting to be rushed. Realizing that there was a more than reasonable explanation for the occurrences at the Convention, he rested his mind and body and decided to approach Rev. Hope before leaving with his family.

It was the next morning and Abunda rose very early to meet with Rev. Hope. He knew that he was to be in town at a designated time to leave with his family and the others. Before he could get to the main house, he saw Rev. Hope coming out of the back door.

"Good morning, Abunda," he said. "I didn't expect to see you this early. I had planned to see you, your family and the others off in town. This is great. You and I can have some private time together."

"Good morning, Rev. Hope. I too am glad that you're up this early because there is an urgent matter that I must speak with you about before leaving. I went pass the church on yesterday and was informed that major changes had been made to the Convention rules during my absence. The person there told me that you agreed with the changes. I'm concerned about this."

"Abunda, they asked my opinion and after listening to their argument I thought it had some credence. I, too, thought that you had taken on a rather aggressive plan and was concerned as to how well it would be executed. But I in no way meant to undermine you."

Responding harshly, "I felt undermined. Why couldn't you wait until my return? I made sure that everything was working well before I left, at a pace that was comfort for Pastor Titus and the others to meet. Who are these strangers, anyway, that had so much power; power enough to get you to change your mind?"

"I was in a very precarious place," Rev. Hope responded in a low somber tone. "I was the lone White man in the midst of the Coloreds who were vehement about what was being presented. A part of me wanted to tell them to wait for you, and in fact I did, but they disagreed. Abunda, when we are in leadership, we must consider the good of the many over the want of the few. It was apparent that the newcomers had been canvassing some of the other members of the Convention and had gained their support."

"Have you spoken with Pastor Titus since all this happened? How is he?"

"No I have not and I am sorry to say that I don't know how he is. I've not been back to the Convention since the meeting, so I don't know if he is participating anymore. Is it too difficult for you to see what the others are saying, Abunda?"

"I have not heard them yet! But unlike them I have been committed and faithful for a long time; both to you and to preparing myself for this work. I do not think it is fair that my dedication was dismissed so easily, especially by you Rev. Hope. You alone should know what this means to me. I want the best for all of my people not just an eager few."

"I'm deeply grieved by this turn of events. I am sorry that you are so hurt," Rev. Hope shared with Abunda.

"I am sorry that you could not share the truth with me from the beginning. If you felt my plans were too aggressive why didn't you say so then? I value your wisdom, don't you know that? I do not mean to be ungrateful, I really do not. I do not know whether to address this matter or let it be. I, too, want what's best. I have been put in a very discomforting place. If I address the matter I will be perceived as a ruler not a leader and who will consider my original intents honorable?"

"Abunda, seek God for what you need. I'm sure, as in the past, He will let you know what to do," Rev. Hope advised.

In anger he answered, "Could not your God have stopped this from happening? I will never understand why your God continues to let bad things happen when He is supposed to be such a loving God. Now my people are beginning to act just like Him."

Rev. Hope hung his head and made no reply. He could see, now, how truly hurt Abunda was and that he had perhaps acted too hesitantly in agreeing with the others.

Walking away, feeling so dejected, Abunda did not bother to look back at Rev Hope. He was too afraid that he might say things that would hurt the only man that had helped him the most. Yet, he could not fathom why Rev. Hope had agreed with total strangers; over their relationship.

The others were all gathered waiting for Abunda to join them. The Baskets were still reeling from their dream of 'a better life' and their departure from Annapolis Grove. Each member of the family acted with the respect and the training of learned people who were no different from White people. They were treated extremely well by the Rouses and the Bishops during the entire trip. Uncertainty started to fill the minds of those waiting because Abunda was almost going to miss their departure.

Momma Basket spoke up, "Where Abunda? He gonna be left. Ain't he goin' wit' us?"

"He be here," Poppa Basket assured the waiting group. "I's feel lik' he al'right. He be y'ere, y'all. He be y'ere."

It was now time for everyone to be leaving and still no Abunda. The family was visibly upset and wanted to stay behind to wait for him, but there was no more time to wait. As they were slowly making their departure, one of them saw a man running in their direction.

"Look, look, it's him," his brother yelled. "Wait, please wait!"

Abunda reached them just in time and joined the others. He was weary from having to rush but more so because of his conversation with Rev. Hope. Because they were leaving, he did not have time to discuss the Convention matters with anyone else.

Concerned about what would take place in his extended absence, again he contemplated whether it was worth it for him to leave his family and be with others who did not support him. The group could tell that something was bothering him because his countenance was sad.

Sha'myla approached her brother and put her arm around him, "Abunda, you all right? What's wrong? Who made you sad?"

Responding to his sister's attention, he rested his head on her shoulder, "I'm just tired, Sha. I had to go back to the Hopes and have a talk with Rev. Hope about a serious matter then rush here to meet the family. This whole experience has been a little much and I have not had much rest since I got home to Annapolis Grove. I have some serious thinking to do, but I will be fine. We will be coming to Crusidea soon and Ja'cin and Makita will be going home, perhaps you want to spend time with them.

"That's a good idea. I wish they'd come with us," Sha'myla said softly in a sad tone of voice. "I want to be there when the baby's born. We have enough money now for us to all live together. Maybe I can make them change their mind before they get home."

Before she could make her case, Makita had persuaded Ja'cin. They agreed that he would stop at Crusidea and sell his business and meet them in Settles Landing. When Makita told Sha'myla she leaped and yelled. She was so glad to have her sister back, especially with the new addition. Ja'cin and Makita told the rest of the family just before reaching Crusidea.

Ja'cin was left in Crusidea and the group continued their travels. It would not be long before they would be in the Bishops' hometown.

Jet, Hais and Abunda discussed the plans for the family to go on to Settles Landing in safety. The town north of where Hais Bishop lived was much more progressive concerning their attitude towards Coloreds than Annapolis Grove and Marantha. Many successful Coloreds were recognized citizens for their work and businesses. Hais did not foresee a serious problem with the Baskets finishing their trip alone. However, he did have a plan. "When we reach my home I will contact some people that I know who will assist with the arrangements for the rest of the trip. They know people along the way that will protect the Baskets and assure that they reach their destination safely. Abunda, I will give you enough money for you to get your family established. You will be able to buy whatever you need and want. My friends will also provide contacts to assist you in purchasing a home and looking for business opportunities for Ja'cin when he rejoins the others. In the meantime, Jet will handle the financial matters here as he did in Annapolis Grove and Marantha."

The Bishops were generous in hosting the Baskets at their home. They too had a celebratory event but it was nothing as lavish as the Hopes. Though the occasion was festive, it was also heavy with sadness, especially for the Rouses and particularly Momma Basket. They had been together for so long no one believed that they would ever separate. The

Rouse household would now have a huge emptiness that probably no one else could fill like Momma Basket.

Mrs. Rouse, in a broken voice, spoke to the Baskets, "I pray that you will have your 'better life'." She starts to cry as she approaches Momma Basket and says, "You are like my family. You have taken care of my children, my husband and me. I've trusted you with the most precious things of my life and you never let me down." Now they are both in tears as the others looked on also teary-eyed.

"Missy Rouse, I gonna miss y'all, too. Ya b'en good ta me 'en my family." Momma Basket could not continued because she broke down in tears. She and Mrs. Rouse embraced each other for a long time.

Hais Bishop had done as promised and some of his contact people met them at his home to discuss the remaining trip plans. Unbelief was evident on Abunda's face as he now greeted people of Color who were distinguished and more progressive than he could ever dream. Thinking that he had great dreams and plans, Abunda was face to face with others who had realized their dreams and were willing to help make his a reality.

Abunda's trance was interrupted by Hais Bishop's voice, "My friends here have something for you. Here is a list of names and safe places for the trip. I assure you that we will meet again soon. Serenity and I would like for you to visit on your return to Marantha from Settles Landing. You will be returning, won't you?"

"Mr. Bishop, I do not have the words to tell you how much this means to me and especially my family. You have been so kind to me since the very first day I met you. Everything you promised to do you have done. If I am passing through, I will be sure to stop by and I am grateful for the invitation."

Abunda was busy considering the rest of the trip. He wanted to make sure that his family would be safe and so he concluded that his matters could wait.

Chapter 14

A Betta Life

The saddest part of the trip had come. The Baskets were now left alone to travel the rest of the way to their new home, Settles Landing. They were all frightened, even Abunda had reservations about the journey. None of them had ever been this far away from safety alone. Somehow their 'better life' now had to be the overwhelming motivation for them to enjoy what they had been blessed with.

Following the plans and information given by Hais Bishop, the Baskets arrived safely in Settles Landing. Abunda was deeply saddened because he knew that he had to make haste, return home and that he had promised the Bishop's he would stop by their place.

Upon their arrival in Settles Landing, the Baskets were met by two very distinguished Colored couples who were adorned in African clothing. Initially, Abunda assumed that they were Africans until they greeted him, "Pastor Abunda Basket?" one inquired.

"Yes, I am," he replied with enthusiasm at hearing the voice.

"Welcome to Settles Landing. My name is Lionel. This is my wife Seanna and my friends, the Snowdens. We're glad that you arrived safely. We received word of your coming and have made some arrangements that we hope are to your liking. Is this your family?"

"Yes. This is Momma, Poppa and my sisters and brothers. Will it be all right if I make formal introductions later? We are very weary from traveling and would like to get settled. Afterwards it will be our pleasure to host you for your kindness."

"That's fine," Lionel answered while he and his contingent were greeting the Baskets. "We only have a little further to travel to your new home. Let's be on our way."

Before long the Baskets were in front of something they had seen many times but was owned by the Whites. It was the most beautiful estate with the rolling grounds, gardens, flowers, trees, a gazebo, and a verandah that they could see from the front and sides. The Baskets were all, including Abunda, paralyzed in awe as they stood motionless before their new home.

The Country Style house, that was fully furnished, was sitting on 10.5 acres, which included a hemlock forest and creek. The house had 13 bed and guest rooms with private baths and entrances, three living rooms and two dining rooms one which could sit 20 people. There was also a huge kitchen with an island and nooks for eating. It was supplied with pots and pans hanging from a wrought iron holder over head. The first level featured 20-foot long, hand-hewn Chestnut beams and original stone walls and a huge fireplace. The house had a two-story porch which spanned the front, sides and back and provided beautiful views of the valley and surrounding mountains. The premises also include a private Innkeeper's residence of approximately 1200 square feet.

Lionel asked, "Well, do you like it? It is the most beautiful piece of property here in Settles Landing. Actually it's on the outskirts of Settles Landing. I was told to find you the best and this is it."

No one was able to give him an answer. The youngest children were now jumping around yelling, "We gonna live here, Momma?"

"Nay, ya kno' we's ain't gonna liv' y'ere," Momma replied embarrassed by the question being asked in front of the new people.

"Mrs. Basket, yes you are," Lionel reassured her. "This is now your new home if you like it."

Abunda, again having to compose himself, says, "It has to be very expensive and we need our money to live off of."

Lionel shared with Abunda and the family how the property was acquired, "The property was owned by a White family that had spent their lives helping people of Color to get free from slavery. This family pledged everything they had to helping others. They taught people of Color, from the south, to read, write and learn trades. They provided the money for many of these people to start their own businesses. When the last family member moved, because the grounds were too large for their family, they decided to cut the price of the property in half for any family or organization of Color to purchase. A friend of mine heard about it and informed me immediately. We got together the deposit to put down to hold the property pending your arrival before anyone else in the area could attempt to purchase it. You all must be really blessed because the timing was uncanny."

"Our Poppa told us that our ancestors have, for years, told of having 'a better life'. We believe that they are looking out for all of us: our people. And we believe that they are with God who is looking out for all people."

"Your philosophy is much like ours," Lionel admitted. "Settles Landing was settled because we people of Color knew that with our rich heritage we had to have 'a better life' than slavery."

"I like that you call us people of Color and not Colored people," Abunda shared.

"Colored people is who the White people call us because they want to be superior to us. You know White stands for purity, therefore, anything that is not white is impure, hence we are Colored. We don't believe that any one people is better than the other, but that God made us all equal in stature."

In absolute awe and excitement, he tells Lionel, "I must spend some time with you to learn of these new things. I must."

"You are more than welcome anytime," Lionel says extending the invitation. "Often a group of us meet to discuss our heritage and our futures. Please join us. By the looks of things you certainly have some things to share with us. None of us have been able, yet, to amass money to purchase properties like this. The opportunities have been available, as we expand our community, but the resources are prohibitive. There may be a business opportunity for your family if your resources are not prohibitive. We can discuss that at a later date."

Instantly Abunda dreaded the thought of returning to Marantha. It was the first time he had seriously wanted to leave and be with his family. Even with the issue at the Colored Convention, he was more emotional than realistic about leaving his home. But now he could stay with his family, start a family business perhaps, and continue helping his people to grow. There must be some people in Settles Landing who were not affluent and would need his assistance.

Up to this point, Poppa Basket has said nothing. He just stands and quietly investigates his surroundings; not being able to fathom that the ancestors really meant this kind of 'a better life'. Poppa maintained an internal dialogue for fear of appearing stupid about what Lionel was telling them. His mind kept telling him that there was no way they could live here let alone own this property. How would they maintain it? How much does it cost? A plethora of questions seemed to invade his mental space without any effort from him.

Lionel invites the family to enter, "Let's go into the house so you can have a good look around. As I said, if you don't want it we can look at something else. I thought that since I was told of your large family that you would want plenty of room. I even bought some groceries knowing that you would stay."

Makita came up with a great idea, "Ja'cin could keep the grounds. He does that for other people. We could hire him."

"That takes care of the grounds problem," Abunda admitted. "You're right Makita. Ja'cin could start his new business with us first. Maybe you boys would like to learn to do what Ja'cin does," Abunda asked directing the question to his other brothers.

"I would," one of the boys replied.

The entire family followed Lionel into the house. It was completely furnished with furnishings that the Baskets only saw in places where they worked. Each member went towards a different room or part of the house; just looking and admiring. Some had gone upstairs to investigate the bedrooms and whatever else was up there. It was the most unbelievable experience of their lives. They thought the trip from Annapolis Grove was awesome, but it paled in comparison to this.

Momma Basket made her way to the formal living room and sat down in absolute awe while the others went to and fro. Poppa Basket found her and sat next to her; still not saying a word. He gently reached over and took her hand into his squeezing it ever so lovingly. She responded by squeezing his hand. They just sat in peace!

After Abunda and Lionel had gone completely through the house, Abunda wanted to discuss the details of the purchase along with the atmosphere of Settles Landing with his family. Lionel provided answers to all his questions and gave a thorough history of Settles Landing: present and past. He was quite eager to discuss the future of their little town, which they had planned would be a major city someday. Everyone that came and stayed in Settles Landing was a part of that master plan.

"Lionel, would you let me discuss this with my family and I will give you our decision in a little while. Can we stay here for a short while?"

"Certainly, I will take a look around the grounds and make myself comfortable under the gazebo until you all have reached a decision."

"Thank you. I don't think this will take long," he advised Lionel.

Abunda returned to gather the family into one room, the formal living room where Momma and Poppa were still seated. "What do we want to do? Do we want to buy this place?" he asked. "I think it would be a great place for Momma and Poppa to spend the rest of their days, not having to work or worry about anything. There is more than enough room for everybody. Makita and Ja'cin can even live here; especially with the baby coming. That's what I think, but everybody has to agree."

Jumba, almost in a yell, "I want to live here." That made the rest of the family join in like a chorus, "yea, we want to live here."

Momma and Poppa still had not spoken a single word until now, "Is dis real? We's kin stay y'ere?" Poppa asked.

All the family members rushed to them. Some sat at their feet, others gathered close behind to demonstrate solidarity. This time Sha'myla, who had also been very quiet, spoke, "Yes, this is real and we can stay here. We can buy this place and live like real people not.... Momma and Poppa, the ancestors kept us together for this day. We want you to live 'the better life' before you die. It's not just for us, y'all earned it."

The decision was unanimous; the Basket Family would buy this property and it would be their home. They named it Buswala Ridge after their African ancestor.

The time was rapidly approaching for Abunda to return to Marantha. Remembering that he had promised to stop by the Bishops on his way, he did not want to delay his departure or prolong his absence.

Abunda announces to the family, "I will be leaving soon. I must return to do my work. I will be making regular trips to visit since you are closer than when you were in Annapolis Grove. I really don't want to go. I don't. At least this time I'm not running away and you know where I am. I will make some arrangements to stay in touch. I love y'all so much. I want you children to take extra special care of Momma and Poppa; give them whatever they want. Don't let them work; but let them do something."

Momma proceeded towards Abunda with her arms stretched out and open wide saying, "Abunda ya's got big things ta do. We's be fine. Me 'en Poppa we's need da rest. Ya's right. But we's want ya y'ere wit' us. We's got 'da betta life' but it ain't 'betta' if ya ain't y'ere."

By now Momma has Abunda in a bear hug and is crying; so is he. The rest of the family joins in for another group hug.

"Ya do wha' cha gotta do," Poppa spoke authoritatively. "Ya betta com' back fo' Momma 'en me is dead. Ya hear?"

Very emotionally Abunda replied, "Oh, Poppa, I'll be back long before that; besides you and Momma ain't gonna die no time soon. You've got to live 'this better life' first. I'll probably be leaving in a few days after I'm sure that everything is settled here.'

The few days came much faster than anyone had imagined. The family was still busy getting settled in and having fun getting what else they wanted in the house. Makita was glad that she decided that she and Ja'cin would live with her family. She was positive that he would be excited and knew that he would welcome the opportunity to start his business with her family.

Momma prepared one of her family feasts for Abunda's departure. It was another very festive occasion like their departure from Annapolis Grove. Now, everyone knew where Abunda was and that he would always be an active member of the family. Abunda requested that he leave from Buswala Ridge alone to minimize the emotional impact on everyone. The family disagreed but finally agreed.

Conflicting emotions were imploding in Abunda's mind as he traveled. Three raging wars were battling within: leaving his family, seeing Serenity again and the Colored Convention back home. He realized that he was in bondage to them all. How he would deal with them needed to be reconciled. With regards to leaving his family, it did not mean just this departure, but whether or not he would eventually return to Buswala Ridge and permanently remain in Settles Landing.

Serenity was the greatest issue of all because it involved two people he loved outside of his natural family. This was Abunda's family, not Poppa's family.

Last, the Colored Convention that represents a divine purpose and destiny was at stake because it was a work for him to perform and cultivate. What would happen to it if he did not remain long enough for a firm foundation to be established? Remaining in Marantha, however, he would again be forfeiting a personal life for a divine mission.

As promised, Abunda's traveling arrangement included stopping by the Bishops' Estate before returning directly to Marantha. He could now see the house from a short distance and thought to himself that he would be glad when the visit was over. Now on the steps of the front door, he used the brass doorknocker to announce his presence.

Much to his surprise, Serenity answered the door and seeing Abunda she nervously extended an invitation, "Well, Abunda, do come in. It is good to see you, again. The others are in the parlor. How was your trip and how is your family? Did everything go well? Let me stop asking so many questions; I'm sure the others will want to know as well."

Abunda could tell that this was very awkward for her and he did not want to add to the awkwardness, so he responded pleasantly yet comforting for her. "It is good to see you, again. Everything will be all right, I promise. I am looking forward to sharing with the others so that I can be on my way to Marantha. It is funny because I do not see it as home anymore, but Settles Landing where my family is, is now home."

Before reaching the parlor they gently held each other's hand briefly to signify unity.

"Look who's here," Serenity announced joyously. When the others saw Abunda, their delight equaled the joy in Serenity's voice.

It was a very special time. The Rouses and the Bishops were informed of the happenings in Settles Landing and all were emotionally touched. Abunda took special care to thank them again and this time an extra thanks to Hais Bishop for the contacts he made.

"I was amazed seeing Colored People, I mean people of Color!" Abunda shared. "They are so learned and affluent. It was like being in another world. Lionel was a huge help and I am sure that we will all be friends. I am looking forward to returning to be with my family again."

Hais Bishop added, "I'm happy for you and your family Abunda. There are many good people in this world, Colored and White. I am glad that I could help. As I told you when I first met you, I want to help your people and I still mean it."

Jet Rouse interjected, "Me, too. You know how we feel about Momma Basket and that includes her family."

"Thank you all, again, very much," Abunda concluded. "Now if you do not mind I am very tired and would like to rest. I will probably be leaving sometime tomorrow."

"I'll show him to his room," Serenity offered. "I'll rejoin you all shortly."

The others nodded in agreement as Abunda and Serenity left the room. They left walking slowly towards the staircase. The moment was very intense, but neither of them made any visible demonstration of their strain.

It was uncommon for a woman to escort a man to a bedroom, especially a White woman with a Colored man, but Hais Bishop had such trust in Abunda and his wife that he gave no thought to any idea of infidelity, after all why should he? Serenity and Abunda were total strangers before their accidental meeting at the Faith Convention in Valentine City.

Almost at the room door, Serenity turns to Abunda and says, "I want to see you before you leave. Can we meet early in the morning on the grounds somewhere? I will pick a safe place. I want us to talk about Joshua and us. I know we said we wouldn't interfere in his life, but I must know your feelings about us all being together while traveling. I had many conversations with him and I'd like to tell you what he shared with me. Please, Abunda, can we do this?"

Before he could answer the question they heard a door shut a distance away. They paid no attention because it could have been one of the servants, but each realized that the sound was distracting.

"Serenity, I do want to meet and hear what you have learned from our son, but we must be very careful," Abunda advised in a concerned tone. "We don't want the others to get suspicious if we go off together alone. I respect your husband deeply and I will not jeopardize that in any way. Perhaps we can get together after breakfast. Can you have breakfast for us all in the gardens, that way we will not be leaving the house alone, but can just stroll the gardens?"

"Yes, I can certainly do that," Serenity responded with delight. "Good night, Abunda, have a wonderful rest. I hope your quarters will be satisfactory."

"Good night, Serenity," Abunda replied as he entered the room.

Serenity immediately rejoined the others as promised. The Rouses and the Bishops were enjoying each others company. Joshua was also enjoying himself on the lavish estate of the Bishops. It was much larger than theirs in Annapolis Grove and they had a game room that he found phenomenal.

"Good morning all," Serenity greeted her guests as they filed in for breakfast. "I trust you all had a good night's rest, especially you Abunda? We're going to have breakfast in the gardens this morning. I thought it would be perfect since it is such a beautiful day. Is that all right with you all?"

The guests were all in agreement with the idea. Joshua was the first one darting towards the gardens; it was apparent that he was very hungry. There was no particular seating order so he took the first seat he came to.

After breakfast, everyone was sifting around in the gardens talking when Serenity offered this suggestion, "Why don't we all take a walk around the gardens? They are absolutely beautiful."

Both Hais and Jet declined because they wanted to spend more time together. It was uncertain when they would see each other again.

"I have a slight headache," Mrs. Rouse informed the others. "I believe that it may be hay fever or something similar. If it's all right with you, Serenity, I'll just rest here on the chaise lounge until you return. Why don't you and Abunda take a leisurely stroll? I'm sure what the other two men want to discuss won't interest either of you."

"Abunda, do you mind being alone with me?" Serenity asked innocently while her heart was leaping for joy.

Hesitating, Abunda replied, "It would be my pleasure for just a little while because I will have to be leaving soon."

Off they went; now free to go anywhere they wanted to. Again, this opportunity was as if God had orchestrated it for them Himself.

Serenity directed them to a beautiful secluded place a distance from the main house. The place looked like it was naturally formed with huge oak trees clumped together forming a conclave. Under the trees was a clearing surrounded by wild ivy growing in an artistic fashion. A small bench was in the clearing that looked like it had been there for years.

"This is my favorite place on the whole estate." Serenity informed Abunda. "I come here when I need to think or just to get away sometimes. It has a very spiritual tone to it that I can't explain. When I'm weary or low and I come here, something seems to make everything all right. It's something like what you say your ancestors do for you all."

"It is a beautiful place," Abunda agreed. "Why do you get low Serenity? You have everything anyone could ever want. You have a great husband, wealth, friends...."

Serenity interrupted, "But I don't have you or our son. I've tried since the day I left Joshua with the Rouses to put it out of my mind, but I just can't. Abunda, I want us all to be together even though I know it will never be. He's such a fine boy. On our way here he told me all the things he likes. He said that he wants to be a lawyer like his father. Oh, Abunda he's so much like you but he will never know that either."

Visibly upset, Serenity was shaking and crying. Abunda reached to take her in his arms to console her. He hesitated momentarily because the moment was too emotional for him as well and he did not want anything to happen. Being a little more in control, he followed through with his plan and took

Serenity into his arms. She gently placed her head on his shoulders and responded to his affection. Once again they were in a hopeless situation but this was different.

"Serenity, it's getting harder and harder for me to see you. Each time I do, I want to tell the whole world of my love for you. I want to take you into my arms and never let you go. I want to kiss your beautiful lips and caress your hair with my fingers. I want us to be together forever but we both know that it is impossible. We have discussed this before; being together would mean ruining other people's lives. But there's something different now that I can't identify."

Abunda took Serenity's face gently into his hands and planted kisses all over it. He kissed her on the forehead, her cheeks, her nose and on her lips. Serenity welcomed every kiss and was quietly hoping for more. Her wish was fulfilled.

Mrs. Rouse was resting quietly on the chaise lounge trying to get rid of her annoying headache when she heard a familiar voice speak directly to her, "Mother. Mother, it is so good to see you. I'm so glad to be here with you. Where is father? He did come, didn't he?"

Forgetting her headache, Mrs. Rouse quickly arose from her lounge speaking all the while, "Storm. Storm, my son it is good to see you. I was hoping that your plans would work out so that you could join us here and we would all travel home together. You look wonderful. How is school? Are you hungry? How did you get in?"

"The servant let me in," Storm answered. "I told him who I was and he told me that you were out here. I wanted to surprise you so I asked him to show me the way and not announce my coming. Yes, I am hungry."

"Let's find something for you," Mrs. Rouse suggested as they walked into the house. We had a great breakfast. There must be some left, I'm sure."

Mrs. Rouse sat and watched quietly as Storm ate like he had not eaten for sometime. She was glad to have her son at home. He was doing well in school like his sister Alyon who would also be home for the summer.

"Mother," a voice blurted out while entering the kitchen. "May I go…? Storm. Storm. You're home, here. When did you get here?"

"Mother, Storm is here," Joshua said loudly. "I didn't know he was going to meet us here. I'm so glad to see him."

"I thought it would be a wonderful surprise for our family," Mrs. Rouse informed Joshua. "Since Storm was traveling this way to come home, I thought that he could meet us and we would all go home together. Sort of like a vacation, but on the way home."

Before Storm could answer Joshua's questions, Joshua was hugging and hanging all over him. He was so glad, like their mother, to see his big brother. Storm released Joshua's hold on him, and stood back to take a look at his little brother that he had not seen in a good while.

"Joshua, you're taller than I am. You've got muscles. You're so much taller. What have you been doing?"

"You know I can't make myself taller, but I've been lifting some weights. You like it?" Joshua questioned Storm because he wanted his brother to be so proud of him.

Storm could not help but notice how different Joshua looked since he last saw him. Not just his size, but his appearance. Physically his body build was contrary to Storm's and his skin color was more like a lasting summer tan which was the same feeling Serenity experienced.

Storm finished his breakfast and the two boys went off to reminisce together. Walking around the grounds, the two talked about what had occurred for each other since being apart. Having no plans in mind, they just aimlessly wandered around the grounds. From a short distance they say two people coming toward them. Joshua said eagerly, "That looks like Ms. Serenity and Pastor Abunda coming this way. They left after breakfast for a walk around the grounds since nobody else wanted to join them. Let's go meet them. I want to introduce you to them." As they came closer, each recognized the other and continued toward one another.

"Hi," Joshua exclaimed. "This is my brother Storm. Storm this is Ms. Serenity and Pastor Abunda. Ms. Serenity is Mr. Bishop's wife; they live here. Pastor Abunda is Momma Basket's runaway son. He came back not long ago."

Everyone exchanged greetings and walked together toward the house. Soon it would be time for Abunda to leave and he wanted to say his farewells to the others.

"Abunda, I really hate to see you go," Serenity admitted quietly so the others could not hear. They had no more opportunity to be affectionate because of their unexpected company.

"We will be in touch," he assured Serenity. "I will be traveling this way to see my family and perhaps I can stop by sometime. Your husband and I will be involved in business affairs and will need to meet from time to time, also."

The four of them had reached the gardens where Mrs. Rouse had resumed resting and the gentlemen were still engaged in their affairs on the inside. Mrs. Rouse was awakened by the gathering. She inquired, "Storm, have you seen your father, yet?"

"No, where is he!" Storm wanted to know. "I'm anxious to see him."

Joshua volunteered to take Storm to their father. "Come I'll take you. He's going to be so surprise to see you."

"Joshua, please ask the others to join us out here", Serenity requested. "Abunda will be leaving soon and he wants to say goodbye."

"Yes, Mrs. Bishop," Joshua politely answered.

Mrs. Rouse turned her attention to Abunda. "Did you enjoy your walk? Aren't the grounds beautiful? It so reminds me of our home in Annapolis Grove."

"It is lovely. I did enjoy my walk and appreciated Mrs. Bishop's company. I will be leaving soon because I have to get back to Marantha and my church. I have enjoyed your company as well and all that your family has done for my family."

At that point the others were returning. Hais Bishop had his hand outstretched as he walked in Abunda's direction. Storm, however, could not take his eyes off of Serenity Bishop.

"Abunda, we hate to see you go," Hais Bishop shared while shaking hands. "Jet has taken care of the business here and everything is in place. I will be sending the financial support monthly as I promised. Arrangements have also been made through the bank in Marantha, so you will have no problems accessing the funds. Serenity and I are so happy for your family. We look forward to hearing the great news of the work you have started, as well."

Jet Rouse adds, "Ditto. Again, we too are happy for your family. If we can help anymore please let us know."

Mrs. Rouse presented Abunda with a warm embrace to express her feelings. Joshua rushed to shake Abunda's hand and Storm followed, but with a fixed eye still on Serenity.

Following Abunda's departure, the others gathered in the gardens. Everybody was eagerly listening to Storm telling some of his adventures from the past school year. Joshua was recklessly excited about his brother's presence and especially the adventures. Serenity excused herself from the group to see about the upcoming meal for her guests. Storm also excused himself because he had a personal need to attend to. On his way back to rejoin the others in the garden, Storm passed the kitchen where Serenity was still making arrangements.

"I know her from somewhere, but I can't remember where," Storm thought to himself. "I would not forget such a pretty lady. She must have been younger? Where do I know her from?"

The thoughts continued to nag him as he reached the others in the gardens but fatigue took over and he sat down quietly on the closest seat and drifted off to sleep, momentarily. No one bothered him as they surmised that he was tired from traveling and it would be a little while before mealtime.

"Storm, wake up," Mrs. Rouse urged. "It's time to eat."

Storm collected himself and rose up to join the others. "Please, excuse me for a moment; I want to clean up a little. I won't be long and you don't have to wait for me."

Serenity also needed to get something from another part of the house, so she accompanied Storm.

"Please excuse me Ms. Serenity," Storm requested. "But I believe that we have met before and I've been trying to figure out where. I think it was a long time ago, maybe that's why I can't remember."

Serenity was dumfounded. She refused to consider that Storm might remotely be talking about their only meeting when she gave her baby away. "He was too young to remember that," she thought. But now she felt compelled to give an answer that would frame his memory.

"I don't think so," she spoke softly so as to take away the stress from Storm's mind. "I have no idea where it could have been because of our age differences. The places where we could have met were limited."

Storm insisted, "I know it sounds bizarre but I'm positive that we've met before."

Serenity has arrived at her destination while Storm continues to his. "I'll see you back downstairs shortly," Serenity informs Storm.

Now really, really concerned, Serenity contemplates how she will handle this new crisis and remain social to her guest. Her life would be ruined if Storm remembers that dreadful day. Explaining to Hais would be impossible and assuming that he would surely want to end their marriage, haunted Serenity's mind. Her wonderful life was being threatened like never before. How she would handle the fallout pounded her every thought.

Everyone was now gathered at the dining table. Storm and Joshua sat next to each other so that they could continue talking. They were extremely engrossed in conversation the others could not hear and it was very bothersome to Serenity.

Serenity is now feeling the brunt of her history. She has been in bondage to her secret but has managed to garner a successful life anyway. Now her past is in the present and the emotions that she controlled for so long may override her ability to mask the truth. "What are you two boys so secretive about," Mrs. Rouse questioned.

Joshua replied swiftly, "Nothing Mother, just boy stuff," as he winked his eye at Storm.

"You two are up to something," Jet Rouse added. "We must gather our things so that we can leave early in the morning. Hais, thanks for your hospitality. We've had a great time. Let's not make it such a long time before we get together again. And thanks for your help, again, with the Baskets."

Hais in a gentleman's voice retorted, "It was my pleasure. I'm glad Serenity wanted to visit her mother so that we could get together; otherwise it would probably have been longer before we got to Annapolis Grove. I'm happy for the Baskets and glad I could help. We certainly won't make our visit too long the next time, either. It was great to have you all here and especially to meet Joshua and to see how Storm has grown."

Storm's ears were tinkling at the statement Hais Bishop made about them being in Annapolis Grove. More than ever he was determined to remember where he had met Serenity. "Could it have been in Annapolis Grove?" he wondered.

The morning came quickly and after breakfast the Bishops were seeing the Rouses off to town. As they were saying their good-byes and embracing each other, Storm made it a point to be the last person to embrace Serenity; even though Joshua did not want to embrace any of the adults.

Whispering in Serenity's ear he said, "Your secret is safe with me." Afterwards he released her without saying any more and headed closer to the area where they were to depart. He never looked back to see Serenity shaking and almost ready to faint.

Returning home, Hais Bishop noticed Serenity's unusually quiet mood but refrained from interrupting it. He thought that she was perhaps being a little melancholy because now the house would be quiet and she would be alone again.

Chapter 15

Reality

A bunda arrived safely back in Marantha but is sad because of leaving his family and Serenity. His thoughts have constantly centered on all that has transpired lately. His family is safe in Settles Landing starting the 'better life'. He had the opportunity to spend some quality time with Serenity even though it was not the right thing to do.

He remembered his meeting with Lionel and the other people of Color, in Settles Landing, who inspired him to do much more than his original plans. There was more than enough money for his family and his work. Ja'cin and Makita would now be living with the family. The first grandchild would be born and all the family would be a part of the birth. Much had taken place! But now Abunda had to concentrate on the issues at hand, the Colored Convention.

Upon arriving at Marantha, he went directly to the farmhouse. He entered on the side and went to the upper level. He slipped out of his clothes, fell on the bed and immediately was asleep.

"Abunda, Abunda, you're home," a startled voice yelped.

Still groggy and tired, Abunda replied, "Bela what are you doing up here? Yes, Bela I'm home and it is so good to see you. How are you and the others doing? I really missed you and wished that you had gone with me. When I go back to visit I'm going to take you and the others, if you want to go, because that's where we were headed in the beginning."

Bubbling with excitement, Bela tells Abunda, "We all doing good. The others are still learning and growing. They are also still excited about your news and can't wait to talk to you. I really missed you too, Abunda. I was scared you wasn't coming back. I understand if you didn't. How is your family? Oh, I had to come up here to get something for Cliff."

"I have so much to tell you, Bela. Settles Landing is unbelievable. Colored people own almost everything in the town. They don't say Colored people they say people of Color. The family is getting settled and is doing well. They are excited about 'the better life' and making plans to 'be better'. Mr. Bishop contacted people to help us on our way and to meet us in Settles Landing. We were met by Lionel and his wife when we got there. They had a house for us with everything we needed to get started. Bela, you need to see it and them. There is so much more to life that people of Color can have and do than we ever knew. We'll talk more later. I want to see Rev. Hope and get to the church. I've been gone so long I don't want our people to think that I don't care anymore."

"Okay, Abunda, I see you later. I'm so glad you home."

Now that Bela had awakened Abunda, he decided to get up so that he could meet with Rev. Hope. But something inside was saying not to go yet but sit and meditate for a while. Abunda was sensing that the ancestors and/or God wanted to tell him something. Obeying the urge, he cleaned himself up, got dressed, and wondered whether to stay inside or find a nice place on the grounds. Remembering his last episode while out on the grounds, he elected to stay inside.

After all, everyone was out working and it was quiet and very peaceful in the farmhouse.

Instead of focusing on the ancestors, this time, Abunda wanted to focus on God. So many of his questions were unanswered, about God, but it seemed that God was always there. Confusion loomed in his mind as to how the ancestors and God interacted. Who was in charge? God? The ancestors? The White man's God who allowed us to be slaves, killed, murdered, taken from our country?

"Why do you have such a difficult time with God?" Abunda heard a voice say but there was no one there.

"Deston, is that you?"

"Yes, Abunda, it is me. What's wrong, now?"

"I want to know who to believe. Who do I follow, the ancestors or God? Both? I still don't understand why God let people kill innocent people, our people."

Deston assures Abunda, "God gives man freedom. Man kills and enslaves his own because of color and differences that they disagree about."

Abunda listening attentively now shares with Deston, "I heard, a long time ago, when I first came to Rev. Hope's that God gave His Son, Jesus Christ for the freedom of all men. But some men killed him because they disagreed with what he was doing. Rev. Hope said that's how God wanted it because Jesus died for everybody to be free from evil. Jesus is dead, but evil is very much alive. I don't understand that."

"That kind of understanding you can only have by faith. Remember I told you that a while back? You must believe that there is a right way to do things even when everything seems wrong. Think Abunda, how did you get this far? Why aren't you dead? Something inside of you keeps driving you to something better and that's what you believe. That's your faith at work!!"

Abunda acknowledged, "I do understand that. I didn't know it was faith, though. So you're saying that God also wants good for us all but He lets man make the decision."

"Right," Deston confirms. "However, all men will answer to God for what they have done against what He wanted done."

A sense of reality filled the room and somehow he knew that Deston was no longer with him. That being the case Abunda was now ready to meet with Rev. Hope. Armed with this new piece of learning, he was also ready to meet with the new comers to the Convention.

Eager for Rev. Hope to be at home, Abunda headed across the estate to the main house. He knocked gently on the back door and was greeted by Mrs. Hope.

"Abunda, you're home. Please come in. I'd like to hear about your trip."

"Thanks, Mrs. Hope but I urgently need to speak with Rev. Hope. Is he in? Perhaps we can discuss my trip at another time?"

"That's fine. And yes, he's in the parlor and I'm sure he's anxious to see you as well. You remember the way to the parlor?"

"Yes, I'll see myself there. Thank you."

The parlor door was ajar and Abunda gave a slight knock before entering. "Come in," Rev Hope announced. Abunda entered the room.

"Welcome home. When did you get back? How was your trip and your family? How are they? Please have a seat and let's talk."

Abunda shared the excitement and details of his trip with Rev. Hope but he sensed that Rev. Hope was preoccupied. He was right. There was something wrong. This was a very difficult moment for Rev. Hope and he was concerned about how to share this with Abunda who he loved and trust dearly. "I don't know how to say this, Abunda, but there is a rumor going around that you were seen in a secret place with a White woman. The story is that you and she were very intimate. Somehow this has gotten back to your church and the Convention and the people are upset. Many are calling for your resignation and do not want you to be apart of the church, either. There have been several meetings. I attended a couple and spoke on your behalf but they will not change their demands. I have defended you unlike the last time, but I'm concerned as to where such a rumor came from. Why would anyone want to spread such a vicious lie? I am so sorry Abunda."

Stymied, Abunda was once again frozen in space and time. "How could this have happened?" he thought privately. "We were so careful. What do I say? Do I tell Rev. Hope the truth? How will he handle it? He should understand because he loves me, he said, and he loves God."

Rev. Hope saw the look of shock on Abunda's face, as he assumed it would be. What he did not know was that the look was there because Abunda never thought anyone would see them. He waited patiently for Abunda to collect himself and perhaps provide some answers to this dilemma.

Abunda wanted to tell Rev. Hope the truth about him and Serenity. Ironically, the new lesson that he learned from Deston was just what was needed here. He knew that Rev. Hope would do the right thing by understanding this dilemma and continue to support him. He knew that Rev. Hope would also help him to make the right decision about any further contact with Serenity. Finally, Abunda could breathe because he could now get counsel from this man who had been like a father, pastor and dear friend. But most of all, he knew of Rev. Hope's love for God that was the core of his life.

"Rev. Hope, I need to share some things with you," Abunda started more nervous than he had ever been in his entire life. "Please, let me finish first and then you can say whatever you want or need to. This is extremely important."

The room was motionless as Abunda was sharing his heart. The air seemed to get cold and clammy. The oxygen was thinning with every word that came out of his mouth. He now needed to breathe deeply as if gasping for air. A thunderstorm preceded by dark clouds affixed themselves to the ceiling of the room. Water could be felt in the room, but it was the stream of tears running down Abunda's face. He was too ashamed to look at Rev. Hope. "Sir, that's honestly the whole truth," he said in conclusion.

"Abunda, I have no idea what to say," Rev. Hope began. "I love you like a son and trust you with my life. You have been everything good to my family and your people. I am so sorry for this, I know that you and your friend, are heartbroken, especially not being able to acknowledge something that is so dear and special to you. But I agree that you should resign from your church and the Convention. This would leave such a negative cloud to everything you would attempt to do."

This was surely not the answer Abunda was expecting. Again, wondering to himself, "Why does anyone have to know? I confessed to you and am asking your wisdom as to what to do. I never thought you would want me to resign. I would never see my friend again if that's what you recommend. But this....?"

Abunda felt betrayed and rejected. "Was this the price to pay for an indiscretion that occurred so many years ago?"

Finally, Abunda relayed exactly what he was thinking to Rev. Hope and concluded with a question, "Where is the forgiveness of God? Your God? Would He strip me of everything because of something I did before I knew Him? My ancestors keep telling me about this 'better life' and an inheritance. Is this my 'better life' or my inheritance to be castrated both mentally and physically? To be denied the opportunity to give birth when I was denied what I loved because of man's decisions?"

Sitting in quietness, neither he nor Rev. Hope spoke. Abunda now realized that the 'better life' and the inheritance were not the same. He, in actuality, has the 'better life' but still has issues with who is controlling his life. He realizes that the best gift he could ever have is to establish his own identity apart from the requirements of society, his family, and others who need him. He also realizes that having freedom of mind is crucial to his existence. He ran away because he would not be enslaved to anyone or anything. He was looking for more than just a place to live but a place to freely live. Did such a place exist externally? Could this kind of freedom be the inheritance?

"Rev. Hope," Abunda said sounding relieved, "Now I understand what our inheritance is. One Plantation is enough; I'll not be in bondage to a New Plantation. I think I might finally have my inheritance!!!! Abunda wakes up!

DEFINITIONS FOR
THE NEW PLANTATION

afta - after; **ag'in** - again; **anuffa** - another; **`at** - that

Buswasla -Bu swa la; **betta** - better; **b'gin** - begin; **bigga** - bigger; **before** - befo'; **brotha** - brother

chi'dren - children; **chil'len** - children; **'cited** - excited

da - the; **d'ere** - there; **dey** - they; **'dem**, them; **d'ese** - these; **dinna** - dinner; **don'cha** - don't you; **d'ose** - out doors; **dis** - this

e'erybody - everybody; **'en** - and; **e'tha** - either; **e'vn** - even; **evr'y** - every; **evr'ythang** - everything

fatha - Father; **fo'** - for; **fraid** - afraid

'gatha - together; **'gin** - begin; **git** - get; **gonna** - going to; **gotta** - got to

hatin' - hating; **hep** - help; **in'tresin'** - interesting **jis'** - just

kil't - killed; **kin'a** - kind of; **kno'** - know

la'fin - laughing; **Lawd** - Lord; **li'l** - little; **los'** - lost; **leas'** - at least

mad' - made; **'memba** - remember; **mo'** - more; **musta** - must have; **moffa** - mother

naw - no; **'new** - knew; **'night** - tonight; **n'body** - nobody; **na'va** - never; **nuffa** - another; **nuff** - enough; **nufin** - nothing

offa - other; **oughta** - ought to; **outcha** - out of your; **o'vah** - over; **ownna** - owner

pasa - pastor; **'posa** - suppose to; **'pose** - suppose; **'portant** - important; **pow'r** - power

'round - around;

sade - said; **scaked** - scared; **sho'** - sure; **'splain** - explain; **sup'in** - something

tawd - tired **use'ta** - use to

wanna - want to; **wan'** - want; **wha'cha** - what you; **whil's** - while; **wit'cha** - with you

wit'out - without: **wonda** - wonder

ya - you; **yasa** - yes sir; **y'ear** - hear; **y'ere** - here; **yistaday** - yesterday; **yu'rs** - yours; **yit** - yet

y'use - you is

The author is available for speaking engagements and book signings to the faith community, or the general public. If you are interested in having the author speak to your group, or would like to purchase additional books, kindly contact wingspancc@yahoo.com.

The author would greatly appreciate your assistance in spreading the word about her book if you found it to be an interesting read. You could begin study groups to investigate what you believe and/or how you think. Are you out of the box or regulated to the norm? You can talk about how you validate your faith as an individual. There is much to investigate!!!

Thanks again for purchasing this book and may God bless your desires and endeavors.

Printed in the United States
135173LV00001B/2/P

9 781606 478943